Diamonds in the Dirt

Sara Powter

Bible Quotes from the King James Version

ISBN:97809945782-7-3
Paperback edition

Pacific Wanderland Publications
ABN 99 768 734 831

Kincumber NSW 2251

saragpowter@gmail.com
sarapowter.com.au

1st Edition 2022 - Amazon/Kindle
Revised 2025
2nd Edition 2022 - Pacific Wanderland Publications
Revised 2025
1st Edition 2022 - Hard Cover Revised 2025
1st Edition 2022 - Large Print Edition Revised 2025

Australian Historical Novels
(All stand-alone books)

A First Fleet Stories (1788+)
Gentle Annie Soames
The Emancipated Potter
Paternity Unknown

The Hunter to Macquarie Collection (1795-1822)
When Upon Life's Billows
The Saddler's Song (2025)
Tuppence to Pass (2025)
His Majesty's Pageboy (2026)
A Fist Full of Holey Dollars (2026)
Far From the Whispering Sheoaks (2026)
Bound Down in Iron Chains (2026)

Unlikely Convict Ladies Trilogy (1792-1840s)
Dancing to Her Own Tune
(co-authored by Sheila Hunter & Sara Powter)
Amelia's Tears
A Lady in Irons

The Lockleys of Parramatta (1800-1901)
Unshackled Lives - *Prequel novella - free with newsletter signup*
Hands Upon the Anvil
Out Where the Brolgas Dance
Diamonds in the Dirt
The Earl's Shadow
Once a Jolly Swagman
Jonty's Journey

The Convict Birthstain Collection (1820-1840s)
No More, My Love
The Vine Weaver
Scotch at The Rocks
Waiting at the Sliprails
Convict Shadows of the Past
In Defence of Her Honour
I Can't Stop Tomorrow
Madeline's Boy
Jam or Marmalade for Tea

Sheila Hunter's
Australian Colonial Trilogy (1840-1850s)
Mattie
Ricky
The Heather to the Hawkesbury

Dedication

For my dad, Norman McLean Hunter, who taught me to find gemstones,
And my mum Sheila, who taught me to cut and polish them.
And to Steve, my own beloved, who took me hunting for more.
He even took me to Bingara in NSW, and we saw some cut lemon diamonds.
And thanks you to the Lord who made them.

Thanks

I wish to thank my beloved husband, Stephen,
for his patience in answering my never-ending questions.
Also, for answering 'does this sound right?' enquiries.

To my mother, Sheila Hunter,
who inspired me to write by writing three herself.
Sadly, she never saw hers in print
and will never know that I followed her lead …
at least not this side of Heaven.

Thanks also to my convict ancestors,
who were ripped from the arms of their loved ones
and sent forever to the other side of the world.
I appreciate their sacrifice and their faith more every day.
Their faith in God still lives on through many of us.
I am astounded that it survived the rigours of the
convict life they were all forced to endure, but it did.

To my husband, Steve,
Thank you for all your support in my writing.
He's my Alpha reader.

To Roby Aiken
for your patience in correcting my punctuation
and to my Beta readers, Noreen Robertson and Anna Marie Leffew
, for doing the final read-throughs.
Anna also does the advertising for me.
And to Annie Seaton, who encouraged me to keep writing.

Table of Contents

The grammar and language in this book are
Australian English spelling.

KEY

~ - Time passing in the same locality

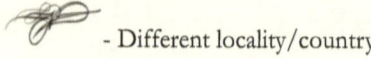 - Different locality/country

Chapter 1   End of Learning

*T*he blonde head was bent over the book, deep in thought. The reader absentmindedly flipped pages without reading. The green leatherbound tome with gold edges was one of Luke's favourite books. He had read it many times over the past ten years. He closed the book, and his hand gently rubbed the green leather. He exhaled. A deep sigh escaped his lips. He stood and walked to the window, deep in thought.

Last night, he'd had a strange dream. It was he and some others on a horse trek; it had haunted him. He didn't understand what it meant. He lived in Sydney. He didn't even own a horse, so he was not likely to have any horse treks. It was early afternoon; he was still unsettled, as his dream had been on his mind all morning. He had nothing to study for, no exams and no plans for the future.

He shrugged it off, thinking that his dream had been inspired by hearing of Sir Thomas Mitchell's death only days before. He knew his brother Wills would be upset. The family had more than enough death lately. Their grandmother and step-grandfather had passed within days of each other. Luke's parents had left for England days after their funerals to tell his aunt in person. He missed them. He released a huge sigh.

Gosh, he wished Wills at least were here; he wanted to talk about things, particularly his future, over with him. He walked back to his desk and sat down again. Flipping the book open to what he'd been reading. He could not concentrate, and his mind wandered.

Luke's mind slipped back to the day he'd been given the books and his stationery travelling case. It was for an early seventeenth birthday. Was that really ten years ago? Wills had bought them for him when on his honeymoon. Luke's eyes misted with the love shown to him. His family were everything to him. That was the last birthday that they had celebrated together. Uncle Ned, Aunt Christina, and Aunt Suze went back to England not long after that. Although they heard from them regularly, it just wasn't the same. Oh, he wished he were seventeen again. He had been in his last year at The King's School. The university was still just a dream back then.

Luke remembered Mr William Wentworth coming to dinner with Governor Fitzroy. At the time, Mr Wentworth had still been speaking to

Dar about the possibility of the colony having a University. Luke sat with them and Mama around the table at the cottage. His eyes were as big as saucers when both Mr Wentworth and Governor Fitzroy asked if they could use Luke's name in Parliament to fast-track a University. That was 1847. Luke had already stayed at The King's School far longer than he should have done, but there was no other avenue open to him where he could study further. Since then, Governor Fitzroy often came alone to the cottage. He could talk to Mama and Dar about Lady Mary. They had both been there for him on that fateful, melancholy day when she'd been killed. Luke would make himself scarce, but as his room was only next door, he could often hear what they spoke about. Dar had called him in and said, "Luke, Governor Fitzroy has a proposition for you. I want Sir Charles to tell you himself. Sit down, lad; you may fall otherwise." Charles Lockley, Earl of Coxheath, pointed to a chair and motioned for his youngest son to sit.

Luke sat on the edge of the chair.

Governor Charles Fitzroy watched as the tall blonde lad sat. "Luke," he rubbed his brow, how exactly to start. "Luke, Mr Wentworth and I have been talking, as you know. We have great plans to start a University and know it's vital to have some excellent candidates to begin this venture. We need one, in particular, to be our test case if you like. I have an idea that could benefit us all, including the Colony."

The Governor mopped his brow again. "Luke, we have spare rooms at Government House in Sydney, and we were wondering if you'd care to reside there while doing a year or two at Sydney College and then starting University once it gets going?"

Luke was still perched on the edge of his chair. He was flabbergasted. "What?" he swallowed, "Why me, sir?"

Sir Charles continued. "Luke, I have watched you over the last couple of years. I have also had others watching you. The work you have done with William, that other amazing son of your Charles, is astounding. Lad, do you know others are now copying your bookkeeping system for their businesses?" He looked at Charles and then Luke, and raised his eyebrows.

Charles nodded for him to continue.

"Luke, this way, there will be no accommodation costs, and you will be close to the College. Government House is just a few blocks away. It's almost a second home to your family anyway. I don't need an answer immediately, but please consider it." He stood to leave.

Luke accepted the offer and went to Sydney the following year. He had studied at Sydney College for more than three years, and in 1852, he was one of the first students, if not the first, to enrol at the new Sydney University. The lectures were held in the main auditorium at Sydney Grammar School. Oh, but they were terrific. Mr Woolley's lectures on Logic were undoubtedly different, but oh, they stretched his thinking. Luke had only stayed at Government House for one year, then Wills bought a house in town on Pitt Street. It was only walking distance from the college. This house was where Luke now called "home" while he was studying. His books were there, as was his chair, lamp and this stationery travelling box. He still had his rooms at Parramatta with Dar and Mama, and at Eddie's place when they were away, but didn't go home as often. Not since Ellen married. He thought they had an understanding. Apparently not so!

Luke shut the book with a slap. He pushed back his chair, walked to the window again, and then ran his fingers through his thick, wavy blonde hair. As he watched, a boy with a fruit barrow pushed his way up the street. A dog followed him for a while before it took off after a stray cat. His eyes followed the various people out and about, getting on with life. He sighed. At twenty-seven, he was no more sure of his path in life than he was at seventeen. At least his parents were there to guide him back then. They had gone to stay with Uncle Ned again in England. Dar had wanted to be with his sister when they heard that their mother, his grandmother, had died.

It had been a double blow as Grandpa Richard had died only the week before her. She died peacefully on the 2nd of September; she had lost the will to live after his passing, and within a week, she, too, was gone. She was only seventy-three. They had nine years together, but Grandpa had promised her wonderful, happy years, and they had been. Luke's eyes welled with unshed tears just thinking about them. They may have found each other late in life. She'd been a widow for decades; they were so happy and spread that happiness to everyone. Now, they were both gone. Dar and Mama had packed quickly and taken the next ship to England only days after the funeral.

Luke watched a carriage come up the street. His eyebrow raised when he saw it was the Hotel town carriage. His eyes widened further when he saw it pull up at the gate.

He waited to see who it was before he took off out of his office and fled downstairs. He threw the door open before his brother had even handed down his wife, Cathy, from the carriage. She was again heavy with child.

Relief washed over Luke. He said, "Wills, Cathy, how wonderful. I was having a melancholy moment, and your timing could not have been more wonderful." He greeted Cathy first with a gentle hug and kissed her cheek. Luke then threw himself into his brother's arms. "Oh, I needed you, brother. But what are you doing here?"

"Let's go inside before I answer that," Will said after greeting his little brother.

Cathy took Wills's arm, and the three walked inside.

"I was sitting upstairs, being sad. Silly, but I know how you felt when you were a kid. Only – here I am, so alone. Your timing could not have been more perfect." Luke opened the door for them as it had slammed shut.

A red-headed man hobbled out from the back rooms.

"Hamish, we have guests. Well, not really, as he actually owns the house." Luke chuckled. "Can we have tea, please?"

Cathy excused herself and went upstairs to refresh.

"Of course, good sirs and ma'am," Hamish replied.

Two years ago, Hamish Macdonald had been a soldier. He had lost his leg and somehow ended up on the wrong ship. Instead of returning to Scotland, he had been placed unconscious on board a vessel heading to Sydney. For ages, no one knew much more about him.

Luke had found him in church one Sunday, sitting in the back row where the convict servants usually sat. Effy, the Evans' maid, called Luke over and introduced them. Luke had been looking for someone to help in Wills's new townhouse.

Hamish obviously had nowhere to go, no money and no idea about much, except that now he was here, it was a better climate. He decided to stay. If God had brought him, it must be for a reason. He bowed and thanked her. "Miss Effy, thank ye for your wonderful and Godly assistance." He kissed her hand and hobbled off after Luke.

When Luke met him, he had been in town for three days. He had slept rough and scavenged food. He had a stump where he once had a strong leg and used a branch as a crutch. His months at sea had healed the wound, but the hurt in his heart was still raw. Now, two years later, that too had gone. He was a cheerful character and a delight to Luke; he was also a fabulous caretaker. He could cook, albeit the same meal repeated, and he could garden, and he loved his "little cookies" in the garden.

Luke found he meant the white cockatoos who visited him and were hand-fed. He'd been nipped a few times but still continued to feed them. Luke explained they were "cockies," not "cookies", but he could not get his Scottish tongue around the word.

Hamish's vibrant red hair was still unruly. His red beard almost totally covered his face. Luke had absolutely no idea how old he was.

Wills put his hand out to shake Hamish's. "How are you, Hamish? Is the leg still painting?"

"Arr, aw getaway wit' you, my lord. It's only the foot that keeps itchin'. It wouldn't matter if I could actually scratch it, but it ain't there now, is it?" He chortled. "Tea are cummin up, your lordship," he said in his broad Scottish brogue. "Miss Cathy, you sit your sle' down, and I'll make yee a nice strong brew." He hobbled.

"Quit the m'lord stuff, Hamish. I'm just Wills, or I'll start m'lording you too." Wills replied in good-hearted banter.

The three watched him go as he tittered with joy as he went. He had a great sense of humour and knew how to rile both the boys.

Wills smiled. "I love that man, you know. His attitude to life could have been so different. But no, he's always joyful. One day, we'll find out God's purpose for him being here." He turned to Luke. "Hope you don't mind, but we're here for a few weeks at least. The luggage is on the way with Martha, Jack, and Colleen. They are to look after the children."

"Why should I mind? It's your house. And to tell the truth, I'm so sick of my own company, I really need you all. But what's it all about?"

Wills looked at Cathy. He smiled, then turned again to look at Luke. "For the most educated person in the family, sometimes you miss the most obvious things. Cathy is just over seven months gone with child."

"Yes, and...?" Luke said innocently.

"Does she look only seven months?" Wills asked with a smile on his face.

"Or err, I don't know, I must admit I don't take much notice of these things." He mused. "I thought she was nearly ready to drop." Luke blushed.

Wills said, "Exactly, Luke. Martha insisted that we had the doctor here check her out last week, and when we did, we got a big shock. He's pretty sure it's twins. Mama calls it the family disease; she's just thrilled that she never had a set. After Uncle Ned had two sets, Charlie one and Eddie and Jen two, and even Grandmother being a twin, we should have thought it a possibility. But it honestly never occurred to us. Well, guess what... twins. So, here we are until after they are born. They aren't due until December, but twins often come more than a month early, at least, so as I said, we're here until they are born. Harry and Vicky have got everything under control at home. So we're having a bit of a holiday. Do you mind?"

"No way, I'm overjoyed," replied Luke. "Your timing could not have been more perfect. I finished my last exam yesterday. I'm now finished University, Wills." He gave a deep sigh. "The problem is, I have no idea what to do next."

Hamish came in with a tea trolley. Luke had purchased this for him the week he arrived. He had dropped only one plate, but the tea spilling was something Hamish himself refused to forgive. He saw one for sale at Lenehan's furniture store and asked if Luke had the means to purchase one similar.

Luke went out that afternoon with Hamish and purchased a Lenehan's Tray-mobile.

Luke had met Andrew Lenehan while living at Government House as the Irishman was refurbishing it. One of the items that had been there was the most exquisite cedar desk. He had been allowed to use this for his study desk while he lived there. It was so beautiful; Luke would take pleasure working from it. Andrew's brother Michael worked with him sometimes.

These two Irishmen were from County Sligo in Ireland; they were regular visitors as Hamish had struck up a friendship with some Gaelic brothers. They were an unlikely trio.

It was not long after Wills bought the house that Luke had

"adopted" Hamish. Only weeks later, Michael arrived one day with a large wrapped parcel under his arm. He asked to see Hamish, but also wanted Luke to stay, too. Hamish joined them in the front sitting room. He hopped in using his roughened branch walking stick. Michael told them both, "Sit, please."

So they did.

Michael then handed Hamish the parcel. He unwrapped it and gasped. "Oh, Micky ma boy, you've gone and made me a leg. How does it work?"

Michael took it from him and, after showing it quickly to Luke, knelt before his friend. "Hamish, do you remember the night when Andrew and I got you plastered with whisky? We did it for a reason. When you were drunk, we took measurements and even did a fitting. You were out cold, so we had plenty of time to work." Michael laughed. "My lovely Jane has made a thick felt lining for the inside, and you will have to wear a sock of sorts to help pad it." He slipped on the leather straps and pulled the leg onto the stump. "You'll get the hang of it so that you won't eventually need your cane. But in the meantime, use both."

Michael turned to Luke. "Luke, help him up." With a friend on either side, they got him standing.

The grin on Hamish's face was worth the effort and secrecy. "Oh, laddie, this is *braw*. All that blathering about me leg, and you go do this for an old Scot." Hamish was as close to tears as possible. "I cun stand, laddie, I CUN STAND AGAIN. On me own two feets," he shouted. He wobbled a bit. Mick and Luke grabbed onto him.

"Take it easy, Hamish, or you'll break the other one," Luke said.

That had been two years ago, and he could walk without the stick now. He named his leg "Mark," and instead of a footprint, it left a foot mark. Andrew and Michael made a couple of other models for him, and the latest one had a hinged foot. This one he called "Mark time." As he could actually March with this one.

By the time Hamish made the tea and pushed in the trolley, Cathy had exited the room again and retreated to the back privy. The second carriage was pulling into the driveway, and the third with the luggage was behind it.

Martha and Jack were accompanied by little Lukie, Philip, called Pip, Catherine Victoria Matilda called Tilda and Aurelia, whom everyone called Goldie.

Lukie and Goldie were as fair as their father, and Pip and Tilda were slightly darker, like Cathy.

Cathy had just managed to sit down before she was covered in small children. Lukie was eight and the oldest of the growing brood. He was typically supposed to be at King's, but they had taken him out to be together as a family. As they lived at Emu Plains, he had been living at his

Uncle Eddie's place and going to school with his cousins, Ned, Kit, and Nick. He shared Kit's room as they were only a day apart in age. He was over the moon that he had a month off to be with his family, let alone his beloved Uncle Luke.

He was the first to leave his mother's side, greeting his uncle with a bow and then throwing himself into his arms.

Luke took the lad in his strong arms. Returning hug for a hug. Young Lukie pulled away and took his Uncle Luke's face in his small hands. He looked him in the eyes and said, "I love you so much, Uncle Luke. You are my Uncle Lucky Lukie," and then he hugged him again.

Luke felt a lump form in his throat. He couldn't say anything, so he hugged him back, burying his face in the young boy's neck. It was just what he needed. They stood locked together until Martha and Jack bustled in. By then, Luke had recovered and gently placed the young lad on the ground. Pip came for a hug, but it was quick. Tilda and Goldie stayed with their mother.

Wills stood watching his family while leaning on the unlit fireplace. As usual, he was dressed in black and white, with the only touches of colour being his silver fob watch chain and large blue sapphire tie pin. He never flashed his wealth, and there was now much of that. It was used to help everywhere, but no one knew where the funds came from. If he heard of a genuine need, the money appeared anonymously. The Benevolent Society and similar needy groups were never short of funds. Only Wills, Cathy and Luke were aware of where the money went. Luke was still doing his "personal" bookwork; it's the only reason he knew. They lived a reasonably simple life. They paid fair wages, and their staff were many of the Murphy family children. They didn't need that many, but the Murphys needed the work. They were really friends with nowhere to live, as there were sixteen children and two adults living in a slab hut with a dirt floor.

Luke adored his older brother. There were only two years between them, and they had always been close. It was because of Wills that he'd been able to spend all these years studying. For Wills to be here now was an answer to Luke's prayers. Luke's heart was full.

Colleen Murphy knocked on the open door frame and asked, "I was wondering if the children would like a run in the backyard." Soon, the room fell quiet. She had made up all the beds and already helped Hamish unload food for a meal for them all.

Wills sat talking with Luke and his in-laws for about fifteen minutes before he excused both himself and Luke as they had things to discuss. As he left, he bent and kissed Cathy. "I love you," he whispered, not so softly.

Luke saw Martha smile and reach out for Jack's hand.

Wills walked to the door, and Luke followed him out.

There was one room in the house that was the den. Luke only went in there to use some of the books.

Wills had installed a wall of bookshelves and told Luke to "Fill them with whatever you want, but don't make yourself too comfortable in that room." Wills smiled as he led the way into the lovely office.

Andrew Lenehan had designed him the most fabulous desk. It was made of deep red cedar with brass inlay. He had added a trick lockable drawer system where the bottom ones were locked unless the others were open an inch, but no more.

Luke discovered that the same cabinetmaker made the presents he had received for his seventeenth birthday. He hadn't been that well-known back then. He still loved running his hand over the lovely, warm grain of the wood.

Wills pulled out the leather upholstered desk chair. "Luke, I need to have a little chat with you. So take a seat." He pointed to the other comfortable chair near the desk.

Luke sat, wondering what was coming. He'd prayed that God would direct him where to "go" next and what to do. He felt he was at a fork in the road, and he could see only empty or flooded roadways in front of him.

"Luke, we didn't need to come for a couple of weeks, but I knew yesterday was your last exam. Reverend Clarke has been keeping us informed of how you are going. He and Reverend Woolley are friends and colleagues."

Luke nodded. "Yes, I know, but huh? Doesn't explain why you're here."

Wills smiled. His little brother was so deep into his books that life completely passed him by. He had to do something. He'd been praying about what to do when he received a visit from an old friend.

"Luke, late one afternoon last week, Cathy's brother Marc Turner knocked on our door." His brother-in-law only lived a couple of streets away in Emu Plains. Marc said, "Reverend Clarke wants a word with you. Any chance you could pop in now? He's leaving early and is going to head to bed." Wills paused. "I went straight away."

Reverend Clarke had explained to Wills. "Finally, the grant has come through for a Government Mineral Survey, Wills and I have to find now a couple of men who can come with me on a long, arduous trip. I want trustworthy men, Wills. I had a dream last night that I had to tell you, my boy. Any idea why that would be?" His old headmaster looked him in the eye.

Blue eyes were meeting blue eyes in a gentle request for help. "Sir, isn't it just as well we both trust our Lord? I had only just finished praying that He'd send me some way I could help Luke. As you know, he's been at University and is due to complete his final exams later this week. He has a double degree in Science and Arts. John Evans has also been doing some courses with him, mostly in Science. But you know that, as you were the one sponsoring him." Wills turned and walked across the room, then back again.

Could he take it upon himself to send his youngest brother into the wilds of the country for goodness knows how long? He took a deep breath. "Sir, why don't you ask Luke and John if they'd come? Neither has a proper job. John only seems to work when you're around. He's skilled at drawing, as is Luke, and they both know their Geology and Natural History."

"Oh, lad! They were the two names I wanted you to give me. I, too, have been praying, and these two faces kept coming into mind, but I wanted someone to confirm my thoughts. I know, and like John, we've worked together often at the Museum along with Dr Homes, but you're right. He needs a bomb under him, but he works when I'm near. He does need direction, something to really motivate him. Luke is a worker, though. Do you think he'd come?"

Reverend Clarke looked lonely and sad. Wills wondered why.

"Will Mrs Clarke join you, sir?" he asked tentatively.

"No, Wills, she's still in London with the children. She's been gone for ages, Wills. I hate that she's not here. I do so miss her."

Reverend Clarke took a deep breath before continuing. "Now I have to get things organised. It will keep my mind occupied. I'm heading to Bathurst for a week, and then on my return, I'd like to run into Sydney and prepare for the trip. Is there any chance you can sound them out for me? If they aren't interested, can you hunt for someone else? I have to arrange transport, and oh, you know everything."

He wiped his hands over his eyes. He took a deep breath. "Wills, she left a long time ago. She took the children home after her nieces' weddings. I want her back."

Wills realised that she had been gone for years, and he missed her. Maria was his rock. She went where he went. The children, too, not that they would be children any more. However, if she wasn't at home, then neither would he be. The Governor needed this survey done, and he was the man to do it. Now was as good a time as any. At fifty-seven, he wasn't as young any more. He had been pushing for these mineral surveys for over a decade. The middle-aged minister was the only person who knew the country and what he was looking for. He had already sourced gold and tin. Who knew what else there might be?

Wills smiled at the memory of the conversation they had had. He was now in Sydney, fulfilling Reverend Clarke's wishes. "Luke, last week Reverend Clarke stayed in Emu on the way to do a wedding in Bathurst." Wills didn't really want to proceed, but knew he had to. "Luke, he wants to know if you and possibly John Evans would be interested in going on a long survey trip with him."

"What?" asked Luke. "What sort of survey trip?"

"Well, that's it. You know his big dream is to conduct *the* mineral survey. He started asking about it when Governor Gipps was in charge. He said, "No," Fitzroy said, "Yes," and got the ball rolling. Denison is pushing for it to be completed now. That all worked in with our plan for the Emporiums, but well, he got busy and never had the time. He is still the Rector of North Sydney, but has other clergy and curates assisting him in that role. He still does the travelling and outback stuff, hence his trip to Bathurst. He's looking for two trustworthy men to go with him and help with record-keeping and the like."

Luke looked astounded. He sat silently, thinking.

Wills waited patiently. He knew Luke. He would make an informed decision, and he would not be hurried. They were so different.

"I'd like to talk to John," he finally said. "Does he know yet?"

"Yes, and no. Yes, he knows about the trip; no, that Reverend Clarke wants him to go, nor about you either. Luke, don't answer yet. Pray about it." Wills looked at him anxiously. He now wished he'd talked it over with his two elder brothers first.

Wills continued, "Luke, it would mean living in a wagon if you're lucky, but knowing Reverend Clarke, most of the places he's going to head have no wagon tracks. So it would be horseback or on foot, possibly a cart if you're lucky. Few supplies, living off the land and no communication for months. It will be rough and no comforts at all."

Luke had not really heard what his brother had been saying. His mind was otherwise occupied with his dream from last night. Is this what it meant? He stood looking out onto the street. He saw the boy with the fruit barrow was coming home. It was empty. Good, he'd had a good day, for he was early.

"Wills, I have to go." He turned to his brother, "I have to do this." Luke looked at his brother and told him of the recurring dream he had had.

"Ahh!" was all that Wills said. He added, "Cathy has dreams like this. I've learnt to trust her too. I spoke to Uncle Ned about them. He calls them 'words of knowledge' or 'visions'. Did you know they are even in the Bible? From Joel chapter 2 v 28: *"And it shall come to pass afterwards, that I will pour out my Spirit on all flesh; your sons and your daughters shall prophesy, your old men shall dream dreams, and your young men shall see visions."*

Luke turned away from Wills and went back to the window. "Wills, I was literally at the window praying for direction as you pulled up. I had this same dream again last night. I wonder if John has had any inclination of any call?" He turned to look at Wills again. "I don't really want to go. I can't take my books, but I know I'm called to do this. It's what I've trained for ten years to do."

Over Luke's shoulder, he saw a man walking in the front yard. He gasped. "Luke, I think we're just about to get an answer to that."

Hamish answered the door.

John Evans stood on the doorstep. He had forgotten to brush his hair before leaving work again.

"Hello, Hamish, I'm here. Not sure why I felt I needed to come.

What's up?" John walked in but went into the office, not the sitting room. Hamish scratched his head; no sound had come from that room; it was usually empty. He shrugged and walked off.

Wills welcomed him with a smile.

Luke swung around and gasped.

John said, "Hi, I don't know why I'm here; I felt I had to come. Got any idea why?" John plopped himself into a chair and looked at his two friends. John was the epitome of an absent-minded professor. At only thirty-three, he was far too young to be so distracted.

Wills and Luke looked at each other. Then Wills smiled. "Well, actually, John, we may. Have your ears been burning? Do you have any plans for the next year or so?" Wills asked tentatively.

"Err, no, not really. Reverend Clarke said something funny the other day. Said something about it 'being time now'. I was hoping he would ask me to go on the survey he wants to do, but he hasn't said a word. Why?"

"Well, it's about that. At least you know what he's got planned. He's asked me to sound out the pair of you. To see if you both want to go?" Wills looked at Luke. His eyebrow cocked. Then he smiled. "John, we were actually talking about you and about the trip when you arrived. Can you tell us what you know?"

John spent the next half an hour telling his two friends about the planned trip. He had helped Reverend Clarke prepare the route maps and did much of the research into possible routes. John had interviewed surviving inland surveyors and sorted the equipment they needed. He was so upset that Reverend Clarke had said nothing to him.

John was depressed and distracted. He had wanted to go on this expedition for years. He'd worked hard for it. Silence. He sighed in frustration.

"Wills, did you not wonder how I knew you would be here? Or even why I'm here? Neither of you even asked." John looked at them both.

Luke said, "John, if you're like me, well, I had a dream. One is about going on a trip with two others and horses. I was standing at the window, praying about it and wondering who I should talk to. Then Wills drives up." Luke looked at his friend's face. "John, we all know God's ways are mysterious. We really shouldn't be surprised that He has already prepared the way for us, should we?"

John said nothing, but he shook his head and gave a half-laugh.

"So it looks like you have a long journey to prepare for. What do we need to do, John?" Wills said.

Half an hour later, the three men rejoined the others in the sitting room.

Hamish had joined them as well. His position in the house was strange as he was neither a guest nor a servant. He cooked for Luke but joined him to eat them. He called it 'earning his keep.' It turned out that he was a Baron's second son. His brother Fergus was the current Baron, but no one knew where he was. Their home had burned down. Hamish had served in the Crimea in the Russian wars with the 1st Battalion of the Royal Scots Regiment and then later the Coldstream Regiment and had planned to return home after he was wounded. A sabre slice to his leg had become infected, and the leg was later amputated at the knee. The next thing he knew, he woke up on board an immigrant ship instead of the hospital. It was filled with Macdonald's and heading to New South Wales. As Hamish was unconscious, one of his distant relatives had made the decision for him.

Hamish's father was dead; his family house had been destroyed, as had the farmland. There was no home to return to. His mother, Amelia Elspeth's, family came from West Sussex, and he didn't know them well, having only met them once, although he had written to his grandmother often when a lad. His cousin, Colin Macdonald, did what he thought best, and that was to bring him with him. Sadly, Colin caught a fever and died on board. Murdoch and Mary Macdonald and their family nursed him back to health. They had their own path to lead. They lived out the Hawkesbury River somewhere.

So once more, Hamish was alone. The only possessions he had were Colin's including his army clothing. His regimental plaid and kilt, thankfully, had not been lost. Hamish wore it whenever they could. His age was indeterminate, but they figured he would be in his mid-forties. They never asked, and he certainly didn't volunteer much more information.

Wills and Cathy loved him. As did Luke.

Martha and Jack Turner loved anyone that their three daughters loved. So that was Harry, Ed, and Wills and their family. They had both arrived as convicts; Jack arrived chained to Charles Lockley, Wills and Luke's father. Charles had later had his conviction quashed. It was also discovered that he was an Earl. He'd had no idea. Martha had arrived the year earlier and had a rotten time on the way out. Jack had been given an Absolute Pardon.

Two of Charles' sons married two of Jack's daughters. Their middle daughter had married Wills's best friend, The Honourable Henry Harlow, known as Harry.

Colleen stood at the sitting-room door. "Mr Hamish, would you like me to *do* dinner tonight? We brought a pile of goodies with us."

"Ooch, lassie, if you'd care to. Unless it's porridge you want, well, I think that's a good idea. It's Mr Wills's kitchen and his food. I cook fine enough for Mr Luke but not good enough for the family. Aye, feel free, lassie. I ken your scran 'n' guid ta a nicht orf."

Colleen looked at Luke, puzzled. "He said he doesn't cook well enough for the family. Then he said he knows your cooking and will enjoy a night off."

"Aye, that's what I say, lassie; what he says," Hamish sat in the sitting room with a broad grin on his hairy, bearded face, knowing perfectly well how to confuse her. He chortled.

Colleen nodded, not really understanding what he had said, but she was happy to cook dinner. Colleen was also not a servant but a live-in friend who helped out.

The children had settled down. Some of the adults were now sitting with some books and toys on the floor. She loved this family; she loved children. One day, she might find someone she'd want to marry herself. She was the same age as Cathy but had not found someone special. At twenty-nine, she had better hurry. Unbeknownst to her, that someone had just noticed her in a way she never expected.

John had been sitting on the floor, playing with the children. She had not noticed him, but he had seen her and sat stunned, just watching her. "Luke, who's that?" John asked quietly.

"Huh? That's Colleen Murphy; you know – Cathy's best friend. Her family are from Emu Plains. Come on, surely you know Colleen, you must met before? She lives with Wills and Cathy, sort of like a paid companion, along with another of her sisters. She earns a pittance but gets free board and lodging for about four of her family. There were twelve children when I first met them, but it's up to about sixteen now. They all have that, well, "joy of life." Colleen is almost one of the family now. I think of her as a sister of sorts."

"Oh, *that* Colleen, she's beautiful, Luke," John said in awe. "Why have we never met? I've heard about her forever. I still think of her as the scruffy child Ed used to tell me about. Luke, she's stunning."

"I suppose she is, I know she has a beautiful soul. I've never really thought about it. As I say, she's like a sister." Luke sat, looking at his friend. "John, would you like me to introduce you to her?"

John didn't know what to say, so he just nodded.

Luke grinned. He'd seen Wills' face when he realised his feelings for Cathy. Wills had been just fourteen.

Later that evening, Colleen was officially introduced to John. Her eyes dropped, and she caught her breath. Throughout the evening, their eyes often met, and each gave a smile.

When the meal was finished, John offered to help her with the dishes while Wills, Luke, and Martha put the children to bed. Cathy and her father sat in the sitting room alone.

Hamish excused himself and disappeared.

Cathy was cuddled under Jack's arm. "Pa, I want to thank you for letting Wills and me get married. I love him as much today as I did as a fourteen-year-old. I still find it hard to believe we've been married for ten years."

Jack loved his baby girl. Cathy had always been special. He knew that her heart had been given early and that Wills had turned out to be even better than the man he had hoped he would be. Not only that, but with savvy business management and with God's blessing, he'd become one of the richest men in the Colony. His second-oldest brother, Ed, had turned a small gift into a business venture also worth a mint. He had built an Emporium at Parramatta and sold farm hardware and tradesman's goods on consignment. Ed was a blacksmith and a very hard worker. The oldest brother, Charlie, Viscount Lockley, was now Viceroy in the colony west of Parramatta on a government allowance.

Wills and Cathy had built him a new house that they named *Willow Grove*. It was just down the road from Eddie's house in Phillip Street, Parramatta.

Wills had built Cathy a magnificent house at Emu Plains called 'Emu Hall'. They also had use of a cottage in Parramatta. Nothing fancy, but they were comfortable.

"Cathy, I just want to say I'm proud of you both. You could have absolutely anything you want. But no, you only take what you need and share the rest. I am truly amazed at the pair of you."

Cathy didn't answer; she just snuggled to him more.

Jack continued, "Do you know I only found out last year how much gold he found. He only ever said, 'a lot'. I knew about the ten pounds in the bag of gold dust. But I had no idea about the hundreds of pounds of rocks they had found at Hartley. He said about 100 pounds; I presumed he meant value, not weight. When he told me only last year, his share was £13,000, I was stunned. Cathy, it didn't change him one bit, nor you." He bent and kissed the top of her head.

"Pa, it doesn't matter to me. All I ever wanted was Wills. Oh, it's nice to have it. The children will want for nothing. We can give where we see any need, and we do, often. We can help people by employing them, rather than giving them money. We train many and pay for apprenticeships rather than giving handouts. Teaching them how to work honestly. Like Colleen. She couldn't read or write when she came to us. Now she can, and so can most of her brothers and sisters. And did you know she can draw too? She's good. And play the piano now as well." She laid her hand on her stomach. "Pa, feel this."

She took her father's hand and laid it on her moving stomach. One baby was doing push-ups on her rib. She then moved his hand, and the other baby was kicking her.

"Active little things, aren't they? I remember when your mother was expecting all of you. You also did push-ups on her rib. I don't remember any of the other six being so active. Jenna, maybe, but the others were quiet, Alex especially. He was so quiet we wondered if he was all right. He smiled as he was kicked.

Like her, Alex had fallen in love early. With the daughter of his boss. She was very young. Only about twelve when they met, and he was about fourteen. But he knew he would marry her one day. He did. Mary Parker, as she had been, and he now had four children.

Cathy sat, thinking about whether she should say anything about the business. She decided not to. Wills shared everything with her. When he wanted to give 10% away, she encouraged him to do more. So the church received a £1,000 ingot, as did Reverend Clarke. It was because of him that Wills had found the gold. Wills gave Mrs Clarke another £100 to return to England with their children. She had not asked for it, but Cathy had seen her in tears one day. She needed to take their children home, but had no way to pay for a ticket for them all. She was going to have to send them unattended. Cathy sorted it. She offered to pay the extra. Unbeknownst to the family, they had upgraded the whole family to cabin class and then provided funds for a return passage.

They had decided not to tell Reverend Clarke about the upgrade until it was too late for him to do more than bluster. He had seen them onto the ship and was surprised that the Captain had greeted them and shown them into three adjoining cabins. Only then did Maria tell him what Cathy had done. Cathy was surprised she had not had a visit from her for ages, for some years actually.

Cathy was also thinking about how much they had slipped to Grandpa Richard over the years, so he could help the little girls at the school. His parting gift to the children was to give each girl a length of new fabric and a pair of shoes. Mrs Jenkins and the ladies' group had helped them make the fabric into pretty church dresses. The boots were hand-made by all the cobblers they knew, including old Mr Iles in Sydney. Some of them were made by his two new junior apprentices but were serviceable for the orphans. They bought all the stock they could and donated it to the school. The girls with the most potential for good work had been given the best shoes, so they presented well. She smiled to herself. Grandmother Elle knew, as did Richard, but no one else knew where the donation had come from. Wills was able to say, "I promise I did not buy it." As Cathy had. With his blessing, of course.

Wills and Cathy thought they had a lot of money until the Emporiums opened. The profit from the turnover of products from both Emporiums was overwhelming. A bad month was a £100 profit, and that was just Wills' share.

Harry, Philip, and Eddie each had 20% of the profits from their investments. In the years since the gold rush started, the income just kept growing. Wills kept donating to the needy.

Their bank account had so much in it, they were embarrassed. Will had built new houses for Liza and Charlie; the more they spent, the more they had.

Eddie had no need for more, and neither did Anna. She had married Tim Miller, who was now a member of the Legislative Assembly.

He would go far. However, Wills had a new office built for him when he was just a lawyer.

Wills had bought the house in Sydney for Luke to live in, but it also meant the family had a home base. Mr Stewart at *the King's Arms Hotel* had bought a new town carriage and let them know it was for their use when required. The other family members still preferred to stay at the Hotel for their frequent official visits to Government House. They had standing invitations to Government House, and Wills often dropped in to update the Governor or his aide on some project or other.

Cathy sat, smiling about all these things. She was content. So content, she fell asleep in her father's arms.

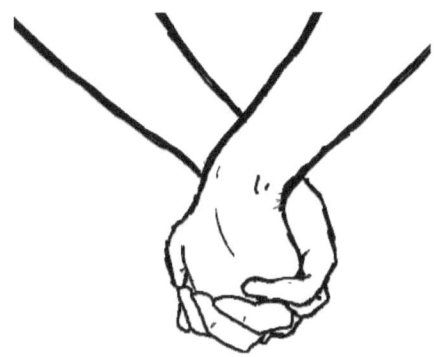

Chapter 2   Smitten

*J*ohn wandered home with much on his mind. For the first time in his life, he had spent over an hour talking with a lady. He had no idea that doing the dishes could be so entertaining. He could not wipe the smile from his face.

Colleen's face and her mischievous smile were firmly fixed in his mind. He had never even noticed a female before. His mind was on beetles and butterflies, surveys and maps. Now, he had a divine, dark-haired, two-legged creature fluttering around his mind. She had inky black hair, vivid blue eyes that laughed, and black eyelashes. He remembered someone once saying that it was like they had been placed in her face with dirty fingers.

Martha and Jack had gone to bed soon after the children. They knew they would have an early morning.

John caught his breath when he first saw her.

She had done the same when they were officially introduced a short while later. She stood bewildered, unable to tear her eyes from his face.

Cathy and Wills both noticed John and Colleen, as did Luke.

When they left to do the dishes a little later, Luke said, "Well, this will complicate things somewhat, Wills. Think he'll still want to come?"

"I dare say we'll find out soon enough," Wills said.

John's arrival at home was uneventful. His parents, Caroline and Douglas Evans, were both already in bed, asleep. He was pleased. His mind was still in turmoil. He wanted to pursue this amazing woman, but he also needed to go on this expedition.

Thankfully, they weren't leaving immediately. He would have time; time to work things out.

John finally made it to his bed and threw himself on it backwards.

His stomach was churning. He had never felt like this before. He had laughed when his older brothers Phil and Stevie fell in love and married. Now it had happened to him.

He let out a big sigh; she really did have the most amazing blue eyes. He had a month to court her, at the most. He would speak to Wills tomorrow, but for now, he needed sleep.

John's dreams were filled with daydreams of long, blue-black hair and blue, blue eyes. He longed to touch her, to hold her, yet he had only met her once; he wished to be with her. He had known *about* her for years, but she looked nothing like how his brothers had described her. He remembered Eddie telling him about a scrawny Irish girl who helped with their surprise engagement party. He knew Colleen was Cathy's best friend, too.

He woke at dawn, knowing he was going to see her again after work. He'd call in to see Wills on the way to work and ask about coming to dinner. He jumped out of bed and dressed. He could hear his mother up and about. She was someone he could confide in. She always had been. He went to talk to her.

Effy, their help, greeted him and passed him a bowl of porridge.

He waited for her to leave. "Mother, may I have a word before I leave for work?"

Caro Evans looked at her youngest son. "Of course, love. Is everything all right?" she asked, concerned.

"Oh, yes! I have met someone, that's all," he smiled a dreamy smile.

"Oh!" she said.

Effy came back in, and she was followed by Douglas. He greeted his son. As he did every morning, he tousled his hair. Usually, John reacted; this morning, he didn't. Douglas looked at Caro with a surprised look.

"Morning, Father, sleep well? I did," John said with a spring in his step.

Douglas looked astounded. "Yes, I did, son. Thank you. Are you all right?"

"Yes, thank you, Father. I'm fine. Looking forward to today, Father. Lots happening." He smiled and looked up to meet his father's eyes.

As much as he loved him, John was much closer to his mother, as his father, a Master Mariner and Sea Captain, had often been away while he was growing up.

Douglas had given up the sea after he had "been missing presumed dead" for eighteen months. His ship had been lost at sea; then he'd been thrown in prison.

On his return, just shy of two years missing, John remembered the great joy his return brought. That was fourteen years before. He loved his father dearly, but it was his mother's counsel he needed now. He tried to keep the conversation flowing over the meal.

Effy was in and out with dishes and clearing plates.

When the tea was served and she finally departed, he said, "Wills and Cathy have arrived. She's having twins, you know. And they plan to be here for about a month. Martha and Jack Turner are with them, and a lady named Colleen Murphy." He had no idea that the way he said her name was different from how he spoke to the others.

His parents, on the other hand, had noticed. Their glances at each other spoke volumes.

Douglas raised an eyebrow when looking at his wife.

Caro shook her head and shrugged. When John wasn't looking, she mouthed "later" to her husband.

He merely nodded. Douglas made an excuse to leave, and Caro and her son were left at the table.

John watched him go. As soon as the door shut, he turned to his mother. "Mother, I am in turmoil. I am all undone. I have worked on the mineral survey with Reverend Clarke, and now it looks as though he wishes me to go with him, along with Luke Lockley. Only I have met someone."

"Oh!" said Caroline lightly. "Would it be Colleen by any chance? We met her out at Wills' place last year," she said, smiling at her youngest boy.

"But Mother, how? What? Ahh! You know me too well," he chuckled. "I only met her last night. We did the dishes together." He looked moonstruck.

Caro smiled to herself. "Tell me about her, son."

"Oh, Mother, she's beautiful. But more than that, she's nice too. She's Irish, of course, one of sixteen children – so far. So she lives with Wills and Cathy, as do two of her sisters and a brother, but you know all that. Two more Murphys work at Marc's inn, some more of the brothers. She's twenty-nine, and oh, Mother, she's beautiful, but it's deeper than that. Did I say that before?"

He sat, beaming. "Oh, her parents came free, escaping the Irish poverty and religious persecution. We talked of many things over the dishes last night." He sat with his chin on his hands. "Mother, she believes too. Really believes. Her parents came because they were not Catholics. She told me about their persecution in Ireland. I've heard all about her for ages, but never met."

Caro looked at him. "Why the concern, son?"

"Well, I want to court her. No! I'm going to court her. But I want to go on this trip as well. What do I do? I don't want to marry her and then leave her. I don't want to become engaged and leave her. And I don't think she'll be allowed to come with us." He put his hands on his head and groaned.

"Oh, my darling boy, you've waited all these years to find your 'someone'." She commiserated with him. "Are you sure? You only met her yesterday." Caro looked at her son lovingly.

"I'm sure, Mother. I was sure the moment I looked at her. That sounds silly, I know. I used to laugh when Eddie told me that's how he felt when he saw Jenna. But now, well, I know it's true. Yes, she's beautiful, but it is so much more than that." He spoke in earnest but repeated himself for the third time.

"Son, I think the first thing you should do is talk to Cathy, Wills, and Reverend Clarke. Sound them out. In the meantime, court her and bring her over to meet us. I'm sure we'll love her too when we get to know her. I liked her when we first met." She patted his hand. "Now, son, you had better get ready for work. You'll be late."

She left the table and stood holding the door for him. She knew he would sit there forgetting time if she didn't.

John rose, and as he left the room, he kissed her cheek on the way out. "Thank you, Mother. I'll ask her to come soon. I might try and stay for dinner again tonight. They are here for a month, or at least until the twins are born. Did I say Wills and Cathy are having twins? My mind is a swirl." He collected his hat and left.

Caro laughed.

His hair was still a mess from his father's teasing; John didn't care. He walked briskly along the street. He had decided to call in at Wills' house on the way to the Museum.

Reverend Clarke wasn't due in this week, and no one would mind if he was a little tardy. He had some newly pressed butterflies to pin out and some beetles to mount. They could wait. He knocked at the door of their house.

Hamish answered the knock. "Greetings, laddie. Who'll you be wantin' at this hour of the day? Everyone is up, though. Come in, Come in." Hamish ushered him into the dining room.

"Good morning, John. To what do we owe this visit? All well at your house?" Wills greeted him warmly.

"Morning, all! Yes, everything is fine. I'm just here to wangle another invite for dinner. I have some thoughts I'd like to run by you. I'm late for work, so I can't stay." John heard hurrying footsteps behind him.

Hamish told Colleen John had arrived.

She had come almost running.

He turned, and again their eyes locked. He stood staring at her. "Morning, Miss Colleen, how are you this morning? Well, I hope?" Aaargh! Cor, he sounded like a lovesick fool, he thought to himself. Well, I am. John turned back to Wills. "Would that be all right, Wills?"

She nodded to Wills behind his back.

Wills saw her gesture and said, "Sure, John. Come as soon as you leave work. No need to change." Wills said.

John turned to leave.

Colleen stood aside to let him pass, then followed him out. She shut the dining room door after her.

John walked to the front door but did not open it.

She followed him.

"I can't talk now, but I would like to after dinner if that's all right?" he said to her softly.

Her eyes shone. "Yes, I'd like that," she put out her hand to him.

He gently took it, turned it over and kissed her palm. "Until tonight," he opened the door himself and departed before he could change his mind.

The conversation in the dining room following their departure was interesting. Luke said, "Well, I think things might be interesting for at least the next month. They remind me of Ed and Jenna. Did you see them both?" He smirked.

"How could I not?" Wills said. "I wonder how this will affect the trip? Luke, you may have some female company with you, and we may have to find a new cook."

Cathy chipped in. "She would be really useful to take. She's good at nearly everything. Roughing it wouldn't be a problem either. How would you feel, though, Luke? Would you mind?"

Luke thought for a while. "No, Cathy, I don't think I would. If I had a girl myself, it might be hard, but I don't. John would be heartbroken if Reverend Clarke said no, though. He will have the last say."

"John may have a tough decision to make," Wills replied.

~

Work passed very slowly for John. He had some beautiful butterfly specimens to set. He loved the taxonomy part of his work. The pinning of the specimens collected from a previous trip. Today it was cathartic. He had placed them in the relaxing jar a few days before, and many had softened enough for him to now mount and label.

He took up his pen and wrote the genus and species name, then the date, locality and collector on the tiny label. Four lines of minute writing. Something he had done a thousand times before.

He smudged the first one and misspelt the second. Finally, on the third go, he got it right. He laughed at himself. He shook his head. He took a long glass-tipped pin and then carefully un-papered the butterfly. He eased open the wings and pinned the thorax. He knew what to expect, but the wings' iridescent blue reminded him of Colleen's eyes. He took great care with it.

Placing it on the mounting board and gently easing the wings further open. He carefully flattened the specimen with two strips of paper and then gently moved the wings into the proper places. With some special thin paper, he pinned them in position, then did the other side.

The butterfly looked as if it were resting. Only it was now surrounded by about a dozen pins. He sat looking at the blue peeping out from under the paper.

He picked up another papered butterfly. This time, a giant citrus butterfly, a *Papilio aegeus* female, was revealed. It had inky black edges and again reminded him of Colleen's hair. He chuckled to himself. "Yeah. I'm smitten."

John worked away all morning until he had filled twenty boards of set butterflies. The rest would need to wait. They were not relaxed enough to set without breaking. These had been collected by Reverend Clarke on one of his last trips south. There had also been beetles, another of his loves. The labels for each had to be accurate and legible. The specimens would be stored in special boxes and drawers and are expected to last over a hundred years.

His office smelled of naphthalene. The odour permeated his clothing.

He checked the beetles, and he was able to pin them more quickly. "Concentrate, John," he told himself as he nearly pinned it in the wrong spot. Pin through the thorax, label and box, and repeat. He had worked out a system to do the labels at once and had them in small piles, cut and ready to pin. All had the same collection data; only the scientific names were different. Depending on where they were found, some specimens needed two or even three labels. If they were found on a specific plant, that, too, had to be recorded. All relevant data were written on the individual papers in which the insects were stored. He loved this work. It was fiddly but rewarding. No one had collected specimens in this land before, and most of them were new species. John Lewin had described many, and John used his work and books to find out if these had names. For many, he had to put 'ssp' next to them, as they were all undescribed species.

John had finished writing over one hundred tiny labels and had the beetles ready to pin. He prepared his desk. A small wooden block held the brown glass-topped one-and-a-half-inch pins, labels, and a cork-lined drawer.

He stretched, cracked his knuckles, then got to work. Doing the beetles took his mind off Colleen. He had a pad and a pencil beside him. He would write thoughts of what to take on the trip as he worked. By three o'clock, he had finished the day's quota and all the prepared specimens. He would put new insects in the now-empty relaxing jars. Most would be ready in a couple of days, but some took a week. He'd recently found a small box of John Lewin's own papered specimens that had been somehow overlooked. It was some of these he'd set to relax. If he tried to set them before they were fully relaxed, they broke.

His next job was preparing more papers for collecting more specimens on the big trip.

John already had a list of approximately what he'd need to either take or send. He smiled. He so wanted to go on this trip. Then he thought of Colleen. What were his choices? He hoped he could take her. Married, of course. Reverend Clarke would be the one to make that decision. He hoped she would want to come. He sighed. He wanted to see her. He packed up quickly and left early to head to Wills' house.

Colleen had been busy with the children. She'd tried to keep herself occupied. Reading to the children helped. But she kept thinking of John. Pip and Lukie noticed she wasn't concentrating. Twice, she had stopped reading mid-sentence.

She had prepared a lovely dinner for tonight: slow-roasted mutton with baked potatoes and fresh beans. Followed by steamed pudding with custard.

Cathy had suggested she join them tonight. She usually did it at home, so she was not surprised by the idea.

She had just taken the children into the nursery, and Martha said she would stay with them for a while. Colleen went to set the dinner table only to find Hamish had just finished it. She had nothing to do and was standing in the hallway, wondering how to occupy her time, when she heard the front door. She answered it to find John standing there.

"Hello, Miss Colleen," he smiled at her. "Have you had a nice day?"

"Yes, thank you, sir. I have. Have you?" she asked. Not really knowing what to say.

He took her hand in greeting but didn't release it.

She closed her fingers over his. "Please come inside, sir." She drew him inside and closed the door.

"Please call me John. May I talk to you a little later? I have to see Wills first." He finally dropped her hand.

She nodded. "I'll be in the kitchen when you need me. Wills is in the office." She gave him a beaming smile, then turned and left him in the corridor.

John walked into Wills' office-cum-library. He knocked and went in without waiting for an invitation.

Wills was standing at the window. He turned on John's entry. "Hello, John. You look as though you have the weight of the world on your shoulders."

John dropped into a large winged leather armchair. He slouched and sighed. "Wills, sometimes God's timing stinks. I really want to go on this trip, but I also want to court Colleen. No, heck, I want to marry Colleen. Why couldn't you have brought her with you before? How come I have not met her earlier?" He dropped his head back on the cushioned headrest. "I used to laugh at Ed when he told me about Jenna. I'm not laughing now."

Wills smiled. "I saw your face when you clapped eyes on her. I knew then. She's been off-keel all day. Pip complained that she even lost her place reading their story twice."

"Really?" John exclaimed, sitting upright quickly. "So it's not just me? Oh, that is a relief." He sighed again. "But the timing... We're supposed to leave on nearly a year-plus long trip. Can I ask her to come? Would Reverend Clarke allow me to bring her along? Would she even want to come? Do I wait and speak to him first? Oh, Wills, what do I do?"

"Well, first thing, I would not wait. Court her, marry her soon if you will. But she must know about the trip. You have to let her decide. Reverend Clarke will not worry, I'm sure. Luke is fine with it. I've already spoken to him about it."

John's eyes flew to his. "When? I only met her yesterday."

"Oh, John, really? It's written on both your faces. This morning, after you left. We three sat and discussed it." Wills walked to his friend. John and his brothers were like family. He squatted next to his chair. He looked at him intently. "John, if God has not brought you two together before now, He has a reason, but now you've met, do you really think that He would do that to you? I suggest you take her for a walk. Hamish can do anything that needs doing towards dinner. Go down to the Botanical Gardens. Tell her about the trip. She needs to know. Go. But also know her father, Finn, will need to be asked, so plan a trip to Emu soon."

John pulled himself upright and stood up. "You think it's all right if I do that, Wills? Shouldn't I ask him first?"

"No, take her now. Just go... now," he replied.

John took a deep breath. "I will." He walked to the door, turned and said, "Thanks, Wills." He was smiling as he left. John was four years older than his friend, but he felt like a young boy in this situation.

John walked to the kitchen and greeted Hamish. Colleen was not there. "Hamish, would you mind if I asked Miss Colleen for a walk?"

"Go, laddie. I have everything under control here. I sent her to collect her bonnet when you went into Wills." Hamish gave him a broad, white, toothy grin.

John heard a sigh behind him. She stood holding her bonnet, looking a little embarrassed.

John looked at her, then dropped his eyes to her bonnet. "May I ask you for a walk with me, Miss Colleen?"

She nodded.

He followed her out of the kitchen. She stopped at the hall mirror, placed her bonnet on, did up the ribbons loosely and then turned and gave him a beaming smile.

His heart did a somersault. "Ready?"

"Yes, John," she said softly.

He opened the back door for her and let her pass through. He offered her his arm, and they walked down the road and toward the Botanical Gardens. He talked about the weather as they walked.

She answered as best she could. She had never walked out with anyone before. This man took her breath away. He was everything she'd heard people saying of him. Her head had been full of his face all day.

They walked in through the garden's south entrance, and John found a seat out of the main thoroughfare. He placed his handkerchief for her to sit upon, then sat near her. Oh, where to start? Boots and all, I suppose. "Miss Colleen, Colleen, where do I start? Firstly, I would dearly love to court you, but before you answer me, I need to tell you something." John felt tongue-tied.

She looked intently at him. "Yes, John, relax. I won't bite," she smiled. She took his hand. "I'm forward, or I wouldn't be here with you, but I want to hear what you need to say."

He nodded. "Colleen, I work with Reverend Clarke at the Museum. I know you know him."

She nodded.

He took a deep breath, trying to control his racing heart. "I'm not sure if you know what he has planned. It's a mineral survey. I've been working with him for the past two years, preparing for it. I need to go with him."

He paused and looked up to find her eyes fixed on him. "Colleen, it will last for the best part of a year. We will either be on horseback or on foot, and it will be rough. I don't know when we leave, but it will be soon."

"Oh, John, really?" She looked sad.

"Colleen, I'd love to say that if things work out, you could come, but it's not my call. Having said that, I'd still like to court you." He took both her hands in his as he was speaking. "May I?"

"Yes, John, I'd love that." She squeezed his fingers. "As I said, John, I'm a little more forward than most well-brought-up girls. I come from a large Irish family, and we don't have much. I've never met anyone I liked before, and well, I don't quite know what to do."

She dropped her eyes and said softly. "But John, you will have to ask my papa, though."

"I will, Colleen, but I wanted to know if that was all right with you first." His heart was racing. "Colleen, I don't know what to do about the trip."

She moved a little closer to him. "John, can we leave that to God? If it's meant to happen, it will; if not, I'll be here when you return." She looked up at him in earnest. "Do you know when you leave?"

John gently took her hand and turned it over; he raised it to his lips. "I never expected to feel like this. I never knew love could happen so fast. No, Colleen, I have no idea. Today is Thursday. I can take the day off tomorrow and head out to see your folks this weekend. I would ask you to come, but we would need someone to accompany us." He sat holding her hand, gazing lovingly at her face. "I think we'll have a month or so."

She asked him more about the trip, where they planned to go, and the sort of things they would do. "At least we have this month."

They tried to work out why they had not met at the various family functions, finally realising that on the ones he had skipped, she had been at.

"John, if Papa says yes, and Reverend Clarke too, would you want me to come?" she asked tentatively.

"Oh, are you serious? Of course, I would – as my wife, of course, but I can't ask you that until I have spoken to your father. Colleen, all I could think of last night was what if Reverend Clarke says no?" He looked sad. "I want to have it both ways. But it will be a hard trip. No luxuries, not even a wagon to sleep in; I couldn't ask that of you. It's no trip for a woman. And I couldn't bear to leave you behind. I'm torn."

She held his hand, "John, I'd love to come. But as I say – if things don't work out – I'll be here waiting for you. I come from a family with sixteen children – so far. We have never had luxuries. We all sleep on the dirt floor. We have no beds; Pa and Mama have a sort of a bed, straw-stuffed inside a hessian cover. I had never slept in a bed until I moved in with Wills and Cathy. I've made do with the bare necessities all my life. We only cooked over an open fire. If you had chosen an 'English Miss' as a partner, then she would not have coped, but I'm not that. I'm an Irish Colleen."

"Do you mean that? You'd come? Or you'd wait?" He searched her face.

"Well, I would prefer not to wait. If I can't come, then maybe we could well…" she couldn't put her desires into words.

"We could marry, and you would be safe with Wills and Cathy until my return?" he finished off for her.

She nodded. "Yes. I will wait if you don't want that. I'll wait for however long. But who knows, I could even be with child before you leave."

He looked around to see no one near. "May I kiss you?"

She nodded, "I said I was forward, but I know what I want, too."

He bent and gently touched her lips with his. He had never kissed anyone before, nor had she.

Neither expected the electricity it would cause between them.

John gently lifted her loosely tied bonnet back from her head. Then he gathered her into his arms, and she reached up and wrapped her arm around his neck.

Her groan of desire made him remember himself.

He gave her another quick kiss. "Mmm, I liked that." He set her bonnet gently back on her head.

"Me too. Please hurry back after you have seen Papa. John, don't just ask to court me, either. He's Irish, but not a prude. The many children prove that. If I can't come with you, I would rather be married before you go than have to wait here alone."

"I shall ask him for your hand, too, my dear." John looked lovingly at her. "We had better head back. However, would you mind detouring past my parents' place? They would like to meet you again. Officially, this time. I think it's funny they met you before I did."

"I'd like that, John. I'd like that a lot. I already love your mother. She was so kind to me." She stood up.

He reached out to collect his handkerchief. Still in the seclusion of the garden, their hands met, and he took hers in his. He stuffed the unfolded cloth in his back pocket, then his other hand slipped around her waist, and he drew her to him. "I could do this all day," he murmured as his head bent to find her lips again.

Her arms slipped around his neck; she stepped closer, pressing herself to his body.

After some minutes in a passionate embrace, "Ohh, Colleen, I am going to find it hard if he makes us wait." He bent to give her a quick peck. "We must go." He took her hand and placed it on his arm. They headed to a different exit and walked down a path towards his parents' house.

They had just started walking when an older couple approached. Caro and Douglas Evans had decided to take an afternoon stroll. That they ended up in the same garden was pure chance. John officially introduced Colleen to his parents.

Caro took Colleen's hand and walked ahead of the men.

John fell back to tell his father that he was heading to Emu Plains to ask for her hand.

Douglas was surprised but pleased. Finally, John had given his heart. Douglas had liked the girl when he'd met her on the last visit to Parramatta. Everything he had ever heard of her was good.

John spoke as highly of her as did Caro. He hoped that they could marry soon and, if Reverend Clarke permitted, she could accompany them on the trip. Towards the top of a slight rise, Colleen had stopped. She turned and waited for John to catch up.

Caro studied her face. In the few minutes she had been talking to this Irish beauty, she, too, had fallen for her. She was open and honest. It was apparent she had fallen as hard for John as he had for her. "Yes, I like her," she thought.

As the men drew close, Colleen said, "John, I must get back. I can't leave Hamish to do all the work." She smiled a melting smile at John. "It has been so lovely meeting you both again," she cooed genuinely. "I look forward to getting to know you better." She gave them a curtsy and then took John's arm. They meandered off down the rise.

Caro turned to Douglas. "I think we are soon to have a new daughter-in-law, Doug."

"I think you're right there, love. I bet it will be a Special Licence marriage too. John is still determined to head off on this trip."

"She said she'll go if she's allowed. She's apparently no shrinking violet and no prim English Miss, but neither would suit John. I think they will do well together." Caro took his arm as they continued their walk. "I think John has found his diamond."

"I think so too, love," Douglas said.

"I certainly like her," Caro murmured. "She is so different from the two other girls, but in a good way, Douglas."

Chapter 3   Permissions

*D*inner the night before was a success. He'd never enjoyed washing the dishes so much. Wash, dry, kiss. He chuckled to himself, remembering.

John caught the early morning ferry to Parramatta. From there, he'd catch the coach to Emu Plains. He'd stop the night with Marc at the Arms of Australia Inn. Colleen and Cathy tried to give him instructions about where her parents lived, but she said, "Just go to Marc; he will take you."

He thought back to his welcome on arrival at Wills' townhouse. Wills opened the door for them and greeted them warmly.

John breezily mentioned that he'd be gone for a couple of days, and Colleen blushed.

She removed her bonnet and departed to help Hamish. His eyes followed her until she was out of sight.

Wills quietly observed him. "Going to see her father?"

John nodded. "And asking for her hand, too, not just to court her. It's not like we're too young or anything. We met my parents on a walk, and they gave me their approval, too. They met her on her last visit to Parramatta." John was sure Wills could hear his heart pounding.

"Come," said Wills. He walked into his study. Once there, he walked to the grog tray that Hamish had placed for him. He was not a drinker. But he could not persuade Hamish that he didn't like whisky. If he had to drink something, it was brandy, but Hamish insisted on the whisky, too. He asked John which he'd prefer.

"Brandy, please. I'm not a drinker. But I need to steady my nerves. Did I really only meet her last night?" He shook his head. "I kissed her, Wills. I shouldn't have, but oh." He sighed. "She wants to come on the trip too. Do you think she'd cope?"

"Hmm, as to the kiss, well, a bit early. As to the trip, she'll cope better than either you or Luke will. But you know that's up to Reverend Clarke," Wills said, looking at his friend. "John, I have to prepare you for her family. I told you there are eighteen in the family. Sixteen of them are children. They range from her oldest brother, Eion, who is thirty-two, and the baby, Mary, who's two. Her mother loves children and pops them out about every two years. They own virtually nothing. The roof over their heads is a wattle and daub hut her father built; it has a dirt floor, which is what they sleep on. Other than growing potatoes, he works wherever he can. We try to give him and the boys lots of work. He and her older brothers are all hard workers, and they will never ask for anything. They will always be first to pitch in when needed, and they do their work and then go, not even waiting for thanks. I have a lot of time for all of them. The small amount of land they do have is under cultivation with potatoes. Have you heard of 'Murphy's Spuds'?"

John nodded. "You mean that's them?" His eyes widened. Everyone in the colony ate Murphy's Spuds when they could buy them.

"Yes, that's Finn's business; they supply the entire community. If it weren't for the number of children, they would be making a large profit. I employ any of them whenever I can, as does Harry. One of their boys, no idea which, is now caretaker at the Emu Emporium; they may even swap, and I'd not realise. And another is at the warehouse in Parramatta. And wow, can that lad work. To this day, I can't work out which one is which, so I just call them all Murphy. There's Eion, Connor, Brodie, Brennan, Shamus and a few more. I think the rest are mostly girls. I lose count." Wills laughed. "John, take them at face value. Be honest and kind. Let them know how much you love her, and you will be fine. Also, tell them you have our blessing. We've had Colleen living with us for nearly five years. We'll miss her. Deidre and Imogen are there often, too."

"Wills, she said she'd never slept in a bed before she came to you. Is that true? They really have nothing?" John was stunned at what he'd heard of her family.

"She only possesses what we've given her. She came to us with one outfit, and that was already too small for her. John, she does not care. Possessions mean nothing to them. Jenna, Vicky, and Cathy make sure all the girls are properly clothed. We tell Maureen, that's her mother, that they must be decently clothed. They won't take new clothing but will accept hand-me-downs or cast-offs. The best thing we can buy them is fabric. She sews so well. I found a bolt of water-damaged material on my last trip to Sydney in a new place called 'The English Emporium'. I went in because of the name. Fabulous place. Anyway, it's a joyous floral print with a watermark. The shopkeeper sold the entire bolt for 1 shilling. She took it and made clothes for her daughters and the orphan girls at Grandmother's school with the leftovers. There was not a scrap left over. Any offcuts were either turned into buttons, headbands, handkerchiefs, or patchwork. Not one minute square left," Wills said, amazed.

"Oh! I came from a family of boys, Wills. I know nothing about females. I've never even been interested before. I'm not one for fribbles or furbelows. I need a girl who's down to earth, with good sense and someone who will rough it with me on my expeditions. I don't care what her background is. Just that she accepts me and my crazy hobby. If she can cook, that's a plus because I can't. I'd starve if it weren't for Mother and Effy."

Wills said, "Then she's the right girl for you, John."

~

John was now on the way to ask for her hand in marriage, and a hasty marriage at that. After he'd arrived home, Father had suggested a marriage by Special Licence as they could at least have some time together before he had to depart. If she could go, well and good, but if not, they could at least have a month or so together before he had to leave.

Last weekend, he would not have dreamed that this was how he'd be spending the following weekend. He smiled. His mind was still whirling. His heart thumped when he thought of her. He sat, thinking as the pounding of the cantering horses beat a tattoo on the dusty road west. He was so deep in thought that he did not hear the lady next to him question him.

She touched his arm. "Are you all right, lad?" she asked with a lovely soft lilt to her voice. She sounded just like Colleen; even her hair was the same.

He smiled. "Pardon, sorry, ma'am. Just deep in thought. Happy thoughts, though," he explained with a smile.

"That's good, laddie, as long as you're all right. I don't like to see the young troubled. There's too much sadness in this world to waste a minute of it. Grasp happiness while you can. That's what I say. Hand problems to the Good Lord, and He fixes them." She sat watching him.

He nodded, then he turned back to the window.

"How far are you going? Bathurst? Not to the diggings, are you?" she asked him once more.

"No, Ma'am, just to Emu, I'm on an errand of the heart. Out to seek permission to court and wed my love. I find it hard to stop thinking of her." He smiled, as did she.

"Ahh! Well, that's good, then. I do hope you will be successful. You go with my blessing for what that's worth." She fell silent.

"Thank you, ma'am," he said sincerely.

They stopped to change the horses and give both the passengers and driver a bit of rest. Many years before, an enterprising person had hollowed out a log and left an old bucket, as well, so water could be drawn from the nearby creek. The old log made a natural water trough. The area had shade and a thicket of trees for ablutions; there had been nothing else there. Now, there was a staging post of sorts built. Wills had constructed it, and the family kept a couple of teams of horses, and they could shave time off the trip. The Mail coach, too, had a swap team stabled here.

They now returned to the Mail Coach in different seating, and it took off. The new horses knew the route well and knew what was before them. They set a good pace as the road was now excellent, with few ruts. The previous rocky sections were now levelled and even.

Governor Fitzroy had kept his word to Wills years before and improved the road west. This was now well-worn, with much traffic heading to Bathurst. The diggings were in full swing, with more miners joining them daily. The coach passed numerous other overloaded wagons, as well as men on foot, all heading to Bathurst to try their luck at the gold.

Wills had told John about his finds at Ophir some years before, but not the volume of what they found. John had gleaned more from Reverend Clarke than from Wills, but he knew that the gold rush was of Wills' doing. His own Uncle Thomas was involved, too, mainly with the smelting of the stuff.

Governor Fitzroy had given them the Government Charter to smelt the colony's gold finds. Somehow, they were ready as soon as gold fever hit. Wills and Eddie had this all set up before the rush even started. Reverend Clarke had let that cat out of the bag one day at work. He would love to know the whole story. Maybe one day they would tell him. Perhaps he would find out on the trip. Luke must know.

The miles passed, and soon the horses were slowed to a walk over the noisy bridge at Emu Plains. It was late afternoon when he finally alighted at the Inn. Marc greeted the coach as he always did, just in case anyone needed accommodation. He greeted John and waved to the lady in the coach. She waved back joyfully.

John greeted Marc; they had met at various Lockley family weddings. Two other passengers were staying.

Marc said that he could have the inside room in the house, but the others could have rooms in the new accommodation block behind the stables.

Milly greeted him with a kiss, and the children swarmed over him. They all knew him from the family get-togethers in Parramatta. He would sit and play with them rather than mingle with the adults.

Marc settled the two other passengers and then returned to John.

"Mill, can we have some tea, please, love?" He gave her a quick kiss. "We'll be out the front." He walked to the front door. No one ever seemed to use this, as most entered the house via the kitchen door. There was a long log slab seat on two stumps on the front verandah. Marc motioned for John to sit.

John was churning inside. How to tell Marc what he had come for.

Milly arrived with a tea tray and placed it between them on the slab. There were two large steaming mugs of tea with a huge chunk of cake. It smelled delicious, and John realised he'd forgotten to eat lunch. He had brought a sandwich that Jenna had made for him, then forgot all about it.

Marc handed him a mug and waited for Milly to leave. "Now, John, we can talk. You don't usually come this way without notice. What's up?"

John looked deeply into the tea. "I finally met Colleen." Then he looked at Marc. Would he know what he meant?

"Ahh, now I understand. I was the same with Milly. I met her at Ed's wedding, I think, or it could have been Liza's, no, definitely Ed and Jenna's. One look, and I was a goner. Same with you, eh? They've only been gone four days." Marc watched John's face.

"Yes, oh, Marc – I didn't know these feelings existed, the joy, the turmoil. I'm to leave on this mineral survey with Reverend Clarke and Luke very soon. Now, this! I wish to take her, and she wants to come. Luke's happy, but I don't know about Reverend Clarke, hence the turmoil."

"Oh! Now I understand. Did you talk to her mother about it?" Marc asked.

"No, how? I haven't met her." John looked puzzled.

"You have; you just don't know it. You see, that was her on the coach. The lady I waved to," Marc said, smiling. "Did you talk to her at all?"

"Oh!" said John, blanching. "Yes, I did, I told her I was on a 'quest of the heart'. Coming to seek permissions to woo and wed."

"Oh, she'll love you for that. Finn will know all about it when you go over it later. Finish your tea, and we'll get a move on. I'm not going to miss this for the world." Marc downed the mug of tea as John finished his. The grin on Marc's face was somewhat disconcerting for John.

"Is it walking distance?" John asked.

"Yes, just down the road. Cheer up; they are lovely. Dear friends, too. True diamonds in the rough." Marc smiled at his friend confidently.

John took both mugs and carried the tray back into the kitchen, leaving it on the table.

Marc greeted him at the back door. "Ditch the top hat. These are the Murphys. You'll scare them off if you go too fancy."

The two men walked out the back door and out through the courtyard.

"John, relax," Marc said.

John's heart was in his mouth. He tried to chat naturally but ended up falling silent. "I can't, Marc, I'm so nervous."

So Marc talked, and he filled in a bit more of their history. They were so admired in not just the local area, but all over the colony, considering they had absolutely nothing. If the lady in the coach was anything to go by, she was scrupulously clean. Well-spoken, and she seemed nice too. She would be his mother-in-law. He smiled to himself; he liked her. With this thought in mind, he brightened.

Marc saw his change in attitude; he, too, smiled. "We're here."

They stood in front of a small, nondescript, wattle and daub hut. It was white-washed inside and out, and everything was spic and span. He saw a tribe of mini Colleens and a smattering of small dark-haired lads, too. At the stick and wire fence, Marc stopped and asked if they could visit.

Two-year-old Mary stood and looked up at him with the same blue eyes as Colleen. John caught his breath. Her children may look like this: his children. The lady from the coach emerged. "Marc, dear, please come inside. Oh, you've brought your friend. Welcome." She ushered them inside. "Finny, this is the nice laddie from the coach I told you about. Marc has brought him for a visit. I missed your name, laddie," she gently coaxed him.

"It's John Evans, ma'am, sir," he nodded to both and swallowed nervously.

"Maureen, is Shamus around? I need to have a chat with him," Marc asked.

"He's around the back, Marc. Go around, and he'll appear," Finn replied for her.

Maureen ushered John to a seat on an upturned tea chest. There was nowhere else to sit. The room was undoubtedly Spartan. Yet it was cheerful, homely, and full of love. He noticed the earthen floor and the pile of folded blankets in the corner. Colleen said they had no beds, but only the ground, and he could now see for himself that she meant it. There was no room to sleep anywhere else. He took a deep breath and steadied his raging emotions.

"Now, lad, what can we help you with ?" Finn asked.

"Oh, Finny, my love, can't you see he's nervous enough as he is? I told you he'd come on an errand of the heart. That's right, isn't it, Johnny?" she said, putting him at ease.

"Yes, ma'am, you see, I met Colleen, and well, I would like to court her. She would not agree unless you both gave permission." He swallowed.

"And why would we withhold permission, lad? We know of your family. You are who our Eddie lived with in Sydney when he was at school there, aren't you? You're young John, who loves bugs?" she said with confidence.

"Yes, ma'am, I am he." He was surprised that they knew so much of him, and he knew nothing of them. Was he so buried in the work that the world so passed him by?

Finn had said little. He had turned his head a little sideways and was looking at John intently. "You want to marry her, don't you? You've been hit by the 'Pixie bow'." He roared with laughter. "Smitten, I've seen it before, first Eddie, then Marc. Now you. I like you, lad." Finn sat back, smiling.

John looked at the Irishman. "Yes, sir, I'd like to marry her. And I would like to do this quickly, too. May I tell you why?"

Maureen took her seat next to her husband. "Tell us, Johnny."

"As you know a bit about me, and I presume you have at some stage then met Reverend Clarke, as he did Harry and Vicky's wedding here, then you may know he wants to do a mineral survey," John said.

"Yes, lad, we've met him quite often. Nice man," Finn said.

John nodded and continued. "I've been working with him on this project for years. With Mrs Clarke in England, he's planning to go soon, but I don't know how soon, nor for how long. He's asked Luke Lockley and me if we will accompany him. It will be rough, horseback and walking, and we'll be gone for up to a year. We plan to cover as much land as we can in the time we have available. I want to marry Colleen and take her with me. She would like to come, but it's not us who will have a say as to whether Colleen can go; it's Reverend Clarke. If we're married already, we won't have to delay if he gives us the word to go. As we're not taking wagons, it's only a matter of finding suitable horses and saddles. Everything else is ready." John looked at his prospective in-laws, hoping for a positive reply.

"You've been honest with us, so we shall be with you too. Colleen is a good girl. We have always wanted the best for our children. I can see that you have great feelings for her. I know that from what you said to Maureen on the coach. So yes, lad, you can marry her. Whenever you wish, if that means by Special Licence, then so be it. I should add that she's not a Catholic, and neither are we; we are Protestant. It's why we're here. Not too popular back in the part of Ireland where we come from. So we came out here. I still find it hard to believe people fight over how to worship the one God." Finn stood and shook John's hand. "Welcome to the family, lad. Bring her back before you go if you can."

"What happens if she isn't allowed to go with you?" Maureen asked. The concerned mother needed answers.

"Wills and Cathy said she can continue to live there. But we haven't even discussed that. It will be her call where we live. I have ample funds from working at the Museum for so long. But I currently reside with my parents. May I leave the choice with her? We could have a room at Wills and Cathy's house, or in my parents' house, or we will probably get our own place on my return. She will be well provided for, no matter what the outcome. We won't leave until after Wills' babies are born. They are having twins, you know." John looked anxious. He had not even thought of where they would live. It wouldn't really matter if they could both go on the trip.

"If my Colleen is happy, that's all that matters. As to the trip, I think she'd like that." Finn was pleased Colleen had waited. She'd found a nice husband in this young man. She'd never shown interest in any other man she'd come across, even the Lockley lads.

Marc knocked and entered. "I have to head back, John."

Finn said, "Congratulate him, Marc. He just became engaged. I presume you asked her first?"

John blushed and nodded. "I broached the subject but didn't exactly ask her."

"I should hope not," said Maureen, smiling.

"Wonderful news, John! Congratulations to you all; you are both wonderful families. I'd stop for a drink, but we have other guests tonight."

John stood and bowed to both Finn and Maureen. He put his hand out to shake theirs.

"Pfaff that, my boy. Give me a hug." She embraced him and kissed his cheek. "Welcome, lad. God put me in the right place at the right time. Do you know that's my first trip back from Parramatta by myself?" She smiled.

"No, ma'am, I didn't know, but as to God's workings, He did that, ma'am, for a good reason," he said quietly.

"Let me get one thing straight: we are Finn and Maureen, none of the sir and ma'am stuff," Finn said.

John grinned. "Done!" He shook Finn's hand again, then departed on Marc's heels. He liked them.

The night passed swiftly, and John caught the mail coach back the next morning. The trip home seemed to take much longer than the way west. He could not wait to propose to Colleen officially. He'd felt he should buy her a ring. No, he'd let her choose one for herself. He'd propose with his signet ring. He knew that Bishop Barker was supposed to be at St Andrew's on Sunday morning; they had said as much the week before at St James. John would introduce Colleen to him and seek a Special Licence. He wanted them to be married before Reverend Clarke returned. If he said, "No," then he would not leave her. He had almost decided that overnight as he lay awake thinking about her. He'd stay at the Museum and work. He knew that this decision was not only the right one but an important one. No, he would not leave her. They pulled into Parramatta an hour before dark. He was dropped off at Glenmere on the corner of Church and Phillip Streets and started to walk down to the Ferry Wharf. He didn't want to see anyone, so he kept his head down. He just wanted to get home. He checked his fob watch and saw that the ferry still had half an hour until it arrived for its last run. It was a full moon tonight, so it would make the last half of the trip by moonlight. He was walking past Eddie's house as he arrived home. Ed waved him over. John rechecked his watch and went over for a quick chat.

"Hi, John, what are you doing out this way?" Ed inquired.

John grinned, "Getting permission to get engaged, Ed. I need to catch the ferry home."

"Oh, congratulations! Anyone we know?" Eddie enquired innocently.

"Err, well, yes. Colleen Murphy." John grinned. "You've kept her well hidden from me all these years. I only met her on Wednesday. Finn gave his permission last night. It's all a rush because of the mineral survey, but I need to catch the ferry tonight to see the Bishop for a Special Licence tomorrow. Finn and Maureen are fine with this, too. Wish me well, Ed. I know how you felt over Jenna now."

Eddie was dumbfounded on various fronts, but managed to ask, "How did you not ever get to meet Colleen? She's almost part of the furniture. I'm over the moon, John; she's a perfect fit for you, too. I don't know why I never thought of her for you before. Give her my love and congratulations."

"I will, but not too much of it. The love that is, I think I will be a jealous husband. It's taken me long enough to find her." John grinned at his friend.

Eddie grinned at his reply. He knew what John meant. He still felt the same for his Jenna after eight children and thirteen years of marriage. "How is Cathy? No baby, sorry, babies yet?" Ed asked.

"No, she was still in one piece when I left yesterday. She still has a couple of weeks, probably. I have a feeling we'll stay there until the babies are born. Ed, we haven't even discussed where we'll live. It's been a bit of a whirlwind, actually, no; a huge whirlwind. I had better go, Ed. Unless you want to walk with me to the ferry." John turned to see it just coming down the channel. He knew he had a few minutes yet.

"Hang on. I'll tell Jenna." He disappeared inside and returned quickly. "Come on, let's go." He took John's bag. He didn't get to see John much; he was like another little brother.

Ed had lived with their family for five years when a lad and this quiet, studious man was very like Luke. They have different interests but are similar in many ways. He loved them both. They chatted about the future trip, about Colleen and suggestions about where they would live.

By the time the ferry pulled out, John had many more things sorted in his mind than he had before.

Ed was right, he said, "Hand it to God, He'll get it sorted." John was happy with that. He had a firm trust in God, too; he knew Ed did as well. He'd seen him pray every night that he lived with them, on his knees at the window. It wasn't long before all five boys did the same. Each night before they slept, they prayed. It was a habit he still kept. Only he now slept alone in the room that once housed five. Maybe soon, it would house two.

When they returned from the trip, he would find a suitable place for them to live.

The ferry chugged up the harbour, the sunset behind him as he sat at the front of the boat. The moon was already up and was beginning to pierce through the darkness. The headlands were outlined in the twilight. He could see the observatory and windmill in silhouette.

Not long now. He wanted to run up the hill and propose to her. He'd call in any way, but it might be too late for a walk. It would have to be tonight if he were to speak to the Bishop tomorrow.

As the ferry pulled into the circular quay wharf in Sydney Cove, he held himself back from jumping over the rails as he wished to do.

Martha, Jack and Colleen were at the dock to meet him. His heart leapt. He groaned that the skipper was so slow at drawing the gangplank into place. His eyes were locked on hers. Finally, the little boat was secured. He forced himself to walk sedately down the final few yards.

Martha walked to him. "Hello, lad; we hoped you'd make it back for this ferry. Someone wanted to come and meet it. I wonder who?" She chuckled as she walked back towards Jack. "Give Jack your bag, John."

"Thank you, Martha," John said.

Colleen stood waiting for him. Her eyes were wide in anxiety.

John walked to her and took both her hands. "Will you walk with me, my dear?"

Colleen nodded.

Martha and Jack started walking up the hill. Jack had John's bag over his shoulder. They were going to dawdle and leave the young lovers to catch them up. They loved Colleen like a daughter; they had known her from when she was born. John, too, had a special place in their hearts.

John took Colleen's hand and tucked it in his arm. They walked up the hill towards the Government House. He was planning to take her far enough that they were hidden from prying eyes. He found a large tree that hid them from view. In the twilight, they were able to be unobserved by anyone passing. He drew her to him and loosened her bonnet. Pushing it back on her head, he bent and brushed her cheek with his thumb. The softness under his touch was tantalising. He bent his head and gently kissed her.

She wrapped her arms around his neck and opened her lips to his. Their kiss deepened far more than he intended. After some minutes, he pulled away from her and dropped to his knee. "My darling Colleen, will you marry me? Soon?"

"Yes, John, I will. And yes, whenever you want. Now, can you kiss me again, my husband-to-be?" she giggled softly. "Oh, I do like the sound of that."

He obliged willingly. He drew her to him; he just needed to hold her. "I can't believe how I need you." He kissed her again. "Are you happy if I speak to the Bishop tomorrow and get married by Special Licence?"

"Really? Can we get married that soon?" She reached up to kiss him again. She murmured, "John, I'll marry you tomorrow if he says yes. Is that too soon?"

"No, love, I'll ask him. I have no idea how long it will take. We also have to work out where we're going to live. I thought you'd like to stay with Wills and Cathy until the babies come. Once Reverend Clarke gets here, we can make more plans then. Is that all right?"

"Truly? You'd do that? Oh, John, that would be perfect. I'm so excited."

"As much as I would like to keep you here forever, Martha and Jack are waiting for us." He leaned over and lifted her bonnet and placed it back on her head. "If the Bishop marries us tomorrow, we will never have to say goodbye again, my sweet, but we must return now." He hooked her hand through his arm and was about to walk her down the hill when he remembered his ring. As he held her hand, he slid off his signet ring from his little finger and slipped it onto hers. "This will have to do until we buy you a proper one."

"Thank you, John. I'll be careful with it. I do love you, you know." She said as she walked. She was clinging to him as they walked up the hill.

Martha and Jack were waiting for them at the corner of Pitt Street. Martha congratulated them.

Colleen returned her hug. "Oh, Martha, I'm so happy."

"So you should be, love. He's a wonderful man. We've known him for some years, lass. I still can't work out how you've not met him before," Martha said, puzzled.

"I'd heard all about him. Of course, I have. I've always been interested in what he and the other Evans boys were up to. He's been at things I missed and vice versa. I knew that God would have the perfect time for our meeting when I met the man for me. I didn't expect it to be so late in my life and so rushed. But Martha, I don't care. John is going to see if we can get married by a Special Licence. Maybe even tomorrow." Colleen looked at him and took his hand. "Cathy has always said, 'John did this', or 'John did that'… I had just never met him."

He stepped closer and hooked her arm in his again; he placed his hand over hers and entwined their fingers. They walked like this until they reached John's house. John had removed his bag from Jack when he had rejoined them. It was now slung over his shoulder. He opened the door and quietly placed his bag just inside the door, then rejoined the others for the short walk to Wills' house. The slow walk from the quay had taken them about fifteen minutes. Once John had rid himself of his bag, they completed the remainder of the distance quickly.

Hamish greeted them at the door.

Martha and Colleen walked in first, followed by Jack, then John. "Well, lad? What did he say?" Hamish whispered as he entered.

"He said, 'yes', as did she. We have just become engaged, Hamish," John said quietly. "Where are Wills and Cathy?"

Hamish pointed to the sitting room. "That's *braw*, laddie. It's good news."

John walked into the sitting room.

Colleen was upstairs, removing her bonnet.

Martha and Jack were in the kitchen. They would join them later. They were giving him space to tell the family.

"Good evening, all! Isn't it a wonderful evening?" said John as he entered. He had a spring in his step and a huge smile on his face.

"Finn said yes, didn't he?" Wills asked.

"Yes, and so did Maureen and then Colleen. We're getting married. I'm seeing the Bishop after Church tomorrow. We're going to see if we can get a Special Licence and marry as soon as possible. It might even be tomorrow." He could not wipe the smile from his face.

Colleen knocked timidly.

John beckoned for her to join them.

Cathy called her to her side.

Colleen sat beside her and received her congratulations. "Cathy, we've been talking, and if it's all right with you, when we get married, John will move in here, and we'll stay until the babies are born or until we leave. I wish to travel with them and do hope that I will be allowed to. Luke, do you mind?"

"No, Colleen, why should I? But remember, I am not the one whose decision matters. Reverend Clarke will and must have the final say about that. He hasn't actually asked either of us yet. He just asked Wills to sound us out. We all have to wait until he comes."

While Luke, Colleen and Cathy were talking, John was standing next to Wills. His eyes were devouring her from across the room.

"You are so lucky, you know. You can get married quickly. I had to wait months to marry Cathy, you know. I had to wait first until she turned eighteen, then until Vicky married, and then again for my parents to return. At eighteen, waiting is very hard. At thirty-two, at least you have no reason to wait. Go for it, John; I'll stand as a witness if your brothers won't, or even your father."

"Wills, I had not even thought about that. Wills, we need two, won't we? I'll ask Father, but if not, will you and Luke stand with us? Or Cathy." John's eyes had still not left Colleen.

"Wills, we were wondering if we could stay here after we're married, at least until the babies are born. We might go to the Hotel for a couple of nights first, but it means if you need to take Cathy, we can babysit the rest."

"That would be wonderful, John. Are you sure? I'll move Colleen into the other visitor's room; it's got a big bed. Her room has a tiny single bed. While we're talking, John. I have to give you some information you need to know." He moved, so his back was to the ladies. He dropped his voice. "Don't use soap 'down there'; it burns them." He had blushed but continued, "I was told when I married and forgot a few times. They were right. Poor Cathy. So, no soap, at least not the course stuff with lye. Just hot water. Remember that." He kept his voice low.

"Are you serious? Soap eh? I'll remember that. I know some are worse than others, especially in the eyes." John smirked, then realised, "You're serious, aren't you?"

Wills nodded. "Really burns them ... there." Pointing to his groin.

"Ohh!" John said.

Wills nodded again.

Martha, Jack, and Hamish joined them. Hamish was pushing a trolley with champagne and glasses. "We've planned a wee celebration for ye both."

John picked up the champagne bottle and popped the top. He poured the glasses and handed them around. The last two he took to Colleen and stood by her with his. He passed his glass to his other hand and put an arm around her shoulders. He bent and kissed the top of her hair.

Everyone toasted them.

John finally made his goodbyes at about nine o'clock. He took her to the corridor and said good night in private. He had yet to tell his parents and inform them that he may even be getting married tomorrow. If so, then he would also be moving out for a while, at least.

"I'll see you tomorrow, love, but I have to go." He gently kissed her and said a final goodnight. "I told Wills that if we can marry tomorrow, we'll spend a couple of days at *the King's Arms Hotel*. A mini honeymoon if you like. Then we'll come back here until we know what's happening. Is that all right?"

"Sounds perfect, John; until tomorrow then, my love." She kissed him again, then pulled away. "Go now, or I won't let you go at all."

He walked the short distance home and was greeted by his parents. They, of course, had seen his bag and waited up for him. He joined them in their sitting room. He plonked himself in an armchair. "Congratulate me. We're engaged. I'm seeing Bishop Barker tomorrow and see if we can marry immediately. If Reverend Clarke says we can both go with him, then we won't have to rush a wedding, as we will have done that already." He smiled. "If not, well, either way, Colleen doesn't want to wait. If Reverend Clarke allows her to come, that is fabulous; if not, we can be together for as long as possible. I may not even go. I've almost decided I won't."

"Oh, John, that is fast. You have not even known her for a week. Are you sure? I thought you'd wait a few weeks at least," Caro said. "Don't get me wrong. I love her, and I think she's perfect for you. But John, it's so fast."

"I know, Mother. Sometimes, God's timing is not something we can understand. I trust Him, and this is how things have worked out. For years, she's been at every Lockley family function that I've had to miss. It just wasn't God's time for us to meet, and now it is. I'm not going to waste a minute of it either. Mother, she's twenty-nine, and I'm thirty-two. We're not teenagers. And she's not exactly a stranger. We've known about each other for years." He turned to his father. "I have a request, Father. Would you be willing to serve as one of our witnesses, please? Wills is to be the other one."

Douglas sat, looking at his son. He had missed a lot of his sons' childhoods due to his work as a sea captain. The memory of the day he came home from being missing was seared in his heart. John was the first of their sons on that day to find out. He was only eighteen. The love shown that day broke down any barriers that may have existed in the family. The overwhelming joy of that reunion kept the bond strong between them all. "Son, I would be honoured."

John sat, rubbing his eyes.

"Go to bed, son. You're exhausted. I'll wake you in time for Church." It would be the last time Caro would send her little boy to bed.

"I will, Mother; suddenly, I am exhausted. And thank you both for supporting me in this." John yawned. "So not the way I expected this week to end."

"Make the most of it, son," his father said as he walked out the door. John looked at him, puzzled.

As he left the room, he heard his mother say, "Doug, shh. He'll hear you. He won't get much sleep tomorrow if he gets married. We both know that." She chuckled.

John swung around, looking at the now-closed door. His mouth dropped open. He smiled, then laughed as he walked off to bed. Yes, he'd get some sleep.

~

The next morning, both households were up and ready early. Colleen had washed, dressed, and fed all the children before the adults were even awake. Luke had slept in.

Colleen sent Wills in to wake him. There was no way she was going to be late. She would go without him if he wasn't ready. She was dressed in a periwinkle blue gown, the exact shade of her eyes. She had put an apron over it while preparing the children. She had taken special care with her hair. Sadly, it would never be in ringlets, but the inky blackness of it was softly coiled on the back of her head. She might be getting married today, and she wished to look her best. She was so excited. She was sure everyone could hear her heart beating.

Cathy greeted her with a big hug. "Oh, Colleen, I'm so excited for you. I'll miss you, but I'm so happy as well."

Finally, the family left the house. Wills had ordered a carriage to be brought up from the hotel, and they travelled to church together. It was not a long trip, but too far for Hamish, the children, and Cathy to walk. They were greeted by John, who was there waiting. As he handed everyone down from the carriage, he said. "We're in luck," he said to the assembled group. "Bishop Barker is here. They said last week at St. James that he would be here this week. I've seen Reverend King already, and he'll speak to Bishop Barker before the service." He turned to Colleen. "You look amazing, sweetheart," he whispered lovingly. He took her hand and hooked it through his arm.

She smiled adoringly up at him. "I just hope he will do it today," she whispered. "I should look after the children, John." She reached down and took Goldie's chubby hand.

Luke had Tilda, and the boys walked together. The group walked into the Cathedral. They were met by Caro and Douglas and greeted each other, Cathy and Caro, with a hug.

Douglas led the group to a pew. It was not quite long enough for them all unless the children sat on the adults' laps.

Hamish and Effy said they would sit at the back.

Phil and Steve were already seated with their wives and nine children. After some shuffling, they squeezed into the pew.

John was able to sit next to Colleen and carefully hold her hand under her shawl. He was intermittently caressing the back of her hand or tracing hearts in the palm throughout the service.

Reverend Attwood gave the sermon.

Neither John nor Colleen had any idea what it was about. Both consumed with the nearness of the other. After what seemed an age, they all rose to take Holy Communion.

Stevie whispered to John, "Isn't that Colleen Murphy?"

"Yes, she's my fiancée," he said as he passed him.

Stevie's jaw dropped in amazement. On return to the pew. Phil and Stevie had shuffled seats. They were in conversation.

Phil had placed himself next to John. "When did this happen?"

"Yesterday! Hoping to marry today… Staying around?" John grinned.

"You bet, sly dog." Phil looked at his youngest brother. John never ceased to amaze him. He was so different from his older brothers. Both had gone into law. John always wanted to be a scientist. It had always been his passion since he was a small child.

John again took Colleen's hand, but this time didn't hide it. They sat with fingers interlocked, occasionally smiling at each other. His heart was joyful.

The service was over, and the families did not move until the rest of the congregation had exited the building. Then, there was a buzz of conversation.

Phil and Stevie took John aside, and Colleen was introduced to their wives, Alice and May, and their children. Both had briefly met her at Lockley family gatherings.

As the murmur of voices faded, John saw Reverend King approaching with Bishop Barker in tow.

John left the family and met the clergy a little further up the aisle. He turned and motioned for Colleen to join him. When she had, he explained to Bishop Barker, "Good morning, Bishop. We were hoping to obtain a Special Licence, please."

Colleen had curtseyed on her arrival. She met his eyes and smiled; he was so tall. "John, what's this all about? Come with me while we change."

John and Colleen followed them into the Vestry, where the Bishop and Minister disrobed. As they did, John explained about the forthcoming mineral survey trip with Reverend Clarke. "Sir, we'd like to marry as soon as possible. We are both of age, though I also have her father's permission. We are also both of the same faith. Miss Murphy is Irish but not Catholic."

"I see no problem then," said Bishop Barker. "When would you like it to happen?"

"We're ready now. Do we need to do anything first?" John asked.

The Bishop turned to Reverend King, "Any objections?"

"No, sir," Reverend King replied.

"Miss Murphy, you are fully content with this young man? You are not being forced into this with any pressure?"

"No pressure, my Lord Bishop, I am in full agreement," Colleen replied.

"I'm just 'Bishop', not 'Lord Bishop', my dear. I have half an hour before I have to leave for St Philip's. Why not? Let's get you two married. I'll need to fill out the register first and get a certificate. Give me ten minutes."

John handed Reverend King a sheet of paper with their details on it. Names, ages, parents, and other required information. He'd taken a moment to ask her last night and scribbled them down on his return home.

The Bishop waved his hand for them to leave and turned to discuss the forthcoming service with Reverends King and Attwood. He retrieved the marriage register, and Reverend Attwood filled it in while Reverend King did the Special Licence. Ten minutes later, all was ready.

The church was empty, bar the two families, who had now moved to the front seats. The three clergymen filed in, and the Bishop called John and Colleen forward.

They were married.

Douglas and Wills signed as witnesses in the register.

The Bishop congratulated the newlyweds and told John he may kiss his bride.

John did.

Colleen had no veil, bouquet, or attendants, but she was so beautiful that she glowed with happiness in her periwinkle blue gown.

They left holding their precious marriage certificate.

Colleen waved it and said, "I'm Mrs John Evans. That's not how I expected this week to turn out." She giggled.

John swung her around, oblivious of who was watching. He then kissed her in front of both families. Caro invited everyone back to their house. Effy had prepared a special morning tea; she'd missed the service intentionally. Hamish had not stayed for the wedding service either but returned to help Effy.

Wills piled Cathy, Caro, and the youngest children into the carriage; the others walked. It was only a few blocks to their Pitt Street house, but as the carriage was there, it could also be used.

John and Colleen fell behind the group. John gazed at the lady on his arm, "My wife, I can't say it often enough. I never thought it would happen to me, my love." He could not drag his eyes from her face.

"Oh, John, it's been so fast, but I have no regrets either. I still can't work out how we never met. What's important is that we now have, I love you so much," she cooed.

"We have a stop to make on the way to the house, love. We're staying at The King's Arms for a short honeymoon, but I have to book in. Sorry, it's not very long, but we'll have the rest of our lives in front of us." John gently squeezed her fingers. They walked into the hotel as they passed, and John booked the double room for the next three days.

Mr Stewart greeted him by name. He had visited often enough when the Lockleys were staying with him.

John introduced his new wife to Mr Stewart and was congratulated. They then departed. Mr Stewart sent the staff scurrying. They would upgrade them to the Master Suite, where he usually housed the Duke of Gracemere on their various stays. The staff were told to prepare everything for a honeymoon couple. He smiled. He loved a good romance.

John and Colleen arrived at the Evans' home. She had heard so much about this house. As she had not been to Sydney before, so she had never seen it. John ushered her inside and was greeted by his brothers and their wives.

Alice and May took her aside and showed her where she could freshen up. She looked at her new sisters-in-law in awe. John said she would love them, and she did. They were so kind. "I vaguely remember meeting you both at Eddie's, but I was always busy with the children," she told them.

John was dragged into their father's office by his brothers. "Spill," said Stevie. "You said nothing about her before. When did you meet?"

"And where?" added Phil.

So John told them. "We only met on Wednesday. Do neither of you remember her? She's been living with Wills and Cathy at Emu for years. I never met her, but I knew all about her. Surely you've both met her before at the Lockleys' gatherings?"

"You mean she's *that* Colleen Murphy? But she was a little scrawny thing and in rags." Stevie said.

"Yes, the same girl, only with good food and nice clothes, she's changed. I went to Emu and got her parents' permission on Friday, back yesterday and married today." John grinned at his older brothers.

"What, you only met her on Wednesday? What's the hurry?" Phil asked.

John looked at his brother with an astounded expression on his face. "Oh, come on, Phil. You know that Reverend Clarke is due back any minute, and the trip is nearly ready to roll. It could even be this week. We either marry and hope she can come, or we get engaged, and I have to leave her for over a year. That wasn't going to happen." John looked at his brothers. "I'm thirty-two, she's twenty-nine, we don't have as much time as you two did. We know what we want. Yes, we may not have known each other long, but we're certainly not strangers. Everything I have heard of her is good; apparently, the same for her. It's quite simple – I love her. She is all that is kind, gentle, and noble. She also has a strong faith. I would not have married her otherwise." He met both pairs of eyes, honestly. "Okay, she's stunningly beautiful too, but ... well, it's far more than that."

"That's good enough for me, lad," said Phil.

"Me too, and congratulations," Stevie added.

They rejoined their parents, and the three younger ladies arrived soon afterwards.

Hamish and Effy had taken all nine children into the backyard, and Hamish was watching them.

Effy returned to the kitchen and was joined by Caro. "Hello, love. Is everything under control? It's a lot to drop on you without much notice."

"I've got it all under control, Mrs Evans. Hamish has been helping; he's watching the children now. Mr John is worth the effort. I'm just glad he's finally found someone." Effy had not stopped preparing the tables while talking. She finished trimming the beans and started making custard.

Caro returned to the now crowded sitting room. She stood at the door, looking at her family. She smiled. Finally, it was complete. John had found his match.

Chapter 4   Preparations

A week later, Reverend Clarke walked into John's office. "Hello John, Terrance said I had to speak to you. What's happened?"

"Hello, Reverend, nothing is wrong. I got married, that's all," John said quietly. He had finished his pinning for the day and was about to place more in the relaxing jar. He decided not to.

"Oh, John, that's good news, but to whom? I didn't know you were seeing anyone?" his mentor said.

"Let's get some tea, and I'll fill you in." John took him along to the tea room, and they settled down for a long chat.

An hour later, Reverend Clarke and John left the Museum to head down to Wills' house. Before he made a decision, he wanted to meet Colleen. Then he also wanted to ask Luke on the trek officially. He also wanted to talk to Luke about Colleen and see how he felt about her joining them without Wills or John around.

Luke reassured him that he was happy about her coming. He knew her to be a great cook and used to roughing it.

By that evening, the group of four were preparing for the start of Reverend Clarke's dream. He had agreed to wait until Wills' babies were born. It would take some weeks to make the arrangements needed anyway; they had yet to buy horses, saddles, more panniers and saddlebags. Colleen wanted to buy some split-skirt habits for her to wear.

The cobbler, Mr Iles, had been commissioned to make her some special walking boots. John also ordered two pairs of riding boots for her. They each bought two new pairs of riding boots for themselves. Mr Iles had two new boys working with him. They were only about ten, but were keen workers.

Colleen went to John's office and helped him pack some of the items they would need for his insect specimens. He showed her around and introduced her to his colleagues. As she left, John turned back to see each of their mouths open. He grinned and winked at them.

"Cor! Now I know why he married her so fast," said one.

Another said softly, "Did you see her? She's stunning."

John heard both comments and smiled to himself. She certainly was beautiful, but there was so much more to her than her looks. Their three days at the Hotel had been everything he could imagine a honeymoon could be. If he thought her kisses were memorable, what followed blew him away.

After Effy's lunch, they returned mid-afternoon to Wills' house, where she packed her bag. The carriage then took them to the hotel. John had repacked his bag the night before, just in case, and he grabbed it on his way out. The carriage had taken the Lockleys back home and returned for the happy couple. Then returned to the hotel.

The Earl, Wills and Luke's father had a standing arrangement with Mr Stewart for a carriage to be available when required for any of his family. The prestige attached to the Earl's family using their vehicle covered the inconvenience the hotel may encounter of having their coach seconded at any moment. Wills and Luke enjoyed the convenience of having it as they wished. Occasionally, having an Earl as their father was nice, one of the perks of the title. Even Charlie and Gracie used it when they came to town, but more to hide in than anything else.

Mr Stewart welcomed John and Colleen like royalty at the hotel. Colleen was overwhelmed. She thought the luxury of Wills' house was terrific. She was used to Eddie's place, too, but this. Velvet drapes, embroidered bedspreads. There was carpet on the floor, an inside privy for each room and a full-size bathtub with a plug to empty the water.

"Oh, John, this is amazing. I feel like a queen," she said after returning from the dining room on their wedding night. After that, they had barely left their room for the next three days. John had intended to buy her a ring on Monday, but it was Wednesday on the way home before they visited Mr Lamb, the jeweller.

They first picked out wedding rings, then Colleen chose a beautiful sapphire engagement ring with a diamond on either side. "John, God sits on a sapphire throne, and we are but little diamonds on either side. It's perfect, and I love it." She returned his signet ring. He slid on her new wedding ring and then her engagement ring. He had also bought a matching one for himself. Wills had one, and he liked it. They had returned to Wills' house that night. A mere week from when they had met. Hamish and Martha had already moved her things into the front upstairs room.

John had to return to work on Thursday. Colleen came in one afternoon, a week later, to help pack.

Caro, Alice, and May had decided to take her shopping, allegedly to buy her some clothes for her trip, but also to buy her a trousseau. For a girl who had two dresses before she married, she was soon in tears. She backed away from them. "I can't take all this. I'll never wear them. I married John because I love him, not for all this. I don't need these."

"Love, sit for a while and listen." Caro shooed the other two girls away. "Colleen, the more I get to know you, the more I love you. You love John; I know that, and so do I. Now that you are married, you need to be able to fill the part you now have. That includes dressing for the role. John mentioned that your folks don't have a lot. Colleen, we do, and we would love to share it with you." Caro took her hand and looked her in the eye. "Colleen, I'll make you a deal. You let us spoil you, and you must remember we're all doing it for John. We shall also outfit you for the trip. Split habits and everything else you need. Will you let me do that – for John?"

"Oh, Mother Caro, I don't want it or deserve it. But I'll do it for John. But I refuse to get more than I need before the trip. When I come back, you can do your darnedest if you insist. I never thought that I would ever need more than I have." She had tears rolling down her cheeks.

Caro drew her into her arms; she smiled. John had chosen well. Caro sat her up and looked into her face. "So are we going to make John proud or you? Even more than he is? You only have to watch his face when you're in the room. He loves you, not your clothes, but we can still make him even more proud. Let's blow him away, eh?"

Colleen nodded, smiled, then sniffed. "All right, make me a clothes horse. I'll do it for him, and only for him, but not too much, just enough for the next few weeks." She shrugged her shoulders and shook her head. "Do your worst," she smiled wanly.

Caro laughed. Yes, she adored this girl.

Alice and May came back in. Effy followed them with a tea tray. They sat drinking tea and comforting Colleen. Both thought it was funny that she didn't feel she needed many clothes. Caro learnt a lot about her girls that day. Mainly, that the two other girls didn't need her; Colleen did, and she needed Colleen.

After they had tea, they left together and started on Colleen's preening. Now resigned to it, she entered into it with joy. Everything she chose was "for John". "Would he like this?" or "What's his favourite colour?" She looked to Caro for advice and took her word as final. It was only when visiting Mr Iles that she voiced her opinion. She accepted a couple of pairs of dancing slippers. However, she chose her own riding and walking boots. The next stop was to purchase her split habits. She refused to go without them. She would allow only one ball gown, and that was because they were going to Government House. Caro suggested one in cream with sapphire blue trim. It set off her eyes, and the jaws of the other two girls dropped when they saw her in it. The rest of the day dresses were to be only for the next month. More than that, she would not allow. She insisted that serviceable dresses in hard-wearing fabrics were what she really needed. She was allocated only one pannier for the horse, which was used for any clothing she needed and her personal items.

Caro listened to her.

Colleen had said to Caro, "Mother Caro, I'm hoping that I'll not need more than these for some time." She looked embarrassed, but Caro knew what she meant. Caro then added a few small items for John's benefit. Colleen's eyes opened wide when she saw the delicate lawn and lacy undergarments. She blushed scarlet.

"These won't take up much room," Caro said.

The other two girls were looking at things for themselves. Caro snuck in a very saucy camisole. It would be at the bottom of her pannier. The fabric was so thin it was almost see-through and was threaded with periwinkle blue ribbons through the lacy edgings at the neck and waist. Caro had seen her fingering them, but she passed over them for something very practical, calico draws. Caro bought both for her.

Luke, too, was in the throes of packing. He had a little more than clothing, new boots, and lots of empty books for journals.

Wills advised him about drawing materials. He had made a trip some ten years earlier. He and six Englishmen had travelled west across the mountains, then out to the wetlands. Wills sat in Luke's room and helped him sort through his things. He was only allocated one double pannier for personal items and a medical kit of sorts. They also had to pack bedrolls, overcoats, canvas, food, and equipment.

Wills sat with the group, discussing their needs. They had worked out that they needed seven horses, one riding horse each, with appropriate panniers for the back and saddlebags at the front. He had also suggested three pack horses, two for food and one for equipment. Or they could also invest in a small cart and take the bulk of the load as far as they could. They would send back many rock specimens along the journey, and if they took the things they couldn't buy, that would be a better idea. This final idea is what they finally settled on, only changing one ridable horse for one that could also pull a cart. They would also pack a spare saddle, should they need to leave the cart somewhere.

Reverend Clarke had previously travelled with Maria. He was not opposed to having a cart, at least with them. They had always taken a wagon. They and their children had lived in it. Colleen had offered to be the cook, and they were thrilled. She grew up cooking on an open fire. It was all they had.

Luke was happy to go along with any of the plans. It was all an adventure for him. Reverend Clarke had initially planned that this trek would head north-west. They were now starting by heading up through the Hunter Valley and over the mountain range at Nowlands Gap above Murrurundi, then through Doughboy Hollow and further north-west. However, the first stop was to be Parramatta to stock up on equipment from the Emporium warehouse, then going west to Emu Plains, then north via The Putty Road. From there, they would rejoin the original route at

Singleton.

Colleen suggested a few specific things. A sizeable waterproofed sail with side ropes was her primary concern. When asked why, she explained that this could be placed over the cart, thus protecting the supplies and pegged to the ground, hence providing weather protection for sleeping. She also listed some equipment for cooking and the basics she'd need.

Wills suggested that they contact Eddie and get him to make some special rock-chipping hammers. Pointed on one end and flat on the other. Years before, he had taken one that Uncle Ned had sent from London when digging for gold at Hartley. Wills had drawn what he wanted and sent the sketch to Eddie. He was sure these would be just the thing for digging out mineral specimens.

~

A week later, Ed sent back six hammerheads and some small metal wedges to attach handles. Each was slightly different but similar, with a pointed end and a flat end. In the bundle of these, he also included a leather roll of tools for changing horseshoes, hoof picks and similar things, a selection of horseshoes and a box of shoe nails. They had forgotten about these.

Luke had done his share at the blacksmith with Eddie and knew how to do most of the essential repairs, including shoeing a horse. He was no blacksmith, though. His work was usable but, as Eddie said, not really saleable. He had not done any for some years now. Luke had preferred to work there as a striker if he had to be at the forge or doing the books. Reverend Clarke had also had to do many a repair on the road. Having Luke along would be a boon.

Wills was almost jealous. With small children, all he could hope for was a week-long holiday now and then at their Hartley cottage. One day, they would get to travel again. He'd had his big trip eleven years before. Then, a few other shorter ones before they had children.

John asked his parents if they could park the small cart in their backyard. They, of course, said yes. This way, they could still be involved with what was happening. They also suggested that the spare room near the back door could be used as the storeroom for the trip's equipment and packing room. Four large leather, watertight, double panniers and four smaller pairs of saddlebags were delivered and duly unpacked into the room. They were made from kangaroo skin, polished and waterproofed. Four thick sheepskins for under the saddles and two small wire brushes for hoof cleaning. Four saddles, harnesses and all the rest of the accoutrements required for riding. Spare harnesses, reins and traces were out of the question. Wills bought them a small box of buckles and two rolls of half-inch wide leather strapping, and one small roll of one-inch wide leather, too. From this, they could replace most of what they needed should one break.

They fitted into the bottom of one pannier.

Into one of the panniers, Caro and Colleen packed and repacked items that Colleen would need. She wanted to take all three habits, but the required boots could only fit two in the box. They sat puzzling over this for some time until Colleen fell back on the floor, giggling. "Mother Caro, I forgot, I have to wear one and a pair of boots too. That will give me much more room." Colleen said, laughing. "I can easily fit everything inside." She had been a little worried about how she was going to cope with her menses. They had included a large package for that, too. A week after they married, she had them. John had no sisters, so this was something new for him. He knew it was science, but had no idea exactly how things like that worked or for how long. She had explained things enough for him to understand. Thankfully, he knew the biology of reproduction. She didn't need to describe that.

She and John had sat and discussed this soon after Caro had brought up another topic they had not had a chance to discuss: children. Hopefully, she would conceive and not have to worry. She didn't want to say anything about that. Caro had mentioned it to John. He just looked stunned and stayed silent on the subject. They had not previously discussed children. Everything had happened too fast.

That night, John and Colleen sat on their bed and discussed children. Colleen had already had to talk to her younger sisters about menses and babies. Talking to your husband wasn't the same. She loved his absolute innocence about such things. Coming from such a large family, babies and their creation were merely a fact of life. John was the youngest of three boys, but fortunately, he studied science, which included biology.

John admitted that when he met her sister, Mary, he had imagined that their children would resemble her. They had gone to bed, still talking about it. She lay with her head on his chest. He was still thinking about babies. "Colly, what happens if you fall while we're away? What will happen? You can't continue with the trip. We'll come home."

She turned on her elbow, "Oh, John, don't be silly. It's just a baby; it's not as if we're galloping everywhere. We're walking. I'll be doing much less than I normally do. My problem will be delivery. I've helped Mama deliver six of hers, but I'll have to teach you what to do. It depends on where we are at the time, though. There might be someone available. I'm not that worried, love." She reached for him. "We could practice making them, though…"

He reached for her and drew her into his arms. "Oh, willingly, love," he murmured against her lips.

Their deep conversation was finished for the evening.

Weeks earlier, on a ship to England

On board the *Donald McKay*, Charles and Sally Lockley travelled with as little fuss as possible. They had managed to catch a coastal steamer from Sydney to Melbourne and obtain the lovely master cabin on the *Donald McKay*. They had asked the Captain to keep their identity quiet as they wanted no fuss. All was well until they reached New Zealand. The news circulated quickly that the Earl of Coxheath was on board. Someone had seen them, and soon, they were lauded by all and sundry. Both hated this status, especially now when all they wished for was invisibility. They ate in their cabin for some time, but it was so small and stuffy that they emerged to get fresh air. Captain Warner insisted they eat at his table, where they could be away from prying eyes. Their grief at the loss of both Charles' beloved mother and stepfather was raw. The Captain suggested that they wear black if possible, or black armbands at least. People would then leave them in peace. Neither wished to socialise. They had waited for the double funeral and then departed in a great hurry. Luke had come for the service and returned immediately as he had exams that afternoon.

Charles wanted to tell his sister and aunt himself; he'd had nine beautiful years reconnecting with his mother. Sally would not consider letting him go back alone. So, two days after his mother's funeral, they were on board the ferry heading to Sydney to catch the next ship heading to London. Only Luke was there to see them off.

"Sal, are we doing the right thing? We're leaving the family alone at a time when they, too, will be hurting," Charles said as he held on to her as they leaned against the railing. The Captain had shown them where to stand out of the spray. Charles didn't care if it was etiquette or not, but by holding the railing with his arms around Sally, he could keep her both close and safe. His previously injured leg meant that his balance was still unsteady.

Sal words brought him comfort. "Yes, love, we are. Lilabet needs to hear it from you. Our children are grown now, whereas you are all she has left. We must be with her."

He was so sad his beloved mother was gone, yet happy that her last years were filled with joy and happiness. He had Richard to thank for that. He had filled her life with purpose; she had come for a visit and stayed for ten years. She had met Richard Childs soon after arrival. They socialised for over a year, neither thinking of marriage. It took for her to leave, and their ship nearly sank before he declared himself. They married three weeks later. She was sixty-four. He was the headmaster of the Female Orphan School, and she had thrown herself into the work with them. She involved the rest of the family, too, changing the lives of many of the girls.

Charles was now going back to England to tell his sister they were both gone.

His sister, Lilabet and her husband, Matthew, had come for a visit four years before. They had brought their two children, Matthew, known as

Matty, and Elizabeth, known as Betty, with them. They were adorable little imps who loved their "Uncle Chas" and "Tant Sal," as Betty called her.

Lilabet was thirty-nine when they married, and Matthew was forty-four. They had not expected to have any children, so being blessed with two perfect angels was truly tremendous. Especially, as young Matty was now the heir to the title.

The *Donald McKay* sailed from Wellington and was heading to South America. The wind was behind them, and they were skimming across the water. The wind was catching every inch of sail and the smaller handkerchief sails, too.

"The one nice thing is we shall get to see Ned and Christina again. Letters are all well and good, but it's not the same as a good belly laugh. I miss that, my love." Charles thought of his friend and cousin.

In the early years, they had to be circumspect in their friendship, as Ned was a Major and Charles a ticketed convict.

It had taken nearly twenty-five years and the discovery that Ned was now the Duke of Gracemere to find Charles was his third cousin and Earl of Coxheath to boot. It was only in the weeks between the near shipwreck and their final departure that Ned finally admitted what had stopped him from looking at Charles' history.

Ned suspected that Charles might have been his father's child, conceived while his mother was expecting twins. He would rather not know. If he had only swallowed his pride and asked earlier...

What was done was done. Ned was his best friend, but he now lived half a world away. Thankfully, with the advent of Clipper ships, it didn't take so long to get there. These 'birds of the sea' filled their sails with wind and flew. They were often shaving some forty days off the trip. It was still not fast enough.

That night, Sal cradled her beloved husband in her arms. He just needed to be held. It was the only time Charles' grief could be released. She understood. She had been the same after her mother had died. He had been her rock.

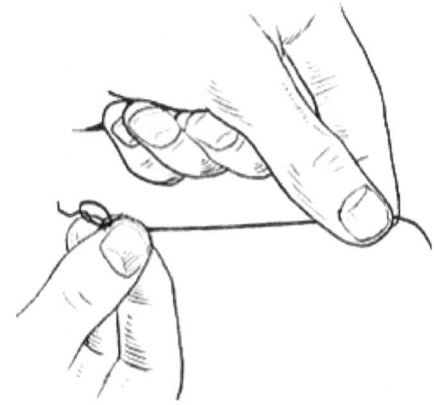

Chapter 5   Pulling Threads

*L*uke and Reverend Clarke were busy each arranging their own packing.

Reverend Clarke still had his parish to administer; his non-ordained assistants needed some instruction. He was seriously distracted, though. Unable to keep his thoughts fixed on the job ahead. He shook them away. He also needed to stock up on Holy Communion wine and ingredients to make his own unleavened bread. It was a stock item for his travels.

He wished he could take his covered wagon, but knew that where they were heading, it would not make the distance. The Communion wine would fit into his pannier bag, and so would his travelling Holy Communion set and black preaching stoles. He usually had his cassock, but he wasn't sure he could fit that in this trip.

He only had to think of a trip, and his thoughts would return to his missing wife. He missed Maria so much. The trips were just not the same any more. What had made him confide in Wills, though?

The past decade had been horrible. At least she wrote often. As did the children. Oh, how he missed them all.

Now, in the Rectory at North Sydney, Reverend William Branwhite Clarke stood looking out the window. The view never changed, and neither did his mood of depression.

William prayed, "Lord, show me a way to bring her back." He had accepted this position in North Sydney to establish a stable home life and a home base to raise his children. However, they had returned to England. He had stayed in North Sydney parish, so she had somewhere to come back to. But she never came. He hated being here without her. He missed the children.

William groaned, praying aloud. "Lord, is this to be my lot forever? Alone? Studying dead rocks?" He stood leaning on the windowsill. Drenched in perspiration and overcome with grief. He had his back to the door. He had heard someone enter just before he prayed. He turned.

Wills Lockley stood, looking at him.

"Did you hear?" The man sounded so absolutely dejected.

Wills nodded. "It's what I've come to talk to you about, sir."

"Oh, lad, I should not have burdened you with my sadness." His mentor and friend looked haggard. He sank into a chair, dejected.

"Reverend Clarke, do you trust me?" Wills asked.

"Of course, lad. You know I do, or I wouldn't have said anything otherwise." William sank into a chair near him. "I'm just down, lad. I miss her sorely; I have done since she left. It's why I travel so much. I hate being here without her."

Wills smiled. "It's where I think I can help, sir. I presume it's just money? I have more than enough. Way more than needed, and most of it is because of you. Sir, the Lord has blessed me a thousandfold and more than the gold I found. You know that. If we send her the money, will she come back? Is that the only problem?"

"Oh, Wills, I wish I could say yes. I just don't know. I want her back so very much." His mentor looked grief-stricken. He smeared a wayward tear away with the heel of his hand.

The student comforted his mentor. "Then let's do our best and just focus on that. Do you have her address?"

"Yes, she writes often." The Reverend felt a glimmer of hope.

"Good, then I can send a letter to Uncle Ned or Dar, and they can do the groundwork from over there. If you can write a letter to her that Uncle Ned can deliver, I think that would do the trick. No one can manage to say 'No' to His Grace, the Duke of Gracemere. We'll send it in one of those new clipper ships, and it will be there in about eighty days. Give her two months to pack up and another eighty days back. Will that give you enough time to get some of your trip done? Let's say August?" Wills was now squatting in front of him. "Sir, let me help. We can work this out."

William's face brightened. "Do you think it will work? Do you think she'll come back? Wills, it's been so long." His eyes were swimming, but he took a deep breath. "I'll do it, Wills. I'll write tonight. Mr Stewart will know when the next ship is to sail."

Wills heart hurt. He said, "Thank you, sir, I do wish you had confided in me before. I could have helped. You know that. If it were not for you, I would have nothing. I, too, would be just a simple blacksmith. This is the least I can do to say thanks. Let's get this done. Let's bring her home. Cathy and I, well, we sort of feel responsible because we bought the ticket for her to go home with the children. We thought she had her ticket back." He met his mentor's eyes and held them. "Cathy said she purchased a return ticket."

"Maria cashed it in and spent it on the children, Wills. I gave her the rest of the gold bar as well, lad." Reverend Clarke took his hand and squeezed in thanks. Unable to speak, he nodded. He took another deep breath. Finally, he said, "August, eh? I can work around that. Maybe not even that long. I'll bring them back in July, Wills." His mentor swallowed. "You've given me hope, my boy." This time, he wiped his eyes on a large linen handkerchief.

Wills smiled, "I'll go and talk to Mr Stewart and see when the next ship leaves. Do you know that my Dar is over there? Uncle Ned may send them back altogether. That means Cabin Class again." He chuckled. "I'll get going. Sir, we'll get her back."

Reverend William Clarke took his hand and shook it vigorously. A broad smile on his bewhiskered face. He was unable to speak due to a large lump that had formed in his throat. His smile said it all. "The Lord does work quickly, doesn't He?" He chuckled.

Smiling, Wills let himself out and walked back down to the wharf.

The ferry was still at the wharf. He had asked them to wait. He walked briskly. They cast off as he walked along the jetty.

Wills pushed the boat off from the wharf as he stepped on board. It had only taken him three minutes longer than he expected.

When the boat arrived at the quay in Sydney, Wills hot-footed it up the hill, stopping in at the hotel and found that a ship was in the harbour and due to leave in three days. It was now taking on cargo and filling with stores. He scribbled a note and asked that it be delivered to Reverend Clarke.

"*Granite City leaving 31st October. Wills.*"

Wills sealed the note and handed over the message.

Mr Stewart sent a bellboy straight down with the letter for the ferry Captain.

Wills then returned to Cathy less than two hours after he left.

Two weeks had passed since they arrived in town. Her time to deliver was getting very close; she was barely eight months old, but she could not get comfortable. Her feet were swollen, and she was so sick of being so large.

As he entered his house, he could hear feet running and movement upstairs.

Hamish was in the kitchen and heard the front door close. "It's time. By tonight, you'll have some babies. Jack has gone to the hospital to prepare the doctor. Martha is getting Cathy ready. John is at work, Colleen is just grabbing her bag, and I'm going to babysit with Luke. Go to her." His accent was nearly non-existent, and Wills chuckled. He knew Hamish could plaster on a thick brogue, but he had not realised just how much.

Wills did, two steps at a time. Cathy was in the middle of a contraction. He was in time for her to grab on to him. He had been with her through the other births. He had told the doctor he was going to be in on this one, too. The doctor was horrified but finally agreed. Martha and Colleen were ready. The contractions were still ten minutes apart. They only had time to walk out the back gate and across the road to the hospital. Once down the stairs, they walked gently; she had a contraction just before they reached the back entrance. Her waters broke, and Wills picked her up and carried her across the road.

"I can walk in, love. Truly," Cathy pleaded for him to put her down.

Wills was adamant. "Love, you need to get to the hospital *now*. Wrap your arms around my neck."

Cathy did, and he carried her quickly across the road and in through the hospital door.

Martha and Colleen were hard on his heels.

Martha heard Cathy start to yell with another contraction. They were hard and fast now.

Jack said he would head back and help Hamish with the other children.

The doctors and nurses came from all corners. Wills had put her down, and she was leaning into him through another contraction. Martha caught up with them and followed the doctor into the room.

Colleen and Wills would bring Cathy in when this one passed. She waddled slowly into her room, Wills and Colleen on each side of her. Less than a minute later, another one hit.

"Oh, Wills, they are coming so fast now," Cathy said.

"Yes, love," he said supportively.

Martha and Wills undid her gown, and Colleen had a nightgown ready. She was in bed and changed before the next contraction hit.

The doctor came in and was followed by two nurses. He had not washed his hands, and Martha refused to let him touch Cathy until he had. He knew he had met his match in her, and he and the nurses all went and scrubbed.

In less than half an hour, Cathy was ready to deliver. She had been having back pain all day before and had not let on.

Wills was upon his knees behind her as he had been with the other deliveries.

Cathy was bracing against him and thankful for his support.

Colleen stood beside her with a basin.

The doctor was in awe of these four people. Obviously old hands at birthing, he waved the nurses to stand by and let Martha and Colleen continue with their help.

Richard Edward Lockley made his entry into the world with little effort; he was a healthy five pounds.

Elizabeth Martha Lockley took another half an hour to arrive.

After Richard was born, Wills had Cathy up and walking around so the second baby could turn.

Martha walked with them.

Colleen again stood in readiness with a basin.

Cathy walked over to her baby boy and stroked his cheek. "Oh, Wills, he's so beautiful." The fair-haired baby grasped her finger as she stroked his face. She felt another contraction coming and turned to Wills for support. From there, they came hard and fast again.

With delivery imminent, Wills eased her up on the bed for the birth. Elizabeth made a quiet entry; she needed a smack to take a breath.

They watched her turn from blue to pink.

"Oh, Wills, she's just like Tilda." She had light brown hair and a dimple in her cheek.

She delivered the afterbirths, and the doctor and nurses cleaned her up. She had not torn and insisted on sitting up and feeding the babies.

Colleen had brought both infants to her, and Cathy adjusted herself to feed them together.

Martha placed two pillows and helped arrange both babies. She'd had plenty of experience with twins, too. Ed and Jenna had a set, and Ned and Christina had produced a set on their last visit, and she had helped with their delivery. Christina had twin girls on the same day Jenna had delivered Kit.

Martha and Colleen had helped deliver many of Maureen Murphy's babies, not to mention many family babies. She stood guard, not letting him near her daughter. "We're not coming back here while he's here." Martha was horrified by the doctor. He had wiped his hands after the births but not washed them.

Wills was blissfully unaware of the politics going on around them. He was still sitting with Cathy. He stayed with her while Martha went to arrange a wheeled chair to take her home.

Martha refused to leave her daughter in this horrible place.

Wills tended to agree. He had noticed the cockroaches running over the floors, and nothing was clean. Surely they had learnt about the bicarbonate of soda and sugar baits? He shuddered; he had to get her home.

The doctor said she was to stay in bed for a week before she was moved, and then he left. Five hours after the babies were born, Wills wheeled her out the front door while all the staff were 'otherwise occupied'; he pushed her across the road and took her back home.

Colleen had set up a diversion, and then the group vanished.

They acted quickly and took her outside.

Martha and Colleen each had a baby, and Wills carried Cathy from the back driveway to their room inside.

Luke took the wheeled chair back to the hospital. He passed a nurse and told her Cathy was home.

No one had seen them leave.

Luke smirked when the doctor blustered out and said, "I would not have let her leave."

"Sir, you are not married to her. He is. It was his choice." Luke did not have a discussion with him. He turned and left the building. A smile on his face as he left, he saw a rat run across the floor. "No wonder Wills wanted to get her home," he thought. He went home.

By the time he returned, Cathy was settled in their room. All the children had piled onto their beds and were watching the new babies. Lukie, Pip, Tilda, and Goldie were in awe at their new brother and sister. They knew they had to be quiet and still. They were.

Luke and Hamish came and took the children away, leaving Martha with Cathy. The babies were placed together in a cot, and they slept.

Cathy settled to sleep; she was tired.

Colleen changed her clothing and then followed John and Hamish out into the back garden. "John, I can't wait until that is us." She slipped her hand into his.

Hamish was lying on the grass with four children tying him down like Gulliver. He had been reading the story to the children during the afternoon. This grizzled red-headed Scotsman was gruff except with the children. He was putty in their hands. He adored them, and they did him. Jack was sitting, watching Hamish, chuckling.

John caressed her cheek. "Colly, I'd love them." He sat on the back steps, and she was nestled under his arm.

Colleen lifted her face to his. "John, I'm so happy. I just wanted you to know that." She smiled lovingly up at him. "Now that the babies are here, we can plan to go. Do you feel like taking a walk to let your parents know they have been delivered and are all safe and well? I need some activity." She pulled him up, and they told Hamish where they were going.

As they walked into the kitchen, he pulled her into his arms. "Colly, I did tell you I love you, didn't I?"

He lowered his head and kissed her. They had been married for ten days; each night was bliss for them both. John could not believe that married life was so good. His concentration at work was nil. The image of her waiting for him at home slipped into his mind often. He disciplined himself to try to control his thoughts. He had been busy packing for the trip, being with her day and night. Today, he had not been successful at keeping his mind on track. He had come home early as he had wanted her for a romantic dalliance.

On his arrival, she was not there. He was disappointed. The house was quiet and devoid of people. Finally, he heard voices in the back garden and looked out to see Luke and Hamish with the children. There was no sign of anyone else.

He had walked out through the kitchen door and was greeted by Pip, with "Hello Uncle John, Mummy had gone to bring the babies home."

Tilda threw herself into his arms, closely followed by Goldie. At four and five, the girls were adorable. They looked like little angels, the littlest one with almost white curls and the other honey-gold like Cathy. They were so unlike his own nephews and nieces, who were prim and proper and not fun to be with. These imps had wormed their way into his heart. They knew how to play without hurting their siblings. Phil's children were constantly pinching each other and generally trying to annoy either their siblings or cousins. More often than not, it was to draw their parents' attention. He had watched Wills. He had a firm hand on their behaviour, but a loving one. They knew when to behave and when to play.

John had never noticed parenting before. He never thought he would need to learn. Now, he soaked up everything he could.

Wills was fully hands-on. He refused to leave everything to Cathy. He could change a child's clothing, bathe them, doctor a scratch and hug them when injured.

John wanted this relationship with their own children. John released Colleen from his embrace and whispered to her. She nodded in reply. They quietly walked upstairs and slipped into their room. He locked the door, and she turned and reached for him. "I want you so much, love. Oh, Colly, I've not been able to get you out of my mind."

John had called her that on their first night together, and she loved it. He gathered her into his arms, and they tumbled on the bed, their desire for each other rising.

Half an hour later, they emerged, relaxed and sated.

Colleen had put her bonnet on, and she smoothed John's clothes. He hated tight-fitting jackets as they hindered his movements, making catching insects difficult. He always looked somewhat creased and crumpled.

They walked downstairs and met Luke on his way up. They explained they were going down to see his parents and tell them the good news about the twins' arrival.

Luke nodded. He had heard them go upstairs some time ago. He wasn't jealous, just lonely. He hoped they would be discreet on the trip, or it would be hard for him. It was hard already. He had known Colleen for ages. He loved her like a sister, but that was all. He was happy that she was content, and so was John. He had seen her grow from a gawky, skinny child into the beauty she was today. Her beauty had not stirred his heart. He had met some of the most beautiful girls; many had been introduced to him over the years with the intention of enticing him. Not one of them had touched his heart in that way. He had given that away years earlier.

He believed God had someone for him. But where? Who? He had

no desire to look, not since Ellen.

Luke had spent more time in prayer. He was looking forward to the trip, but then what? He presumed he would have to look for a teaching post. It was about the only thing he was trained for. He almost wished he didn't have brains. At twenty-seven, all his brothers were married and had families. He had not even met his "someone." He sighed and continued up to his room.

He shut the door quietly behind him. With the babies now here, the trip could proceed. He stood in his room looking out the window again, as he had only three weeks before; in that time, John had married, his brother and sister-in-law had twins, and he was preparing for a trip. He still felt empty. He had been deeply hurt when, twelve years before, Wills had left without a word and, in essence, run away. At fifteen, he'd felt abandoned. They were both living at their older brother Eddie's house; he had a room to himself, access to every book he could possibly desire and more luxuries than he could believe. His parents were in England back then, as they were now. Luke had never understood how Wills could leave… until now. Now he knew how he felt, alone in a house full of a loving family.

Unsettled, yet he felt called for something, he just did not know what. He stood before his window, praying as he had before. He wanted to talk to Wills, but he was busy with Cathy. He had bigger things on his mind. How long he stood there, he did not know. He heard a knock on his door. He turned as it opened.

"May I come in, Luke?" Wills was there.

"Sure, Wills," Luke welcomed his brother.

Wills entered and softly closed the door behind him. "Luke, Cathy said I needed to talk to you. You know her dreams. She said we needed to talk." He sat on Luke's bed.

Luke gave a half-laugh. "You have to admire God. I've been standing here, thinking back to you, actually, Wills. You know, when you ran away. I never understood how you could be lonely in a house full of loving family until now. It has taken me long enough, but I finally understand. I am so sorry."

"Ahh! I was wondering if that was it." Wills stretched himself on Luke's bed. Half lying against his pillows. "It's a horrible feeling, isn't it? A deep ache, and you don't know what is causing it."

Luke nodded. Wills was only two years older than him, and he was happily married with six children. Luke sighed. "Wills, I feel lost. What do I do with my life? Okay, I have a University Degree, actually a double, or will do; but I have no job and no prospects. What the hell am I going to do with my life? Charlie has the inn and his role as Viceroy, and Eddie has the forge and his Emporium. You – well, you've built a huge empire for yourself, and I think that's fabulous. But I'm nearly thirty, and I have nothing. Absolutely blooming nothing. No money, no job, no house, and no one to come home to."

The look he gave his brother made Wills gasp. There was a deep, haunted look in his eyes. Wills stood and went to him. "Luke, I feel this trip will help somehow. So does Cathy. I don't know God's will any better than you, but this is the door He's opened for you, and you have to walk in confidence and faith along that pathway. Let the future look after itself." Wills wished Dar or Eddie were here to talk to him, but it was just like so many years ago.

Luke nodded. He didn't want to be alone. He wanted Ellen.

Wills continued. "John felt the same, you know. He had been saying something similar on our last visit. We've sat trying to work out how he and Colleen have not met in all the years we've known her. But God's timing was not right for them." He looked at his little brother.

Luke had sunk onto the floor, looking dejected. Tears were not far away.

Wills continued, "The waiting is hard, but Luke, I have found that it's when we get this disquiet that God is beginning to 'do His stuff'. Trust Him. It will work out. Until then, we have to follow where He's leading us. For you, right now, it's going on this trip. That's your start. Plan for that and leave the rest to him."

Luke held his brother's eyes. He nodded. "All right. I'll try to. I'll throw myself into this and do my very best. I suppose seeing John and Colleen together makes it just that bit harder too."

"You're not wrong there." Wills stood looking at Luke. "As you're going with him, Luke, I'll let you know that Reverend Clarke's wife left him not long after Lew and Aidan's double wedding to Mrs Clarke's nieces."

He heard Luke gasp. And utter a soft, "No…"

"Well, I'm not sure she actually left him, but she took the children home for an education and has not returned. She has been gone for that long. He never said anything until I saw him at Emu Plains a month ago." Wills met his brother's sad look. "Luke, he didn't have the money to get her back here. It's where I was this morning. We have a plan. I'm hoping she'll return with Dar and Mama mid-year. Luke, I think you need to help him on this trip. It's why *you* have to go."

"Oh, yes, Wills, of course. Why didn't he say anything? Why, that's nearly five; no, it's over eight years ago. Oh, Wills. I thought she was just staying at the Rectory while he travelled," Luke exclaimed. His melancholy had seemingly vanished.

"It's what we all thought, but Luke, it's been over ten years. He only let it slip to me by accident. I caught him at a vulnerable time. Our plan is now in action; you're part of that. You'll now be returning in about July, August at the latest. Hopefully, she will be here then or soon after, and hopefully with Dar and Mama. That will give you all the time to sort the specimens collected and tidy up before she arrives."

Wills noticed the change in Luke's attitude. He now had someone else to think about, and his woes were insignificant to Reverend Clarke's. "Good," thought Wills. "Do you need help with anything? Packing, sorting, or need any more equipment? Money?"

"No thanks, Wills. Just a good kick up the backside is all I needed. Only a brother could do that; I'm just feeling sorry for myself. I'm good now. Honestly, at least I know one way I can help. I'll leave the rest to Him." Luke pointed upwards and smiled.

Wills noticed that the haunted look had already flown from his brother's face. "Trust God, Luke. He already has all this sorted."

Luke nodded. The words and promises were easy to make, but some doubt still remained.

Chapter 6   Directions

*R*everend Clarke came to visit the next day. He came with his letter to Maria in hand. He was overjoyed to hear of the birth of the twins, congratulating Wills joyously. He handed the letter to him. His attitude was bubbling. So different from the melancholy man of yesterday morning. Hope had finally returned to him. Wills took him into his office; he shared that he had told Luke and why.

When Wills told Reverend Clarke of Luke's own melancholy, the Reverend's eyes lit up. "We will help each other, lad." Reverend Clarke smiled at Wills. "Can you bring him in? I actually have something to ask him. It's why I have come up here rather than dropping in the letter. I had two more visitors yesterday afternoon, Bishop Barker and Mr Armitage. I'll wait until Luke comes before I tell you the rest."

Wills went and called Luke in to join them.

On their return, Wills motioned for them all to be seated.

Luke sat silently, looking from one to the other. He had no idea what this was about.

Reverend Clarke looked at Luke and said, "After Wills left yesterday, I had two more visitors. One was Bishop Barker and the other was the new Headmaster for the King's School, Mr Armitage. I'm not sure if you know, but there has been a, shall I say, 'readjustment' of the school again. Mr Armitage has finally taken over the school and is in the process of reworking both the curriculum and the school. He wanted me back on staff to teach. However, I have refused. I need to focus on my parish, my writing, and, hopefully, my wife and family. After this trip, nothing will be planned for the foreseeable future. Maria will get my full attention."

Both Lockleys nodded.

The minister continued. "Luke, I have put your name forward

instead, as the new Geography and Science teacher for The King's School. You have all the qualifications needed, and this trip will give you some practical skills that will be useful. I do not know if you have a job lined up already, but this one is a fantastic opportunity." He paused, watching the astonished look that appeared on Luke's face. Reverend Clarke was intrigued that Luke was staring at Wills, not at him.

Slowly, a smile spread across Luke's face. He turned to look at Reverend Clarke's face. "Really, sir, you gave my name? Why?" Luke was stunned.

"Luke, you have been preparing for this for years. Now is your time. It's why I wanted you with me on this trip. I feel all that was missing from your education is a bit of practical knowledge. What do you think? Are you ready to take on a classroom full of boys?" He bit his lips, trying to stop smiling. "Mr Armitage has instilled some discipline into the students, drills and some military education. The school has grown substantially. Do you know that now it's mostly live-in students? Over one hundred board at school now. Very different to when you were both there."

Luke and Wills remembered the years fondly. Reverend Clarke had been one of their teachers. He had even been the headmaster, for a time. He taught them what he now wished Luke to teach: Science and Geography. It was in these same classes that Wills learnt about the presence of gold in the quartz reefs. After class one day, Reverend Clarke had privately told Wills about some traces he had found in the creek at Hartley. Wills, however, discovered the actual reef when he had run away. Then he bought the land it was on. He had since built a cabin, and they all used it for weekends away.

Reverend Clark said, "Wills, when you came yesterday, I knew they would be there that afternoon. I knew what they wanted and was tempted to say yes myself. But if Maria comes back, as I'm sure she now will, I need and want to be with her." He looked at Luke, "Luke, I'll be available for any help you need, but I think it's too good an opportunity to pass up."

Luke threw back his head and laughed.

Again, this was not the reaction Reverend Clarke had expected.

Luke explained. "Sir, nearly three weeks ago, I was standing upstairs in my room in a very melancholy mood. I was alone, but for Hamish. I had finished all my studies and had no prospect of work. I had sought a position here in town, but there were no upcoming tutoring positions and no vacancies at any local schools. As I stood praying, a carriage pulled up at the door. It was Wills and the family. To say the past weeks have been a whirlwind is an understatement. First came the prospect of the trip with you, then John and Colleen's marriage, and now the twins. Sir, only yesterday did I confide in Wills. Again, he told me to trust God. The good Lord already had it under control." Luke looked at his brother and smiled. "Against my will, I said I would, but sir, I did feel better. I'm no longer seventeen, carefree, with the world waiting for me. I know that I have to work in my trained field. I had no option but to trust God." He chuckled. "Today, you come to me with this. How can I not laugh? I doubted when Wills was actually correct – God already has it sorted. Sir, I accept with pleasure. I will learn as much as I can on this trip and turn to you for help often, both during and after my return. I have much more to learn; I am aware of that. Is Mr Armitage still in town? Or has he returned to school?"

Luke was relaxed. The way forward was now open to him, with a clear pathway. He gave a deep sigh of relief.

Reverend Clarke quietly said, "Bishop Barker wants to see you this afternoon if it's convenient. As to the trip, we're now ready to leave. We will go via Parramatta, then Emu and up through the Putty Road. I was going to head via Newcastle, but that will add a couple of weeks to the trip. I have done all that area, so we will bypass it and go on the Putty Road, as John and Colleen will want to visit Emu Plains, too. Now, we have a goal, purpose, and a time frame. Let us not waste any time. We leave on Monday, Luke. Lots to do."

"Six days; whoa! I'll be ready," Luke said gleefully.

"Luke, can you come with me now, and I'll introduce you to Bishop Barker? I think you've already met. However, he wants to question you further. Grab your hat. Wills, don't lose that letter." Reverend Clarke stood to leave. He turned to Wills and said, "God's pulling his threads again, eh? If you had come today instead of yesterday, things would have all been different. I would have taken that job, Wills, and Luke wouldn't have one." He was chuckling to himself as he left. "God's perfect timing." He waited for Luke to get his hat, and they departed. "We have to see him at the Cathedral; otherwise, we would have to travel to Randwick to his house. Let us hasten." He jovially led the way out the front door. It was the happiest they had seen him for years. And now they knew why. They walked briskly past St James' church, then through Hyde Park, along Park Street and to the Cathedral. Reverend Clarke walked in through the transept door without knocking. He closed it quietly and stood listening.

"Is that you, Clarke?" came a voice from just beside them.

"Yes, sir, I've brought Luke Lockley with me, Bishop," he answered brightly.

"Good, good, bring him through and leave him here while you go and find Armitage. He's poking about the place somewhere. I'll call you when we're done." He waited for him to leave.

Bishop Barker was tall, very tall. Luke stood at six feet two inches, and Luke needed to look up to him.

Bishop Barker looked at him. "How's the happy couple?" he asked.

"Ecstatic! Couldn't be happier, sir," Luke sat where the Bishop pointed and waited.

"Well, you come with good recommendations. Clarke can't speak highly enough about both you and your family. I gather you are an Old Boy yourself?" The Bishop reclined in his office chair, spread his fingers and tapped them together.

"Yes, sir, I spent a few years at King's, then a few more at Sydney College and the last three at Sydney University," Luke replied.

"Hmm, so you know the school. That's good; it solves a few problems. You know of its history and issues they have been having?" the Bishop said enquiringly.

"Yes, err, there have been a few of late. My father, Charles, has been helping out where possible with what he can do."

"Oh, you're *that* Lockley family. That explains a lot. That said, what makes you want to teach? You have no experience, do you?" the Bishop asked.

"Well, sir, none at all with boys, but I have a love of learning. I wish to instil that love in others. If you do that, you have won the battle. Making learning relevant and important in their lives is what is needed. After that, each student needs to have their passions developed. Reverend Clarke possessed this ability and taught both my brother, William, and me about that passion. We are very different from each other, and he worked on our skills and interests. We each followed in our own path. Wills is the one who built the big warehouse in Parramatta and the emporiums. They supply the diggings. He is pouring some of the profits back into the community. He's starting by educating every child possible. Our grandmother, Elizabeth, was married to Richard Childs from the Female Orphan School, and over the years, we have all worked there, teaching them," Luke explained quietly.

"I'm so sorry about their passing. They were good people. I was pleased to be able to meet them earlier this year. A tragic loss." He commiserated with Luke.

The Bishop sat thinking, "If you know this about learning, you have won half the battle. I think you will do, lad. Now, I believe you are to leave soon on some trek with Clarke and our young bride and groom. Sounds interesting. A mineral survey, I believe. That will stand you in good stead. I'm sure Clarke will teach you as you travel. I believe you should now return mid-year."

Luke nodded in affirmation.

The Bishop continued. "Armitage should have things worked out by then. Be ready to start soon after your return; he'll have to muddle on if you're not back in time. Congratulations, you have your first job."

"Thank you so much, Bishop. I shall use this trip wisely. Reverend Clarke said I could use his syllabus. He will not be using it again as he's going to concentrate on other things." Luke was ecstatic but had to contain his joy.

"Wait there, lad." The Bishop stood and walked out.

Luke dropped his head and prayed. "Thank you, Lord. I'm sorry for my lack of faith in you." His head was still bowed in prayer when the Bishop returned a few minutes later.

Mr Armitage and Reverend Clarke accompanied him. He looked up as they entered, not at all embarrassed that he'd been caught praying.

The Bishop noted his stance and smiled. "Yes, I've made the right choice," he thought. "He's a man of faith."

Mr Armitage was introduced to him, and the Bishop left them together to get acquainted. He told Clarke to follow him.

Reverend Clarke followed the Bishop to the other transept.

The Bishop motioned for Reverend Clarke to sit beside him on a bench seat. "William, why didn't you tell me about Maria before? I saw your letter on the desk yesterday. Sorry, but I feel I was meant to know. Are you all right? Is there anything I can do to help?" The Bishop looked at him with compassion.

"Oh!" He looked somewhat confused. "I'm hoping that this will be sorted by mid-next year, but I miss her so. Bishop, I took the Parish at North Sydney to give her a permanent home. She left before the house was completed. I didn't mind as I thought she would only stay to place the children in school and then return. She kept extending it, but it's been over ten years. Wills Lockley has arranged a passage for her, and hopefully, she will return with his parents next year. I gave her all the money that Wills had given us. He gave me some gold as a 'thank you'." He looked at the Bishop shyly. "I hope so anyway. Oh, Bishop, I miss her so much."

He paused mournfully, then continued, "We used to travel and live in covered wagons. I look back, and I see how hard it was for her. I never thought I never dreamed I was hurting her. The children loved it; of course, children do. She, however, didn't. She hated it. She put on a brave face, but in the end, she couldn't hide it from me. I pushed her too far. I gave her too little. If she does come back, I will stay at home as much as possible. I'm getting too old to travel now. I turn sixty the year after next. I shall then write. I have a lot to record, many journals to reply to, and books to produce. Yes, that is what I shall do. My poor dear will have me under her feet so much, she'll wish I'd go travelling again." He wiped his fingers over his brow. "This may well be my last trip, Bishop. I now have a purpose, too. I shall teach Luke what I know and how to do what I do. Then I shall return and wait for her." He sighed in both resignation and contentment.

Mr Armitage and Luke emerged from the office. They shook hands, and the Bishop and Reverend Clarke stood to join them.

The Bishop looked up and saw them. "William, come and talk to me again before you leave; I have an idea." The Bishop laid his hand on his shoulder and gently gave it a pat. "I shall pray that your letter will be well received."

Reverend Clarke nodded and walked to join the others. "I have to come back tomorrow. Would that be convenient?"

The Bishop smiled, "Here at ten."

William nodded again, unable to trust his voice.

Luke and he departed.

Mr Armitage waited for the Bishop to join him. They walked into the Bishop's office, and neither sat. "I think you have found me the right teacher. He has a love of knowledge and the passion for sharing it," Mr Armitage said. "I did not arrive expecting to find a teacher, but I do feel the Lord has opened a door for this young man. He's an Old Boy, too. Did you know?"

The Bishop nodded. "I think you will find there is much about this young fellow that will please. I found him praying when I walked back in. He is a man of faith from a good family. Surely you have heard of the Earl?"

"You mean he's one of *those* Lockleys? No! Why, that's wonderful," Mr Armitage smiled. "It says much for him that he did not mention it to me. I think we shall get on well." Mr Armitage took his leave of the Bishop, gave a bow and departed. He had much to think about on the return trip to school. By the time Luke returned from their survey, he should be ready for him to start teaching. He rubbed his hands with glee; the Earl was a benefit already; Luke would be a double blessing. He headed back to his lodgings to collect his bag and head back to Parramatta.

Reverend Clarke and Luke were on their way back to Wills' house. They walked in silence, each deep in thought. As they approached the house, Luke said, "Sir, I want to thank you so much. This is really an answer to prayer, literally an answer to my prayer. It is God pulling His threads again, isn't it?"

"Yes, son, He works in very mysterious ways. I said as much yesterday. The Bishop wants to see me again tomorrow, so I'll bring a load of my gear over on the morning ferry, then head down to see him. Just as well, John's parents don't mind us traipsing in there with all sorts of paraphernalia at all times of the day. I'll have to get help with the last big load. I may have to blinker the horse and bring him loaded up. Can't bring that on the ferry, but the barge should do the trick. We'll talk about that inside, eh?"

Luke nodded as they walked down the street.

~

The next day, Reverend Clarke brought his sturdy little horse with him on the barge. It was saddled and loaded with his well-used panniers, sleeping roll and all sorts of other paraphernalia. They still had no cooking utensils or mining equipment except for the hammers, but Wills' contribution to the trip was to stock them up at the warehouse. The Reverend gentleman departed for his meeting with the Bishop.

When Reverend Clarke arrived back at Wills' house a few hours later, he stood in the office, stunned. He had just had an interview with the

Bishop. "Wills, the Bishop has said that if Maria comes, he's to make me Assistant Commissary for the Northside of the Harbour. This will give her a place and a role that she would enjoy. I will have to write and let her know." He turned to look at Wills, then chortled. "God pulling strings again. Wills, two letters are going from me."

Cathy suggested that Wills travel to Parramatta with them. He refused to go. He sent them with a sealed letter to Eddie and didn't tell them what it contained. They found out later that it was *carte blanche* to take what they wanted from the hundreds of stock items at the Warehouse. Ed was to pack what they refused to take.

~

Very early on the morning of the 5th of November, the little caravan of horses, a small cart and three pack horses were hitched and saddled in the Evans' backyard. Colleen was driving the cart. If she were seen astride riding through town, people would be horrified. She had never ridden a side saddle, and even having a saddle was a delight to her. John rode behind her with a packhorse behind him. The other two pack horses were tied to the saddles of the other two riders.

Wills was there to see them leave and rode on the cart with Colleen to his house. The caravan called in to say their farewells and kiss the children.

Cathy came down and hugged Colleen. Cathy may be married to an Earl's youngest son, but she was a convict's daughter at heart. Colleen, however, had been born free of free parents. Yet it was Colleen who had worked for Cathy. They were friends, always had been. It was with great sadness that Cathy waved her goodbye. She would miss her. She turned to Wills, who cradled her in his arms. "She's always been there for me; I'll miss her."

"She'll be back next year, love. Hopefully with her own child, or nearly ready to have one," Wills added lovingly. "It's what we've always wanted for her."

Cathy nodded, "I know. I'm happy for my friend but still sad for myself." She sniffed. "I'm just selfish, love. She's such good company."

Wills hugged her gently. "Immi, Deirdre, and Kerry will still be at home, and Fiona can join them now that there's room. Siobhan is really too young to live away from home, but you know she's always welcome. Give her a year or so. If we keep the house full, it won't be so bad, love. The children love them all; we will need some help at least for the next few months." Wills said.

They stayed watching until the cart was out of sight. The dawn had passed, and the sun was above the headlands. The empty streets were beginning to come to life. Wills pulled Cathy inside as she was still only in her dressing gown and closed the door. As they padded down the hall, Cathy heard the first of the babies' wake. The others would follow soon, and then the pandemonium would start all over again. "Ready for another day of noise, love?" Wills bent and kissed Cathy's neck. "Go back to bed, sweeting, and I'll bring them into you." He walked into the nursery; thankfully, the babies had not woken the other children. He quickly picked up Rick and changed him, taking him to Cathy before he fully woke Bette. He returned and changed Bette while she was still sleepy, then carried her to Cathy, too. He placed the babe in position on the pillow, and Cathy fed them both together.

Wills sat, talking quietly to her while she fed their new offspring. They were a week old already. Rick finished feeding first, and Wills took him and burped him. He was an old hand at this, as he'd burped each of the others. For a couple who had trouble conceiving in the first years of their marriage they now had six beautiful children. "Cathy, we are so very blessed. Look at these two. They are perfect." He was sitting, rubbing his thumb against Ricky's cheek. "I'm in love all over again, sweetheart."

Cathy sat, cuddling Bette. She had finished feeding. A baby let out an almighty burp, and Cathy giggled. "Not very ladylike, my sweet." She lay her back in her arms, and she gave a windy smile. Cathy gasped. "Wills, she has dimples, she's so cute. Look." Sure enough, Bette did it again, and her dimples darted in her cheeks.

"Oh, how sweet," Wills exclaimed. He rubbed Rick's cheek, and his popped too. "They both have them, Cathy."

Cathy covered up; she pulled her shawl around her. She'd heard noises and recognised her mother's footsteps. There was a gentle tap on the door. Cathy called, "Enter Maa."

Martha stuck her head in the door. "Is everything all right? It's so quiet."

Cathy laughed. "Yes, Maa, we're just relishing the peace. Come in and have a look. Bette has dimples."

She brushed her cheek, and the baby smiled. "Oooh, so adorable," said Martha. "None of the others have them, do they?"

"Hmm, none of the older ones, no." She said, "But Wills does if he gives a cheesy grin. It's why you don't see him do it often. He hates them," Cathy chuckled.

"They are cute on girls," he said, embarrassed.

"Oh, Wills, why have I never noticed?" said Martha.

"As Cathy said – I hide them." He gave a big grin, and sure enough, they popped. "Luke and Eddie both have them, but not as big. You never see theirs either."

Martha stood there with her hands on her hips. "You've been married for ten years, and I find something new about you." She left laughing.

Chapter 7   Westward Ho

*T*he cart and horses headed west.

Colleen was content, as she hadn't expected to be able to come. She would do whatever she could to help, or whatever they asked. If that meant she was a cart driver, then so be it. She had moved the extra sheepskin and laid it folded on the cart seat, nice. She was with John, and she was happy.

The week before leaving, she had had her menses, and she was pleased that it was done and dusted for another month. She worked out that the cart could come in handy next month. By then, they should be some hundred miles or so away.

Colleen was overjoyed when John told her they were going via Emu Plains so she could say goodbye to her parents.

John rode beside her where he could when the road was wide enough.

Before the gold rush, Governor Fitzroy had doubled the road's width to Parramatta and paved it with gravel. They should be there by nightfall. Lunch was to be at Canada Bay by the water or near there. Ed was expecting them, and they could stable the animals in his yard.

They pulled into Ed's front yard just at twilight.

Eddie and Jenna came out to greet them.

Luke greeted his brother, and Ed congratulated him on completing his University Degree.

Meanwhile, Jenna enfolded Colleen in her arms. "I can't believe it, Colleen. Married already, that's excellent news."

Colleen was glowing, "Jen, I'm so happy. I still can't work out how, after all these years, I had not met him before. Why had God kept us apart for so long?" Colleen was watching John as she spoke. "I'd heard you talk about him for, well, forever. He had never come to Emu, and well, we have never been to the same family functions. I had met Phil and Stevie, but I was only a scrawny child back then."

Jenna hugged her again. "Coll, and you've filled out beautifully. John obviously thinks so too," she giggled.

They walked inside arm in arm.

John brought in her pannier bag as well as his.

Luke went directly to his old room. It was now empty of all his personal items, but it still felt a bit like home. He would not bother opening up his parents' cottage to stay there, and Reverend Clarke took Wills's old room.

John closed the door and took Colleen in his arms. "Sweetheart, this will probably be our last night in a nice soft bed for some time." He drew her into his arms and gently brushed her lips with his. She stepped closer, pulling his body against hers. He groaned with passion. He was about to lay her on the bed when there was a knock at the door. It was Cara bringing some hot water.

John took the cans and thanked her politely. He put them down and locked the door. "Now, where were we?" He resumed their previous occupation.

Downstairs, Reverend Clarke and Luke handed Eddie Wills' letter. They told him what they knew about the twins' birth, which was very little.

Luke said something about Bette's dimples, and Jenna got the giggles.

Ed gave her a dirty look.

Luke was smirking so much that he revealed his much-hidden secret. He, too, had them.

Noises were heard in the kitchen.

Charlie, Gracie, and their children had arrived.

Luke was surrounded by the children. Teddy, John, and Emma were all clambering for his attention. Then, someone else walked into the room, and Luke froze.

Ellen followed her sister Gracie into the room.

Luke kept watching the door to see who her husband was. He had heard she was married, yet no one followed her. She stood looking at him, his eyes now locked to hers. His heart was beating like a galloping horse. Why was she here? He had not seen her for four years. He had avoided any family gathering where she might have been since he had heard of her marriage. He managed to greet his eldest brother and his sister-in-law, Gracie, then politely bowed to Ellen. As he took her hand, there was no ring on either hand. He finally found his voice. "Is your husband here too, Ellen?" He asked her quietly.

"Lukie, I'm not married. I have never been." She dropped her eyes. "Did you hear I was?"

He nodded, unable to speak. The massive lump in his throat would not allow him to answer. He nodded again and groaned. Finally, he swallowed and uttered, "Oh, Ellen. Who could have been so cruel to tell me so?" He spoke so softly that only she could hear.

"I waited for you, Lukie. You never came," she whispered. She still held his hand and squeezed it.

Luke turned to Ed. "We'll be back in a bit."

Without asking, they left. Walking out through the kitchen, almost dragging her, he walked into the privacy of the backyard. He had not dropped her hand. She was almost running to keep up with him. In the quiet of the garden, they could talk.

Luke stopped and turned. "Ellen, I stayed away because I was told you had married. For four years, four horrible years, I have avoided coming home, as you were with someone else." He was frozen in grief for the wasted time. "How could they say something so cruel, Elle?" He looked stricken.

"Four years? Oh, Luke, that will teach you to listen. Not 'Elle' but Isabelle 'Belle' Ellis married my brother, Sammy, back then. Lukie, I waited; I'm still waiting." She took one hand from his and touched his cheek. "I will wait forever, Lukie."

"Oh, Elle, what have I done?" He gently drew her into his arms, and he buried his face in her neck. "My heart had smashed, Elle. Oh, my Elle," he muttered. He was holding her tightly.

She felt the dampness on her neck. "Love, it's not too late. I'll wait forever." She pulled him away. "Lukie, I have always loved you, and only you. Do I need to ask you? Or do you no longer care?" She grinned but looked up at him coyly.

Luke had dropped to one knee. "Ellen Miller, would you do the honour of accepting my hand in marriage?" He had hold of both of her hands, and their eyes locked together.

"Yes, Lukie, of course I will. Now kiss me, you foolish man." She drew him to his feet, then stepped into his arms.

He enfolded her to him again. His pent-up hunger for her was released in the passion of his kisses. He was burning with desire and crushed her in his arms; then he kissed her eyes, cheeks, and forehead before again finding her lips. "Elle, I love you so much; I have done for so long." Reality hit. He stopped and held her away from him. "Oh, my love, we are leaving on an eight or nine-month trek tomorrow. If I had known, I could have got a Special Licence. I'll pull out love, we'll marry, and I'll start teaching now."

She put her fingers on his lips to stop him from talking. "No, Lukie, I have waited this long. I will be here when you return, but we will marry as soon as you get back. I will have everything arranged, so be warned. July, my love, August at the latest, but I'll be here."

He drew her to him again. "My love, my wife-to-be. I'll be here, even if I have to return alone." He kissed her again. Nothing gentle but hungry, passionate, emotional kisses. No gentle caress, but filled with passionate desire from them both.

After a few minutes, he lifted his head. "Elle, I have not told you my other news. I've been pleasantly occupied otherwise." He dropped a quick kiss on her lips. "I have been offered a teaching position at The King's School next year. So we'll be able to live here in Parramatta."

"Oh, Lukie, that's wonderful, but I don't care. As long as I'm with you," she said against his lips, kissing him as she spoke. She shivered. "We had better go in. Luke, I'm so happy. I just want you to know that. You are worth waiting for, my beloved."

He realised she was only dressed in a thin gown. They had stood embracing in the cool spring evening.

Cara poked her head out the door and told them dinner was ready. It was she who had suggested to Gracie that Ellen come to dinner.

Neither had told anyone of their feelings.

Cara, however, had seen the looks between them and even noticed Luke's extended absence. She smiled to herself. She could see them enfolded in each other's arms. "Finally! Star-crossed lovers indeed, but what timing."

They strolled in the back door.

Ellen was leading Luke inside, still clasping his hand. She would not let it go now. He was hers; she would wait forever if necessary.

They said nothing to Cara as they passed, but the look on Luke's face said it all. He was grinning so much his dimples were evident. He was beaming. They paused outside the sitting room door.

Luke kissed Ellen again; then they opened the door. One arm draped around her shoulders. The other reached for her hand.

As they entered, everyone fell silent.

The look on Luke's face was enough for Gracie to say, "Finally."

Ellen giggled.

Luke coughed, then made the announcement, "We're engaged."

Ed and Charlie made a beeline for him. "What's this lad? Engaged?" They dragged him away to pummel him with questions.

Luke nodded. "Long story. I had heard she married someone else four years ago. It wasn't Elle, but Belle - Isabelle Ellis, Bertie's sister. It's why I haven't been home much. I couldn't bear to see her with anyone else. Oh, I have been such a fool. I should have come and fought for her." He looked sheepish; then his eyes caught hers across the room. She was being congratulated by her sister, as well as Jenna, and Colleen.

To his brothers, he said, "We'll marry as soon as I get back – so you are going to have to prepare a wedding in my absence. I'll see if I can delay here a day and get the legal side done and buy her a ring and..." He stopped mid-sentence.

Charlie interrupted his reverie. "Have you asked Bill yet?"

Luke swung around and faced his brother. "Oh, cripes! No! I'll go straight after dinner. These next months will be so hard. But now I have not only a wife but a job to return to."

"What?" said Eddie, startled.

"Oh, I haven't had time to tell you about that. Bishop Barker and Mr Armitage have offered me a post at King's. I'm the new Science and Geography teacher, replacing Reverend Clarke. I start in August. So I can support her now, no more handouts. Only have to find somewhere to live."

"Ah! About that," Charlie said with a smile. "*Gracemere Cottage* will soon be vacant. How about that?"

"I'd love it, but that's where Wills and Cathy stay when they come to town." Luke looked puzzled.

Charlie explained, "Harry asked me to see if I could find a buyer for *Roseneath*. He and Vicky are now settled in Emu Plains at *Yodalla* and rarely use it. They can stay either here at *Bramblemere Close* or next door with me at *Willow Grove*. Wills needs a more significant base here in Parramatta as all the children no longer fit in the cottage, and I suggested we keep it in the family. He's just bought it. Six children won't fit in the cottage's second bedroom. Looks like you have a home yourself now, too, Lukie boy."

"Are you all right, lad?" Ed asked. He had seen the wave of anguish wash over his face, then joy.

Luke nodded. "If you had heard the conversation I had with Wills a couple of weeks ago, you would laugh. I had just finished my Uni exams, no job, even though I had tried every school in town. I had no girl, for I thought she'd married someone else, and well, life didn't look too appealing. I was standing at my window, praying about how lonely I was and with no direction. My actual words were, 'What the hell am I going to do now?' and pleading with God." Luke smiled. "Well, Wills pulled in at the gate as I was praying. I poured out my feelings to him, and we prayed together. He told me to trust God. He was sure it was sorted already. I laughed. I had stupidly begun to doubt god and His plans."

Charlie nodded, "I know that feeling, but go on."

Luke knew his brother had problems with that. Ignoring the comment, he continued. "Well, we were in the sitting room, and John was sitting playing with the children, and Colleen walked in. It was like you and Jenna all over again, Ed. Anyway, what was great for them was making it harder for me. Don't get me wrong, I wasn't jealous, just empty," Luke sighed. "Wills told me that Reverend Clarke wanted John and me on his trip. I was thrilled. Those were months I didn't need to be around Parramatta; the further away, the better. Then John married, well, that was hard. I knew Colleen would come. Oh, they have been fabulous. No touching or anything in front of me, but they were together, and that alone made it hard. I thought I had lost Ellen."

Charlie put a hand on his shoulder.

Luke continued, "Reverend Clarke arrived one day and told me of the Bishop's offer to him. My heart sank; I thought the trip was off. But, no, he'd refused it and suggested my name instead. We went straight down, and I met with the Bishop and Mr Armitage, and I got the job. My heart was in my mouth. I'd have to live here, in Parramatta and see her husband flaunting her. Last week, I alternately thought about throwing in the job and moving to Melbourne, and just clearing out or coming and putting on a brave face. I chose the latter. Then Ellen walked in tonight. I asked her about her husband. She just said she doesn't have one and never did. That's when I took her outside, Ed, and now we're engaged."

At that moment, Ellen arrived next to him.

Luke slipped his arm around her and drew her to him. "I am such a fool. All these years wasted." He bent and kissed the top of her head.

"Dinner is served, everyone," Cara said as she came in.

"We'll have the best wedding ever planned for your return," Eddie said.

"I don't care about the best wedding, just as long as there *is* one and it's ours." Luke dropped a kiss on Ellen's lips as they walked into the dining room.

Reverend Clarke had stood watching everything. He smiled to himself. "One more day here won't hurt," he whispered to Luke as he walked past him in the dining room.

"Thank you, sir, I really appreciate that." Luke glowed with joy.

William said, "We have yet to raid the Warehouse, but John, Colleen, and I can do that. You get things sorted on your end."

Luke nodded and gave him a beaming smile. He bent and whispered something to Ellen.

She replied with a nod.

Dinner was a joyous event. Eleven-year-old twins Teddy and John and nine-year-old Emma were overjoyed. Uncle Lukie and Aunty Ellen were getting married. Molly, at five, didn't understand but knew everyone was especially happy.

As soon as dessert was finished, Luke and Ellen left to see her father. Their journey was slow, as they stopped often. Luke could not get enough of her. Finally, they made it to the Rear Admiral Duncan Inn. Luke sent her in to wait with her mother while he spoke to her father.

Bill Miller was one of his father's good friends. Luke's sister Anna married Tim; their eldest son, Charlie, was married to Gracie. Luke had known Sam was married, but he hadn't heard to whom it was. Isabelle Ellis, 'Belle'. Her sister Milly was married to Cathy and Jenna's brother, Marc. Her brother Robert was married to Cara and Paddy's daughter Maryanne, and Liza was married to Belle's brother Bertie. He laughed again when he thought of all the interfamily marriages. It was often very confusing when they were all together. Three siblings married other siblings, and the other were in-laws. Now he was engaged to Ellen, at least he hoped to be, as Bill still had to give his permission.

Mr Miller was in the taproom. Luke walked in and asked if he could have a word privately.

Bill called Sam over and asked him to take over. They walked out onto the verandah. "Hello, Luke, I haven't seen you for years. Have you finished your studies yet?" Bill asked.

"Yes, sir, a couple of weeks ago." Luke was strangely relaxed.

"Well, it's nice to have you home again, lad. You always brighten our days. What can I help you with?" Bill asked. Bill saw a frown cross Luke's brow.

"Mr Miller, can I explain something before I tell you?" He swallowed, wondering where to start. "I thought I heard four years ago that Elle had married. Since then, I have stayed in Sydney as much as possible. I threw myself into the study and even did a second degree, then tried to get on with my life." Luke paused.

"I don't understand, Luke. Huh?" Bill said.

"I have loved Elle for years, sir. I could not speak to her while I was at school or even studying, but she knew how I felt. Then I heard four years ago that Elle had got married, as someone mentioned Miller. I only heard tonight that it was Belle, not Elle, who married. Sir, I would like permission to ask for Ellen's hand in marriage. She's in with Molly now."

"Oh, Luke, Belle married Sam four years ago. Is that what happened? Ellen only told us two days ago when she heard you were coming. She wanted to see if she could find out what happened." He smiled. Please call me Bill, as I have been all your life." Bill stood, thinking. "You know, we never guessed. She kept it close. We weren't worried; it's good having her here. We just want our children happy." Bill looked at the man Luke had become and smiled, "Luke, you are the only one who has ever called her Elle; she is Ellen to everyone else."

Luke released a long sigh. He had wasted so much time. "I know. Anna and Charlie are very happily married to Elle's siblings, Bill. I can't believe how stupid I've been. Bill, I need to tell you a bit more. I'm literally heading off on an eight or nine-month trek with Reverend Clarke and John Evans and his new wife, Colleen Murphy. We'll be back in July or August at the latest, and if you say yes, then we can get married straight away. I have a teaching position at King's, and we'll live at Gracemere Cottage."

Luke admired Bill. He was a hard worker, and he had the very best Inn in town. The *Rear Admiral Duncan Inn* was top-class. He and Charlie worked together now, as the gold rush meant that all the rooms were often full at the larger inn on the main street.

"Before I say yes, let's bring out Ellen and Molly." Bill poked his head in the kitchen window. "Love, can you both come out?"

Molly and Ellen were waiting to be called and came directly.

Ellen went straight to Luke and took his hand.

Molly and Bill looked at each other, and then Bill said. "Well, I'm guessing you've already asked her?" He said, grinning.

"Yes, sir, but if you disapprove, I'll honour that. It would break my heart again, but I would go." He could hardly take his eyes from her.

Bill chuckled. "Well, Luke, I'm not going to. I could not imagine my beautiful Ellen going to a better man. I wish we had realised sooner. However, now you are in a position to support her. Before, you were living on your brother's kindness. So, in the long run, I feel this is better. God's timing and all you know."

Molly went to her husband and put her arm around him. "Give him an answer, Bill."

"Yes, you may marry her, and, with our blessing," Bill said.

Luke replied by shaking Bill's hand and kissing Molly on the cheek.

Then he turned and swung Ellen around. Her arms were wrapped around his neck, and she drew his head down for a very passionate kiss.

"I think he likes her, love," Molly said and chuckled. "How did we not guess? Here was I thinking she didn't like boys. But no, she was waiting for her one special man."

Bill bent his head and gave Molly a kiss. "I'd better get back to work, Mol. When they come up for air, congratulate them for me."

"Oh, Papa, we can hear you, you know." Ellen was still wrapped in Luke's arms. She looked adoringly up at him. "I have so little time with him. I want every moment to count."

"I know, love, make the most of it, but go down the other end of the verandah out of sight of the road," suggested her concerned father. "You'll give our inn a bad name." He laughed as he led his wife inside, leaving the young lovers alone.

"Sorry, sir." Luke led Ellen around the verandah. He reached for her as soon as they were out of sight from the roadway. He drew her into his arms again, but did not kiss her.

She had her cheek on his chest as they talked. He had not told her of the cottage yet. However, there was one more thing he wanted to do, and that was to pray a prayer of thanks together. He contemplated how to bring it up when she pulled back in his arms and looked at him. "Luke, can we thank God for opening the door for us to finally be together? I know you believe too. I mean, really believe. I want our faith to be strong in our marriage." She looked him in the face as she spoke.

He bent and gently kissed her lips, then said, "I was about to suggest the same thing, sweeting." He drew her to him again.

Wrapped securely in each other's arms, they prayed. He promised he'd write whenever he could.

At ten o'clock, Molly came and told Ellen to come inside. She could have the day off tomorrow and spend it with him.

He said his goodnights and went back to Eddie's place. He passed

Old Tom on his way. It was late for him to be out.

They stopped, and as he was about to leave, Tom turned to him and said, "Farewell, lad, I'll not see you again before I go. Take care. Trust in the Maker, and all will be well. Never forget that lad. Just trust Him."

"I do, Tom, and thank you. Are you going somewhere?"

Tom smiled, but didn't answer, and he almost shook off Luke's hand, then walked off into the evening gloom. He had been part of the town for so long that he seemed ageless. He had arrived with Bill years earlier and had become a well-known entity.

Luke could not remember a week that Old Tom did not visit their inn for a weekly free meal. Once Eddie opened the Emporium, Tom had taken it upon himself to act as a groom cum footman, taking care of the clients' horses. Tom was both liked and loved by all. Luke stood watching him until the darkness swallowed him, then turned and walked back to Ed's. All the way back to Ed's, he praised God for how He had worked things out. First, the family arriving; then a direction for the future; next, a job, and now Ellen, God's plan was perfect as usual. All his heart's desires had come true. The following months would be challenging but worth it, knowing she was waiting for him. She had been waiting for years. At twenty-seven and twenty-four, they had time.

Luke intended to learn all he could in the next months and return as a better teacher. He entered the now-quiet house via the kitchen. He thought everyone would have either gone home or to bed.

Ed was waiting for him. "I just wanted to make sure everything was all right before I went to bed."

"Thanks, Ed. Everything is brilliant. Bill said yes. Ellen had said nothing to them either. We both bottled it up. It's like a dam has burst. I'm so thrilled. Sad that I have to leave her, but I'll use this time constructively. We'll see the Reverend tomorrow and make a booking for the end of July next year. I'll keep in contact with you all as much as we can, but we'll be out of range most of the trip. We have limited room, so I can't even take my stationery kit. Expect my letters to be somewhat dirty when they arrive." He laughed. "I think you know who will receive most of them." Luke's face glowed; he looked happier and more relaxed than he had for years. "Oh, Ed, I can breathe again. I've felt almost suffocated in town, yet I've not wanted to leave. I could have finished ages ago, but I added a second degree to keep me occupied. Now... well, it's like life is all new."

Ed smiled at his youngest brother, "At least you have tomorrow. Oh, we have a new jeweller in town too. You had better head down there first thing. Do you have funds?"

Luke nodded. "Thanks, Ed. Yes, I do." He had £20 saved from his allowance over the years; it would have to do.

Eddie rose to leave. "I'm thrilled for you, Luke, I really am." He tousled his youngest brother's hair as he left for bed. Luke followed him up the stairs.

"Thanks, Ed," he said quietly as they parted in the hallway.

~

A rooster woke Luke at dawn; he had not heard one for some years, as no one near the house in Sydney had one. The bird was sitting on the trellis outside his room.

Luke turned over in bed, smiled and stretched, then rose and dressed quickly. He would go down to his room at his parents' cottage and collect the few items he wanted to take with him. Things that he had not needed in town. His waterproof greatcoat, work riding boots, long work leather gloves and other rugged items from his smithing days. All would be required. As he turned to leave the room he'd called his for years, it suddenly occurred to him that he would probably not stay in it again. On his return, his things would be moved two doors up into the other cottage. What a blessing Uncle Ned was! What a blessing the two cottages were too; Gracemere Cottage had been Uncle Ned's and Christina's Cottage had been Aunt Christina's.

When Uncle Ned and Christina married, they gave them to Dar and Mama. Dar had later bought the centre cottage too. They laughed and called it Coxheath, after the town where he had grown up. "So I have something to be Earl of, now," Dar had said.

He was the Earl of Coxheath, but that was in England. He had no land nor income from there and decided to name the centre cottage somewhat of a joke. With Grandmother's work at the Female Orphans School, Dar had turned it into a new Women's Craft Group, a thriving cottage industry. It also had a bed as a 'safe room' for any woman in urgent need. The older girls from the school came and learnt all sorts of crafts and skills from the town womenfolk. Jam making, preserving fruit and vegetables, cooking, sewing, spinning, and weaving. The backyard had been turned into a playground, and it had become a women's hub most days and a safe house if needed. The gardens on either side were vegetable gardens as they were fenced and kept out the animals.

Luke looked forward to Ellen being part of this group. Once married, she'd be released from most, if not all, of her work at the inn. If they were blessed with children, this would give her companionship. Molly and Mama would be close at hand, and so too would Liza, Jenna, and Gracie. Anna and Tim moved around a lot, so that she couldn't come often. He looked forward to being home again and being back with those he loved. How different his thoughts were from a month ago; he smiled and nearly closed his bedroom door.

Luke stood with his hand on the door handle, then reopened it again. On the top shelf was a small wooden barrel with tarnished brass bands and a lid. It sat in the corner of the top shelf. It looked like a toy keg. He reached up and took it down. Inside were a roll of banknotes and a leather pouch of coins. Smiling, he emptied the contents into his pocket. Then placed the empty barrel back on the shelf. This was his earnings from Wills for his bookkeeping before he had started at school in Sydney. He laughed; he'd never banked it. He'd all but forgotten about it and the near £200 it contained. There was more than enough for a specific item of jewellery he wanted to buy later that day. Wills had insisted on paying him one per cent of the profits for the years he worked for him. After five years, it had added up. This was his money, earned, not given to him by his family. Ellen was worth every penny of it. For a second time, he left the room. He returned to Ed's house and took the items of clothing up to his room. Everyone was either stirring or already up.

Cara was already in the kitchen, and Moira and Shauna were filling jugs with hot water for the rooms. He thanked them and took his own as he walked through. He needed to shave.

Eddie, John, Colleen, and Reverend Clarke joined him for an early breakfast. They were heading straight down to the warehouse. They'd gather what was required for the journey.

Colleen had a list, but Reverend Clarke knew better than anyone what they'd need. Luke would only be in the way anyway.

Reverend Clarke said they would only take it if they could return it for resale after the trek. The gold miners weren't fussy about used goods, and they could still sell them at cost price.

Ed agreed, even if only to silence him. He smiled to himself. This way, everyone was happy.

For Wills, it was a mere drop in the ocean from what they sold daily.

John had harnessed up the little cart; the sturdy little horse was waiting patiently outside under the awning. They had chosen two stackable camp ovens, two medium billys, and one large one with a lid. There were plates, tongs, and an iron tripod with a chain and hook, as well as two frying pans and other assorted cooking paraphernalia. There was more mining equipment and camping goods, hammers, picks, a shovel, swags and food and water storage containers.

Colleen looked at the waterproof sheeting pieces. She decided on a large oiled sail sheet, with rope edging. It could cover the cart and extend down the sides to protect them all if it rained. It took them some three hours to choose, carry, and pack all the goods. As they had nearly finished, Colleen spied some tent pegs. She grabbed eight large, square steel pegs and stowed them in the cart, too.

Ed took two sets of sieves and four gold pans and added them to the pile. "You never know. I mean, you are going on a mineral survey. Pans will be useful, so will sieves."

~

Luke had left the house as they did and headed directly to Ellen. They would go now to the church and book the wedding together. As they arrived at St John's church, Luke stood rooted to the ground. It looked so different. Gone was the derelict building. The entire structure looked different, almost new. He looked around to see if he was actually at the right place. He had been somewhat distracted by Ellen on his way there.

She giggled. "I wondered if you'd notice. We had a service in July to open the new building."

"Wow! I didn't even recognise it. It's totally different." He stood, looking at St John's church. Taking her hand, he started walking around it. "Amazing, even the windows are a different shape. It was brick before, wasn't it? Now it's sandstone. Look, even the steeple has new shingles on it. Oh, Elle, it's beautiful."

They had reached the side of the rectory. "Have I been away that long? Oh, love, I'm so sorry." He had just drawn her into his arms as Reverend Gore emerged from the office.

"Well, Miss Miller, I never expected this," he said in a surprised voice. He had not recognised Luke until he drew apart from her.

"Luke Lockley, is that you? Are you back from Sydney now? Good to see you, lad. But ... err, I gather you two are here for a reason?" He smiled at them both.

They were now holding hands and returning his smile. "Yes, sir, we'd like to book our wedding in, please. At the moment, we're looking at about July 26th next year. Although we might have to be a little flexible, as I shall be away for the next eight months. We aim to return in July, but if anything unforeseen happens, we will be back at the latest by August. I'm due to start teaching at The King's School in August on the 6th, and I don't intend to be late. Mr Armitage knows, though." Luke looked at the minister. "Sir, don't get me wrong, but I didn't expect to see you here. Where's Reverend Bobart?"

"Oh, Lukie, he died last year," said Ellen, grabbing his arm lovingly. "Did no one tell you?"

He gasped. He shook his head. "No, I had no idea."

"Oh, lad, I'm so sorry. He was your headmaster, wasn't he?" Reverend Gore commiserated with him. "He died at school, horrible for everyone. It happened suddenly in July last year."

"Yes, he was a friend of my parents as well. The timing explains it. I was in exams then, and I bet the family wouldn't want to have told me. I'm just surprised, that's all. He wasn't all that old." Luke was still shocked.

"No, only forty-seven, I believe," Reverend Gore said.

"That's only fifteen years older than I am now. He was a great teacher. We had fun at school. He was a bit like one of the boys sometimes. He and Reverend Clarke made lessons fun. They gave me my love of learning." He swallowed.

"Come into the office, I have a few minutes until Matins starts." He led them back into the office, and they sat down. He took his diary and flicked it to the back cover. He then added the prospective date, with a question mark next to it, followed by their names.

Luke said, "I'll attempt to keep in contact as much as I can, especially with Elle, but we're heading as far northwest as we can get. Maybe I should take a carrier pigeon or fifty." Luke grinned and squeezed Ellen's hand. "More like two hundred and forty of them, so I can send a letter a day. They might overload the horses, though." Luke chuckled.

"All right, all right, being serious." Reverend Gore gave a laugh. "I'll start to read the Banns in mid-June; you have three months from the end of them to then get married. If something happens and you get delayed, then we still have a month or more up our sleeve." Reverend Gore wrote in the details, then put his pen down. "I must go. I'll be late for services. Congratulations to you both!"

"Thank you, sir, we'll behave." Luke gave a mischievous smile and winked at Ellen. They thanked him, then left.

They walked down Church Street. This time, Ellen was oblivious of where they were walking.

Luke steered them towards the jewellers.

The bell jingled as they entered. A kindly gentleman appeared from the back room. "How can I help you today?" It suddenly dawned on him who they were. "Oh Miss Miller, sir, welcome."

Luke introduced himself then said, "We would like to look at some engagement rings, please." To Elle, he asked, "What would you like, love?"

"Oh, Lukie, you choose. I have no idea. Certainly, nothing too fancy," she said softly. "You should have given me some warning," she said dreamily.

"Diamonds, then, please; nothing too big, but nothing small either." He turned to Elle and whispered, "You should have seen what Wills first bought for Cathy. It was so huge that when they swapped it, they got a necklace, bracelet, ear-bobs and matching wedding rings too." The jeweller brought out a small tray of lovely, medium-sized diamond rings.

"Luke, they are nice, but..." Elle wasn't really sure she wanted a diamond.

Luke understood. "Can you bring out a selection of other stones?" he asked the jeweller. "Is the size right, love?" Luke asked.

She nodded, "Yes, not too big." As the jeweller placed six small trays of different stones on the bench in front of them, one jumped at her.

It was the most beautiful dark green emerald in a Florentine setting with a *fleur-de-lis* on either side. "Oh, Luke, this is perfect."

There were two similar ones. She tried on each, and one fitted perfectly.

Luke asked the price, expecting it to be the top end of £100. He had two hundred and twenty pounds and some coins on him.

The jeweller said, "£33 for the ring, sir."

Luke smiled and asked for some matching items to be produced, as well as wedding rings. The jeweller put the trays of rings away and brought out a selection of bracelets, ear-bobs and necklaces, one after the other.

Ellen chose a stunning bracelet and a pair of simple pear-shaped emerald earbobs. There was a matching necklace, but she did not even look at it. It was very chunky and not something he'd like to see her wearing. While she was admiring some other items and looking at wedding rings, he quickly sketched a heart-shaped necklace with tiny diamonds in the lower half of a heart, and a strand of small diamonds as a row of *fleur-de-lis* on each side and a pear-shaped emerald at the bottom. He asked the jeweller to make it and send it to Eddie; it was simple yet stunning. She was still browsing, and he also drew a pair of earbobs that matched. He asked for an estimate and was told £50. The jeweller folded the design and put the emeralds away.

Luke then asked for some wedding rings to be brought out. "Elle, love, come and choose one."

Ellen again chose a very plain one. Not too wide, not too thin, but in perfect taste. "This one, Luke, but I'm not going to try it on." She took off her emerald ring to make sure they fitted together.

Luke noticed she was admiring a strand of pearls. They had screw-on earrings that matched. "Those, too, please, but please send them with the necklace to Ed. All individually gift boxed."

The jeweller nodded.

Luke then asked if he had men's rings. A tray was produced, and Luke chose one. "Can you engrave these with 'Forever yours' in both rings, please? Send them with the rest," Luke whispered.

Again, the jeweller nodded. He tucked the ring and paper in the same pocket.

"Brooches?" Luke asked.

Again, the jeweller nodded. He swapped trays and brought out some brooches.

"Elle, I'd like you to have one of these, too. Do you like this one?" Luke asked.

She had come over while he was speaking. She looked at the one he'd selected. "Oh, Luke, is stunning, but it's too much. I have enough already."

"Thank you. We'll have this today and the bobs. Do you have boxes for these, please?"

"Oh, Luke, really? Thank you so much." She reached over and kissed his cheek.

"She's worth it, sir," the jeweller said.

"Oh, I know," Luke said.

The jeweller brought out a little velvet bag, and in it was the brooch in the box and the empty ring box.

Luke handed Ellen the bag and asked her to wait at the door. He asked for the total price.

The jeweller tallied up the total and gave him a good discount. £160. 10/-. The jeweller said that he'd sort out the other items and deliver them to the desired address when it was ready. Luke was happy, as was the jeweller. He'd just had a year's worth of sales in one day.

Ellen linked her arm through Luke's. "Luke, that's so much."

"Sweetheart, you are so worth it. I want everyone to know you are now taken. Mine – hands off." He wished to kiss her, but wasn't able to in the middle of the road. They had one more stop to make. Again, she did not watch where they were walking. She was somewhat puzzled when Luke opened the door of the Gazette's office. He walked to the desk and took a slip of paper from his top pocket. "Can this be in the next edition, please?"

"Yes, sir, that's 6d, please." The clerk read the note and finally looked up. "Luke, Ellen, oh, great news; congratulations!"

Luke recognised Wills' old school friend George Allen. He'd run away with Wills, but only stayed one night before he returned home. Luke knew his father had arranged a junior job for him at the paper. Eleven years later, George was still there, having climbed the work ladder. Luke merely thanked him, smiled, paid the sixpence, and they left. "I don't know why I bothered paying that. He is better than any newspaper, but at least it's official." He checked that no one was around and bent and gave her a quick kiss. "I love you!"

"And I love you too. Now, can we go home, or Eddie's or somewhere I can kiss you properly?" she asked.

"Let's go to Eddie's. I still need to finish packing, and you're welcome to help if you'd like. The door is to be kept open." He bent and whispered, "I don't really trust myself. I want to kidnap you and take you with me," he said. He kissed her hand. "Let's hurry." They picked up their pace.

Old Tom waved from a distance; he was on his way up to the Emporium to care for the horses.

Luke told her of his strange conversation with him the night before.

She skipped.

Luke laughed. Oh, if only he didn't have to go away. They arrived back at the same time as Reverend Clarke, Ed, John, and Colleen.

Cara had the kettle boiling and served tea in the sitting room. Cara's husband, Paddy, took the cart to the stables and unhitched it. She took a mug of tea out to him and sat outside drinking it with him. "Luke is going to find it hard to leave tomorrow. At least they have finally got themselves sorted out. Bad timing, though. They will all be out after the tea to do the final packing."

In the sitting room, everyone had gathered around Ellen, admiring her ring. Luke was sitting in an armchair watching her. "Show them the other two boxes, love." She returned to the settee and took out two small boxes. She flipped them open, and Jenna gasped.

"Oh, Elle, they are stunning." She waxed poetically over the beauty of the emeralds.

"The green reminds me of God's plants all around me, Jen. My love for Luke is like that. It's always been there; he was always with me when we were young. This makes it official, but I fell in love with this for many reasons."

Colleen was holding her hand. "It's spectacular, Ellen."

Luke was listening. "Just to make it doubly official, it will be in tomorrow's Gazette. Ed, keep a copy or three for me, please." He grinned, and Ellen came and sat beside him, reaching for his hand.

"I hate to tear you two away from each other, but we have some packing to do. Drink up, peoples." Reverend Clarke downed the contents of his mug and wiped his beard. "Ready?"

Everyone else did likewise, and they filed outside to the stables. Paddy was waiting for them. Once the new items had been packed to the satisfaction of everyone, the group returned inside. They spent the afternoon preparing for the next stage of their journey. The first night would be at Emu Plains, then back across the Nepean River, down through Castlereagh and out to Windsor. From there, they would head along the Putty Road to Singleton. During the afternoon, they sat poring over their map. It was drawn by John Tallis. The scale was small, but it was all they had. The area they were heading to was surveyed. Others had been before, but not with a focus on the geology. Even Reverend Clarke had traversed some of the northern roads, but not the Putty Road. Nor had he ventured further west than Singleton. As he explained, the purpose was not exploration or surveying, but discovering and mapping minerals.

Reverend Clarke produced a new map. It was of a much larger scale and covered many pages. Major Mitchell's route from his last trip was the route that they planned to follow.

"I haven't seen this map, sir; is that one even available yet?" Eddie asked.

Reverend Clarke smiled and said, "Err, no, actually, Tom's wife just sent it to me. Tom and I were at college together. I had been hoping to ask him more about his trip, but I had not met with him since his last trip. Now he's gone. I was saddened to hear the news of his passing. I have now only our past conversations to go on. Mary Mitchell kindly gave me a copy of Thomas' latest map. Also, that one from a man named Tallis."

Ellen followed Luke upstairs and into his room. She went to shut the door.

Luke simply said, "No, love. I really don't trust myself. But come, give me a hug."

She walked into his arms. It was there that she finally gave way to her tears. She'd held them in all day. Her heart was full of love, but also breaking.

He held her gently until her sobs subsided.

"I'm so sorry, Luke. It's just not fair. I feel you are being torn from me. I know you're not. I'm just selfish." She pulled away from him and wiped her eyes with the backs of her hands.

"I'll pull out, Elle, I'll stay with you. I hate to see you so sad." He wanted to stay, but he also wanted to go. How much easier it could have been if she could have come, but that just was not possible. Not unless… No! There was not enough time. The thought of getting Reverend Clarke to marry them had crossed his mind, but that meant travelling with her for three weeks before that. No, he'd return in July for her.

She looked at him angrily. "You will not stay. I'm just being ridiculous. I've waited four years for you; I'll wait a few more months. I will have everything ready for your return. I just needed a good cry, Lukie. Call it an excuse for a big, long hug." She gave him a teary smile, then reached up and drew his head to hers. They stood forehead to forehead, talking softly, for some time. They drew apart when they heard footsteps on the stairs. Luke went back to his packing, while she sat on his bed and watched.

~

At pre-dawn the following day. Bill, Molly, and Ellen arrived breathless. She had hurried her parents to make sure she would not miss Luke's leaving. They forbade her from coming alone.

Paddy was leading out the packhorses, Reverend Clarke and John had the three saddled horses, and Luke was leading the cart with Colleen on the nice sheepskin-padded seat. They were all taken to the front verandah and hitched to the railing.

Ellen ran to Luke and threw herself into his arms. "I didn't want to miss you. I couldn't get them to hurry." She giggled. She looked over her shoulder at Bill and Molly, who were still some distance behind. "They insisted on coming too."

Luke bent and gave her a deep, good morning welcome kiss.

Other voices were heard approaching. Charlie, Grace, and the children were on the way over. Luke tied on his saddlebags and panniers, then checked the girth straps. John did the same. Reverend Clarke had just done likewise. "I'm getting too old for this caper. I enjoyed my nice soft bed too much." He chuckled softly. His warm breath clouded in the chill of the morning. "I shall enjoy it again in July or thereabout."

They each took their leave of everyone.

Luke stood with Ellen in his arms, oblivious to everyone watching. He gently brushed a wayward tear from rolling down her cheek. "No 'what if's' love. I'll be back in July. Have everything ready, then we have the rest of our lives together."

She nodded, not trusting her voice. She reached up and pulled his head down to hers for a final kiss.

He crushed her to him. It was deep and passionate.

She finally pushed him away. "Remember, I love you, but go. Go now before I lose my resolve and come running after you."

He dropped a final kiss and whispered, "I love you, always have, always will." They said farewell to the rest of his family.

Liza and Anna had arrived while he was saying his goodbyes to Elle. They were both astounded by what was unfolding before them. He'd not even noticed his sisters' arrival. When he did, he gave them a quick wave, then returned to Elle. He kissed her eyes. "Pray for me daily, love. I'll be careful and will return to you." With a final peck of her still-reddened lips, he mounted, and they were off.

The sun was just appearing as they turned around the corner of Phillip Street. Luke turned and waved as they disappeared from sight. He took a deep breath. "Eight months," he mused.

She stood waving until they were out of sight, then turned to her mother and sobbed. Molly was expecting this and was beside her, waiting.

The trip to Emu Plains was uneventful, but slow. The horses were settling into the pace. Colleen was so pleased that she had added her thick sheepskin to the rough wooden seat of the cart. She had found a small square of oilskin to cover the skin if it rained. It was stowed under the seat, along with Reverend Clarke's Communion wine and the camp ovens. The wine would fit in his pannier, but it didn't get quite as juggled under the cart seat. She'd insisted on them being accessible rather than under the long-term stores. It would take a few days to settle everything, but they had started. They took the first half day for a walk.

Over lunch at the small stage post at Rooty Hill, the halfway area, Reverend Clarke spoke as they stood stretching their legs. "Right – let's get one thing sorted. We're together for the next eight months; I'm William to you all, like it or not. We'll likely get to know each other very well on this trip. So it's all first names."

A little later as they rode west, he pulled up alongside Luke. "Lad, we are going to find the next months hard. Each waiting for the loves of our lives. At least we have that in common. But it's more than we each had a week ago. I've had to wait for years, too. I hope she will return. I won't know until we get back. It's a hard road, lad, but one I've been called to walk. Up until now, I've had to walk it alone."

Luke looked at his brother's mentor. He was a man he looked forward to getting to know better. "Yes, sir, sorry, William, oh, this will be hard. You were my teacher, no, you are my teacher," he said shyly.

"You'll cope, Luke." William grinned bashfully.

Luke returned the smile he'd received. "Yes, all right, William, I'll try. No, I will."

An hour before dusk, they were leaving Penrith. Twenty minutes later, they were pulling into the inn, and Marc came out to take the horses into the holding yard.

William shooed away John and Colleen. "Go see your folks, dear. Stay for a meal if you like; we'll see you both later."

Colleen grabbed John's arm, and they walked quickly out of the stable yard and down the road. They were greeted warmly. It had been only a couple of weeks since John was last here. Now he was here with his wife. Finn and Maureen welcomed them with open arms; they were soon surrounded by many little Murphys. John was somewhat overwhelmed. Wills was right; he didn't know one from another, except Mary, whom he took up in his arms.

Mary wrapped one arm around his neck and gave him a wet, sticky kiss. "Wuv vu," she rested her head on his shoulder, thumb in her mouth and fell asleep.

John had not had much to do with small children until he moved into Wills' house with Colleen. This feeling of absolute trust from a child was almost overwhelming.

"Oh, John, don't pander to her," Colleen said.

"I'm not. I'm enjoying this. Colly, she's adorable. I look forward to having our own." The thought made his heart do a flip.

Mary's even breath on his neck was so comforting. The child's trust was astounding. Yes, he looked forward to having his own child. Something he'd never thought about before. They spent a few hours with her family. John was beginning to sort out who was who. Mary stayed in his arms for about an hour before she woke and struggled to get down. He chuckled as she toddled off, totally oblivious to the feelings she had stirred in him.

Maureen had been watching him. She sat beside him. "They worm their way into your heart, John. No matter how many you have, each is different, each with its own needs."

"I have much to learn, Maureen," he smiled, "Much!" In the short time they had been married, his feelings for Colleen had already changed and deepened. His eyes followed her as she spent time with her family.

Finn's eyes watched him. He sat smiling to himself, watching his new son-in-law. Yes, he liked him. John had known her less than a month, married for even less, but he felt she'd been part of his life forever. He'd certainly known about her for a long time. It was always 'Colleen this' or 'Colleen that', from Wills and Cathy.

The time soon drew to a close. They said their goodbyes and departed for the inn. Maureen and Finn stood arm-in-arm as they departed. "Finny, she found a good one, love. She had to wait long enough. But I think he's worth it."

"I think you're right, me love." Finn bent and gave Maureen a quick kiss.

On arrival back at the Arms of Australia Inn, Milly and Marc met them and told them to make themselves comfortable.

Reverend Clarke and Luke had gone for a walk to stretch their legs. John asked where they were sleeping, and on being told they had rooms out the back of the stables, Marc took them and showed them their room. He told John that Wills and Harry had both insisted and supplied funds for a dedicated accommodation block, as there would be all sorts of undesirable types coming through for the gold diggings.

Marc agreed with his brothers-in-law and willingly allowed them to plan for whatever they thought the inn could use. So Milly's leather-working office had been moved to a side room in the barn, and a new accommodation building had been built behind the stables. One of the guest rooms had a double bed; they had been allocated this room.

Colleen helped where she could. After dinner, they would walk up to Wills' house just down the street, as Colleen needed to get some items she'd need. Her work clothing and overcoat that Cathy had bought her when she had given hers away. She had not required them in Sydney. Imogen and Deidre were there, and she said goodbye to them. She also introduced John to them.

Chapter 8 Into the Unknown

*T*hey were following wheel tracks, so someone had been this way

before. Hopefully, this would be the case all through their route. It had been three weeks since leaving Emu Plains. They had travelled through the Putty Road. The bush was thick, but the track was in reasonable condition, and they had prayed nightly; they did not meet any 'poddy dodgers' stealing cattle as there was nowhere they could hide. Thankfully, that part of their trip had been uneventful.

Luke had managed to send two letters home, both to Ellen. One was posted at Singleton, and another a squatter took near Muswellbrook as they passed through the day before.

William had recorded various geological outcrops and gathered a few rock samples. He noted the different fascinating valleys between Singleton and Muswellbrook, which contain coal, shale, or other sedimentary rocks. It was this he was particularly looking for, but he wondered what other finds they could make. He noted, "There is probably coal in this area."

~

Every creek they passed, they would not only water the horses and refill their own barrels, but William also took samples. Luke panned the gravel, and John chipped off some rocks and kept his eyes open for butterflies and beetles.

Colleen would always have something ready to eat on their return from their various wanderings. They were all on the watch for snakes.

William showed John and Luke what he was looking for, the different sorts of rocks: basalts, quartz, shales, and granites—pointing out the difference between Metamorphic, Igneous and Sedimentary rocks and formations.

They spent a few days around Christmas with a family who lived a few days north of Muswellbrook.

They suggested a tour on horseback. It was the first time Colleen had been able to ride, and she was thrilled. They had a camp set up not far from the creek.

The family showed the travellers around Wingen, then up to the foot of the 'Wingen Maid' and finally took them up to The Burning Mountain. It was a place where wisps of smoke emerged from the ground. It smelt sulphurous, yet the hole was surrounded by red brick-like rock with ash of some sort.

William became so excited over this. It proved that there was coal underground as it was sedimentary rock, not volcanic as he'd previously heard. He made copious notes and collected lots of samples to reinforce his findings.

Luke shot a scrub turkey and celebrated with a Christmas feast.

William had bartered some flour for some vegetables, and these were included in their feast.

Luke showed them how to cook the bird in a clay ball. When they were children, he and Wills had seen the local Aboriginals cooking waterfowl in this way. They had often shared what food they had and were taken on local hunting jaunts by them.

Sadly, as they grew older, the locals had either been forced out of the area or had died. Some were still around but were not encouraged to hang around the towns.

Luke still remembered many of the lessons he'd been taught as a child. He missed those carefree days when there was no bias as to whom he could play with, except the Irish or convicts on the chain gangs, whom they had to stay away from. He thought this funny as his mother was Irish, as were Cara and Paddy, as well as the Murphys'. Many lessons he never forgot.

Wills had told him they had used this skill to cook wild ducks on his "runaway" trip. His English friends were stunned. They had had no idea how to prepare them, and the ducks had been delicious.

Colleen had a good fire burning. Luke encased the dead bird, feathers and all, in damp clay.

Once the fire burned down somewhat, he set the clay ball in the coals and covered it well.

It took some hours, turning it twice, but he reasoned that it should be done by dinner time.

They had been 'working' the river all day. Many interesting finds were recorded. In the creek, there were various sorts of agates. None of the beautiful jaspers from Muswellbrook, but nice finds anyway.

They were settling into the routine well; Colleen was delighted not to have to do any digging. She made biscuits, damper and sometimes griddle cakes.

The men were all very appreciative. She enjoyed being able to make each campsite 'home'.

She was in her element, cooking over an open fire.

They enjoyed their Christmas turkey, and they sang carols around the fireplace at night in the starlight. She would have loved to sit in John's arms, but that was not fair for the other two, so they just sat close. That would come later when they would sleep in each other's arms.

~

From Wingen, they headed through Murrurundi with a detour out to Timor and the big rock mountain called Wallabadah Rock out in that valley. This sat on the Hibbs property, descendants of Peter Hibbs, from the First Fleet. He had only died some eight years before.

From there, they doubled back and headed up through Nowlands Gap to Doughboy Hollow. Whilst in this area, they planned a bit of fun. They hoped to be in Wallabadah for the New Year. Apparently, local horse races were held there on New Year's Day, and they thought they'd join in. They discovered a spot where they could see the Wallabadah Rock from a location near the small hamlet. They were shown it by one of the locals.

Luke took the opportunity to write a few more letters and sent them south with one of the racehorse owners. From Wallabadah, they decided to head north instead of further west.

William studied the terrain as they travelled; he added to his pocket notebook often.

Sometimes, they made a detour to check some geological outcrop; all the while, he was instructing Luke on their structure and makeup. As they were heading up north, William suggested they head via Swamp Creek and Oakville Creek and see how the diggings were going. He wanted to see if there was more than gold up there.

In one creek to the north of the main gold diggings, Luke found the first sign of the 'something else' that William was looking for. He had been panning in the river gravel.

The sunlight caught something in the pan, and William heard him gasp. Luke grabbed the little pebble and took it to show William. It was a beautiful blue sapphire.

"Ahh!" said William. "I'll show you how to pan these. It's similar but different to gold."

He scooped up a sieve load of creek gravel. Fitted the fine sieve under the coarse one. He sloshed it around with a gold pan under them. The contents divided into three sizes. The big rocks stayed on top; he quickly checked these before throwing them away. The medium ones caught in the fine sieve, and the fine dirt fell into the gold pan. He washed out the pan until the water ran clear, then flipped it upside down on the riverbank. The middle of the wet pile of rocks was slightly darker than the surrounding gravel.

William started picking out small black stones. Then, as he was still sorting, "Oh, look. There's black spinel; these are garnets, sapphires, and nice, even some amethyst. The darker stones are the heavier ones, so they should be the sapphires, rubies, and spinel. But those stones come in different colours as well. I'm on the lookout for diamonds. I'm sure they will appear where the sapphires occur, but I've never panned them before. We'll do a few more scoops here and see what else turns up. I want to stop for a week somewhere up the road."

William then washed out the sieves and whistled. "Look!" He picked up one ugly-looking rock. "Doesn't look much, does it? This is a star sapphire. See, it looks a bit shiny, like glass in this spot." He pointed to a chipped section. There was a flash of shiny stone, and they could see it was not ordinary gravel. "You can't see through these, but when polished properly, they make a star on top." He popped it in his pocket.

~

They stayed overnight at Oakenville Creek, near Nundle Station and then spent the next weeks on the road, continuing on to the Peel River some weeks later.

They decided to stay at the Royal Oak Hotel in Tamworth. Each member of the team delighted in a long, hot bath and enjoyed sleeping in a real bed as a bit of luxury.

Colleen and John asked if they would mind spending a day or so in town, and William and Luke agreed.

William agreed, as he wanted to pan some samples along the riverbanks anyway. The hotel was comfortable, and the food was excellent and cheap.

Colleen and John went into town, allegedly to "go shopping"; although they did have some shopping to do too, this wasn't exactly their intention; they needed to find a doctor just to confirm Colleen's suspicions of her condition. She had not had her menses since they left home. She was hoping that she would have a child on the way. The last weeks, she had felt a little ill, and John had concerns about her health. She had not said anything to him until recently.

The night before they left Oakenville Creek, she had asked if John would like a moonlight walk. It was something they often did as it meant they could have some personal alone time. They would take a blanket and some food and find a private spot. He agreed willingly.

"John, love, remember I told you about menses when we married?" she asked breezily.

"Yes, Colly. Why?" he asked in all innocence.

"Well, I had them the week before we left home, as you know." She was a little embarrassed, but there was no other way to tell him.

"Yes, love, I remember." He stopped walking. "But that was nearly three months ago." He swung around and looked at her. "You mean, well, you haven't had them since, have you?"

She shook her head. Phew! She didn't have to explain, "No, John. I should have had them twice more." She smiled at her husband lovingly. She let him figure out the rest.

"Oh, Colly, really? We're going to have a baby? Are you sure?" he asked, stunned.

"Well, that's it. I think I'd like to see a doctor in Tamworth if there is one. Do you think we could go 'shopping' together while we're there?" she asked.

"Of course, love. You really think it's possible? Do you really want to continue on? You're feeling all right?" John was full of questions.

"John, love, settle down. It's just a baby. I'm fine. I wouldn't mind being near another woman or a town when it's born, but really being with child is not being sick. I'll be fine."

He was over the moon. "A baby, love. And you've known for how long? Weeks?"

She nodded, "Some. I wanted to be reasonably sure."

"How could you keep this from me? How did I not guess?" He took her in his arms. "Colly, have I said I love you? Really, I love you so much, and this is so exciting."

"John, don't say anything until we're sure," she asked demurely.

"How? I don't have a poker face, love. They'll know as soon as we go back." He stood gently, rubbing his thumb along her jawline. "You are so beautiful, you know. You glow with happiness. Is this what they mean when they say a woman 'glows' when she falls with child?"

"I don't know, John. Except that I, too, am overjoyed." She stood on her tiptoes. "And of course, very excited," she murmured on his lips, then nibbled his bottom lip, then giggled as she started undoing his shirt.

Then he crushed her to him, and he kissed her passionately. After a few moments, he released her a little. "Colly, can we still...? Well, you know?"

This was something she had asked her mother. "Yes, John, of course, but as things progress, we just have to be a little more careful. If we're still due home in July, we should be home before it's born. But I'd like to buy a few things just in case. We can do with the minimum, but some linens, wraps, six or more flannel napkins, blankets, and maybe an outfit or two for the child. A newborn doesn't need much more than napkins and wraps. It's all Mama had anyway for us all, but we should have something just in case it comes early. They sometimes do."

John chuckled. "Yes, of course, love. I'm just stunned you didn't say anything to me, but oh, so excited. Stupid me! I should have guessed, though, shouldn't I?"

She smiled, loving his adorable naivety.

They had sat on a rocky outcrop, talking until it was dark enough for them to return without William and Luke seeing John's face.

Colleen had made a loaf of soda bread and set it in the camp oven in the coals to cook on their return. They sat around the fire in the firelight.

John normally didn't hug her much in front of the others, but tonight, he just needed to touch her. To keep touching her. She was carrying his child, and he just needed her close.

John still hovered close by.

~

In Tamworth, Luke remained at her side.

The following day, William went off with Luke, and they checked out the riverbank. They found little but some small dark garnets.

They returned to the hotel, and William decided they should pack up some samples and send them to Eddie. He had an extensive cellar and said he'd store anything for them.

They had found that there was a regular wagon to and from Port Macquarie. It took mail, produce, and goods to the coast and brought back supplies. This would lighten the load considerably for the next stage of the trip.

They found three wooden crates and Luke and William packed them so that the labels would not be separated from the specimens. Each was wrapped in paper and layered in the boxes. They tied up the box and nailed the lid down. The packages were addressed to Eddie then they carried them downstairs. The carrier would be passing around noon, and they were ready and waiting.

They had just completed the job when John and Colleen returned.

They had a small parcel wrapped in brown paper and string. John asked if they could all go into the sitting room. They found a corner and sat.

John looked at Colly; he smiled. "Colly and I have had an interesting morning; what about you two? Find anything?"

"No, a few small garnets, that's all. What about you two? Find what you were looking for?" Luke asked.

Colleen looked at John. "Yes, we did. We err, well, we visited a doctor or as good as they have here. The 'hospital' is a small slab building on a side street."

"She's dithering. We're having a baby." John almost shouted the news.

"John, love, shh," she giggled.

William grinned. "Wonderful, fabulous news. What an adventure for us all. Maria had two of ours while on the road."

Luke looked from one to the other. Hopefully, this would be Ellen and him the following year, if not before. "I think it's wonderful too."

He looked at them both, now more than just good friends. They had been travelling for nearly three months. No cross words, no embarrassing moments, no flaunting their relationship.

Luke said, "And I think you are both wonderful, too. You could have made being newlywed and travelling with two single men very awkward, but you haven't. You're both amazing, and I want to thank you. This news is just wonderful."

"Thank you, Luke. I grew up in an overloaded house. I know how important privacy is. My parents certainly never displayed the private side of their marriage to us. And with sixteen children, they certainly have one." She smiled. "Our shopping was some emergency baby items in case it comes early. This may be the last place we can buy any. Otherwise, the baby could be wrapped in sailcloth and oilskins." She took John's hand. Not something she often did in public.

He lifted hers to his lips. "It is not due until after we're due home, but we'd rather be prepared."

"I think this deserves a few more letters homeward bound. Are you going to write?" Luke asked.

"Yes, we're still somewhat in shock. At least I am," added John. "Colly has known for some time before she told me last week."

"Do you mind if I go and put my parcel upstairs? I also need to wash up. I'm so hot."

John stood and helped her up.

She gave a small chuckle. "Thanks, love; I'll need that a lot more in a few months. I might have a nap while I can. You stay here chatting. I'll have a bath, so don't hurry."

They stayed in Tamworth for an extra day to celebrate the baby's news.

Colleen luxuriated in their soft, good feather bed. She had welcomed John when he'd arrived not long after she left him, and held her arms out to him and invited him to join her on the bed. With her riding habit removed, she was covered by just a sheet. She'd thrown this back when he'd closed the door. "Join me, my love."

John didn't need a second invitation. He'd already taken off his coat; his perspiration had soaked it. He had a wash first, then joined her on the bed.

They emerged after a long afternoon rest to enjoy what would possibly be their last special dinner for some time.

John had lain beside her with his hand sitting gently on her stomach. "I'm overwhelmed, love. If this little one is anything like your sister Mary. then I'm in love with it already. God was softening my heart that day. I had never thought about children before I visited your parents. I had spent a little bit of time around Wills' children, but I avoided Phil's and Stevie's like the plague. The difference between them all is astounding."

"It's the discipline, John. My parents say that. Wills and Cathy are strict but very loving and hands-on. I only saw the others for a little bit of time. But they have nannies and seem to play up when their parents are around. I feel sad for them, love. They just want their parents' attention. No nannies for us, love. Sorry, but my foot is down on that one." She fell silent for a while.

John was thinking, "No arguments from me, sweetheart."

"John, I don't really want sixteen children either, but I want ours to be loved and wanted, not that we weren't. I'll be happy with however many God blesses us with. Mind you, we're starting later than my parents."

"I agree, Colly. My brother's children annoy me no end, hence my avoidance of them. It's why I fell for little Mary. Oh, Colly, I'm really looking forward to this. Wills' children are so different, disciplined and loved."

Regardless of the heat outside, she curled up in his arms. "So am I, John, so am I."

Dinner, later that night, was a large juicy T-bone steak each. When it was placed on the table in front of Colleen, she was pleased she had not had to cook them. Her stomach did a flip, then settled. She smiled. Her mother had been the same with both meat and soft eggs. It was then it became real for her. She met John's eyes across the table and beamed.

~

The small group departed Tamworth after a seventy-two-hour respite. Everything was washed and repacked. Stores restocked, and samples were sent home.

Colleen also made a purchase of extra bicarbonate of soda and powdered sugar. She also bought six small screw-top jars to store the mix in. Her mother had used a combination of this with lemon juice to ease her morning sickness. She hoped she would only need it for the next few months, but didn't wish to run out. So far, on the whole, she had been well.

They crossed the Peel River and headed to Manilla. It was a four-day trek, and they pulled into town late one afternoon. They had stopped at a creek about halfway between the two villages and only found more poor-quality garnets. William was busy recording the different strata of rocks in the area. The garnets were of nice quality and had a lovely, deep red glow, but they were not worth much.

Manilla was much busier than they expected, with bullock wagons and shops. Having the cart with them was proving no obstacle at all. There was a beautiful church and even a dress shop of sorts, more like a general store. Colleen realised she'd need to buy some fabric for some sort of gowns for herself. She should have bought it in Tamworth, but had been so excited about the baby she forgot. Her riding habits would soon become unwearable as they were reasonably tight-fitting. She found three lengths, one heavy-duty surge fabric in brown and two lighter-weight drills, one green and one blue, both in practical colours. She also purchased a pair of scissors, it was something they had not thought of packing. Her little sewing kit was in her pannier. Papa called it a 'hussif,' short for "housewife". She had laughed as a child when she'd first heard the name. The scissors in that were minute.

The blue of the drill was the same colour as her eyes, and she decided to make this first. As she was driving the cart, she decided to make smocks as they were comfortable to wear. She could even swim in these, and they would fit no matter what her size.

From Manilla, they kept heading northwest and stopped at a tiny place named Barraba. A new post office was being built, and although not yet open, Luke discovered that he could still leave a letter sent from the pub. The Inn Keeper would see that it got posted. It was sixpence when it should have only been a penny. He presumed the transport cost more; Luke didn't care. The convenience was worth it.

~

William fell into conversation with anyone he could. He would pump them for information on gold, minerals, and other finds. Farmers knew about soils, and he asked everyone about them. There were black soils, loam, sand, silt, clay, and many others; each different sort gave William an idea of that area's geological structure. Even the shape and some kinds of trees helped with his survey. He could identify where water was from a vast distance.

Without giving too much away, one local old-timer suggested that they stay for a few weeks around the next stop, and then head east on Cope's Creek Road. All he would say was, "No end of what you're looking for at both spots." The old man smiled and walked away, whistling.

~

William pushed forward on the expedition, and two weeks on, they came into another town named Bingera.

It again was a thriving town for an area in the middle of nowhere; this astounded them all. It housed no more than one hundred in the entire area. Most would have lived on farms.

William announced that they were to stay in this area for a few weeks, as he had heard of many interesting possibilities for minerals.

Colleen set up a proper camp on the town outskirts near the river bend. They set up some distance from the river in case there was a flash flood. She had Luke and John tie a rope between two trees, and over that, they ran the large sail. The ropes along the side of the sheet were pegged down and formed a makeshift tent. They could pull the cart under it and also have some protection from the sun.

Although now autumn, the days were still hot. It was in a quiet area by the river, away from any mining, so the water was clear.

William was not surprised to find some gold mines at the tops of the hills rather than just in the river. He explained how quartz reefs were formed and that reef gold was found in the veins of the white quartz. Erosion of hills caused the gold to wash down the hills and into the creeks.

The men left Colleen at the camp and walked down to the nearby riverbed. Another wagon was camped nearby and had a family in it. Their campsite was three times the size of theirs.

Colleen introduced herself to the wife. It was nice to have some female company for a change.

The lady's name was Sadie Cambridge. Her husband, Simon, was helping in the mine's office. Hence, the size of their camp. They had four children, and the two camps soon became friends.

Colleen would spend the days at camp with Sadie, and the men would head off "to work," as William termed it.

Sometimes, the men went further down the creek and took one or two horses. The panniers on the horses were all emptied and readied for samples.

John always took his butterfly net, a graphite pencil and a box of 'paper triangles' for the butterfly specimens. He had a small box with cork sides, and once caught in the net, he would squeeze the thorax of his captured specimen and kill it quickly. He would place them carefully in a paper triangle, write on the relevant data, and then place them into his box. He only took non-tattered ones and only one of each type; many were released. Some were mating, so he knew the male and female of the various species. Those papered specimens were wrapped together.

Colleen asked, "What is the unusual smell when you opened the boxes, love?" Her nose wrinkled whenever he opened the box.

John was so used to it that it had not occurred to him that others could smell it. "Look, these are called mothballs. It is made from naphthalene. WE use other chemicals at the museum, but these are suitable for transport." He pointed to a white lump of smelly stuff pinned in the corner of each box. "It keeps the bad bugs away." His saddle had a unique holder on the back of it for his net. The front saddlebags carried a small bundle of pencils and a small box filled with "butterfly papers".

She was willing to learn about anything related to John, and that included his work.

Chapter 9   Diamonds in the Dirt

Willliam arrived back at camp one day looking very pleased with himself. At the campfire later that night, he pulled out a small box. "Look. I found them." In his hand was a nondescript rock. Clear and shiny, and has an odd triangular shape. It was about half an inch long and didn't look that interesting as it had no colour.

Luke's jaw dropped open. "Is that what you got today? I was wondering why you looked so pleased with yourself."

"Yes, Luke, I found four, but the others are tiny," William replied. The excitement in his voice captured Colleen's attention.

"What is it?" enquired Colleen. She had carefully taken it in her hands. In the firelight, she could see it was entirely transparent. "It's quite pretty." She was spinning it between two fingers.

"Quick! Hide it," William said quietly as Simon came to their campsite.

Colleen closed her fist around it and carefully placed it in her pocket. She would not let it go; she had no idea what it was, but William was happy with it, so it must be valuable. With one hand, she opened her handkerchief and wrapped it up.

Simon made himself at home and sat with a mug of tea.

Colleen excused herself. "I'll leave you, men, if I may." She went to the cart and found one of her small jars. She carefully placed the small stone in it and hid it in her bedroll.

She returned to the fire with a loaf of sweet damper. She sliced it, trickled it with honey and handed it around.

It seemed an age before Simon left.

"Where is it?" William asked anxiously.

"Safe," she went and collected the small jar and handed it to him.

He held it to his chest. "This, my dear, is wonderful. You have no idea what this is, do you?"

She shook her head.

William lowered his voice. "It's a diamond and a large one at that." He carefully removed his handkerchief and unwrapped it to reveal three smaller stones. He added these to the jar. "It's what I hoped to find here. And this one, which I showed you, is a perfect specimen. Its value could make Wills' finds of gold just mere pocket money."

The three gasped.

"How much is it worth?" Luke finally asked.

"At a guess, that one stone could sell for about £5,000, possibly more. Twice that if we could sell in Europe. If Simon finds out before I register the find, well, let's just say I don't want that to happen. Not a word of this to anyone! Is that understood?"

"Of course, William, I said that we are only looking for tin and hopefully some gold. I know they are both found here." Colleen smiled.

Luke pulled out his handkerchief and handed it to William. "I found some colour, mostly sapphires, garnets and some clear quartz crystals."

"Luke, these aren't quartz; those are topaz, and look, you have one as well. What a corker, even bigger than mine."

Luke looked stunned. "What? That's a diamond?"

"Shhh! Yes," said William, waving his hands for Luke to keep his voice down.

Luke took the small rock in his hand. Holding it as Colleen held it to the flames. It had a small dent on the side of it, but was perfectly clear. "Ohh! This will come in very useful for when I get married." The smile spread across his face, and his dimples sank deep into his cheeks. He threw his head back and laughed.

John and Colleen watched their two friends. He had found some pretty stones and folded them in his handkerchief. "William, can you check these out?" He, too, drew a bundle from his pocket.

William unwrapped his stones. "John, you have four small ones too and some nice sapphires. Look at that blue. Luke, that will bring a small fortune in itself. It must be …" He bounced it in his hand. "About thirty carats uncut, but the colour. It's pure blue." He looked at his three companions. "I do think we may stay here for a while. What do you think? Refresh the coffers."

Each nodded. Stunned at the revelation.

"Diamonds are not recorded from this country yet. I had so hoped to find some, but it was only a dream. The geology is right. I knew they'd found some sapphires and the gold, of course, too." William sat holding his small jar in his hand. "But I'd be happy to go back where we were today and try again. Colleen, bring your smock and have a swim." William said, "It will also be a good 'cover' for us."

"I'd love that, William. I'll do some digging, too. Contribute to our tally." She handed John another small jar, and he slid his stones into it. "John, put them away carefully, please. Luke, here's one for you." She handed him another small jar. "What an amazing start for us all." She had bought six small jars for her bicarbonate of soda medicine mix, but had only used one, as she had minimal sickness. She smiled as she put William's stone in the first one. "God even provided these." She laughed softly as she told John.

~

The next day, they all walked to the creek. They took their precious pots with them. Hopefully, now that they knew what they were looking for, they hoped to find more. They wandered back down to the sandy creek in an area not far from their camp and started looking.

William showed them all how the currents worked in floods and where to look. He pointed out rock shelves and boulders. Then, he also showed them the layers in the soil. They spread out and were all soon sifting through gravel, looking for stones. They only had two sets of sieves, but they also had the four gold pans.

Colleen was hot, so she was sitting in the water working.

John soon joined her. He had stripped off all but his trousers.

"Don't burn love," she said to him, noticing his very fair skin was already going pink. "You're not used to working without a shirt." He put his shirt back on but didn't do it up.

Luke and William were working in the shade. Both also had fair skin and burned easily.

They worked steadily for some hours, and each added to their haul. There was a small pile lying on a rag on the riverbank.

William had told them to collect anything that had colour or was see-through or anything that looked like broken glass. It actually was harder to pick them out while wet than dry.

Colleen had easily found some just sitting on the dry river gravels.

At lunchtime, Colleen unwrapped the packed pannier bag she had brought. It contained hard-boiled eggs, damper, and a selection of fruit; there were mugs too. They ate quickly. She then retrieved a large covered billy of cold tea to which she'd added honey to sweeten. She had made a hole in the wet gravel and set it in the water when they arrived. It was now cool and refreshing.

Everyone moved their spots so they could continue working out of the direct sun.

Colleen walked up the creek a little and found a huge boulder.

William had suggested that these may be good to hunt around. She scooped up a few handfuls of gravel from underwater. What she saw amazed her. In her hand were five blue stones and some other little rocks that looked like glass. There were other colours, too, amongst the river gravels. "John, come here, look."

He joined her and saw what she'd found.

Luke and William were called over, and soon, they were panning the gravel between the big rocks.

Colleen retrieved the now-empty billy, and they started filling it.

Handful after handful of the dirt revealed so many coloured gems that soon the billy was half full.

"Colly, what made you look over here? It's on the wrong side of the creek," John asked.

"Well, there isn't a privy around here, is there? I thought I would get some privacy here. I got so excited about my finds, I forgot to relieve myself." She laughed. "I'll go across the island and go over there." She waded through the water and walked over to the island. She proceeded to find a suitable site and looked around her while squatting. She spied some more gravel deposits in some rock crevices and, when she was finished, went to investigate them. Sure enough, it was similar to the previous area. She picked out some of the larger gems; one, in particular, caught her eye, very large and clear, just like William said. She soon had a handful and walked back to John.

"William, Luke, John, look," she held out her hand. It was filled with rocks. They could see lots of colours and the large, clear, chunky ones too, mostly hidden by the colours. "There are many more out on the island," she stated. As they had now cleared the gravel from around the boulders, they took the billy, sieves, and pans and followed her. She showed them the crevices, and they scooped up the gravel and panned it.

They didn't have to sieve it there, only pan it, but before they did, Colleen said, "Stop; before you do that, pick out the ones on top. Look, they are easily found." They realised that the sapphires

So the men worked panning while she sat on the riverbank. Once washed, they flipped the pans on the riverbank next to her. The stones were in a pile on top of the wet gravel. She sat, picking out the colours and clear ones. Take only the nice-sized ones. William dug in a few deeper spots, then sieved and panned the dirt; she picked and sorted. After three hours, the big billy was full.

William gave a quick look. "A few diamonds, lots of sapphires, look! Some rubies as well." He poked through the stones, "That's topaz, clear like the diamonds but cloudy on the outside." He held a few to the light. "Oh, these are perfectly clear. They will be great to cut. Nice specimens and those are agates, Colleen; nice finds, too. The red is jasper; it also polishes nicely and is often used for seals in rings and the like." He'd dug in his hand and placed a handful in the billy lid. "Colleen, look at this. You see this?" He picked out one sizeable clear stone. "It's huge. Do you know what this one is?" It was another half-inch one.

"They're about six like that and lots of smaller ones. You said to look for things like broken glass. They look like the ones you showed us last night. Are they, well, you know?" she asked.

"Yes, Colleen, they are even bigger than the last ones. I don't know why we bothered going all the way out to Copeton last week. Oh, you have done well. Very, very well, my dear."

"My back is killing me," Luke said.

"Mine too. Colly, are you all right?" John was pulling her up.

"Fine, love, I've been sitting with my feet in the water playing with gemstones. I've had a wonderful time, but I think I'd like to change if that's all right." As she stood up, she swayed. "Hmm, a bit light-headed, love." She murmured as she fell into a faint.

"Colly! Love!" John raced to her. Nothing was worth her not being well. He scooped her up in his arms and, wading across the shallow river, headed off the island and back to their camp a little further along the river.

Luke and William collected all the equipment and the billy. They followed as hard on his heels as they could.

She was stirring by the time they reached the campsite. John had placed her under the tent cover. "Oh, Colly. Sweetheart? Are you all right?" He sat her on the ground next to the cart. The sail provided some shade, and there was a breeze from the water. She was lying on their sleeping mat. She was trying to sit up when he returned to her. "You need to drink something, love. I watched you hand us all the tea, but didn't see you drink any yourself. I think you're dehydrated."

Colleen said, "I forgot."

Sadie saw them fussing over her and came over to help. "Anything I can do? I saw you arrive with her, John. Is she all right?"

"I don't know, Sadie. She might be dehydrated. Or it could be the baby," he explained. "She's been sitting with her feet in the water for most of the day, but it's so hot, and I don't think she's had enough to drink."

"I am right here, you know," Colleen said with confidence.
John was on his knees beside her. "Oh, love, you gave me such a scare. Are you sure you're all right?"

"I think so, John; I've just overdone it a bit. I think you're right; I kept forgetting to drink anything." He handed her a mug of cooled, boiled water, and she downed it. He refilled it and made her drink that, too. She was still resting against his shoulder.

Sadie felt her forehead. "I think she's had a bit too much sun, John. Sponge her forehead and make her keep drinking. Did you say, baby? Is she with child? If so, she'll feel a bit hotter anyway. Make her keep drinking, John. Make sure the water is boiled. I'll come and check on her later." Sadie went back to her children. Simon wasn't back from work, and the children could not be left alone for long.

William and Luke had arrived. William placed the billy near the fireplace; the lid was tightly jammed on. They had watched his careful placement and smiled. It was safe in full view.

Colleen was feeling better, but John refused to let her move.

"Colly, you have done enough today. We'll cook something to eat and serve you for a change. You stay put." He bent and kissed her. "Keep your eyes on that billy," he whispered. Then kissed her again. "Are you really better? Sure?"

"Yes, John, really, I've just overdone it a bit, I think. I'll stay here tomorrow. Sadie can watch me. I'll help her with the children." She lay back against the cartwheel. She was still a little lightheaded, so she stayed still. "John, the stew should already be done."

Luke stood watching Sadie leave. "She's gone. Can we do something with that?" he pointed to the billy.

William said, "We certainly can't leave them in there." He wandered to the back of the cart. He poked around for some time and finally said, "Ahh! This will do." He pulled out an empty flour bag, flipped it inside out, gave it a good shake and sent flour dust everywhere. Turning it the right way out, he said, "Luke, pour them in here; we'll sort them later." William held the floury bag as Luke poured the contents into the bag. "Colleen, you found some good ones there. Good girl!" He handed the bag to Colleen.

"You all found most of them; I just picked them out," she said quietly. "William, there are some really big ones in there. One is twice the size of yours yesterday."

"What? Was it shiny or dull?" He'd shown her the difference between a diamond and a topaz.

"Shiny, William and it had the double points too. A perfect one, about an inch, there are also some pink ones. Are they rubies? They are pink, aren't they? Lots of sapphires of all sorts of colours. There are purple stones. What are they?" She put her hand in the bag to see if she could find the stone she was talking about. She should be able to find it by feeling. Her hand was digging around. It pulled out one. "No, that was the big blue one. Oh, this is it." She had the stone in her fist and passed it to William. "This one," when she unfurled her fingers, the largest, most perfect diamond sat in her hand. At an inch long, it wasn't difficult to locate in the bag due to its size.

"Oh, Colleen!" John was on his knees, looking at it.

Luke picked it up and held it. "It's enormous."

"This is the one I first found on the island. It's why I called you all over. So it is one?" she asked.

"Yes, Colleen, it is. And this one is all yours. The rest we'll split four ways." William said.

"No!" Colleen stated adamantly. "Three ways, John and I get one share only. I'm only here because John is here. This is adequate for my share; I'll put it in our jar. The rest we split, sorry, no arguments. Right, John?"

"Absolutely, Colly, thirds," he said, reinforcing her decision. "Colly's stone alone will mean we can buy a house in Sydney. The rest is cream."

"John, with what is in that billy, we'll each be able to buy the entire blooming dairy farm rather than just the cream." William chuckled. "I'll be able to buy Maria whatever she wants, and I'll be able to pay back Wills too."

Luke grinned. "Well, this will mean that Ellen and I can buy our own house, and I'll look when I get back. I might get Ed to go hunting, though." Luke had a handful of raw gems in his hand. "These will make a huge difference."

"These will make an immense difference to a lot of people, Luke," John said quietly.

"It certainly will," William said, smiling at both the younger men.

William marked his journals with records of the various basalt, granite, or sedimentary outcrops. He had developed a code for the various gems years ago, and although he knew it by memory, he had recorded the cypher in another journal at home.

They stayed collecting for another day, finding lots more sapphires and small diamonds, but no more large ones. The flour bag was three-quarters full. They decided to look around the area.

Colleen was feeling well again. She made sure she did not dehydrate again. She said, "I feel so silly, John. I just forgot to drink. I was cool as I had my feet in the water, but I was so sidetracked."

~

They broke camp four days later and headed eastward down the mining road. William wanted to investigate this area a little more, which meant traversing most of the tracks in the area and checking each stream and riverbed. Cope's Creek was the closest, so it was first visited. William and Luke were in the lead, with their two pack animals following. Colleen was on the cart with the third packhorse tied behind.

John brought up the rear on his steed. He had a loaded pistol on his saddle. As he had the gun, it was decided that his horse be unencumbered by a packhorse. His wife and child were his number one priority. He was now on protective patrol.

They followed the track down until the river branched.

William consulted his map. Tea Tree Swamp Creek and the flood plain on the bend of the river opposite looked like a good spot. They travelled until they found a good campsite.

William saw someone had felled a huge tree, and it was obviously used as a walking bridge across to the other side of the river. He was intrigued by the change in rocks in the landscapes. From quartzite, then basalt, and back to granite. No wonder this area was littered with minerals.

He decided to camp near the creek. This would give them access to all three areas. Again, they strung the rope between the trees to provide shade. A few days here, and they would move on again.

Colleen decided to stay at camp, guard the finds, and bake some bread. She had a craving for some real bread rather than soda bread. She also craved fresh cabbage, which was strange, as she didn't like it in general.

Sadly, she had to leave that craving unsatisfied as she couldn't buy any anywhere. John had purchased a small jar of sauerkraut for her before they left their Bingera campground.

Luke and William went across the river on the huge log.

John stayed and investigated the riverbanks near the camp. He refused to leave Colleen totally alone. Miners passed along the track, and she was too beautiful not to be a temptation for them.

~

At each campsite they stopped in, they found more gems and other minerals. Some creeks were heavy with tin, others with gold. They kept a small sample of the tin and put the gold in another small jar with what they had previously found.

William placed the jar of gold in his spare boot, then promptly forgot all about it. At one place, they found a silver outcrop but only took a small specimen of the rock. William recorded each find and the stratigraphy of the samples taken.

The further east they went, the more sapphires were found. The diamonds were found to be on the western end of the river, closer to Bingera.

~

After three weeks of exploring, they had emerged at Green Swamp. They had travelled through the rough mining town of Copeton, but didn't stay.

Luke, who had written more letters, posted them in the town. The post office in Green Swamp had only opened the year before. Postage from here was once again 1d. He was told that they were thinking about changing the name to 'Inver-elle', which meant 'meeting place of swans'. Luke laughed as they had not seen a single swan. He was reliably told that they did fly in huge flocks.

William insisted on investigating around the area more, and they headed further west along Frasers Creek. They discovered many more amazing blue sapphires, as well as some bi-coloured ones. One had a yellow centre that looked like an eye. They had found so many that they became picky. Only taking what William called "cutters".

Colleen found a beautiful peridot-green sapphire. It was huge and perfectly clear, and she gave it to Luke for Ellen. "Get this cut for her, Luke. She loves greens."

Luke had found a stunning yellow one and said, "I'll have the green if you will accept the yellow."

Colleen laughed but accepted the stone as a swap. Each was popped the gems into their private jars.

~

They explored and dug in the area for a month before heading back west again. This time the group took the road to Warialda.

In the creek there, they found traces of more sapphires and a few tiny diamonds.

From there, they kept heading northwest to Moree. This was mainly a basalt area. They were once more surprised to find a small town with a general store. The storekeepers, James and Mary Brand, told them there were hot springs in the area.

William wanted to investigate this phenomenon, as this also meant volcanic vents. Mary introduced them to a local Aboriginal man and his lovely family. She sent them to camp near them, which they called "the long water hole."

The Aboriginal family found that Colleen was expecting a child and would not let her swim in the very hot water. They took them further down the river, where the water was perfect for swimming in.

Instead of the chilled icy waters of the river, it was delightfully warm. The mineral waters were luxurious, although Colleen's hair didn't like the minerals in the water. It felt strange, almost stiff. They swam twice a day, and Colleen did her washing.

As it was March, they celebrated Easter while there. William held a service for everyone on the riverbank. Some forty people attended. It was the first Easter service that some had been to for over a decade.

After a delightful week relishing the warm waters, they broke camp.

They moved on.

They were still heading north, and William said that Tom Mitchell's map took them to Goondiwindi.

They crossed the Macintyre River at a ford, checking for more minerals, of course, then north to St George's Bridge. They followed the road north again, seeking more minerals and mapping the terrain.

William surmised that there could be coal in the St George area. They marked it on his map and moved further north.

Although the days were sometimes hot, the nights were now chilly, and they built a big campfire each evening.

Colleen was now over four months gone with child. She was beginning to feel it moving. Small flutters, but she knew it was there. John couldn't feel anything yet.

Her split habits were beginning to get a little tight, but she could still wear them. Soon, she would have to put them away in favour of her new smocks. She had cut out the fabric at Bingera, but they had been busy there. Now, as she drove the cart, the pony was so docile that it followed the lead horses with its head down. She would lay the reins on her lap and use the time industriously.

It was some weeks after leaving the last big river that John first felt the movement of the child.

Colleen lay next to him that night, and she could feel the baby moving. She had placed his hand on her stomach as she could feel where it was moving.

His eyes flew open in wonderment at the experience. "Oh, Colly, this is amazing." They had fallen asleep in each other's arms.

~

The further north they went, the fewer people they met, but the cart was still following existing tracks. Every now and then, when discovering that William was actually Reverend William Branwhite Clarke, various people made comments like, "It's eleven years since I have had the benefit of a minister." "Can we have a service, please?", "Would you marry us?", "We can't get to town. We have three children we want to be Baptised, can you do them too?" One man said it had been fifteen years since he'd been able to be in a church. It was on occasions like these that William felt all the trips were worth every step.

William travelled with a special "Travelling Register" to keep a record of all the occasions, including services, baptisms, weddings and the like.

While in discussion with John one day, Luke said, "I remember reading an article William wrote from a trip in about 1852. He said something like. *'I have never felt so much as, on late occasions, the value of the office of a messenger of grace and salvation. The most gorgeous cathedral, filled with holiday worshippers, is not more pleasing in my recollection than that noble landscape by which we were surrounded and the company of pilgrims who stood by me under a burning sun on the side of the hill, listening to my homely words of encouragement and exhortation. It is to be hoped that I may never be reproached with forsaking my calling to seek for the gold that perisheth, for the judgments of the Lord, which I proclaimed amidst the mountains to those benighted souls are more to be desired than gold, yea, than much fine gold."*

Luke didn't realise William was listening.

William chuckled when he heard Luke. "Yes, lad, I feel like this often. With every unexpected service I do, I know I'm doing God's work." He loved it so much. "Good memory, lad."

Luke grinned, a little embarrassed.

Luke, John, and Colleen also took the opportunity to share what they knew of God's love and absolute forgiveness with the people who attended. In reality, the mineral survey was only secondary to this work.

The four travellers showed and lived the love that God showered upon them; they wished to share that.

Luke remembered that whatever they found, this trip's real purpose would be to prosper God's work. The discoveries from there were mere coincidences. William was merely putting God's handiwork into a written order for others to read and use. In every tiny hamlet they had passed through, they had held Divine Service, and as many who had heard about it attended. Very rarely were there only the four of them. They sent word ahead wherever possible. Services were rarely on Sundays and, more often than not, held under trees. All were held in the glory of God's creation.

Luke was also in awe of William's turn of phrase. He really had a way with words; he had memorised quite a few. Luke remembered saying to Wills shortly before they left home, "Do you know, when I rise after a night sleeping on the ground, I would not be waxing lyrical about the beauty of the morning, I'd be complaining about having to get up so darned early from a hard ground bed. Listen to this, Wills…" Luke recited a section of a clipping from the newspaper he had read shortly before leaving on their mission. *"I lay facing the east and saw all the processes of dressing the day and wished I had been a Turner to have transferred the tints of that glorious drapery, in which morning marched along the horizon, to my canvas."* Luke smiled at the descriptive words. "Wills, his words paint the entire picture in your mind. Oh, to have skills like that."

Luke knew his ability lay in physical descriptions via his art. He could look at something and reproduce it in an instant. Every now and then, he would look at his amazing teacher and just shake his head in awe. William's use of words made pictures jump from the page. He often would make up a poem around a campfire.

Luke tried to write them all down.

William would write scientific journals as quickly as Luke would pen a letter, and he was the most fantastic teacher. He had learned so much in the preceding months. Yet, he knew there was so much more to learn. This trip turned out to be a real blessing.

William kept telling him. "Luke, to be able to teach, you must teach the students why they need to learn. If you can only teach them that, you have succeeded. You have to start with their knowledge and experience and work from there. Identify that in each and every child."

Even the previously absent-minded John was concentrating and dedicated to his work. He was passionate about what he, too, was learning. They took another week to travel north; they planned to head south at Surat or Roma at the latest. In Surat, William discovered traces of opal and took extensive notes on the geological formations of the area. William had also been seeking fossils and had many theories about their age. He had instructed Luke in all he found and why it was interesting. By this stage, Luke was as efficient as William at identifying the types, strata and what could be found in each area.

Major Mitchell had gone further north. They would all have liked to, but each had a deadline to return home.

It was already May. In this area, they found a crossroad. This was not expected. It was not on the map.

William was surprised to see a bullock wagon arriving in town from the east. The place was so small that it could not really be called a town, more like a locality.

They stopped and talked to the driver.

The bullocky told them there was a rough track from there east to

Brisbane. They could reach the coast in less than a month.

William asked for more information; he had an idea. If they travelled north for a short while more, they could then take the other road to the coast and sail home, but they wouldn't make it home by the end of July as he wished. The more he thought about it, the better it would be to turn east and head to Brisbane. They sat around the fire and discussed it that night.

William, as team leader, was in a quandary. His urge to explore was almost overwhelming. Yet, if they explored further north, they could and probably would be delayed by at least a month. He gazed longingly at the northern road, knowing he must leave the road untravelled.

He was the team leader, and he had responsibilities. Luke's wedding awaited, as did Maria and the birth of John and Colleen's child. His decision was to turn east and travel along this bullock route to Ipswich. From there, they could load up on a coastal transport and return to Sydney by ship, but it would mean they could explore some new land between here and Brisbane. He put it to the group that night.

They each decided that returning in July would be it.

Brisbane was their next destination, but they would dawdle.

There was now too much at stake. With Maria's possible return, Ellen is waiting for Luke and, of course, the baby's birth.

The return trip would be quicker, as they would not have the month they spent on the gem fields.

They would map and explore the new road from north of Surat, then head to Brisbane. The mountain range would be interesting. William's fossil collection had grown somewhat, as they were bulkier than the gems.

The flour bag of gems was now divided into two, as it could no longer be twisted closed. They were both safely stored in a wooden box in the middle of the cart. There was a third bag they were now working on filling. No more diamonds or sapphires, but often areas of semi-precious stones were found. As they travelled eastwards, William recorded more potential Coal areas. This was desperately needed in the colony.

~

On entering Drayton Swamp, they kept travelling down the only street named Darling Street. There was only a newspaper shop, a general store, a trading post, and the Royal Bull's Head Inn.

They asked about a campsite from a William Horton, who owned the inn, and he directed them to a camp spot near a creek. There were very few people in view.

Mr Horton told them, "If you continue a little further down, you'll come to the newly cleared area with a dubious name of The Swamp. The new town of Toowoomba is to be built in this area. The area has already been subdivided, and houses are already being constructed. It's okay to camp there for the moment."

William asked if there was indeed a church in the area, and the reply was, "Yes, the incumbent's name is Mr Benjamin Glennie."

William had performed many weddings and baptisms on his trip. This was something he regularly did as part of his pastoral work. He requested that they call in and meet with this gentleman. He never called these services a delay, as they were the primary purpose for the trips in reality.

Reverend Glennie was a tall, thin man with intense eyes and a smiling mouth. His 'church' was a room on the side of his slab-built residence. It had a shingle roof.

William took one look at it and was pleased that they at least had a sail to sleep under. This church was vastly different from his beautiful North Sydney church. He found that Reverend Glennie had arrived with Bishop Tyrrell. He had only been in the colony for eight years and was very glad of some companionship.

Reverend Glennie welcomed them warmly and invited them to tea. This consisted of mugs of hot black liquid sweetened with honey while sitting on tree stumps outside. Living in this settlement was sparse to say the least. William remarked that this man had a joy of life that one could only admire.

Reverend Glennie explained his plans for a church in the new town and already had the land.

William liked him. He had no money to give him, but around their campfire that night, they discussed this quandary and thought they could give him a few sapphires to sell as a donation towards the new church.

But the time they departed, William and Benjamin were on first-name terms.

Benjamin was most appreciative. He knew little about stones, less about gems.

William suggested where he should take them to sell, as he'd previously heard of a good jeweller in Ipswich and recommended him. He may not get full value, but it would be something.

The jeweller's name was Bigot and Parkes Jewellers in Union Street. He had heard they were honest and had good-quality stock. William suggested to Reverend Glennie that he mention his name regarding the authenticity of the specimens.

The ten stones they gave him could bring in as much as £100, possibly more, as they have not been able to inspect them thoroughly.

They left him and went to find another campsite. They spent the next day sieving the creeks in the area and found traces of more sapphires, garnets, and zircons, but none really spectacular.

Colleen collected some lovely pale green rocks.

William told her it was olivine. He found some small specimens of silver-bearing rock and even some traces of lead.

As they now had a bit of time up their sleeve, they decided to take a couple of days and follow a creek northwards.

They travelled about fourteen miles and found a good campsite with easy access to the creek bed gravels.

They panned again and found more alluvial gold traces, some smaller sapphires and some stones William thought may have been spinel. These didn't interest him much, but he recorded their presence.

The silver-lead minerals were again found, and he duly recorded them.

They returned along the track and headed back down the main wagon trail eastwards again.

In Parramatta, Reverend Gore read the Banns for the first time in June as he told Luke he would.

Ellen informed them that they were on schedule for a late July wedding. However, Charlie had heard that their parents would be back in August, so Ellen booked each Saturday through August to make sure. Even if Luke wanted it earlier, she would make him wait unless they both arrived earlier.

Reverend Gore said he would fit them in when suitable; he pencilled in all the Saturdays in August at various times, as some days he already had bookings.

In the months that Ellen had been waiting, she had put her time to good use. She had started volunteering at the new Orphanage School. The old state orphanage had closed, and the Roman Catholics had a new one next to the old Female Factory. Since Elle and Richard Childs retired and then died, many extended families have taken to helping out there. The children were so desperate for affection, they missed the physical touch that the Childs' had given them, hugging and sitting on laps while stories were read to them. Ellen loved the little children.

Elizabeth, or Elle Childs, previously the Dowager Countess of Coxheath, Luke's grandmother, had instilled cleanliness and manners in the children. Their deaths had left a massive void in these children's lives. Richard had been far more than just a headmaster; he had been their grandfather figure. Elle had been far more than just the headmaster's wife. Occasional outbreaks of lice still occurred. Mostly head lice, and these were all promptly treated with overproof spirits directly into the hair. They were dealt with quickly and rarely spread too far. The children would then have to sit outside for over an hour with their alcohol-soaked, wet hair wrapped in a damp towel. All the bedding was then washed, and the dormitories aired thoroughly. The outbreaks did not often occur now, and the children were happy, fed, and well-clothed.

Ellen had gone with Liza one day and participated in story time with the younger girls. She loved it and had started going regularly. There were only about ten girls in each small group, so she could take the three and four-year-olds at the same time. They would sit close to her, even just holding her skirt. Her heart melted. These poor dears just wanted to be touched and hugged. She loved doing both. She decided to enlist the older girls' help in making some gowns for her. The offcuts she then turned into clothes, small garments for the little children.

Wills had bought some half bolts of water-damaged fabric for her from The English Emporium in Sydney. There was ample for her gowns, much more than she could use. The remainder she took to the orphanage for the children to sew their own clothing.

Cara, Jenna, and Grace joined her most weeks.

Ellen's mother, Molly, had helped her make a gown in the lightest shade of blue. The fabric was super fine linen and easy to sew. They had already completed her wedding gown. It had numerous ruffled petticoats with flounces on them to give the gown body. All the exotic fabrics were from the new Emporium in Sydney. If anyone was heading to Sydney, some money was given to them to buy material there.

Molly had purchased some locally made lace and added it to Ellen's wedding gown.

Jenna had bought Ellen a small net veil.

Ellen was ready; all she needed was her groom.

Ed and Jenna had helped Wills and Cathy move their things into *Roseneath*. As they lived at Emu Plains, too, there was not much to actually move. They had completed the purchase of it from Harry and Vicky, but they stipulated that they stay there when they wished it would be mostly vacant.

Ed had found a house for Luke. His brother's letter to him required that Ed find and put a deposit on a sizeable house for him. He had funds to pay for it and would reimburse all costs on his return.

This puzzled Ed, and he had not been earning anything from Reverend Clarke. It was an unpaid trip so he must have found something.

Ed himself had learnt never to underestimate his little brothers. Wills' gold find had taught him that. He was wondering what Luke's story was. He was sure to hear, but he was intrigued. There had been no hint of such finds in his many letters. The only place they seemed to have spent quite some time was around Bingera.

He had heard of gold being found in that area, so maybe he, too, had found some gold. Whatever they had uncovered, Eddie was happy to look for a house for his little brother. He had put a deposit on one on the corner of Philip and Church Streets. It was called *Glenmere*.

Ed had laughed as it was in keeping with the "mere" house names in the family. It was due to go to auction in August, but the owner was happy to sell beforehand if Luke liked it. They all knew the house well.

Their father had worked here for over a year when first in the colony; Charlie and Ed had actually both been born in the rooms above the stables.

Ed just hoped he would return in time. It was a two-story residence with seven bedrooms. It was just down the street from Molly and Bill's inn; it was on the same street as the rest of the Lockleys.

He said to Jenna, "I think he'll be happy. Hopefully, Luke will be back before the auction, because it is due to be held in August."

As per Luke's request, Ellen knew nothing about it. Eddie had been able to keep it quiet. Eddie felt the house would be perfect, as he had said that there must be room for Molly and Bill one day, so Sammy could take over the inn full-time. It also had enough guest rooms for all the visitors he was sure Luke and Ellen would have.

When Eddie saw the established orchard in the backyard of the house, he was almost jealous. His father had tended to their care when they were but saplings. The house had been built by a man known in the town as Perry White, but he had been hiding his title. He was, in truth, the Earl of Collingsford. Since his father's death two decades earlier, Perry was now the Duke of Cheatham and a friend of Uncle Ned, Duke of Gracemere. His trees had taken years to get to this stage. Yes, he was sure Luke would like it. If not, he would purchase it for his parents. This lovely home held fond memories for all the family. The large table in his own dining room had once resided in this house. He knew he needed to talk to his brother-in-law, Tim, and submit an offer. He would buy it anyway.

Chapter 10   Down the Incline

Over the next week, the four travellers dawdled down the steep road off the plateau. They were passed by overloaded wagons, both coming and going. The ones heading east were filled with bags of wool, grain, and produce. The westbound ones were piled high with stores and groceries. Occasionally, when they stopped, one would pull up near them and pass the time of day. More often, to cadge a mug of hot tea and a slice or two of the damper. They spent two delightful days at Gatton Creek, again panning and fossicking. The nights now were freezing. Camping out was not that much fun.

Colleen had to crack the ice on the water every morning. At least she and John could stay warm in each other's arms at night. Luke and William, however, froze. They moved their swags next to the fire in an effort to stay warm. It didn't work.

Gatton was a new town, and they stopped at the inn for what was supposed to be a night and enjoyed a long, hot bath for the first time in a long time. Warm at last. They ended up spending some days here, sampling the ground, escarpments, and also insect collecting, although there were not many of those, as it was mid-winter.

By June, they reached Rosewood. It was really only an inn and a tiny one at that. Again, they stopped for a few nights, relishing the luxury of a bed and the warmth of a fire inside.

Colleen was beginning to feel ungainly. Her condition was now unable to be hidden. Secretly, she was pleased that the trip would be finished by water, although she would not say anything to John. She knew he would head directly to Brisbane and get her home if she even hinted at her discomfort.

They kept taking their time traversing down the picturesque valley. It was an area that had not been previously investigated for minerals, so it needed to be charted. They pulled over often to allow other vehicles to pass, especially whenever one came up behind them. They would stop in natural cuttings, embankments or rock walls and take mineral samples. They travelled further east, always heading downhill. It became warmer as they descended from the tablelands. They still camped near creeks, even though it was extremely cold, and generally had a relaxing travel time. The worst of the rough, winding road was now far behind them. The further they travelled along the road and closer to Brisbane, the better the road became. The farms were lush and full of produce. Many, if not most, had stalls at the farm gates. They regularly stopped and purchased fresh food from them, which they ate with relish. The eggs, especially, were a delight.

Colleen had bought eggs whenever she could. Twice on their trip, they'd found emu nests and raided them. Once was perfect, and they ate 'Australian French Toast' and scrambled eggs. Luke had told Colleen about Wills and Harry's "Emu egg damper toast", so she tried it. It was damper slices, soaked in beaten egg and fried in dripping; they were delicious. The other time, the one egg they had taken was addled. When they cracked it, it stank. They didn't take any more after that.

William decided to do some local investigation and asked if they'd mind; only he and Luke went. They left John and Colleen at an inn in Ipswich. They took two pack horses and their riding horses and did a week's reconnaissance. On their return, they had their panniers full of specimens. William had many fossils, dolomites, moss agates, and a variety of jaspers, quartz, as well as a selection of petrified woods and other rock samples.

John collected the occasional beetle from around the local inn. He would not, however, leave Colleen alone long at any inn. She luxuriated in a comfortable bed and warm fire with no cooking to do.

By the time they had left Ipswich to continue their journey for the final land leg, it was nearing the end of June. It would still take three days until they reached Brisbane. They had been told they could catch a coastal steamer from Petrie's Bight to Sydney. This was a wharf where stores, wool, and other produce were loaded. They found they could not take their animals on a passenger ship, but the coastal freight ships would take them if they had the room. William had been assured that the horses and cart would be no trouble to handle. However, they had to wait a week in town before a suitable ship arrived.

They booked on the *Vanquish,* a schooner under Captain Scott, which was due to leave on July 17th. They were cutting it fine, but should be in Sydney in a week. The schooner was loading sheepskins, tallow hides and wool. Captain Scott took a look at the animals and the cart and told them that, as the weather looked good, he'd take them, but they would have to be on the deck as the hold would be full. They could sleep in the galley on the bench seats.

Colleen again luxuriated in long, hot baths at the Grand View

Hotel. Luke had seen an advertisement for the place in the local newspaper and brought it to William's attention. They all jumped at the chance for a bit of pampering. They also had one other project.

In the seclusion of Colleen and John's large double room, the four carefully washed and spread out the two flour bags full of gemstones. From the time they had been stored in the unwashed flour sacks, no one had again even looked at them. Often, new stones were added damp, and over time, many had been covered with a thin glue of flour. Now washed off, they needed sorting. They moved a table into the sunlight and spread a towel on it. On this, they placed the washed and cleaned gems. The sunlight caught the stones and shone through them. Sadly, the gems got caught in the towelling.

Colleen had an idea and took a mirror from the wall, laying it on the table. She placed a handful of gems on it, and when the sun hit them, it made sorting very easy.

Now they could see them clearly; they all made short work of the sorting. The final result was a pile of more than sixty lovely diamonds and some small ones and shards or fragments; the large ones were cuttable, but a few were broken or dirty, as were some small ones. There was more than half a flour bag of sapphires, including all the star sapphires. They sorted these into colours and would do a thorough sort later. There were so many of them in a myriad of colours. Blues, of course, were the most popular, but there were yellows, greens, and ones that William called "parties". These were different colours in the same stone. One was half green and half blue, another blue one had a centre that was yellow. Some had stripes, and one half clear and half blue. It was hard to imagine that there were so many different colours. William explained that the blues were the most popular, but he preferred the multi coloured ones as they had "character".

There was another pile full of topaz. In amongst them were some lovely light blues, golds and clear ones. One, in particular, was an enormous light blue. There were piles of zircons, some red, some black; another pile of what William suspected was spinel, and some assorted quartz specimens, including many lovely, clear, smoky quartz crystals and some beautiful purple amethyst crystals too. Along the route, they had also collected some really red jaspers and other semi-precious gemstones. William's instruction was "throw it in if it's pretty". The jaspers also had a retail value, but it was pennies compared to the other gemstones.

William gave a rough estimate of £50 for the bulk of zircons, some small sapphires, and smaller topaz, and another £50 for the blue topaz alone. He estimated it weighed about 50 carats uncut. It could bring a lot more when cut and set. The smaller good sapphires made him rub his forehead. "I'm not that good at valuing these, but they would have to bring at least £1000."

The others gasped. Luke knew a teacher's wage to be £40 a year.

"The large ones, oh, I don't know, those big ones could be up to £100 each. They would be thirty carats each, and the colour is good, and then there are the diamonds. They alone would be thousands of pounds, and that wouldn't include the ones you each have in your jars. I think we should get hundreds, if not thousands, for each third."

Colleen gasped again. She grabbed John's hand. To her, £1 was a lot of money.

He looked at her and saw tears rolling down her cheeks. "Love, what's wrong?" he asked.

"John, I've never seen £10, let alone £100. I'm just totally overwhelmed." She wiped her eyes but smiled.

Colleen had been brought up to never waste anything, so from the offcuts of the smocks she'd made herself earlier, she'd made lots of small drawstring bags. It was something she could do to occupy her time whilst both driving and sitting around a campfire. She now unpacked these, and they put the separate piles of gems in them. Soon, only the sapphires and diamonds remained. The sapphires they sorted into varieties, colours and sizes. They then bagged these and placed the smaller bags into one large bag.

With the mirror now empty, they wiped it clean and spread out the diamonds.

There were some sixty decent-sized ones in all. Twelve were large ones, between half and three-quarters of an inch for the largest, but most were small. Among them was one lemon-yellow-coloured one. Some had inclusions or were damaged.

William picked up the lemon one. He held it to the light. "This one is a bit special. I didn't know they came in this colour, but it is definitely a diamond. I think we should put this one aside… or add it to those twelve at least."

Luke sat, running his hands through his fair hair. He had a strange look on his face. It was almost horror, but his mouth was smiling. He had done a rough tally of the stones and was aghast at the immense value sitting before them. He now had something to offer Ellen, and he could repay Ed and Wills for their financial support over the last years. He would do something for his parents. He had no idea what, but he would love to install a new septic tank and an indoor privy for their cottage. They, like most houses, still had to use an outside privy. He had come across some of these new plans in Sydney. His mind was swirling.

Colleen was leaning against John, who had moved his chair next to her. She relaxed onto his shoulder. She was resting with her hands sitting on her stomach. The baby decided it didn't like the angle and started objecting. "Ouch! Behave, junior," she said. She drew the fabric tight across her stomach, and they could see the baby doing push-ups.

Everyone laughed as the baby made its presence felt.

Luke was somewhat embarrassed. However, he hoped this could be Ellen next year.

William laughed. "At least it's still got a bit of room to move now; give it a month. We have four; each one had its own antics before birth. Each is unique after birth. What an adventure you three have in front of you."

They sat watching the baby's movements against the fabric of her smock.

William said, "Luke, John, make your family a priority. Others can replace you at work, no matter what your job. For work, you are not indispensable, remember that. However, you are the only father your children will ever have; make the most of every minute with them. Put your life partner first. I didn't go with Maria and have suffered from my error. Remember that, never, and I mean never, put them in second place, except to God." He looked sad. "I do hope that Maria comes back. I do miss her so. All this..." waving to the diamonds still sitting on the table in the bags, "...Well, nothing is worth it. I should have returned to England with her. Never make a decision that you are both, do you hear me? ... Both of you must be 100% in agreement with the decision. God will never call just one of you. He's brought you together; make sure you stay that way." He sat, thinking.

The others did not know how to respond, so they, too, remained silent.

William continued somewhat forlorn, "I thought I was doing the right thing, you know. But Maria was just resigned to life on the road. It was only when she was leaving with the children that I found she hated it, not me, just the lifestyle." He took a large handkerchief from his pocket; a stone fell from it. He watched the diamond roll across the table; no one moved. Then blew his nose. "No! Just not worth it, not even for these." He reached out and added the stone to the pile – "Sixty-one."

Four pairs of eyes were glued to the pile of stones. Each deep in thought.

The afternoon was drawing to a close, and they decided to bathe and change.

Colleen had little choice in what to wear. Her new smocks were now almost threadbare. She said nothing, but surprisingly, John had noticed the darns. He told Luke he needed to go shopping. He would do this while she rested. Colleen decided to luxuriate in a bath again. He had arranged for a hotel maid to be with her in case she fell. She remained lazing in her bath until the water went cold. The maid helped her out and emptied the tub.

Once she had got into the bath, John quietly took one of her other smocks and then went to meet Luke.

The hotel manager had given them directions on where to purchase appropriate clothing for her. They bought her three lovely high-waisted gowns and a warm overcoat. They also bought new shirts for all the men. They also purchased new smalls for each of them and linens for themselves. And a length of fine lawn fabric for Colleen to make some for herself.

They arrived back at the hotel in good time, and although Colleen was out of the bath, she had not yet bothered to dress fully. She had, therefore, not noticed her missing smock. The hotel had supplied her with a luxurious bathrobe that she was snuggled up in.

When John entered, she was asleep on the bed.

In the seven months they had been travelling, she had not made a single complaint. The only incident was when she had become dehydrated in Bingera.

They had seen snakes, scorpions, hundreds of kangaroos, emus and assorted other wildlife, but none had injured any of them. There had been splinters and blisters, even some sunburn; however, no one had become ill. The rain had been so minimal that it was not more than an inconvenience. Only on a very few nights had they actually needed to put up the sail cover. There were odd scratches and bruises, but nothing major. William had got a few leech bites which itched intensely. Luke told him to rub milk thistle sap on them. That had helped a lot. Luke remembered a time as a child when he had been attacked by three of them while swimming. The Aboriginal children with him grabbed a few of the milk thistles and squeezed the sap on the bites. It worked brilliantly. ,

John had let her sleep for about twenty minutes. He gently lay beside her and stroked her cheek with his finger. Her inky black hair was spread out on the pillow, drying. She opened her eyes to see him looking down at her. She reached out her arms and drew him down to her, offering him her kisses. Although somewhat delayed, they finally joined their friends, with Colleen dressed in one of her new gowns.

She was thrilled with John's gift. She was happier, though, that he'd also bought himself a few new shirts and new smalls. She was also thrilled with the length of the fabric he had purchased so that she could make some smalls for herself. Her pre-pregnancy ones were both threadbare and unable to reach around her waist.

Luke had made sure William, too, had two new shirts. With what they would make from the sale of the stones, a little expenditure now would be worth it. There had been few places to spend the money they had each brought with them. The food and other needs were well covered with the small notes and coins they had taken. Luke felt that the sixpence he had spent on postage for most of his letters was the most significant expense. Postage at home was only a penny.

Colleen threw herself into John's arms when he opened her parcel. She burst into tears with joy. "Oh, John, love, I'm so big. Mama used to say this each time; now I know what she means. And I still have about two months to go."

He had purchased one gown in sapphire blue, another in deep emerald green, and a third in dark golden yellow. She looked spectacular in each.

She chose to wear blue that night. The cut of the gowns nearly hid her condition. The thick shawl he had also purchased for her indeed completed the illusion. It enveloped her, both keeping her warm and covered. He had also added a bonnet to her parcel, and this she donned too. She had only packed a serviceable straw sun hat. It had become so tattered that she wanted to throw it away.

They were ushered into the dining room and shown to a table. It was only when John helped her to sit that the staff realised her condition. From then on, nothing was too much trouble.

She ordered a steak with lightly steamed cabbage and pickles, followed by spotted dick and clotted cream with strawberry jam on top.

John looked at her and laughed.

"I've been craving cabbage for so long, John. Every stall and shop we've been in, I have looked for them. None, not even on the roadside stalls. And I simply love spotted-dick." She smiled. "Blame him," she pointed to the baby.

"Oh, it's a boy, is it?" William asked. "We were sure each time. I mean, you only have a 50/50 chance. We were wrong every time."

Luke laughed. "What names have you thought about?"

"Ahh! Well, we haven't really finalised a choice, have we? We've thrown some names around, but no earnest discussion. Finn Douglas was one."

"And Caroline Maureen for a girl, but we really don't like either. Aren't we horrible?" she grimaced.

"I like Rose for a girl." John said, "Rosie."

"And I like both Jonathon and Benjamin," she added, "Benjie."

"Oh, I like both of those," Luke replied. "But they aren't family names, are they?"

"No," they added in unison.

They looked at each other and laughed.

"Hence our problem," John said.

"Use the other names as middle names. Rose and Jon for their 'real' names." William thought for a while, then added, "At least they are real names. You can tell if they are boys or girls. I've been asked to baptise children with many unusual names, like Asher or Charlie, who was a girl, and Manasseh, a boy. But what a moniker the poor child has to live with. And then there are the doubles. Do not call your child Evan."

"Evan Evans, oh, now that is cruel." Luke was laughing so hard he nearly choked. "Luke Lockley is bad enough."

"The worst I heard was a miner named Leonard St Leonards," Colleen giggled. "How could parents do that to a child?"

"I also like Jonathon, it means God's gift, and Hannah, which means, favour of God. Also, Thea, which means, blessing of God. For that's what this child is. It's what our marriage is, John, an absolute blessing from God." She reached out and took John's hand. "I want to reflect that in our children."

"I dare say we will have to wait until we see the child," John said. "I believe that at the time, we will agree."

Coming from England

"The winds are behind us; we should have a good trip across the bight," Charles said to Sal as they stood at the bow of the *Red Jacket*. They loved standing in what Charles called "their special spot".

Captain Mathias O'Hallorhan had permitted them to be there in calm weather. From here, they avoided the splash of the waves, and they had the wind in their faces.

Charles would turn with his back to the wind and watch the sails. He drew Sal into his arms, so many beautiful full sails. At fifty-six, he thought this could probably be his final voyage. Sal was the love of his life and had stood beside him through everything, from convict to countess. She rose to everything life had thrown at her. With hardly a day's warning, she had packed her bags and joined him on another trip across the world to tell his sister personally that their mother had died. He also met with his Aunt Emily to let her know her twin sister had died. It was six years since Emily and Mark Saunders had come for a visit. It had been a delight for the twin sisters to catch up after so many years. Charles was astounded that, after so many years apart, how similar they still were in everything.

Charles thought back to their first trip to Sydney in 1820; they were both in the holds in chains, locked in cell blocks. Now they were in the Master Cabin, travelling as Earl and Countess. This trip had been unexpected, but once again, they were where God needed them. They had been at Gracemere Castle only three weeks when Wills letters had arrived.

He and Ned had to find Maria Clarke and then persuade her to return home to William. A tough ask, but they would cover all her costs. He needn't have worried, as God had been working in her life too.

Maria knew that it was time to head back to William, but had no funds to buy a ticket. She needed a miracle; she had already written to William and was awaiting his reply. It would not come for at least six months. Somehow, she would have to manage until she heard from him. Her money was gone.

It took only a week from receiving Wills letter until they found her. Charles and Ned visited her; she had welcomed them in, and they handed her the letter from her husband.

Maria poured out her story to them and her decision to return.

Ned looked at Charles, then asked her, "Mrs Clarke, would you be prepared to accompany Sal and Charles on the *Red Jacket* in May? Of course, all costs would be covered. Will you accept and return to Australia?"

She was looking at her visitors. Tears were streaming down her cheeks. "Yes, of course, we'll accept." Her children were all now adults; however, they would accompany her. None had formed ties in England, and all wished to return to the land they called home.

Ned had arranged cabins for their large family group and now more for the Clarkes.

They were collected and taken to Liverpool along with Charles, Sal, Lilabet, Matthew, Ned and Christina. On this trip, all the children stayed at the Castle with Gerry and Annabella Winslow-Smythe. They were now known as Uncle Gerry and Aunt Bell. They were caring for some nine children. Grandma Suze had moved to the castle on her return from their trip from Australia, as she no longer relished living alone in the Dower House without Elle. Her friend's death hit her hard.

Ned had welcomed her.

Suze was now content. Loved and cherished, she adored the children, especially her three granddaughters. All perfect little rosebuds. Fair with blue eyes and perfectly behaved. Sarah was fourteen, and the twins were nine. They all adored her. She travelled to the local school with them most days and helped the students with reading and sewing. It gave her purpose, and she loved it. She was sad her friend Elle had died, but was thrilled she'd had nine wonderful years of happiness with Richard.

~

They had two days to wait for the ship in Liverpool.

On the day they were to board, Charles had seen a man, a lad really, after his own heart. This lad had a way with horses; Charles could only call him a horse whisperer. He witnessed one of the horses in a team was champing at the bit, rearing and generally playing up. This young lad braved injury and walked to the horse. Within minutes, the horse settled, and peace once more reigned on the dock. A few had stood watching; none had moved to assist. Charles's leg injury from over a decade ago, precluded him from becoming involved, as he could no longer move quickly. What could have become a catastrophic situation became a joy to watch.

Charles noted an older man waiting for him, obviously the lad's father. The father had not lifted a finger to help, knowing the younger man would be able to control the situation.

Charles stood watching the men for a while before walking over and congratulating the young man. He introduced himself, but only as Charles Lockley. He found out their names were John and James Leslie. The young man, James, was known as Jim, and he was boarding the ship and heading to a new life. John, his father, was there to see him off.

Jim excused himself as he had yet to check in to confirm his berth. John stood talking to Charles for some time. After watching Jim depart, Charles revealed his true identity to the lad's father. "Don't tell him, but I'll take care of him."

John gasped. Then he smiled sadly, knowing he would likely never see his son again. He was miserable. "Jim became unsettled when my wife died some years ago. It is his health that was the turning point for him, though. The cold here is not good for his hands. Jim goes with my blessing. I knew the good Lord would watch over him; I didn't think it would involve a cantankerous horse and a peer of the realm. Our trust in the Lord is strong. I could not let him go otherwise."

Charles said, "I'm always looking for worthy people. They are what we need in the colony." Charles gave him his card and asked him to write if he wished to. Charles had no way to know if this man could even read or write.

John took the card and read, "Parramatta, hmm, pity that's not near Melbourne, is it? It is where Jim is going."

Charles shook his head. So John could read. "No, sadly, it's a long way away. Can your son read as well?"

John nodded. "He has lived with my sister and her husband since he was a child. They have no children and have educated him. Sadly, they, too, are dead."

Once on board, Charles asked if there were any spare intermediate cabins. When he received news that there were some, he requested that Jim be upgraded from steerage to intermediate. He called him up to the dining room and got to know the lad a little better. Charles had been disappointed to learn Jim was only heading to Melbourne. However, he felt he still wished to get to know him.

Jim had seen advertisements for the diggings, not for gold mining, but for horsemen. He wanted to get a job as a driving coach. He had a bad chest, and the bitter cold of the Durham and northern winters was not good for his health. Jim assured him, "I will certainly call in if I ever come to Parramatta, sir."

~

Over the next two months, they met often, as the ship was not very large. Jim was always exceptionally polite. Charles learnt more about him. He had been living with his aunt and uncle in Newcastle since he was twelve. Lancelot Usher was a carriage builder, and as they had no children, Jim moved in with them. He did an apprenticeship with his firm, but fell in love with the horses instead of just wanting to build the carriages. He had finished his apprenticeship years before, but chose to use his driving skills instead. He had an excellent education in Newcastle-on-Tyne. He had been given everything he could wish for with his aunt and uncle. He had loved them dearly. Jim had told Charles that he had been asked to take a carriage from Newcastle to Liverpool soon after he moved in with them. As a twelve-year-old lad, the trust in his ability astounded Charles. Since then, Jim had been in charge of delivering carriages throughout the north of the country. Sadly, his health was severely affected by the cold weather.

The more Charles saw him, the more he liked him. He hoped Jim would eventually come to New South Wales. He would welcome him warmly.

Jim was a good traveller, but not so Maria and her children. Even the very stable movement of the deck while still tied to the wharf caused the four Clarkes to be prostrated with seasickness. They remained so for the majority of the trip. Jim, however, was seen out and about in even the roughest weather. He would be lending a hand wherever he was needed, and even when a sailor fell from the rigging, Jim was first to attend to him. He loved the outdoors. Being cooped up in a cabin was not his thing.

Charles watched the sheer exhilaration on the lad's face. The Captain had allowed him to steer; he felt the pull of the ship against the wind. The power of the wind in the sails and movement of the waves underfoot, the handkerchief sails to the side, lifted the vessel as though almost flying. Charles requested that Jim be permitted to have this experience. Captain O'Hallorhan finally gave Jim free range of the ship, but not the first-class cabin areas unless invited. Even allowing him to assist with hoisting the sails and tacking when required. Jim was thoroughly enjoying the journey. Charles introduced him to the Clarkes and the other first-class passengers. Before they reached Melbourne, Charles decided that he would provide him with a written reference.

The winds and the weather held good, and the weeks passed quickly. By the time they left Fremantle, they were a week ahead of schedule.

As they crossed the Great Australian Bight, Jim knocked on their cabin door. The captain had sent word that Jim was to see Charles.

Charles had delayed his interview with him until they were nearly at Melbourne; now, he needed a word. Charles and Jim retired to the dining room. "Jim, I know you didn't ask for this, but I have written you a reference. Use it as you will, or not. I have seen your skill with horses. I spoke to your father about your training and have come to know you as a worthy man and, I might add, a faithful person. Hence, I have no hesitation in giving you this. I have signed it officially; you can find me in Parramatta under both my name and my title. I am also Viceroy to the Governor in the area. Although I'll be handing that over to my son as soon as I return."

Charles heard Jim draw a quick breath.

"Sir, you do not need to do this for me. Your friendship is all I sought, and by that, I am overwhelmed. I am but a simple man who loves his horses," Jim stated. He, however, grinned. Meeting Charles' eye, he said, "What you do not know, sir, is that today is my twentieth birthday. So I will accept this gracefully and say thank you. When the Lord is working His purposes out, I am not one to say no. He knows I may need this one day." Jim tucked the reference in his top pocket. He had not even opened it, let alone read it. Jim thanked him, bowed, and departed without further conversation.

Charles stood thinking. He headed along to the Captain. "Any ideas about how we could celebrate a birthday, Captain? Jim turns twenty today."

Captain O'Hallorhan smiled. "Actually, sir, yes, I do. He's been wanting to steer while tacking. Merely holding the wheel is good, but actually turning the ship when under full sail takes a lot of strength. I think today might be the day." He grinned. "He has certainly got the strength. Have you watched him on the sails?"

Charles nodded. "It's the horses. They take strength to hold. Do you know he can drive a team of twelve?" Charles was in awe of the young man. That took skill. Charles thanked the Captain and retired to bring Sal up into their favourite spot near the bow. They were rugged up from the bitterly cold winds, even icy winds.

For the second time in an hour, Jim received a summons from the Captain. This time, he was instructed to divest his pockets of valuables, and he was handed a waterproof oilskin coat.

Jim's heart was pounding with excitement. He had to wear a similar waterproof coat when steering last time. He loved the feel of the wheel with the wind in the sails, of the lift of the ship when a strong gust hit. He said nothing but followed the messenger with a grin set on his lips.

When Jim appeared at the helm, Captain O'Hallorhan congratulated him on his birthday. Jim smiled, knowing that Charles had told the Captain. He turned and waved a hand of thanks to Charles, who was at the bow with Sal.

Captain O'Hallorhan told him to take the wheel. They were about to tack, and Jim was to steer the ship as they did so.

Jim's muscles were strong from the years of driving teams of horses. His hands were large from physical work. Yet he held the wheel lovingly, as he would have held the reins. The captain gave him blow-by-blow instructions, and he followed them perfectly. The two-hundred and fifty-foot ship moved smoothly in the rolling sea. Jim was in complete control and needed no help with the job before him. His strong arms were vital for the coaching skills he acquired from childhood. He held the wheel effortlessly for the tack and kept his balance. The captain left the wheel with him for some time, and Jim kept the ship on an even keel. When the captain returned an hour later and finally relieved him, Jim thanked him profusely. It was a birthday he would never forget.

The Captain permitted him to stay close by if he wished.

Jim did. He sat on the deck behind him, savouring the gentle, salty spray on his face. As much as he enjoyed the experience, he could not wait to have a horse in front of him again. They were his passion.

Chapter 11   Ships Converge

*T*he trip from Brisbane involved much tacking on the *Vanquish* as
the wind was a headwind. Once Captain Scott discovered Colleen's
advanced condition, he cleared out one of the cabins he had used as storage
and allowed them to have some privacy. William made them take the gem
laden flour bags and lock them securely in their room.

Colleen kept them wrapped in her new undergarments. She had
learnt men hated touching women's smalls. She chuckled. Even John didn't
like handling her clean underclothing unless he was removing it from her.
She blushed at that thought; yet, she had to wash their clothing. She
chuckled to herself. Her condition had heightened her desire for him, and
they were pleased to have the privacy of their cabin. They often retired for a
mid-afternoon rest.

John was astounded by her appetite for him but was happy to
comply with her desires. This had become twice daily, at least since they had
privacy again. They had not been able to slip away as often as they had
wished on their trip. They had been exceptionally discreet, often taking a
blanket and going for a walk after evening meals. They took whatever
opportunities that were offered. Swims were often something they could
have together, but these interludes were few and far between. Most evenings
around the campfires, they sat together but not overly touching each other
until they retired for bed. Any activities had to be silent, which was often
difficult, so John instigated their evening walks. Now on board, their cabin
became a refuge for her desire. The tiny bed enabled them to sleep
cocooned; wrapped in each other's arms. As the ship moved with the waves,
John could hold her against him. Every now and then, the sturdy ship
would crash down a particularly large wave, and she would be thrown
against the bulkhead. As they were tacking, this could occur sideways.

The two masts were in full sail. By Port Macquarie, the wind turned offshore and slightly from the South, so the journey, although dry, was slow.

The days were often spent in the shade of the sails where possible. Luke and John often attend to the needs of the horses and make the cart secure. John then retired to Colleen's side and stood holding her so she would not stumble or fall.

William did not like the sea and remained as still as possible. He discovered that above deck was much better than below. By the third day, he had his sea legs and could walk around reasonably well. He would sit on whatever was close when he heard the "tacking" call from the helmsman. Then he grasped on to something, or plonked himself on the deck until the ship settled down again.

John and Luke were each offered a turn at the wheel and grasped the opportunity. Loving the feel of the power of the wind pulling at the ship, both men helped with the sails.

Colleen was neither offered the chance to steer nor did she ask. She sat in uncomfortable silence. Uncomfortable only because, as she was so ungainly, she dared not move by herself, lest she fall overboard. She was content to have John close. She was also content with their frequent rest time. He had learnt to read her face and knew when she wished to retire. Often to sleep, but he always accompanied her, then he would take her in his arms as soon as the cabin door closed.

These days at sea were a joy for them both. They could be as close as they wished to be and were not confined to a blanket in the bush. No spiders or snakes either.

She was now about eight months along in her confinement and was unsteady on her feet. Their bunk was squishy for three. She would be glad when they arrived in Sydney. She sat on the deck as they drew into the harbour in Newcastle at dusk. John was beside her, and William was next to him. Luke saw to the horses' needs again, taking advantage of the calm water to spend a little more time with them. They had settled on the deck well. The ship obviously often brought stock, as it was well-prepared for it with a specially built on-deck fenced area.

Captain Scott unloaded some of the cargo and reloaded more, and set off again before nightfall. Two more days with this wind before they reached Sydney.

Luke was getting agitated. It was July 22 when they left Newcastle; he wanted to see Ellen.

William, too, was unsettled, eager to see if there was a letter awaiting him at home.

John and Colleen were content to enjoy their trip. They knew he would have to return to work soon after their return. Luke and William would as well, but they each had two weeks before that happened.

Luke had sent a letter home from Brisbane by passenger ship and told Eddie when they were due to arrive. He had also written to Ellen again.

He was hoping that Ellen would come to meet him in Sydney.

Molly and Bill would probably have to come too, but he would love to see them all. He was anxiously awaiting details of their wedding.

Coming from England.

Many miles to the South, the *Red Jacket* was being propelled past Tasmania and the mainland's southern coast. She was being carried by a tailwind and was moving quickly. She was now only a day from Melbourne. From there, Charles, Sal and the Clarkes would disembark and catch a coastal steamer or whatever would get them home fastest.

Charles would say goodbye to Jim, with further instructions for him to make contact on his eventual arrival in Parramatta, whenever that would occur.

Captain O'Hallorhan brought the ship gracefully to the harbour entrance and dropped all the sails. They glided along with the inertia of her own weight. The steam tugs came alongside and moved her to the dock.

On berthing, the cabin passengers alighted first. Charles and Sal waited for Jim and the Clarkes. They had decided to take Jim to the hotel with them and pay for a few nights' accommodation until he found his feet. He let slip that he had no contacts there. It had not been an intentional plea for help but rather a simple explanation.

The hotel staff were efficient and had the shipping plans on hand. They booked to leave the next day on the *City of Sydney*. A letter awaited them to tell of Luke's upcoming nuptial date, and they hoped to arrive before the 2nd of August.

The hotel manager in Melbourne greeted them on arrival. Charles had an idea and asked about employment with horses for Jim.

The manager laughed. "Not a problem, My Lord, for two men are staying here now, and I shall introduce them."

Charles told the manager that he had provided a reference. "James may not produce it, but he has it."

They settled into their rooms and all met later in the dining room. Jim was invited to join them. Jim was only a little older than the oldest Clarke lad, so he agreed, as he had already met them on the ship. He wore his best clothes, which were clean and tidy but nowhere near fashionable.

Charles informed Jim, "Lad, I have found that two gentlemen are currently staying at the hotel, and I've arranged an introduction. The rest is up to you."

Jim was again overwhelmed that an Earl would take any interest in him. A mere farmer's lad with a passion for horses. He thanked him and assured him he would certainly follow up on the introduction.

It didn't take long for the meeting to occur. As they all retired to the sitting room after dinner, the manager brought two men over to introduce them, two American gentlemen. Mr James Swanton and Mr John Peck bowed, and Charles invited them both to join them.

Mrs Clarke and her children withdrew and retired to their rooms. They were pleased they could sleep in a bed that didn't move.

Charles, Sal, Jim, Mr Swanton, and Mr Peck sat talking for some time. Charles had asked them about what they did. The manager had not actually told them.

Jim's interest was aroused when he heard about their business.

The newcomers noticed his interest.

Charles turned the conversation around to the diggings and asked, "How has the gold affected your business?"

Mr Swanton replied. "Well, four of us started this caper some time ago. We have just bought out the other two. We have been unable to get enough qualified drivers, though. We have resorted to advertising in England and America. We just can't get anyone who doesn't leave and go prospecting. The diggings have taken off, and we've had some problems hiring trustworthy men. They also have to carry the gold back to town, as well as the mail and passengers. This can be dangerous as there have been some holdups by bushrangers."

Mr Peck noted the quick look from Charles to Jim and raised an eyebrow. "Mr Leslie, do I see some interest in this area?"

Jim was somewhat overwhelmed. Not only was he sitting in a luxurious hotel, rather than a poor wayside inn, but he was also meeting the two men who may be able to help him, and his following comments could change his life. "Yes, sir, my passion is horses. I read about a group of four men, a Mr Cobb and Co., who were running coaches to and from the diggings." He unfolded an advertisement from his pocket. It was much read. "I have come to meet them; unfortunately, only one name is given and no direction. Are you in the same business?"

Mr Peck laughed. "Yes, lad, we're two of the 'Co'. We're all American, and we two have just bought Mr Cobb and Mr Lamber out. They have gone home. So it's us you are actually looking for."

With his brash American accent, Jim took a moment to fully comprehend that he'd been led to the exact persons he sought. "Oh," Jim simply said, smiling broadly.

"So you like horses, eh? Tell us about yourself." Mr Swanton asked.

Charles relaxed back into his seat, listening intently. His smile said it all. God was weaving His treads again.

Jim filled them in. "I was brought up on a farm in Durham, England. Horses had always been my passion. However, I am the second son, and my older brother, John, will inherit the farm. Our father, also named John, had a sister, Sarah, who was married to a coach builder, Lancelot Usher. They had no children. Years ago, my father asked if I would be interested in living with them and learning the coach trade. Although not farming, it had a lot to do with horses. I left home at twelve and moved to Newcastle-on-Tyne, and I learnt my uncle's trade, who was building and repairing coaches. For many years, I delivered Uncle Lance's coaches around the north of the country. My first one was soon after I moved in with them. Uncle Lance already knew my skill with the reins and dispatched me with a team of four and a new coach from Newcastle to Liverpool. It's a trip of just under one hundred and eighty miles. It took me two weeks each way. I had to take it slowly as I had to make sure the carriage was delivered in perfect condition." It was.

Jim fell silent.

Mr Peck started. "Jeepers! One hundred and eighty miles with a coach and a twelve-year-old kiddie? My, that's a trip and a half; it's only about seventy-five miles from Melbourne to Ballarat. How many horses can you handle, lad?"

"Four, that trip, sir. I've since driven many with much larger teams. I even delivered a custom-built ten-passenger coach with twelve horses once; I was eighteen then," James volunteered.

"Why did you leave, son?" Mr Swanton asked as he lay back in his chair.

"My uncle died, sir, simple as that. As did my Aunt Sarah, and recently my mother too. My father has three more sons, as well as daughters. I wanted to get back to the horses. Then I saw this advertisement, and the one about the *Red Jacket*, and I thought I could combine adventure with a new life. If you need a driver, then I have the experience." Jim was youthfully confident. He knew his own skills, but so many young men thought they could drive when they were actually useless. "Sirs, I have a suggestion. I know I'm young; I'm only twenty, sirs; however, I know my ability. There is no one here, not even this very kind gentleman, who can vouch for my skills. I suggest I show you. If I can drive the biggest coach with the largest team, I'll work for you for a week for free. I only need accommodation, as I am unable to stay here." He waved his hand around. "I am here at the generosity of Lord Charles."

"I, too, have a suggestion. If you love horses as much as you say, we have some small accommodations over the stables. There's a bed and a communal cooking area, and an outdoor privy. It's basic, but if you get the job, it's free for as long as you like or until you want to find somewhere permanent."

"Thank you, sir. I'll take it. When travelling, I have often had to sleep in the stables with the horses. A bed would be a luxury," James said with thanks. "I can drive all sorts of configurations too, from the standard two by two, to two by three abreast and even four wide."

"Good, then we'll meet you here in the dining room at eight in the morning," Mr Peck said.

They stood and departed.

Jim dropped his head and gave the Lord a word of thanks. When he lifted his head, he met Charles's eyes. "Why me, sir? With all the men on the ship, why me?" Jim asked softly.

"Let me ask you this. Did you just give the Lord thanks?"

Jim nodded.

"That is why. I saw you do that in Liverpool after calming the horse. You are a man of God, as am I, as you know. One day, I hope to tell you my story, all of it. It will astound you. It will be worth your coming to Parramatta to hear it. When I was your age, someone took care of me. My life today is because of that man. So call it 'payback' or 'pay it forward'. Do something with your life and help people. I'm sure you will. And Jim, maybe one day you can help someone else."

"Lord Charles, I can never thank you enough. You achieved in one evening what would have taken me months." He bowed his head as thanks.

"No, lad, that was our Lord," Charles said. "I asked a question, that's all. God did the rest. Now it's time for us to away. I shall look forward to when you eventually come north." Charles stood, as did Jim.

He took Sal's hand and bowed over it. "Thank you, Lady Sarah. You have no idea how much you have helped. You remind me of my mother, Susanna. You are very like, m'am. I miss her," Jim said sadly.

"Oh, Susanna is the name of a very dear friend." Sal smiled at him. "I shall pray for you, too, Jim. Take care."

~

The following morning, they all arrived in the dining room at the same time. Charles, Sal and Jim had already eaten before Mrs Clarke and her family appeared. They had two hours before they needed to be at the dock, and Mr Peck had invited them to meet Jim at the stables. They had met him as he was leaving with Jim.

Charles jumped at the chance to see Jim's test. Sal also wanted to watch, so they quickly ate, packed, and arranged for the luggage to be loaded on the connecting ship. They had enough time to leave a message with Mrs Clarke and then hurried away.

The manager handed them into a waiting carriage. It took them to the Cobb and Co stables.

Mr Peck greeted them. "I told Jim to choose his own team. This is one of the hardest things to do with unknown steeds, as normally the grooms do this. Let's see what he does, eh?"

They arrived some minutes before and sent Jim into the stable and told him to choose and harness up a team of up to six. There were over twenty horses available. Jim chose four horses and quickly had them in their traces and attached to the shafts. The two leaders he had chosen were strong beasts; they had attitude. Their counterparts were of equal size, but their temperaments were less assertive. They would be robust and responsive.

Mr Peck stood watching how efficient his actions were. He did it in half the time that many experienced men would do.

He leaned over to Charles. "If he drives like he works, he's hired. I would have taken hours to choose and harness a team from scratch," he chuckled loudly.

Minutes later, Jim led out the team attached to a large carriage. He was surprised to see Charles and Sal. He thought they had gone.

Mr Peck said, "Lord Charles wanted to see if you are as good as he thinks you will be. He has dismissed their carriage, so I'm presuming you will have to drop them at the dock." He turned to Charles and Sal. "Hop in. I'll ride with you, lad, as you don't know the area."

Charles smiled and gave a half-bow in acknowledgement.

Mr Peck and Charles handed Sal into the carriage. Charles followed her.

Mr Swanton joined them inside. "The skill of driving is not just about horses, but about the journey," he said softly so Jim couldn't hear. "If the passengers are thrown around, then the driving is bad. I'm normally the one to see how smooth the trip is, so it's nice to have company."

Sally sat looking out the window as Jim walked the horses out of the stables.

Mr Peck gave directions, and Jim had the horses responding quickly. His turns were smooth, as was his driving. Although he had a long driving whip, he only hit the shaft between the horses. It gave a cracking sound. Then Jim caught the thong end in his hand. An expert move, from someone used to doing it.

Mr Peck smiled; he directed Jim to the docks, giving him intricate directions as he drove. He directed him along narrow lanes and tight corners. Jim didn't quaver and never hesitated along the route directed.

It had taken him only twenty-five minutes to harness the team. Mr Peck marvelled at how skilfully Jim manoeuvred the team through the chaotic traffic. Considering he'd never seen the street before, nor the team or carriage. Mr Peck thought to himself, "This lad knows his stuff."

Inside the carriage, the ride was comfortable. The starts and stops were smooth. The passengers were not thrown around at all.

Mr Swanton said, "He'll get my vote, my lord. He certainly knows his stuff." He spoke in his thick American accent. He was impressed.

Ten minutes later, Jim turned onto the docks. The traffic was different, as were the noises. The lead horses were flighty, but Jim controlled them to perfection. On arrival, he drew them to a gentle stop. He pulled on the brake but stayed seated.

"What ya waitin' for, lad?" Mr Peck asked.

"I'll stay here until someone can hold the horses. They are flighty and don't know the sounds," Jim simply stated.

That was the final test for Mr Peck. He had seen many drivers trust the brake, and the horses took off on them. Any team of horses can override a simple brake. "Well, lad, you have my vote. It was the smoothest ride I've had in a long while. Let's see what they say inside." He hopped down and led the lead horses to a hitching rail.

Only when the beasts were secured did Jim step down.

Mr Swanton alighted. He took Sal's hand as Charles hopped out the other side.

"Lovely, smooth trip, James. Thank you. I knew you were all I expected you to be," Charles said.

The two owners stood talking, and each nodded. "You'd better congratulate him. He's just scored a cushy job," Mr Peck said. "If he can drive through a town he's never been in, with a team he's never even seen before and drive that smoothly, well, he's good enough for me."

Jim smiled. "Thank you, sirs. Thank you so much. You will not regret this." He turned to Charles. "My Lord, I didn't even need the reference. But thank you anyway."

"What? You have a reference?" Mr Peck sounded surprised. "But you said you knew no one but Lord Charles here."

Jim laughed. "Sir, the reference is from Lord Charles." His eyes were smiling, but the words were said with unuttered laughter. He offered his arm to Sal. "Ma'am, the dockland is an unsafe place to walk. May I escort you to the ship?"

She took Jim's arm, and they walked off towards the boat.

Charles took the opportunity to give his direction to the two men, and he told them of his connections to the diggings with the Emporiums. He gave them each his cards and said, "Do not hesitate to contact either my family or me. If you mention the name of Lockley at Bathurst, Emu Plains, Parramatta, or Sydney, we may be able to help in some small way. Especially if you decide to open up a route up there." He glanced at Jim. "Look after Jim for me. For some reason, I feel our paths will cross again, often. Use my name if you wish." Charles bowed and left them. The men stayed with the carriage. Charles walked in the path of Jim and Sal, meeting them at the gangplank.

Jim again said thanks, bowed and stood back. He felt like throwing his arms around this couple. Lady Lockley reminded him of his mother, and he missed her so much. He fingered the fob watch his mother had given him not long before she'd died.

The time had come for Charles and Sal to step on board. They said a final farewell.

Charles put his hand on his shoulder. "Take care, lad. I feel we will meet again, in the not-so-distant future. I shall hold you to your promise of looking me up. And, please write. I am interested in how you settle in. I have your address here."

Jim promised he would. Still amazed that a man like this could be interested in him.

The three men waited for twenty minutes until the ship pulled away from the dock, then they departed. All three were now up on the driver's seat of the carriage.

Jim was given a tour of the city and shown around town. All the time, his two new bosses were watching how he handled his horses. Never once did he whip the horses. The shaft got the occasional flick, but never once did he hurt them. He didn't fail them. Arriving back at the stables, he waited until Mr Peck was holding the horses before alighting.

Mr Peck saw Jim's luggage in the corner of the stall of the lead horse. He smiled. Only a man who knew horses would have chosen that stall to leave his luggage. No one would have entered that stall willingly; he was known as a cantankerous brute.

Jim was watched while he unharnessed the team. Everything was put away, and the animals were not only fed and watered but also groomed. Only then did he see to his own comfort.

Jim walked up the stairs to the allocated room.

Unbeknownst to him, Mr Peck had followed him. He watched as the lad fell to his knees and gave thanks to his real "boss." Mr Peck smiled and walked off to find his friend. He'd ask him to dinner later.

~

As the *City of Sydney* drew away from the pier, Charles and Sal waved to Jim, then went to their cabin.

The Clarkes were on board, and so was all their luggage, from the *Red Jacket*. They had only taken an overnight bag each to the hotel; everything else was moved from one ship to the other. Once on board and checked that their bags were in their cabin, Charles and Sal returned to the deck. They stood watching the ship move out of the harbour.

In less than a week, they would be home. Once the ship reached the sea, she turned northwards and the wind filled her sails.

Charles was intrigued to see the different set of sails. The *Red Jacket* was a clipper ship with square sails on the three masts and handkerchief sails off to the sides. Every breath of wind was caught and carried the ship as if on wings. This one was a schooner and was double-masted. The front jibs were a set of three triangular, triple sails.

The Captain explained to Charles the names of them all, which Charles immediately forgot. He simply enjoyed the experience and the sensation of the breeze's power.

He hoped that the wind would stay behind them the entire trip. If not, they would have had to tack often, and it would have added an extra day or more.

Three days later, soon after dawn, they were pulling into the heads off Sydney.

Charles and Sal were standing in the bow as they entered the harbour. They followed another schooner, and they could hear yelling from the deck of the other ship. Someone was waving, but they were too far away to see who it was. It looked like Luke, but what was he doing on a schooner? It pulled away from them and went further along the cove into the cargo wharves. Charles waved acknowledgment, then almost forgot about it as they moored at the Phoenix Wharf in the next bay, where their vessel docked in Circular Quay. Before they had time to bring their hand luggage from the cabin, they could again hear yelling from the dock. Only this time, they both recognised their youngest son's voice and could see him through the tiny porthole. He was waiting for them on the wharf. He was bouncing like a child.

Sal was over the moon. She grabbed her reticule and headed outside.

Charles was hard on her heels.

As soon as the gangplank was secured, Luke was up on deck and in his mother's arms. He had done much the same some ten years ago. He was ecstatic; they would be here for his wedding. Last time it was Wills and Cathy's wedding, this time it would be for Ellen and his. He had so much to tell them, but it could wait. They retreated back into their cabin to continue the welcome.

Luke was not the only person waiting on the dock.

William had also made a beeline for the ship. He realised that if the Earl were onboard, then hopefully Maria would be too. However, he waited on the dock.

John and Colleen were to oversee the removal of the stock and cart. They could all join them later.

William's eyes were searching the deck. Finally, his eyes fell on his goal. Maria had come. He walked to the gangplank and waited. The children, now adults, came first, and he tousled their hair, then kissed them.

Maria came last. She had no idea what to expect. She certainly did not expect that he would enfold her in his arms and kiss her passionately in public. Neither caring who was watching, she clung to him, sobbing.

Their children had no idea where to look, so they just moved away from them and left them alone.

William kissed her wet eyes, her cheeks and her lips again. Finally, he took her beloved face in his hands and looked her directly in the eye. "Maria, my dearest, thank you for coming back to me. I have not told you often enough, but I love you." He enfolded her in his arms again, just holding her. He just held her until her sobs subsided once more.

Her arms were wrapped around his neck as though she'd never let him go. "Oh, William, I'm so sorry. I'll never go again. I missed you so much."

He kissed her again, then, tucking her under his arm, he said. "I have so much to tell you, but first, let's get your luggage. I'll send it over to the house. Then I'll get my things and will join you."

"No," she said adamantly. "My dear, we shall go together. Everywhere together again." She called the children over. "Go and get the luggage, my dears. We're going home."

William grinned.

As she said it, Hamish appeared on the dock.

Wills and Cathy were hard on his heels. "Hello, all." Wills greeted the Clarkes *en masse* and welcomed Mrs Clarke home.

She gave him a teary smile and said, "Thank you, Wills, for everything." She took his hand a gave it a slight squeeze.

Hamish turned and called over some of the dock workers. Within minutes, he had arranged to empty all the cabins and bring the luggage off the ship. It was stacked into two piles: the Clarkes and the Lockleys.

Wills went on board to greet his parents, who had not yet reappeared. Once again, the four met in private, and any emotions were shielded from public view.

Cathy stayed on the wharf. She was looking around for John and Colleen; finally, she asked Reverend Clarke where they were.

"Ahh! They are still on board over there," he pointed to the other ship. "I suppose I should go and help." He was about to walk off when he turned and took Maria's hand and drew it through his arm. "Come, love." He walked over to the second ship docked in the next wharf.

Cathy could hear Colleen yelling. "Hello, Cathy."

She could not see her.

"Over here, Cathy," Colleen's voice carried.

Cathy followed the direction and then caught sight of her friend. She could see seven sturdy horses. She walked over to her and greeted her with a kiss, then realised her condition, exclaimed, "Oh, Colleen, how exciting. Is this why you've come back by ship?"

"Partially, over there is the real reason." They turned and saw William still holding Maria's hand. She was following willingly, her face creased in smiles. "There is no way he was not going to be here when she got back. We had to wait six days in Moreton Bay, waiting for a ship that would bring these fellows home. The wait nearly killed the pair of them. I've never seen two people so eager to get moving. He and Luke were unable to sit still. Let's get the rest of the luggage unloaded from the boat, then we can go home. Cathy, can we stay with you tonight? We haven't arranged anything."

"Oh, Colleen, your room is still there waiting. I don't think your new clothes will fit, though." Cathy giggled.

"Err, no. I can't say anything yet, but Cathy, we have so much to tell you. If we can get Hamish to help William and Maria home, they can leave their children there and come back later. We need to get home for Luke to see Ellen."

"Oh no, you don't. Look." Cathy pointed to a small group coming down the hill.

As they walked on to the dock area, they caught sight of Luke running down the gangplank. It bounced. Moments later, Ellen was enfolded in his arms.

Nothing was said. He held her at arm's length, devouring her with his eyes. Decorum and her parents were totally ignored. He drew her gently into his arms, and she welcomed him home properly. Their kiss was deep and passionate; neither was aware of anyone around them, and not a word had been spoken. The rest of the world disappeared for them both. His parents, brother, sapphires, diamonds, and his new wealth were not important. Ellen was here to welcome him. That's all that mattered.

Finally, he heard a cough beside him. He looked up and saw her parents standing nearby. Luke grinned, then gave Ellen another quick kiss. "Hello, love. I missed you."

Her father said, "Um, I think we might realise that. Just as well, it's mutual. Ellen, it looks like the wedding is next Saturday. So you only have to wait a few more days. We had it originally booked for August 30. But she insisted we reserve each other Saturday from this weekend just in case both ships arrived earlier. Here you are, arriving together." Bill stood laughing. Molly was clinging to his arm, grinning too. Ellen smiled at her parents.

Within two hours, the *Vengeance* was fully unloaded. Hamish took control of everyone's luggage, sorting everything faster than expected. Getting the cart unloaded from the boat was the hardest thing. They had to borrow the second gangplank from the other ship before it could be removed. Once off, it was able to be repacked with the Clarks' luggage from both ships.

Colleen oversaw the unloading from their ship and sorted out who owned what.

With the Clarkes' luggage loaded onto the cart, they took an afternoon barge home to North Sydney. William said they would visit at 3 pm. "Have the flour bags ready. We'll leave the children at home, but we will be there."

Wills and Cathy looked at each other enquiringly, but Wills shrugged.

~

Sure enough, at three o'clock precisely, there was a knock on Wills' front door.

Maria still looked somewhat worried.

William turned to her. "Trust me, love, this is worth it."

Maria merely nodded and followed him into the house.

Colleen held out her hand to him and greeted him with "Hello, William. Hello, Mrs Clarke."

She replied, "If he's William, then I'm Maria."

Colleen nodded.

Cathy and Wills greeted and welcomed them both. Hamish brought in the tea trolley, then left them all alone, while he went and looked after the children.

Charles and Sal were sitting just observing the happenings, both sure something momentous was about to be revealed, but no one was quite knowing what it would be.

In the middle of the room was a small round table. Luke moved it a little, so it was sitting in the afternoon sun.

Ellen, Molly, and Bill sat near Charles and Sal, all unsure of what the afternoon would reveal.

William placed a chair for Maria and asked her to sit near him. It was near the small table; William stood beside her.

Luke turned and picked up a large round mirror that was usually on the wall in his room. He carefully put it on the table.

William turned to Colleen. "Do you have them?"

She nodded and produced two bulky flour bags from under her shawl. One by one, she handed them to him.

Luke and she had carried them in and placed them under her shawl.

"Luke, John, come and help," William called over to the two young men. They carefully unpacked a bunch of small bags. The bags were of three colours, and the blue ones were pushed aside; the brown and green bags were placed together.

Each bag was emptied into small piles around the mirror. The sun caught the red of the garnets, topaz, and other gems.

Maria gasped.

"Wait for it, love," William said to his wife, grinning.

Ellen was now on her knees at the table, Sal and Molly standing behind her, their arms hooked.

Luke opened the green bags. He emptied each one onto the mirror. The blues, greens, and yellows were caught by the sun and reflected on the ceiling, a kaleidoscope of colours.

There were so many bags. Finally, John and William started opening the smaller bags to help him. Shiny, clear stones like prisms sat on the mirror but reflected rainbows around the room.

Wills and Cathy gasped.

Wills asked, "Sir, the clear ones are they...? Really... diamonds?" Wills was looking up at the ceiling, not down at the table. The rainbows from the clear ones shining on the ceiling were a giveaway. The sun shining through them was astounding. The other stones were like stained glass, but these were true rainbows.

The extended family followed his gaze and looked up too. Then they gathered around them and "ohh'd" and "ahh'd" at the fabulous finds.

The four travellers knew of some special stones, stored in small jars in their rooms. They agreed that if they mined them together, they shared that hoard. If someone, like Colleen's diamond, was found alone, they got to keep it themselves.

Each had found some unique and very special stones. Their jars were each more than half full.

Most of the vast haul was to be shared; it was sorted and packed in bags. Once all the stones were on the table and the bags removed, the rainbow of colours shone like an enormous kaleidoscope. Everyone was speechless. The ceiling looked like stained glass. The sun was making rainbows as it flickered in the window.

William said, "Maria, my dear, you can have whatever you want, my love. We are going thirds on the value of these."

He looked at Wills, "And yes, these are diamonds, Wills. We won't be able to sell these here, though. I'm not quite sure what we're to do with them, but those sapphires are certainly saleable, as are the topaz, rubies, amethysts, and even the nice garnets and Jasper for a cash price. Before we do anything with those, we also have to report the finds to Governor-General Denison. He'll be rubbing his hands with glee. The smaller gemstones we can sell immediately. There is a not-so-small fortune in these alone, Luke, enough for your needs, John the same."

Maria could only look at him. Her eyes were glassy, knowing how short of money they had been, now this. She stifled a sob.

"Wills, you said you knew one of the jewellers in town. Is he trustworthy?" William asked.

"Yes, sir, Mr Richard Lamb, in George Street, he's honest. He's often called in to do Government work. Yes, I would trust him with some, at least. Take some of the smaller ones and the star sapphires first and see what he says. We really only have this week, though. We have a wedding next Saturday. It's actually booked for every Saturday in August. You could have it this Saturday, but even two days is not long enough for Cara to cook everything."

Luke roared with laughter. Looking at his Fiancé, "Every Saturday?"

"Yes," said Ellen, while nodding vigorously. "I had no idea that you would both be home on the same day. We knew you wouldn't wait, so I booked each weekend."

She walked up to Luke, and he placed his arm around her shoulders.

He bent and gave her a quick kiss. "I love the way you think, sweetheart," he whispered.

She laid her hand on his chest possessively and snuggled as close as she could.

"William, I was wondering if you would be free to come. I'd love you to do the service, but if not, you can at least be part of it. That would be wonderful," Luke asked.

Reverend Clarke looked at his wife. He raised his eyebrows. "What do you think, Maria? Feel like a trip to Parramatta on Saturday week? All my samples are at Eddie's, so we have to go sometime."

She was still somewhat overwhelmed by the tray of rainbow rocks still sitting in front of her. "William, I will go where you go and do what you do. The children can make up their own minds. They are old enough now. I don't need to be there to look after them." She looked around the room. "I think it would be wonderful to see everyone again. Yes, William, I would like … no, I'd love to go."

William turned to Luke. "Book us in then, lad. Now talking of our children, I think we'll head off home. We have much catching up to do. John, Luke, can you put these away? Keep them here until tomorrow. I'll… no, we'll come back again. I'll bring my little jar too. Then we'll head to Government House and do an initial verbal report." He gave them all a slight bow. He then took his wife's hand and said their farewells. The carriage was still at the door, and it took them to the ferry.

Bill and Molly had also sat listening to what was playing out in front of them. The gemstones on the table they knew were worth a king's fortune. Their inn in Parramatta, The Rear Admiral Duncan, was one of the best ones in Parramatta and was doing very well. Tim, their eldest son, was now a successful lawyer and politician, working in his own law firm, and was also Anna, Luke's older sister. He was also up for election again and would probably win his seat again. Gracie was married to Luke's oldest brother, Charlie; she was Viscountess Lockley. Samuel had taken over the inn and married Belle Ellis, and now Ellen was to benefit from this bounty.

Molly was overwhelmed. A tear trickled down her cheek.

Bill saw it and asked her quietly, "What's wrong, love?"

"Nothing, absolutely nothing, Billy boy! This…" Molly said, waving her hand towards the gems, "…This will see the last of our children so well set up. I have always been worried about her. Now, this!"

He squeezed her hand lovingly. "Oh, yes, I was thinking much the same. I must admit, I was wondering how he was going to support her. Teaching, at King's of late, has not been that stable a job. Whatever happens now, they have some funds behind them."

"I think we should leave them alone for a while. We'll see you at home." Bill turned to suggest they go; however, Charles asked if they wouldn't mind staying. He'd like to spend some time catching up with his friend. They never had time to socialise when back at home. So Bill and Molly settled down and relaxed with Sal and Charles for the afternoon.

Ellen, Luke, Colleen and John carefully re-sorted the gems into three bundles. All the diamonds were separated and kept aside. None of those could be sold until their diamond finds had first been reported to

Governor-General Denison. They went back into their own blue bags and put them away.

Another bag was sorted into various stone groups to be taken directly to the jeweller. It contained the garnets, topaz, in brown bags, and most of the smaller sapphires, including most of the star sapphires, in green bags. The large blue star sapphire was not included; there were some two hundred plus stones in this package. The volume of sapphires alone equalled about three mugs full. It was the only way they had to measure them. There was a selection of the larger, better sapphires, rubies, and the finest garnets, amethysts, and a giant blue topaz, among others, in another bag.

William Clarke said he would submit a summary report outlining the findings as quickly as possible, along with his initial mineral survey. The complete official survey would take months, if not years, to be fully completed.

Chapter 12   Finds Reported

$\mathcal{B}$ill, Molly, and Ellen stayed for dinner. Luke walked with them back to *the King's Arms Hotel*. He arranged to meet them after he had seen the Governor and the jeweller. He then strolled back to Wills' house.

John had sent word to his parents, and they arrived for supper. Caro and Douglas were delighted with the news of an impending new family member.

Colleen was glowing, and she greeted them warmly. They didn't stay long, but promised to return the next morning.

~

The next morning, with time now to talk, John told his parents briefly of the momentous gemstone finds and that they planned to set up their own house. Not too far away, but a place to call home.

Caro saw Colleen's face fall, but said nothing.

Douglas had a newspaper under his arm on arrival. After John greeted them, he borrowed it and flicked it open, turning to the sales pages. On running his finger down the page, he said, "Yes, perfect."

Colleen ventured to ask him of his find. He replied by reading her an advertisement. "Listen to this love…

A Four-roomed House, near College Street, a little to the south of Francis Street. BOWDEN and THRELKELD will sell by Auction, at the City Mart, 211, George Street, on THURSDAY next, the 7th instant, at 11 o'clock, The Interest of the lessee in and to the house and ground now occupied by Mrs. Haydon, having 21 months to run, at a rental of one peppercorn per month. The house contains four rooms and shed. A backyard, and entrance from a street in the rear. On the first floor is a small balcony overlooking Woolloomooloo. Immediate possession may be had. Terms, cash.

John looked up, "Love, this will be perfect. I'll be working, so we can't cope with a big backyard, but it does have a yard at the back. It's close to both my work and my family. What do you think?" John asked her. "I'm sure we can stay either here or with my parents until Mrs Haydon's lease runs out. She may even move earlier," John added.

Caro jumped at the opening. "Of course, you can stay with us. You can even make your home with us if you'd like. I know you young people, though, you want your own space."

"Actually, Mrs Evans, Mother Caro, I'd love to stay with you. I'm not used to having no one around me. I think I'd get lonely all by myself all day. But it's nearly two years. Could you put up with us for that long?" She looked at her husband, "Are there any other houses? Is that the only one?"

John kept reading, "I'll look, sweeting, but it's the only one in this paper. We may not like it anyway; we'll keep looking. There might be something later in the year. Mother, Father, would you mind some long-term boarders?" John asked his parents.

"Mind? Son, we'd love it," his father interjected. "We're rattling around in a large empty house. We would love some company. Not to mention a hands-on grandchild."

"Looks like that's settled then, love. We're moving back home, at least for the time being," John said.

Colleen relaxed. She'd not relished being alone in a house, especially with a baby. Now she'd have some female company. Effy and her mother-in-law would both be wonderful. She didn't want to tell John that they were his dreams, not hers. She had grown up in a slab hut with no beds, sharing with all her siblings. For her to be alone was not a pleasant experience.

"You didn't want to move, did you?" John had been watching her face.

She shook her head. "No love, but I know you did. If I can be happy in a cart with you roaming around the country, I can be happy wherever you are. I need, nor want much, just you." She gave him a beaming smile.

He handed the paper back to his father. "I don't think we'll be needing that then, Father. Thank you, though."

"Colleen, do you mean it?" Caro said excitedly. "You'll stay with us? Really? I could not be happier. We've missed John so much over the past months. The house positively rattles. To think we can have the pitter-patter of little feet again would be wonderful," Caro added.

"Mrs Evans, Mother Caro … What should I call you by the way?" Colleen asked

"Mother or Mother Caro would be fine, dear, whatever you feel comfortable with."

"Mother Caro, then. We accept, on one condition, that if we get too much, you will say we're too much, especially when more children arrive. I know how disruptive they can be." Colleen looked at her husband and in-laws.

Caro, who was sitting next to her, took her hand and patted it. "I promise. But that is not going to happen." Her face was radiating joy.

"While the others are away, we have something to show you." John took a small jar from his pocket. He opened the lid and poured the contents into his mother's hand. There were ten clear stones, one a large, clear, double-pointed one and seven smaller sapphires, including a giant blue sapphire, a yellow one of assorted sizes and colours.

Caro gasped.

Douglas fingered them. "What's that? No, it can't be a diamond?" He held the perfect inch-long stone in his fingers.

They nodded.

"But where did you find it? Is this how you were going to purchase the house? I know you have money in the bank, but well, John, these are worth a small fortune."

"We know. But more like a large fortune. And these are but a sample of what our share is. It's why the others have gone to see Governor Denison. They have to report the find. We can't attempt to sell the diamonds until they are officially reported. So our problem is how to sell them." John looked at his wife, who nodded. "As a group, we have quite a few of them."

Douglas looked up quickly. "Ahh! Well, I may be able to help you there." He gave them a whiskered grin. "When I came home from my extended stay in China all those years ago, I didn't completely come home with empty pockets." He looked at Caro. "As it happened, one pocket, in particular, was quite full. I've been eking out the sales over the past years. It's how we've been living. I still have more, but they aren't as good as this one, but I'm sure no one will realise. I take them to Richard Lamb. We have a good arrangement. He knows the source of mine, they are from China."

At that moment, a carriage was heard at the front of the house. Charles, Sal, Wills, Cathy, and Luke had arrived back from Government House. Colleen put away their stones.

John met them as they entered. "I think you'd better come and have a seat," he said as they came in. "Father has something interesting to tell you." Over the next hour, they exchanged information they had discovered during the morning.

~

Two hours later, Douglas, Luke, and John took the big diamond and the sorted packets of sapphires and smaller gems and semi-precious stones to Mr Lamb.

Douglas produced "his" diamond, and Mr Lamb had to sit down quickly. "Mr Evans, this stone is astounding." He had picked it up and was inspecting it with his eye-glass. He brought out a small scale measure. Then had to get a larger one. "It's a perfect diamond, Mr Evans. I've never seen anything like it. I recently heard of a five-carat diamond selling in America for over $8,000. This is well over twice the size; I'd estimate over £10,000, probably more. I don't have money like that. I'd have to send it to Antwerp and sell it on consignment. I don't know what else to do with it."

The jeweller was sitting holding the stone. His hands were shaking. "I'm privileged to think you can bring it to me. It is a once-in-a-lifetime dream to see a rough diamond like this. But I can't really help at this time. I do, however, have a buyer due in soon. With the new sapphire source from up north, I've had notice of a fellow arriving from Europe. I'll sound him out for you."

Douglas said thank you and placed the diamond in a bag, then returned it to his top pocket.

Luke and John then stepped forward and spoke to Mr Lamb. "We've just returned from the gem fields ourselves and have some for sale. We also have others and would be interested in meeting the buyer, too."

Luke took a medium-sized bag from his pocket and tipped them onto the glass countertop. These were hundreds of garnets, topaz, and some of the smaller sapphires, all nice but nothing spectacular. About two cups full in total.

Mr Lamb sorted through them and offered what he thought was a reasonable price for the entire contents, £1000.

Luke looked at John; he made a face. They were hoping for £500 for that lot. He turned back and said. "Thank you, yes, we won't haggle on those. John has some more, though; some may need an individual price. We have to split the tally three ways."

The jeweller collected his new stones and put them in a large glass container.

John drew out a slightly larger bag. He opened the string and tipped them out where the others had sat.

Mr Lamb exclaimed, "Oh, my. You have had a good collecting session." He left them at the counter and walked to lock the door. "Just a precaution," he said, smiling at them.

The first ones that caught his eye were the blue topaz and the huge sapphires. He could see the colours and inspected each for clarity, imperfections and colour. He umm'd and arr'd; eventually, he said, "The only way I could do these is as you say, individually." After some time, "However, I could only afford a few, so the European buyer is your best bet too. Your timing is perfect, as prices are at record highs at the moment, not just for diamonds but also for good sapphires, rubies, and topaz. Her Majesty had brought beautiful gems back into vogue. They are all the rage. Prince Albert is assisting by buying many for her. Mr Evans, I suggest that if you have more of the little 'glass' baubles at home, the buyer might be your best bet, especially as the quality has significantly improved. I'll let you know when he arrives. In the meantime, let me look at these again." He went back to the second parcel of stones.

"That alone is £3,000," pushing the blue sapphire away from him. "I'd love to buy it, but can't afford it. Start at £5,000 when he comes. Don't go lower than £4000. The topaz, well, it too is magnificent, at least £ 500. It's a pity you have to sell it. As to the rest …" He picked out eight smaller but lovely stones. "I'll give you another £800 for those eight. These may be the smaller ones, but they should cut to about five carats each." He knew his offer to be reasonable. He still had to cut and polish them, but they would cut beautifully. There was a yellow, a green, and six blues of various shades. He knew that he could not sell the more expensive stones, but that the European buyer would jump at them.

John and Luke had their heads together on the far side of the store. They agreed that £800 was far above what William had estimated. They'd take it; that was a neat £600 each, and that was just from the smaller stones.

They turned back, and John said, "Thank you, we agree. Please let us know when the buyer comes in. We do have more he may be interested in."

"I do too," said Douglas. "Do you know when he's due? Days, weeks, or months?"

"I'm thinking weeks, but it could be months, Captain Evans. If you have more like that, he'll be your only chance of selling them. I can't cut diamonds. I've had to send yours away to Antwerp to sell, then repurchase them as cut stones. I send them gems to a place called *Tiffany's* in Antwerp. They are the only ones I trust."

John took his father aside. "I don't know how many you have, Father, but we have a few more large ones and a bag of about sixty small ones. We may as well sell them while we have the chance. What do you think?"

"I think you're correct. I'll bring the rest of mine too and sell them in two parcels," Douglas said.

"Err, no, Father, a few more than that. We each have some nice ones. And one parcel to divide. We can sort that out later," John said. He returned to the jeweller.

"We have some more stones that we'll bring along. Father will bring his remaining stones, as will we. Even if you can value them for us, so we know if he's going to cheat us," John said with confidence.

"If he doesn't offer you near the price, then don't sell them. That one stone, Captain Evans, is worth a trip to Europe to sell it. If you have more like that big one, I wouldn't trust a buyer with it unless they pay you cash for it. The more I think about it, the more it could be, even as high as over £20,000. Don't sell yourself short. A passage to Europe is only about £50 for cabin class, and you could make £10,000 more." Mr Lamb looked in earnest at Captain Evans. He was somewhat suspicious as this stone was far beyond the quality of the previous ones. It was not for him to judge, though. Mr Lamb said, "I'll close the shop and come directly to the bank with you now. I don't have that kind of money on me."

They walked to the Bank of Australasia, and Mr Lamb withdrew the money.

John, who had an account at the same branch, immediately deposited £550 of his share.

Luke took his share and walked up the street to his bank and did likewise, depositing £550 into his account.

The final £600, they decided on a draft in William Clarke's name instead of cash. However, they arranged that he could cash it in today if he wished for cash.

Mr Lamb took the bag of sapphires and assorted gems he had purchased and returned to the shop.

John had the larger sapphires and topaz, and Douglas handed back the diamonds to him.

They returned to Wills' house and sorted the remaining stones; Douglas helped them. The lemony yellow diamond they kept aside, as they did with the twelve large ones. They had Colleen's big one, plus her ten smaller ones, Luke's smaller 3/4 inch one and the other sixty-one or so smaller ones belonging to them all.

William had his jar full at home, and he'd have to bring that over later. They knew he had at least four large ones of the half-inch size. Each had kept their private finds and only knew of some of the stones each had.

When Douglas saw the gems in their jars, he was astounded. The large diamond from Colleen's jar was impressive enough; he had seen that already. John had decided to get his blue topaz cut for Colleen instead of selling it. He took it back to Mr Lamb and asked that it be set in a heart-shaped pendant once it was cut. He gave him a drawing of what he wanted. He also had the yellow sapphire and asked that it be made up into another ring for her.

~

William and Maria Clarke arrived mid-morning the next day, and the group once more set out for the jeweller. Douglas had taken possession of all the diamonds. He had them in five bags. His gems were in a small leather bag, Luke's in a blue bag, along with the green sapphire Colleen had given him. John's big blue sapphire and smaller diamonds in a green bag, and Williams's in a brown bag. The remaining diamonds, including the six larger group-owned ones and the yellow diamond, were in a larger blue bag.

Mr Lamb welcomed them and then locked the door after them. He valued them, separating the yellow diamond and the finest sapphires; he itemised the gems and estimated their value. "John, your large blue stone is stunning. I heard of one poor miner selling one similar for £4. It weighed thirty carats. The buyer later sold it for £120, saying it could be cut into two £60 stones. I heard the same stone later went for several thousand pounds. It's about finding the right buyer. As I said before, ask for £5000; don't settle on less than £3000." He continued valuing and writing.

"Luke, that green is superb. As so is the yellow." He picked up the yellow diamond. "Ohh! Oh my! That's not a sapphire, is it?" He looked at William.

William shook his head.

"I read your article from your trip some time ago. I'm not even going to ask, but I bet you found these on your wanderings. So let me see them. I won't let on, but it will be interesting to see what the buyer says. Captain Evans, I'm guessing that, um, 'your' big one is from them?"

Douglas looked at William.

"Yes," William replied gruffly. "As the cat is out of the bag, let's get on with it. Separate valuations on this, this and this." He said, pulling out the three special big ones. "A group price on the bag. There are sixty-one good diamonds, not including the yellow, in there. All cutters, and then there's that fancy yellow."

Douglas said, "The leather bag is full of ones from China. They are mine, as are the others I've previously brought you. It's only these that aren't." He pointed out the new finds.

Mr Lamb valued Douglas's diamonds at a rough £2500, but said he had also to take them to the dealer. Mr Lamb said to ask for £3300. He should get somewhere near that.

Douglas was over the moon.

Mr Lamb was kept busy for some time. He finally gave them a rough estimate. As a group price, he estimated it to be over £50,000. He handed them the sheet of paper with the itemised estimates.

William's hand was shaking when he took it. "What did you say?" he asked quietly.

Richard Lams said, "You heard, sir, and I think that could be on the low end of the assessment. I think those fourteen stones alone could be worth that. That doesn't include the big ones in the individual parcels. They are some of the best stones I have ever seen, and I learned my trade in India. Some mighty fine gems are sourced from there. These are better; actually, all are better than any I ever saw before anywhere, even in Antwerp." After looking through them again, he looked up and said, "I thank you so much for trusting me with these dirt stones. I shall keep your secret. Let me know if you have anything else I can help you with." Mr Lamb hoped there would be more.

William looked at him, then at John, "Show him."

John pulled out the final bag; it was all the top-quality sapphires and the enormous, clear topaz. He placed the little unopened pouch on the counter.

Mr Lamb carefully put the diamonds away. Keeping them separated as when they arrived. He didn't know what to expect from the last bag. His hands were becoming sweaty.

When the last of the diamonds was away, he gingerly opened the larger blue bag. He tipped them out and gasped at the rainbow of colours on the bench before him. Greens, blues, reds and yellows; sapphires, rubies, and topazes. All were large and top-quality stones. "Oh, now, these are lovely." One by one, he checked each stone. Only one did he set aside. "This has a colour change in it." It was green, but when viewed through an eyeglass, it appeared to be half blue, half yellow, rather than a true green. The stone, however, had no flaws. "This one they call a 'pharaoh's eye'. See the yellow centre. These cut beautifully brilliantly. These are even better than the diamonds to me. I can facet these myself. Sadly, I'm not in the position to buy more. Not even the 'pharaoh's eye' one. It's superb. What I can do is sell them to other jewellers for you. I'll take a 10% commission, but I guarantee I'll get more for them individually than I'd be able to pay you anyway."

He separated each one and gave them an estimate for each stone. The minimum was a large green at £150. These were the ones William had valued at about £100 each. "There are thirty-two of them. I'd be surprised if I sell them at less than £200 each, though. That's the difference between retail and wholesale. It's your call. You don't have to make a decision now; wait and see what the buyer says. He may want them, but don't go lower than £200 each. He'll be on the lookout for some good stuff. I can assure him of provenance too, as I know you, Reverend Clarke, and can show him your article."

They decided that John would keep his own and William's stones until the foreign dealer came, because Douglas had a safe, and they would stay there until needed. They thanked the jeweller and looked forward to working with him. William turned back to Richard and said. "Call them if you hear of a possible good buyer," pointing to Douglas and John.

Mr Lamb nodded. He wiped his brow with his kerchief. What a day!

Once outside, John handed William his bank draft for £600. As he took it, he looked astounded. "This is for the garnets and bundle of small stuff? Surely you are joking? I valued that at £100. Ooh, that was seriously underestimated, wasn't it?" William chortled.

"We got £800 for them and £1000 for the other sapphires, so that's £600 each. We have banked ours already. This is your share," John said.

"What? My share? Are you kidding? And this doesn't include any of the good stones. Oh my! Ohh, my, my!" He brushed at his nose, and he chuckled. "Oh, my!" He looked from John to Luke and back to John. "Really?" His eyes twinkled with delight.

They both nodded, smiling.

Douglas was keeping his hand in his pocket with his leather pouch firmly in it. He was still overwhelmed that his bag was worth £2500. He'd been eking them out at about £100 to £200 each every year or so.

William asked them to accompany him to the bank. He banked at the same bank but used a different branch. He deposited the draft and then took out £50; it would be his gift to Maria. It was more than a year's wages for him; she was worth every penny. She'd done without for so long. He smiled to himself as he pocketed the crisp banknote. He clipped it to the outside of his note wallet.

They walked to Douglas' house and placed the gems in the safe. From there, they returned to Wills' house and reported to the rest of the family.

Ellen, Bill, and Molly had arrived again.

Luke took Ellen for a walk into the backyard.

Wills had told Luke that Eddie had placed a deposit on a house, *Glenmere*, near Ellen's parents' inn. Luke knew the building well, but had not been inside it for some years. He laughed, thinking that the name fitted with the family homes of Bramblemere, Gracemere.

They sat in the winter sun, and Luke asked Ellen if she knew of the place. She did. "Yes, I know it, it's called Glenmere."

"Yes, that's it," he then admitted that Eddie had put a deposit on it for them if she wished to live there. Luke said, "The house is perfect for us, Elle. With seven bedrooms and an office, there will be room for your parents to move in with us, but close enough for your Pa to still work at the inn. Sam and Belle could then have the inn to themselves. And we would have your parents close by for when we have children." He sat, looking at her.

Her reaction was not what he expected. She threw his arms around his neck and burst into tears. He was stunned. Not knowing if she was happy or sad. He was still not accustomed to the emotions of females. He knew to hold her until her sobs subsided. He pulled her onto his lap.

She drew away from him. "Oh, Lukie, I'm sorry. It's just that, well, that is my dream home. Every time I've walked past it, I've fallen more and more in love with it. I knew it was for sale and was sad as I knew it had sat empty for so long."

"Oh, that's a relief, because I sent a message for Eddie to go ahead and buy it." He drew her back to his chest. "We'll stay in *Gracemere Cottage* until the sale is finalised. Wills has also offered us *Roseneath*, but I think the cottage is more intimate. However, it has no staff and fewer amenities. We'll only get a few days together until I have to start teaching, but we'll have a long holiday at Christmas and a short one at midterm; that's one of the benefits of teaching. Two long paid holidays each year."

She gave a watery chuckle. She pulled away slightly, only to pull his head down to her and kiss her. They sat happily occupied for some time.

"I don't care about a honeymoon straight away, as long as we can be together at night. Well, maybe some other times too." She giggled mischievously. "I'm looking forward to that, and also to looking like Colleen. And you do not need to warn me that I could be bigger; you

Lockley men seem to like producing twins. How many in your family now?"

"Five or six sets, I've lost count. And then there are Uncle Ned's brothers, and Uncle Ned had got two sets too. Oh, and don't forget Grandmother Elle. She was an identical twin." Luke said nonchalantly.

"What? I didn't know that," Ellen said. "How did I not know that?"

"You know Wills' friend John Saunders? His mother, Emily, was Grandmother's identical twin. They came out about six years ago. Great-Aunt Emily married late in life and only had one child, John. She named him after our grandfather, Dar's papa, to annoy her father, as he disliked him. We had no idea. It was only when Grandmother arrived that John found out he had an aunt. His mother had never said. His mother and Grandmother were identical twins. So it's on both sides. Sorry, love, but yes, it's a distinct possibility that we, too, could have them. Would you mind? Not that there's much I could do about it."

She wrapped her arms around his waist. "Lukie, any child of yours is my dream child. If it's twins, then I'll be doubly blessed. I'll certainly need Mother on hand, though. Oh, I meant to tell you, both Liza and Anna are expecting babies again. Neither is impressed. Their youngest children are ten and eleven years old, respectively. What's even funnier and why it came to mind is that by the size of them both, I think it's possible they could be twins as they are showing already. Albie and William, at fourteen and fifteen, are disgusted with them. It's hilarious." She snuggled closer in the chilly winter afternoon.

Luke looked around and, seeing no one there, hauled her onto his lap. From here, he proceeded to wrap his arms around her. "I'm now going to do what I've wanted to do for a long time and kiss you silly." He proceeded to do just that.

She was a willing participant in the afternoon's activities. Being so close to the house would stop them from further indiscretion, not that Luke would do that to her. However, his hand did, at one stage, started caressing her through her bodice.

Her sigh of desire stopped him. "Oh, Lukie, I can't wait to be married." She kissed him again.

"Easy, love. Give me a bit of time. But, hmm, you're not wrong, how I would love to take you inside and truly make you mine. But I won't, don't worry. We'll wait."

She gave him a quick peck and sat up a little. "Luke, would Reverend Clarke be able to marry us? Do you think Reverend Gore will mind?"

"I hope not, love; I've grown so close to William while we've been away. It would be so special if he could." Luke gently kissed her again. "We'd better go inside, love. I think we'll head home tomorrow. That will give us a week before the wedding. But it will give me a chance to finalise the house."

She didn't move. Instead, she wrapped her arms around his neck again. Running her fingers through his thick, blonde, wavy hair, she pulled his head down to her. "Not yet, love. My turn to 'kiss you silly'." She chuckled. She opened her mouth to his and ran her tongue over his teeth.

He groaned and crushed her to him.

She only pulled away when they heard the back door open.

"Stay sitting, love, just for a bit. You'll find out why after we're married," he whispered.

"I can feel Luke. I have brothers, you know," she whispered back, giggling, "Nightshirts don't hide much, sweetheart."

Thankfully, it was Hamish. He knew where they were and knew it was about time that he interrupted them.

"Tea is being served in the sitting room; I think you two had better come inside," he said softly.

"Thanks, Hamish. We will," Luke replied. "We'll be in soon."

"Good, laddie," Hamish said as he retreated inside.

"Can I get up now?" she looked at him saucily.

"If you must." He gave her another quick kiss, "Minx."

She stood and pulled him up.

He carefully adjusted himself while she was smoothing her gown. "I know what I have to tell you. We sold the cheap packet of gems for £1800, so my share is £600, which is enough for the house and then some, so no debt. There will be more to come, but not until the buyer from Antwerp arrives. Lots more, love."

She walked into his arms.

"Oh, Luke, really?"

"Ellen, we will be financially secure. My job will keep the cash coming in. But even if it folds, we will have a firm base. We will own our house, and I can always work back at the Orphanage again to keep occupied. I won't care as long as you're with me. Bread and dripping will suffice." He slid his arm along her shoulder and turned her to walk inside.

"I'm hoping that we will start a family quickly to keep me occupied." Ellen blushed. "We're starting a little later than the others. Jenna 'fell' on the honeymoon, so did Liza and Gracie. I hope I can too. One, two, or even triplets. We'll have to practise a lot, Lukie." She stood on her tiptoes and kissed him before skipping and heading inside.

"I'm up for that, my darling one." He was smirking to himself as he followed her. Oh, he looked forward to that practice.

~

In Parramatta, Eddie received a note from Luke.

Dear Ed,

I love the sound of the house on Philip/Church Sts. 'Glenmere', I believe it's called. Funny eh? Thanks for finding it. Could you please get the ball rolling so I can purchase it as soon as possible? I have £550 available, with more coming later. Have to sort it tomorrow. I will fill you in when I see you later this week. If we can't settle before the wedding, we'll move into 'Gracemere Cottage' until it's ready.

Do you realise it's the house that Dar and Mama were first working in when they arrived? It was built by a friend of Uncle Ned's. I think you and Charlie were both born there. It's where Dar's table came from, the one now in your dining room.

I look forward to seeing you all and rejoining the family. Dar and Mama send their love. See you soon.

Luke

Ed visited Tim's office and asked if Tim was available.

Tim stuck his head out of his office and called him in. "Hi, Ed, how can I help?" Tim asked.

"I've had a note from Luke. He wants to go ahead with the house purchase. Any chance they will do the sale quickly?" Ed plonked himself down in a chair.

"Funny you should say that. They wanted to proceed with the Auction. I told him, in this case, it could work against him. The corner houses are notoriously hard to sell. So he decided to let Luke have it. He wants a quick settlement, though. Has he got the funds?" Tim was seated in a fancy swivel chair.

"Yes, he says he has enough, but it depends on what the owner wants. Did he have a final figure?"

"£375 cash. It's a goodly amount. If we settle earlier, he might even drop it a bit more. I'll go see him today and get it moving." Tim smiled at Ed. "I'd better get on with the day, Ed."

Ed shook his hand. As he left, he said, "Thanks, Tim, he'll be here in a day or so. Had some business to sort. Thanks again, Tim. See you at the wedding, if not before."

Ed left and went straight to work, and explained to Mr Tindale why he was late. "Oh, wonderful news, Ed, so they are all back then? Charles and Sal, too?" The older man chuckled. "Ed, it's not like I'm your boss any more. We are part-owners, remember. No need to explain anything unless you wish to."

"Yes, Uncle Thomas, Dar's letter said they pulled into the harbour together. I dare say we will hear the full story later this week. Come for dinner Sunday as usual, and I think we'll hear it all," Ed said as he put on his thick leather apron. As usual, the shed was hot, and the apprentices had the forge already working. They were busy making pick heads for the diggings. They had a mini foundry on the site now and could pour the pick and mattock heads themselves. These were still only cast iron. The old way of smithing them and joining two sides together was nowhere near as strong. He'd had many complaints of the pick heads splitting at the join. Casting them made them solid. Ed's dream was to have a proper foundry making steel, and this was his latest unfulfilled project. They had three large crucibles and a small one. The new blast furnace could melt enough iron with the carbon and make proper steel. It was slow going, but they had a system where they had three crucibles on the go at once. The new furnace was able to make a different sort of metal. The furnace could burn for up to three days and then pour a super-purified carbonised iron known as steel. This was even better than the cast-iron ones, and this showed in the price.

Uncle Ned had sent over various moulds from England many years ago. He'd been able to buy them cheaply and brought them as a wedding present for Wills and Cathy, along with a load of pig iron. He had sent more later. Then the gold rush in California hit, and suddenly nothing was available any more.

Initially, they had stored them and wondered if they would ever need to use them. Now Ed wished they had more. When they would do a pouring day, the six apprentices would be working nonstop. The moulds were quenched and reused as soon as the poured metal was cooled.

Ed's mind was full of things he needed to do for the next week. Luke and Ellen's wedding party was again at Charlie's inn. Anna, Belle and Gracie had sorted all the details for the wedding with Ellen. All that was needed was the groom, and he was about to arrive. Ed threw himself into the day's work. There was always much to be done. With three Emporiums and the Warehouse to supply, the work was never-ending. He loved it. Ed's dreams were nearly achieved; the new foundry oven would see a change in the sort of work they could do.

Over thirty years ago, Thomas Tindale wondered if he'd have enough work for six-year-old Eddie when he first came to work for him. However, work had picked up so much that over the years, Charlie, Wills, and even Luke had each learned the trade. Now Ed's own sons were working with him. His eldest son, Neddie, had married Tom Tindale's great niece four years before, and they and their two small children were now living with the Tindales at their house. Another of Eddie's sons, Kit, was loving the blacksmithing. Wills and Charlie occasionally still came to keep their hand in, or if a particularly urgent or intricate order were required, then one or the other would be called in to assist.

Wills' skill with welding was still unsurpassed. He just had the knack. Even Ed couldn't do it as neatly. Ed was now "melt welding" as the volume of mesh needed to make sieves was astounding. "Melt welding" was the easiest way to make large sheets. They would then cut the mesh to the required sizes for the sieves. Now his youngest studious brother was getting married. He'd landed a good job, landed a beautiful fiancé, albeit after a hiccup of an identity mix-up, and now, by the sound of it, landed a fortune. All through it, Ellen had waited for him.

Ed smiled to himself. When Uncle Ned had given him a £1000 wedding present, he was determined to help the community, so he built the Emporium. It brought together all the best tradesmen in the towns. Since then, the business has taken off. Wills initially built two more, and then more followed. His chain of stores was still growing. In the past decade and a half, the town had grown immensely. Parramatta had an extra fifteen hundred houses. He kept thinking back to the census results he'd recently read; in those fifteen years, the population of New South Wales had grown from 48,000 to 120,000. No wonder trade had picked up. In 1841, there were only twenty-six towns in the colony; now, there were eighty-six gazetted towns, and more were listed monthly.

Ed kept working. His mind was running over the statistics he had been reading. When he showed Uncle Thomas the newspaper, they were astounded by the growth. Parramatta was 20% bigger, but the passing traffic was over 250% more. Yes, no wonder they were busier.

The Emporium that he and Thomas had built, initially financed with the £1000 wedding gift from Uncle Ned, was a huge success. The money that had poured in from the profits was astounding. Even with wages, costs, and the original 20% for Uncle Thomas, his investment had netted him thousands of pounds every year. He'd upped Uncle Thomas' percentage to 30% of the profits, and he was still raking in the profit. He paid for the new forge, the foundry extension of the blast furnace, and a new all-weather seating area for customers, friends, and family to come and have a cup of tea and place orders.

The original Tea House at his Emporium had been far too small, and he ended up expanding the Tea Rooms into a quaint little building next door to the Emporium. It now had a micro-bakery attached and was about the same size as the original Emporium showroom. The bakery only made things for the Tea Rooms. It served delicious items, like cakes, biscuits and pies, but not bread.

Maryanne and Robert Ellis, and their three children, lived in their own new residence. Their old house had been converted into a small stockroom, as the Warehouse on the outskirts of Parramatta would sometimes take too long to get goods to the shop floor.

Robert's salary had multiplied, as well. It had enabled them to buy a small house for themselves. Maryanne's parents were the Connors. They were life convicts who were assigned to Ed.

There were four families intertwined. The Lockley family were the centre, the Turners at Emu Plains were family number two, with Eddie and Wills marrying sisters. The Miller's three siblings are soon to be married into the family, with Anna to Tim, Grace and Charlie, and soon Ellen to Luke. The fourth family were the Ellis family. George had married Liza Lockley, Sam Miller had married George's sister Belle and Jenna and Cathy's brother, Marc, had married George's other sister Milly.

Chapter 13   Homecoming

On Thursday morning, July 24th, the majority of the travellers were heading home to Parramatta. Charles and Sal, Wills and Cathy, Bill and Molly, with Ellen and Luke, would leave Sydney as the wedding was now imminent and they had things to do.

The group gathered on the Phoenix Wharf in Sydney at 9.15 am. The ferry was due to depart at 9.30 am; they had a lot of luggage to load on board, and they knew it would take some time. Wills and Luke took that in hand. They said their farewells as they left the various houses. Mr Stewart sent two carriages to the house to collect them and their luggage.

Doug, Caro, John, and Colleen would follow them to Parramatta next week, and the Clarke family would travel with them. They would all stay for the wedding. Sadly, John had returned to work and was unhappy that their wondrous adventure had finally drawn to a close.

Colleen would stay at Wills's house with Hamish while John returned to work. This was because the house all but backed onto the hospital. She could literally walk across the road when in labour.

Caro was planning to be with her each day. She would leave when John arrived home. Colleen was feeling well, and the baby had not dropped. So she was sure that it would be some weeks yet. She knew to keep active, so she was often found outside in the back garden, attempting to weed the vegetables. This astounded both Hamish and Caro. John just chuckled. He had seen her home and what she had put up with on their trip. He knew her well enough now to let her do just what she felt like. He also knew she would ask for assistance if she needed it.

Hamish was to stay in residence for as long as he wished. He was now to be the caretaker of an empty house. It was now the only home he had. He had loved it when Luke was in residence. He had something to do.

Every evening that Luke wasn't studying, they sat around and talked. He gardened during the day, but even then, the vegetables would mostly look after themselves. He kept a wary eye on Colleen's activities, but he was bored. They usually retired to bed after dinner and he fouls being alone was frustrating.

~

One afternoon, Douglas came with Caro, and he sat in the kitchen chatting to Hamish and Stephen Roberts, who had arrived a bit earlier. It was raining outside, and Stephen and Douglas were as bored as Hamish. All were frustrated with the lack of functional activity. They had various skills between them and thought they should use these in some way to help others.

Hamish laughed when he admitted that his skills were not teachable or really useful; hunting, salmon fishing, and falconry were not skills that could be taught. Douglas raised his eyebrows, "Falconry? Really, Hamish, you never cease to surprise me." He grinned. Hamish gave a mischievous grin in reply, showing his perfectly straight teeth. "I can also carve and whittle. I did some dry rock walling when young for fun. It's not much use for that here either. Effy had to teach me to cook, so it is no use my teaching that." They had, however, come up with an idea. They had become close friends with Captain Stephen Roberts, the retired ferry master. It was he who had introduced them to Ricky and Will English, who now ran the fabric emporium.

Stephen told them the lad's story before introducing them. "Ricky was a street child, a waif, at only ten. He had arrived with his mother. They waited for his father to come and collect them, but he never came. When his mother died shortly after their arrival, Ricky ended up on the street, with no money and no friends. He befriended an ex-convict who looked out for him. He found a safe bolt hole in a stable and slept in the straw with the beasts at night. As thanks, he kept the stables clean. In the middle of a storm, he came across another street child. This boy, too, was alone. He did not know his family. His name was Tad. He had an interesting story, as years later, his grandfather had come looking for his lost grandson. I met the grandfather as a passenger on the ferry. I was the one to tell him of Ricky. Mr Falconer-Meade had found his grandson; it was Tad English, he'd taken Ricky's name. They had all travelled back to England on the same ship as the Major and his wife, Christina, in 1842. Tad was only about twelve. He was the image of his cousin who came out with his grandfather."

Captain Roberts sat thinking over the story he had heard. "Ricky had also met a second boy, whom he adopted. Found again during another storm. They sheltered together with Tad. Will has a dud leg. Ricky, Will, and Tad sheltered other street boys and eventually found a building where they could live. John Landon had a hand in that. Ricky had found his young daughter, Amabel, when she had been kidnapped and rescued her. Ricky would accept nothing for himself, but assistance for the other boys was appreciated. Ricky made a living selling fruit and vegetables from a wheelbarrow, then eventually worked up and got a shopfront, and so it grew. By this stage, they were nearly grown, in their late teens. All three worked hard and stayed out of trouble. Tad returned from England and was working as a roving journalist. He had rejected the life of luxury his grandfather offered him. Young Will turned out to be an amazing artist. He even went to Europe to pursue his studies. Tad and Will both took Ricky's surname of English and call themselves brothers. When Will left for Europe, he had a hard time of it, he studied art, but did not cope with the loneliness. So he came home to Ricky. He stayed in the colony and kept working with the stray children. Surely you know of the English Emporium? The big fabric warehouse."

Douglas and Hamish nodded. They were astounded that the young man they saw weekly at church had such a history. It was working with such lads that Douglas suggested to Hamish that they might help with.

Stephen continued, "John Landon told me there's a bit more to his story. About five years ago, Ricky's missing father, Richard, turned up. Richard had been injured up the Hawkesbury and had been taken in by an Aboriginal man named Durren. He never spoke, so they didn't know who he was. After some years, the man got sick and they decided to take him to Mr Forrest's place on the Hawkesbury River. Durren then led them to where he had stashed the man's only possession, an old tin box. In it was the identification of who he was. Major Tim Hinds took control of the situation. The man was brought to Sydney Hospital. It turned out to be Ricky's missing father, Richard English, and they finally managed to be reunited. He was taken to the hospital, where for some weeks Ricky rarely left his bedside. Then, after some time, he was discharged to Ricky's home. Ricky was able to spend his final months with his papa. Sadly, the time was all too short, and Richard died some three months later. That, I suppose, was a comfort in itself that he had been found. Richard took solace in watching Will paint." Stephen looked at the saddened faces of his two friends.

Douglas said, "Ricky is only twenty-five. He is too young to do this work by himself, and he's all alone now. He does have his two adopted brothers, but all the rest of their helpers are just volunteers. I was thinking about joining that volume of helpers." Douglas looked over to Hamish. "Interested?"

"Am I what? Ooch, Douggie, ma boy, I'd love that. I'll be at a loose end soon. Time on my hands and all that; just the thing." Hamish was excited. "Ay Douggie, why don't we go over and see him now? I'll take the girls a cuppa, and we can go."

"Sounds like an idea, Hamish. I'll go and tell Caro." He walked off while Hamish made them some tea.

Within half an hour, the three men were leaving and heading down to Ricky English's house.

They spent an hour talking to the impressive young man. Then they met Will. They had heard about his artwork; to see it for themselves was terrific.

Ricky showed them two of the paintings Will had painted of his father, Richard senior. One as he was shortly after he had been found, and one as Ricky had last seen him.

Will had turned back time, and the resulting painting astounded Ricky. He would sometimes tear up when looking at it. The work was so realistic.

In the course of the conversation, Will revealed that one of his early works was of a blacksmith, based on someone he had met when he was young. He was a blonde lad who had befriended him and went by the name of Ed. He was living in Sydney while at school. Will had only been a very young boy; the smithy was about fifteen. He had never forgotten him; Ed had shown he cared. The smithy's boy told Will that if he could learn to read and write, he could do anything. Without those skills, he would probably never get a job. That one conversation changed Will's attitude toward learning. Ed helped when he could, but then he left and didn't know where he had gone. Douglas looked astounded; that lad could only be Eddie.

"Where is this painting now, lad?" Douglas asked him keenly, hoping it was close by.

"Ahh! Well, I gave it away to our sponsor. He's an importer and salesman of sorts, Mr John Landon."

"I know Landon. He goes to St James as well," Hamish said, more and more amazed at the various coincidences. Hamish looked at Douglas and raised his eyebrows questioningly.

Will nodded and looked at him, puzzled.

Douglas looked at him and explained. A smile spread on his face. "Will, in 1831, we had two young lads come to live with us. They went to Cape's Academy. One stayed for five years, the other for eight. Their names were Edward Lockley, known as Eddie, a blacksmith from Parramatta, and Tim Miller, who is now a member of Parliament in Parramatta. I think it was this 'Ed' whom you painted in your first painting. I'd like to see them."

Realisation spread over Will's face. "That's the story he told me. I only remembered his name was Ed. I would sneak into Mr Cape's free classes. He kept slates at the door, and Ricky told me to go and learn, so Tad and I did. Ricky did too, when he could, but he could already read and write."

Douglas sat looking at him. "Will, have you heard of Lockleys Emporium out at Parramatta?"

Both Ricky and Will English looked at each other, then both nodded. "Yes, sir, but why? It's actually from that I chose the name of our store."

Douglas added, "Eddie is the owner of the Emporium in Parramatta. His next brother, Wills, built the two in Emu Plains and Bathurst." The two young men were astounded. "Now, can you both agree that God has drawn us together for a reason?" Douglas turned his attention to Ricky. "Do you know when I first heard about you, lad? It was November 1841. We were at Liza Lockley's wedding, and a rotund gentleman appeared. He was looking for his son, Matthew. Ricky, his name was Falconer-Meade. I believe you know the name."

Both young men gasped and nodded. "Stephen knew of you and suggested Mr Falconer-Meade see you. I gather he found you, as it's old history now." Douglas said, looking at his friend as he spoke of him.

Stephen nodded in agreement.

Ricky said, "Yes, sir, Theodore, or Tad, is his grandson, but he came back here to Sydney rather than stay in England. He married Amabel Landon, the young girl I rescued many years ago. They, of course, have married under the name of Falconer-Meade." Ricky laughed. "He's in his grandfather's bad books as he kept the name of English as a pen name, even though his real and legal name is Theodore Falconer-Meade; he insists on using Tad English as his name; he calls it his 'professional name'." Ricky flopped back in his chair, stunned.

"Right," said Douglas. "Now we have that sorted. How can we help? I believe you have other boys living in a group house, and girls, too, in another? 'Landon Homes' and 'Sadie House'? Am I correct?"

Ricky nodded. "Well, we have a suggestion," Douglas continued. "We'd like to help. We three are all at a loose end—nothing to do and bored out of our brains. We can teach woodwork, rope work, knot tying, splicing, whittling, and carving. Stephen can teach us all to splice ropes. Oh, lots of practical skills, but if that's not your cup of tea, grooming and deportment for men, and dancing classes. We'll bring the ladies and girls in for that, too. Such skills would enhance a person's ability to live and move up in society. And as Ed told Will and Tad, reading and writing are a way out of poverty."

Ricky looked astounded. "All I can say is that we would love your help. How? Well, we're not quite sure. If you came along occasionally and met the boys, see what they each need. We try to teach them to read and write. Mr Cape was great, but he's long gone, and the schools don't encourage the boys like he used to. If they can do that, life becomes much easier for them. Eddie was correct; many jobs were available at the time. The rope splicing sounds great."

"So we start with reading and writing? It's a good place to start. If we start by showing them *why* they need to read and write, they will *want* to learn. How about that?" Doug said.

Stephen Roberts volunteered some information to Ricky. "I have various sizes of 'fids' at home for rope splicing. I would love to teach the boys to splice rope, as they are needed for every ship. They could make a lot of money if they could learn that skill."

"Thank you, Captain Roberts. That would be fabulous, but may I ask what exactly is a 'fid'?" Ricky looked confused.

Stephen chuckled, "Ah, yes, well, it's not a tool many would know unless you are into rope splicing. It's a concave spike that you poke through the weave in a rope to then splice another through it. They come in various shapes and sizes. There is also the thin twine that you finish the ropes with. It's an art, but worthwhile, and you can make a business of just doing this alone."

The five spent the remainder of the hour discussing the method. The three enthused gentlemen returned to Wills' house. "Where do we source slates and chalk, Hamish?"

Hamish shrugged. "I dunno, but will hunt around. I'll ask Luke; he might know or the reverend gentleman."

~

Colleen and Caro welcomed their return.

They were intrigued by the project.

Caro said, "We've decided that once the baby is born, we will help out at Sadie House with the babies and small children. It will give us something worthwhile to do."

Colleen grasped her hand. "Oh, Mother Caro, that would be so exciting. It would certainly give us a purpose, well, me, anyway. I've worked all my life; I'm not going to stop now, and I positively love babies. If I can live helping others, then that's what I'll do. I grew up poor in pocket but rich in love. If I can help show that love to others, I will." She felt the baby kick as she spoke so excitedly. "It wants to come too," she giggled.

John returned from work early and joined his wife, parents and Hamish for luncheon. When he heard of the proposed work, he was thrilled and knew that his father was bored. He knew Hamish was at a loose end as well, and it would also give his mother and wife a way to help people. He had actually heard of the Sadie House from William Clarke and suggested that they visit the English Emporium to buy some fabrics for Colleen. Mrs Yeats, who worked there, was one of the homeless people that Ricky had found. She now runs the store. "If one young boy can make a difference, then we can make a massive difference to many."

After they had spoken about the new project for some time, Douglas told them about the artist, Will English. "The first painting he did that was noticed was a blacksmith triple panel. He gave it to Ricky's mentor, one John Landon—fancy that. I must ask him if he still has it. Because I believe that it's for Eddie, love."

Caro looked puzzled, then it dawned. "You mean John and Sadie

Landon from St James?"

Douglas grinned and replied, "One and the same love. Landon Homes is the name of the children's home, and Sadie House is for the babies and infants. Sound familiar? Will filled me in on quite a bit. I told you Ricky rescued Amabel Landon years ago. John told me the lad would not accept help, even from him. Ricky insisted that he work hard to stand on his own two feet. Will and Tad literally landed on his doorsteps during separate storms, just as Mrs Yates and her son Phil did. Ricky helped them, as he was supported as a child. It's an astounding story. I just never put all the pieces together before today." He paused, thinking. "Love, do you know this is who Ned Grace's friend Amelia lived with for a year or so. It's just all ties in together, doesn't it?" Doug thought a little about his morning. "He reminds me a lot of Eddie, you know. He has that same sort of gentle soul. What's funny is that Tad wasn't there, as he's on his honeymoon with, wait for it... Amabel Landon. I did hear she was getting married, but I didn't know to whom. The other funny thing is, Caro, we met Tad's grandfather. Remember the big man who came to Liza and Bertie's wedding in 1841. The ferry passenger was looking for his grandson. Well, he found him. It turned out to be this Tad; it was young Theodore. The lad is apparently the spitting image of his other grandson, Joshua. Only Tad has refused his wealth or to use his real name of Falconer-Meade. He has kept the name of English and returned to the colony to work as a journalist. Says a lot for both Ricky and the lad. He could have chosen a comfortable life."

Douglas thought back to that wedding sixteen years before. Now they were heading west for another one next weekend, the last Lockley sibling. This new venture would be something they could all throw themselves into.

Caro decided on a trip to the English Emporium for some fabric. For some reason, she'd never been in there. Martha Turner had mentioned the new store, as had Molly Miller.

It was to become a regular haunt, and she would spread the word too. Both Wills and Martha had already told her about the place, but she'd just never been there. She was determined; her attitude showed through her actions, as Colleen's certainly did. She later found out that it had started when the Female Factory closed down.

Ricky filled her in on the visit that afternoon. John Landon had no outlet for the damaged fabrics, and he was intending to throw them out. Ricky offered to try to sell them at cost price, and John allowed him to use a small shopfront he owned. From there, the idea grew into a huge emporium. The store has been growing for seven years and has been getting busier every month.

Colleen was fast becoming a close friend to her new mother-in-law.

John had seen past Colleen's stunning beauty, which was astounding, to the beautiful soul inside her.

Colleen, in turn, oozed love for John, for her and Douglas, for Cathy and Wills, and of course for any children nearby.

Caro and Doug felt they were coming out of stasis. Colleen had refreshed them all. Caro asked, "Colleen, are you up for an outing? I feel like a spot of gentle shopping this afternoon. Then we can sit here sewing while we wait for Junior to arrive. What do you think?" Caro looked at her daughter-in-law hopefully.

"Oh, Mother Caro, I would love that. John, do you have to go back to work?" After spending the past eight months in each other's company, she still wished to be with him whenever he was around.

"Well, love, I think I would like to come. Do you mind?" He looked lovingly at her as he spoke.

Colleen giggled. "Why should I mind? You can carry our shopping."

John grinned, "Willing to, Colly."

"Looks like we have a family outing. Hamish, that includes you, of course," Douglas said, grinning widely. "You *are* family now; I'll go and hail a carriage."

"Ooch, Douggie boy, I wouldna miss this for anything. For me not to have to walk that far, it's gonna be guid too." He'd lapsed back to a Scottish lilt.

Doug smiled. Yes, Hamish was family, too. God would one day reveal why this gentle, loving soul had been brought into their lives, as they were sure He had a purpose. God didn't make coincidences; He made God incidents.

Their outing was a tremendous success.

The fabrics that Caro and Colleen purchased were of exceptional quality. They would certainly spread the word amongst their friends. A few had minor faults or water damage. They bought far more than was required, but knew that Colleen's mother or any Orphanage could use any excess fabric. They would be easily able to cut around the stains.

They met Mrs Yates, and Colleen loved her too. She felt that they could be friends; she needed friends her own age, and Mrs Yates would be her first.

For the first time in a while, Colleen was not fearful for the future. John and Caro would always be there for her, but she needed more. Colleen needed to be needed. She released a deep sigh of contentment; life looked good.

While at the shop, Douglas had an idea and went to find Ricky and Will English again. He thought he would invite them to the wedding next week. It was about time Will and Ricky met Eddie again. He wanted to be at that meeting, and this is the way he could be there. Doug thought there were two other people he wanted to ask to the wedding, John and Sadie Landon. He needed to bring these two influential family groups together, one group based in Sydney and the other in Parramatta. Oh, the works that they could and probably would achieve. Yes, this was going to happen. For a link already existed between them all; however, it had just been revealed to them both. And then there was the link through Amelia West and Ned. Doug smiled and shook his head over that revelation.

On the way home that afternoon, Douglas and Caro discussed their vision of how they could help had been far too small. They were each energised, excited.

On Friday, August 1, 1857, a large group was gathered on the Phoenix Wharf to catch the Parramatta Ferry. They had eaten luncheon and gathered just before one o'clock. The group consisted of Reverend William and Maria Clarke and their children; Doug and Caro Evans with John and Colleen, Phil, Alice and their children, Stevie and May with their children, nine in all; Ricky and Will English, Hamish and finally John and Sadie Landon.

Douglas made various introductions. He was looking forward to this weekend, and being used as an instrument of God was fun. He was also looking forward to introducing the Lockleys and Landons to each other.

In Parramatta, the first day of August dawned cold and crisp. Luke woke in his old room at his parents' house for the last time. He lay in bed in the dawn light, looking around. His books were once again on the shelves. His desk again had the two beautiful mahogany and brass boxes sitting on it. They had been given to him over ten years before. When he thought about that day, he caught his breath. It was then he realised the depth of the family's love for him. It still brought a tear to his eye. Even then, he loved Ellen, even though she was only just a teen herself, and he was a quiet and studious teenager. He had been way too frightened to show any feelings for her. If they happened to be in the same room, he would sit looking at her.

He remembered hearing of her supposed marriage, or at least the rumour of it, over four years before. He had felt gutted. Unable to breathe or cry, he was stunned. He had been starting university, and he threw himself into his studies. He had not been in any financial position to have done more than declare himself to her anyway. He had managed to tell her that he really liked her, and she said she liked him too. He thought they had reached an understanding; they had walked back from church one particular Sunday during his holidays. He was still at school in Sydney. She had tripped, and he saved her from falling. She had ended up in his arms. When he had assured himself she was uninjured, he had kissed her on the forehead. Nothing more, but for the rest of the journey home, she clung to his arm far more closely than she should have done. His fingers were interwoven with hers.

Each Sunday after that, when Luke was home from Sydney, he offered to walk her home from church. Always the perfect gentleman, he never overstepped the bounds of propriety. She was just twenty. One day, she thanked him with a quick peck on his lips.

He was unable to do or say more as her parents rounded the building moments later. She had, however, noticed the look of joy on his face. He squeezed her fingers and stroked her hand, but was unable to speak up. It was only weeks after that someone mentioned a wedding, and what he heard was about Elle Miller; however, it was actually about Sam Miller and Belle Ellis.

Luke punched the bedcovers; what a stupid, blooming fool he had been. Groaning in anger at himself. He had stayed away from home from then on. He had returned for as short a time as possible for his grandmother's funeral, returning the same day to Sydney. Not even staying the night just in case he met her. It was only last year that he realised his error.

Now, for the first time in years, he had relaxed. Everything in his life had changed that month. He finished university, the Bishop had offered him a job at King's, Reverend Clarke had asked him to go on a trip with him, and to top it off, Ellen accepted his proposal. He had written to her from every town and many campsites between towns. He had inundated her with letters, and yet he was still anxious on his return to see if she had changed her mind. He need not have worried.

He wouldn't be allowed to see her today; he knew that. So this morning, he did not have to rush to get up. The day after tomorrow, when he woke, she'd be beside him, for tomorrow they would finally marry. He still had things to do. He had to move his clothing to the cottage two doors up, but that would not take long. He didn't possess much.

The new house would not be theirs for a few weeks. He had to start teaching on Wednesday, so they would only have a few days together. They decided to stay at the cottage for their honeymoon and go away later in the year. He roused himself to get up. He would pack his books and move them. He knew he would need them for the lessons. He had not unpacked his notes from university. There were some boxes he required to be taken down. They had not been unpacked since Hamish packed his things in Sydney.

A pile of journals from his trip lay stacked on his desk. He leafed through them. He had given William Clarke the set of research notes for his writing, but these were educational journals with personal observations. The finds from that trip would set them up for life. They had yet to secure a sale for all the gems, but the few they had already sold allowed him to buy a house. It had turned out cheaper than he had first hoped. He was left with more than three years' wages in the bank.

He stood in his room in his nightshirt. His breath clouding in the chilled morning air, he shivered and decided to dress. He had just finished when his mother knocked on his door gently.

Sal had heard her son up and brought him a mug of strong, black, sweet tea. "Only one more of these, and you'll be making them for Ellen," she said lovingly to her youngest son. "It's the little things you do for her that will make a difference in your marriage, not the big things. Remember the hug each morning, the kiss good night, and the cup of tea in the morning. They mean far more to her than a new house, fancy dresses or expensive gifts. Notice her; a stroke of her cheek with love is far more loving than a new dress. It's the fact that you think of her comfort or telling her she has been on your mind. That's what matters. When walking, pick her a flower; take her on impromptu picnics; spend time with her; love her; spoil her with your time, and involve her in your interests. Do not shut her out. That's what she'll want. That doesn't mean you can't buy her things too, but it's your time and presence that she will crave and the little things you do for her. Do not come home from work and ask where your dinner is, especially once you have children. Instead, kiss her and ask if you can look after them for her while she gets their dinner ready, or even to have a break from them. Or, even better, if you can help her. Be involved with your children as early as possible. You will not regret that." She bent and kissed his blonde hair. "I'll be washing that and your neck today. Just saying," Sal smiled as she left.

Luke thought about her words. He had watched his parents and his siblings over the years. He had seen the little gifts his father gave her and how his mother loved the tiny flowers his father had picked for her. A bottle brush flower would often sit in a glass on the table, or a sprig of lemon myrtle blossom he had plucked for her. They were just a symbol of his father's love for his mother. These things were part of his childhood, and he'd never realised their importance. They were far more valuable than his father's title or fancy clothes. His mother had those as well and hated them. Luke realised what she meant. He smiled. Ellen would have expensive gifts too, but he'd not forget the little things.

He jerked himself from his reverie. "Ohh! I have to get the gifts from Eddie. I had better go."

Luke kissed his mother's cheek. He knew Ed left early for work. He wanted to collect the chosen gifts for his betrothed. He wanted Ellen to wear the pearls tomorrow. He would drop them off at Bill's or Molly's at the inn. Hopefully, the jeweller had done what he required of him.

He quickly walked to Ed's house and went in through the kitchen door, knowing that no one would hear if he knocked on the main entrance.

Luke was greeted, teased and handed tea by his brother. He ignored it and asked, "Ed, did the jeweller deliver a parcel to you after I left?" Luke asked.

"Yes, little brother, he did." He took a mouthful of soft egg on toast. "Let me finish this, then I'll get it for you."

Cara put a plate with an egg on toast in front of Luke.

She cooked it perfectly. Set but not hard. He hated gooey eggs as they tended to dribble. He grinned at her. "Thanks, Cara. It's perfect." He cut the toast crusts and folded the slice with the egg in the middle.

Cara had seen him do this a hundred times over the years. Luke was never one to sit over his food. He would eat and head back to his desk. "Make the most of it, Luke, from tomorrow, you'll be sitting with your wife eating breakfast. Do you understand me?" She tipped her head sideways, looking at this handsome young man.

"Oh, um, thanks. Ohh!" Understanding dawning on him. Yes, from now on, he'd have to sit and eat with Ellen. "Thanks, Cara. Okay, yes, I will, won't I?" He gave her the eggy grin.

Cara had also seen it many times before.

Luke winked at her, and nodded.

Ed finished his breakfast, and Luke followed him out. He was still munching on his toast.

They went to his office and walked to his safe. He unlocked it with a huge key. He withdrew a packet and handed it to Luke.

"Want a look?" Luke asked.

"Silly question, of course..." Ed answered.

Luke carefully unwrapped the big package; it contained various bags and boxes. The velvet bag was first; hopefully, it would be the pearls and matching earbobs.

"Beautiful, Luke, she'll love them," Ed admired the gift.

Then Luke took the larger box.

Eddie drew his breath. Inside it was the exquisite emerald and diamond necklace. The emerald drop was a teardrop shape, and the diamonds were set in little flowers on a heart-shaped setting. There were matching earrings; each had a diamond star just above the emerald.

Ed fingered it. "It's stunning, Luke, but how did you afford that? You bought them before you found the gems."

"Ed, I forgot I had my earnings from Wills after doing his bookwork. Ed, Wills paid me 1% of profits for those first five years. I had ample funds for these."

Luke smiled. He handed Ed a ten inch, long box. It had a bracelet in it. One by one, Luke opened and inspected each item before passing them to Eddie; one contained a simple emerald drop necklace, and in the last box, a small square box held the two matching wedding rings.

Luke said, "Ed, I like that Wills wears a wedding ring. You can't because you work with your hands all the time. And I couldn't either if I were a farmer or blacksmith, but I'll only be teaching, so I want to wear a ring too. They are engraved. 'Forever yours', have a look."

Luke picked up his ring and checked inside each ring, then handed it to Ed. He studied Ellen's too and smiled. "Perfect," Luke simply said.

Ed congratulated him. He smiled and looked at his youngest brother. He was always understated, just like Wills.

Luke packed up the jewellery and said both thanks and farewell to Ed.

He was about to leave the room when Ed said, "Luke, just a warning, Mama will want to wash your hair and scrub your neck today, and Dar will want to have a long pre-marriage 'talk' tonight. Odds on it will include the topic of soap, but it's true. Just so you know. So take note."

"Thanks, Ed; Mama has already told me she wants to do that. But thanks for the warning about Dar." Luke smiled to himself as he walked home.

On arrival at home, his Father met him at the door. "Hello, son, you're up early."

Luke explained and said, "Hello, Dar, can you hold these for a bit. Have a look while I'm gone."

He handed his father the bulk of the jewels and said he'd be back in about ten minutes. He had taken just the bag of pearls and stuffed it in his pocket.

Luke walked briskly up the street and down Church Street to the Rear Admiral Duncan Inn.

Bill was on the front verandah. "Morning, Luke, you can't come in, you know. I'd be drummed out if I allowed you to enter," Bill said as he walked off the verandah to greet Luke.

Luke chuckled. "I know, sir. No worries. I am just dropping something in for Ellen for tomorrow. From me to her. I would really like her to wear them for the service if possible."

He handed the bag to Bill and walked off.

Bill opened the string and peeked inside. He wasn't quite sure what it would have inside, but when he saw a string of pea-size pearls, he gasped, then whistled. He did up the ribbon of the bag and, after watching Luke vanish around the street corner, Bill took it to his daughter. "Love, Luke just dropped these in for you for tomorrow. Wait until you see them. Sorry, I peeked." He gave her a cheeky grin.

Molly came and stood beside her as Ellen opened the bag. "Oh, Mother, look. He shouldn't have. I saw these when we bought my ring. Aren't they perfect?"

Ellen had the necklace in her hand. She ran the strand through her fingers. "Oh, Mother, they are so beautiful."

Her father picked up the bag; it wasn't empty. "There's more in here, love." He handed it back to her.

She tipped it up, and the ear-bobs fell into her hand. "Oh, they are perfect. And look, no hooks either. Luke has even noticed I don't have my ears pierced." She screwed them onto her ears. They jiggled beautifully.

Ellen smiled. "Oh, Lukie, I don't know whether to be angry at him or hug him," she said with a beaming smile on her face.

Her parents both had wondrous smiles on their faces as they watched her joy.

Chapter 14   Forever Yours

*A*t quarter past two on Friday afternoon, the Sydney Ferry pulled into the wharf at Parramatta.

Ed, Charlie, Luke and many of the family were there to greet them.

Wills arrived just after the ferry. "Sorry, I'm late. The children wanted to come." Little Lukie, Pip, Tilda and Goldie sat on the seat with him. "Stay there, children. I won't be long."

They worked out who would stay with whom. The Clarke family would stay at *Roseneath* with Wills and Cathy. Hamish would go with them, too. John, Colleen, Douglas, and Caro would stay at Eddie's. Margaret Tindale was not well, so staying with them was out of the question. Thomas had their hands full looking after her.

Martha and Jack were due to arrive later that night from Emu Plains; they would be at Eddie's with John and Sadie Landon. There were still two spare rooms just in case they were needed. The final group would stay at Charlie and Gracie's new house, *Willow Grove*. That group consisted of Phil, Alice, Stevie, and May, and their children, plus Ricky and Will English, and Hamish Macdonald.

Ed asked Luke to take everyone to his home, and he would join them as soon as he could. He planned to take Ricky and Will English to Charlie's home personally. More to discover why Douglas Evans had brought strangers to a family wedding.

Ricky and Will English were a bit uncomfortable about staying with the family.

Douglas had planned to introduce them to Eddie before they separated but he didn't have the chance.

Ed looked at the young men with interest. Finally, he said. "You both look familiar. Have we met before?" Ed asked as they walked together.

They looked at each other, then at him. Ricky explained about Cape's Academy.

"I remember now. You two used to sit at the door. Wasn't there another lad as well?" Ed asked.

"Fancy you remembering that," Will stated, surprised. "I can't believe you even recognise us. Let alone remember there was another."

"Yes, that's Tad. He's not here as he's on his honeymoon. He married John and Sadie's Landon's daughter, Amabel," Ricky explained.

Ed's brow creased. "Tad? By any chance, Tad Falconer-Meade?" he queried.

"Yes, I believe you all met his grandfather. But how...?"

"Remember that I wasn't always a well-dressed, well-educated person. I was a barefoot convict's child who was so jealous of you three. I would sit and think how nice it would be to ditch the shoes and run wild with you all. Then one day, something Mrs Evans said made it sink in. I understood the privilege I had been given, and I threw myself into the studies, not that I was very good at them, but I never forgot the three of you. You took every opportunity given to you and grasped it tightly. It's nice to meet you both again. I would like to spend more time talking to you both, but I don't think I'll get much time this weekend. Can you come and stay again sometime?"

Both nodded. How could a convict's child have risen so high?

Will said, "I never forgot you either, Ed. It was you who encouraged me to draw and to learn to read. One lunchtime, you gave me a lead pencil, just a broken stub and showed me the rudiments of shading. You even shared your lunch with me when you found we had nothing to eat. I never forgot that. You told me to learn to read and write, so I did. Do you know, the first big painting I did was of you. It was a triple. I gave it to John Landon. He still has it." Will looked embarrassed. He did not usually tell people he was an artist. Certainly not to a stranger, but Ed wasn't. He was a re-found friend. To paint that first picture, Will had haunted the town's blacksmith, learning the nuances of smithing. He'd never seen Eddie at work, so he used his artistic skills to imagine him as a young man at work over the anvil. All who'd seen the work were dumbfounded.

Ed was somewhat taken aback, but did not reply. He presumed that it was amateur work. One day, he may be privileged to see it. As they had arrived at Charlie's house, he ushered them inside and introduced them to both Charlie and Gracie. Now the pieces had fallen into place. Ed knew they would become good friends now. He was delighted that things had worked out well for them both. Ed left them in good hands with Charlie and returned to his own guests.

Phil and Stevie were heading out for a walk to Tim's office. They joined Ed as he walked to his house before they continued on up the street. Ed told them he'd catch them later. Ed told them Tim had gone home. So the two men were headed up to see Tim and Anna at their home instead of his office. They all worked for the same company in Sydney, and the brothers had not seen him since he'd stood for the local seat and won. He was now the member for Parramatta, but he was still working at his law firm as well. Tim had lived with them for eight years when they were young.

Douglas and Caro were like another set of parents for Ed. He'd missed them. John was the youngest of their three sons and the one he actually loved like a brother. John had a passion for nature, as did Ed. He remembered the day they had first met; John showed him a gigantic stick insect with pink wings. He had never forgotten that. Now John and Colleen were staying at his house too. He looked forward to his company again. He was still as nature-obsessed as when he was a child.

Douglas had brought John and Sadie Landon to stay. Ed recognised them from his Sydney days as they had worshipped at the same church. Yet, he wondered why Douglas had brought them. He had faith in both the Evans' and in God; there would be a good reason. He walked in through the kitchen; Cara told him they were all in the sitting room.

"Ed, Colleen said her back ached. Makes me wonder if she ain't ready to birth. That would make the weekend interesting, wouldn't it?" Cara laughed. "I think I'll word up Martha when she comes tonight."

"Add Mrs Evans, too, Cara," Eddie said. He was about to leave the room when he remembered a message Wills gave him. "Cara, can you get Shauna and Moira to prepare the other two rooms, too, please. Cathy said something about Finn and Maureen coming as well. They might be needed if Colleen goes into labour."

"Will do, Ed," she said breezily. "I'll be delighted to see my friend again." She sent her girls to prepare the last two rooms.

Eddie walked in and joined his guests.

Cara brought a tea tray in, then sat and joined them for a short while. She always sat and chatted with Colleen whenever she was here. Colleen had enough of the Irish lilt in her voice to make Cara feel at home. She was thrilled Finn and Maureen Murphy were coming, making this a fabulous weekend for her. It was only with them that they could all babble away in Gaelic. The four had come from a similar area in Ireland. They were all political refugees. Finn had managed to get his family out before they were arrested, but not so Paddy. At least they were transported rather than killed. They had been assigned to a farm on the Windsor Road and only came to Ed after they found the work was becoming too hard. The farmer wanted a younger couple. Ed's news of the Murphy's arrival was exciting. She kissed Colleen as she left, assuring her of her prayers for the birth. She then went to find Paddy.

Unbeknownst to Colleen, Cara had noticed how uncomfortable she was. Cara was actually assessing her as they spoke. The babe had certainly dropped. It was ready to arrive.

John and Sadie watched, amazed by the freedom the convict servant had to mingle with guests.

Caro drew them into the conversation, explaining the connection between the two families.

Ed told the Evanses and the Landons all about the conversation he'd just had with Ricky and Will English.

John Landon's eyes flew to Douglas. "You knew, didn't you?"

"I was pretty sure it was the same blacksmith who was in your painting. Young Will mentioned he had done one. One day I would love to see it," Douglas said, grinning innocently.

Caro laughed at his blunt subtlety.

John turned his attention to Eddie. "You're the lad in my painting?" He sat studying at Ed, and yes, he could see the similarity. The subject was bent over the horse's hoof, searing on the new shoe. He tipped his head, then, with a broad smile on his face. "Yes, it is you. Will captured you very differently, though. You would only have been about ten."

Eddie nodded, grinning. If he were identifiable, maybe this painting was better than he thought. This time, he did not mind being investigated. They were happy days, even though he missed his family. "I was a bit older, actually, but I was small back when I first met the three boys. Ricky was about ten; I was about fourteen, and Will was a bit younger than Ricky, probably about eight. Tad was somewhere in between." Ed explained, filling in a bit more information. "If you can identify me from it, it must be quite detailed."

John smiled knowingly, "You have no idea, sir. You have no idea."

The story of the Landons, Ricky, Will, and Tad unfolded. Tad was now their son-in-law. Meeting him was something for the future, another tie that joined the families. There were still some missing links, but they were drawing closer.

Charles and Sal arrived through the back door, as did most of the family; Luke was with them. He had gone back to get the cottage. They joined the throng in the sitting room and learnt about the connections. All just smiled. This had happened so often in their lives that they were no longer surprised.

Two more joined the group, Thomas and Margaret Tindale, although, as she had a cold, she kept well away from everyone.

Doug and Caro greeted them warmly. When introduced to John Langdon, Thomas greeted him as a friend on first-name terms.

"Huh? How do you know each other?" Douglas asked.

"At St James, Doug. We first met when the ladies were conversing after church and struck up a friendship," Thomas said.

John Landon looked at Thomas, then Eddie. "Don't tell me you are Tom and that Eddie is your student? I never heard his surname. Well, another thread being pulled, eh? This is so good." John Landon roared with laughter. "And don't forget that we had Major Ned's friend living with us for over a year. Amelia West, er Black, so another tie with Parramatta. I presume that you know Major Ned Grace?"

Considering John Landon had never met Charles before, he thought he looked familiar. With the mention of Ned, John's eyes took in Charles' smiling face. "Another link?"

Charles' eyes were dancing, but he merely replied that he knew him.

Sadie had kept quiet, observing during all this conversation. She was sitting near Sally.

One conversation spurred another, and soon Caro mentioned that they were considering working at Sadie House. "I presume you are the 'Sadie' it was named after?"

Sadie laughed. "Err, yes, but it was the old Female Orphans Home out here that inspired it. I heard of a grand lady who was working there. I liked what she did."

Sal almost choked on her tea.

Caro's eyes flew to her with a smile on her face.

Sadie looked from one to another, "I feel another story. Is there a link?"

Sal looked at Charles. "Yes, Sadie, there is. The 'grand lady' was Charles' mother, Elizabeth."

Sadie said, "But I heard she was a titled lady."

Caro laughed this time. "Maybe you should introduce yourself properly, Sal."

Sadie looked puzzled.

Sal blushed.

Caro continued, "May I introduce you to the Earl and Countess of Coxheath?" She pointed to Charles and Sal. "Charlie and Gracie are Viscount and Viscountess Lockley."

Sadie gasped breathlessly. "No! Really?"

"Yes, sorry," Sal said apologetically and shrugged. "It's a long story, but we arrived as convicts, Sadie," Sal said. "We are still convicts at heart. We've learnt there's a lot more to people than a title."

The afternoon passed with much conversation.

Sal suggested that before it got dark, they take a stroll along the riverbank. Everyone wished to stretch their legs except Colleen, who decided to have a rest instead. John stayed with her.

They would not be alone, as Cara and the girls were in the kitchen cooking madly. She had made pastry rolls, homemade sausage slices, egg and bacon pies, stuffed eggs, boiled eggs, vegetable fingers, mini pies, and sandwiches. Trays of each sort of food. Lots and lots of what she called 'finger food'. Dessert was to be a large apple cobbler. She had made three substantial baking trays of it. There was clotted cream and custard to eat with it.

Jenna arrived from the Miller's inn. "Hello, Cara, where is everyone? I don't hear any noise."

"They have all gone for a walk, Jenna." Cara kept making her pastry.

"What time are the 'Emu'ites due, any idea?" Jenna was picking at the plates of food. "I am so hungry. I haven't been this hungry since … Ohh!" She put her fingers over her mouth and froze.

"Since when, dear?" Cara looked at her, puzzled, then, when she saw the shocked look on Jenna's face, she said, "Ohh!" herself. "Could you be?" she asked. "

"Well, of course, I could be, more than likely I am. I've been so busy with Henry and the wedding, I forgot." She counted on her fingers. She giggled. "Don't say anything to Ed yet, will you?"

"Of course not, Jenna, I wouldn't do that, nor will I tell you know who outside. He can't keep quiet," she grinned. Her husband, Paddy, was known to love a good chat with anyone who would pass the time of day. "Congratulations, love. Know when?"

Jenna pulled a face. "I'm not sure, Cara, December, January, something like that, about when Liza and Anna are due. I couldn't do up my dress today and thought I was eating too much" She heard voices. She turned and waved goodbye, putting her finger to her lips and signalled for her to not say anything; she went to greet her guests, who were all returning from their walk.

Ed introduced Jenna to everyone. They had collected Ricky and Will from Charlie's house, and they would stay for the evening meal.

The smell of cooking onions met them as they entered. They were just settling down to chat when they heard carriage wheels on the front gravel.

Colleen's voice carried down from their room upstairs. "They are here." John helped her downstairs.

She waddled outside to greet her parents.

Jenna let them pass her, and she pulled Eddie into his office. "What's wrong, love?" he asked.

"Nothing, Ed, but I know mother will guess, and I wanted to tell you first. I've just realised I think I'm expecting again. I've been so busy with the wedding and eight children, it just slipped my mind that I haven't had my menses for the last few months. The last one I remember was just after Easter." She quickly kissed him and pushed him out the door.

He was stunned. A house full of people, and Jenna drops this bit of information onto him. Looking back at her as she was still pushing him to the front door. "Sure?"

She nodded in reply, "Shh, yes."

He smiled, "Wow. Okay. We'll talk later." Ed shook his head as if to clear his thoughts. They already had eight children. He smiled. The night they married, she said she wanted a quiver full. Their first two, Ned and Tina, arrived one month early, just eight months after they married. They were followed by Lily, Kit, Nick, Shannon, Toria, and Henry, aged three. The twins would celebrate their fifteenth birthday in two weeks. He took a deep breath and went to greet the next group of visitors. He arrived in time to help Martha alight. Jack helped Maureen down, then Finn. The other two were Harry and Vicky.

Harry was still in the driver's seat. They had been determined to come and see all the family at once. To think they were expecting much the same time as both of his sisters. He gave a laugh.

The Turner sisters greeted each other.

Vicky was glowing. As a mother of four, she should have looked exhausted.

Jenna looked at her with a raised eyebrow.

Vicky smiled, blushed, and dropped her head, but nodded.

"Ahh, when are you due?" Jenna whispered.

"Before Christmas, what about you?" Vicky asked.

"Trust you, Vicks. I only realised I was an hour ago. With eight children and the wedding, I've been frantically busy. Probably January, maybe a bit earlier." She giggled, "I'm about four months and I didn't realise. I thought I was just putting on weight." She went and greeted her mother and father.

Martha also took a look at her and held her at arm's length. "When?" was all she asked.

Jenna laughed. "Shh, January possibly, I've only just told Ed. Don't say anything more, please, Maa."

Martha nodded, hugged her and turned when they heard another vehicle coming down the street.

Jenna hugged her father. "All good, kitten?" he asked.

"Yes, Papa, all good," Jenna simply said. "We have a house full, but you'll love them all. Well, that's what Ed said; I haven't met them all myself yet."

Finn and Maureen greeted Colleen, then Ed took them inside.

Harry drove the vehicle to the stables and passed it over to Paddy. As he drove around the side of the house, he saw Wills' gig arrive.

Wills jumped out and tied the reins to the railing at the front, then assisted Cathy out.

Ed, Luke, Ricky, and Will carried more chairs into the sitting room. They decided that everyone else would just have to stand. There was no way they could all sit down to eat. There were twenty-five people to feed at least. Cara's finger food and a stack of plates on the sideboard would have to suffice.

Moira and Shauna brought in platter after platter of food.

The table was set for those who wished to sit. Most, however, retired back into the sitting room and ate from a plate on their laps.

Ricky and Will sat talking to Luke. They recognised him from church.

Some time ago, Will English had thought Luke looked familiar, but it was his likeness to Ed that had confused him. Sitting in the same room, he could now compare them. His artistic eyes flicked from one to the other, then over to Wills and Charlie. With the four brothers in the one room, it was easy to compare them. Their father was an older version of the four of them.

The evening broke up at about nine with Charles, Luke, and Sal walking Ricky and Will back to Charlie's house.

Charles, Sal and Luke said goodnight, then returned to their home at Christina's Cottage.

Sal walked into the kitchen while Charles led Luke into the darkened sitting room, closing the door behind him.

Charles made no attempt to light a lamp; instead, sitting in the darkness. The only light was from the coals in the fireplace. "Son, there are some things better said in the darkness. This is one such time." Charles swallowed uncomfortably and cleared his throat.

Luke sat listening, ahh, yes, the expected conversation. Ed had warned him about this.

Charles had an in-depth, serious talk with his youngest son. Repeating what he had told the other three boys years ago. It never got any easier. "Be gentle, don't force her, make it fun. The first time will hurt her. Don't make that encounter very long; be gentle. Give her time and follow her lead."

Luke's eyes were as big as saucers. He had not been with a woman that way, but he was not ignorant of the ways of a man with a woman. First time? More than once? That alone was enough to shock him. He shook his head to concentrate on his father's words.

Charles went into some detail. "Son, never force her. I mean, never, or it becomes about power, not love. It must be freely given or not at all. Likewise, do not use that side of marriage as a bartering thing. It must be for mutual pleasure; it's why it's called the 'joy of marriage'. God made it so, for procreation, relaxation, and recreation. I emphasise, make it fun, then it will always be pleasurable for you both. Above all, do not wash with hard soaps down there. It remains on the skin and burns them. Take this warning to heart. Soap is caustic; I'm sure you've had it in your eyes sometimes. Luke, also make sure you keep your marriage bed pure. Never be tempted by another. It can, and probably would, destroy your marriage in an instant. Make this decision now, and stick to it." Charles asked him if he had any questions.

Luke asked a few, but was so stunned by what he heard, he didn't know what to ask.

His father took the wind totally out of his sails when he said, "Make sure you rest well tonight, my boy; you will not get much over the next few days."

"Huh?" Luke said.

"Let me just say that a honeymoon is aptly named. The days are sweet and nights are sweeter. Your desires will be sated, many times over." Charles laughed.

Luke looked at his father in the gloom. "More than once, Father?"

"Oh yes, many more than once, lad, especially over the first few days, you will both make gluttons of yourselves, that is totally normal. Enjoy it. And every time will be more enjoyable than the last. Now off to bed," his father said.

Luke stumbled to the door. Stunned. Would she want it more than once a week or so? If Father was correct, it could be more than once a night. A slow smile spread across his dimpled cheeks. Luke went to his room at his parents' cottage for the last time. He lay in bed, thinking of that conversation. Blushing, whilst remembering, he had no idea what awaited him. He rolled onto his stomach and up onto his elbows. He prayed, dedicating himself to being a good husband. He rolled over and slept. He felt both so young and so old, yet so ready to be a husband.

Meanwhile, in the Rear Admiral Duncan, Molly had gone into Ellen's room and had 'the talk' with her too. Molly said much the same about not defiling the marriage bed. However, being available to sate his needs, if it were fun and enjoyable for both, time together becomes very desirable, not a chore. In the darkness of Ellen's room, Molly was a lot more explicit than Charles had been with Luke.

Ellen, too, knew about the act of procreation and how it was done. But not that it could or should be either enjoyable or fun; this was a revelation to her. Her mother's description was shocking and exciting. She listened to every word. "Mama, you say fun. How so? Really fun? Is that all right to really enjoy yourself that way?"

"Yes, dear, perfectly, all right. That is part of the joys of marriage. Try different things, on top, or even sitting up. The more fun you make it, the more enjoyable it is for you both. It doesn't always have to be in a bed, or at night, either. Nor does it have to take long. That's what I mean by fun. It's up to you. Impromptu, seize the opportunities. It does not always have to be unclad. Elle, the first time will hurt, sometimes a lot; once he's in, take your time, relax. That initial pain eases, and then it's fine to let him move again. That's how he'll know if you've been with anyone before, and there will be some blood, but not like your menses."

Molly went into a little more detail. "And love, the joys of marriage commonly occur many more than once on the honeymoon night and following days. Wash with water and no soap, but you know how that hurts. Just hot water."

Finally, Ellen said, "Mama, I think I understand. I shall remember what you said, truly, I will."

"Good, now sleep, love. Once you have discovered the joyous side of marriage, it works both ways; you will want it as much as he will." Molly bent and kissed her daughter. "You won't get much sleep tomorrow night," she said as she was walking out.

"Mother!" Ellen said, shocked, and she blushed.

Molly smiled, biting her lips to stop from giggling as she left.

Ellen went to sleep alone for the last time.

~

In the various rooms around town, many private conversations were taking place. Harry and Vicky were discussing the possible names for their fifth child. Sixth, really, as they had lost their first one.

Ed and Jenna put their youngest children to bed. They had turned the nursery into the girls' room and the room next door into the boys' room. Now they were to have another one.

Jenna lay in bed with her hands on her stomach. "Ed, if I am four months, then I shouldn't be showing. Vicky isn't yet, and she's due in December." She flipped over in bed, "Ed, what if it's twins again?"

He drew her into his arms, "My darling Jenna, we shall love whatever God sends us. Girls, boys, one of each or just one. Just never love it or them more than you love me." He drew her down to him. "Jenna, I am available at your command, love." He chuckled; he knew that her ardour was elevated when pregnant. He had noticed her demands on him had been somewhat elevated of late. This side of their marriage had diminished little in the sixteen years of marriage.

"Goodie," she said as she nibbled his bottom lip. "Ed, do you know I love you as much now, if not more, than when we married so long ago?"

He gently rolled her onto her back. "Do you remember the first few days of our marriage? We made a total glutton of ourselves. Even delaying our honeymoon trip for a day, as we didn't make it out of bed in time." He kissed her again.

When he tried to pull away, she said, "Not so fast, love, I'm only getting started."

"Oh, I'm not pulling away, I'm just getting comfortable," he chuckled.

Eddie kept her occupied for some time before they finally fell asleep in each other's arms.

~

John and Colleen lay in bed, talking about the imminent birth of their child. Colleen had back pain for a day and was feeling very uncomfortable. She knew the signs and remained silent. The baby was moving quite a bit, and she had been unable to sleep. She realised it had finally turned; she had felt her mother's babies often enough. She had been resting whenever she could; she wanted and needed John close. She was pleased her mother had arrived. She had expected three-year-old Mary to come with her, but she had stayed at home with Deidre. Her sister usually lived at Wills and Cathy's house, but as they were here, she was free to babysit Mary.

Colleen, like Jenna, found that her desire for her husband had increased while she was in the family way. She turned to John. "Love, are you tired? I'm not yet."

He just grinned as his reply. He just reached for her and murmured, "No, Colly, I'm ready anytime, my sweet."

~

In John and Sadie's room, the conversation was not so amorous, but certainly interesting.

Sadie had listened to many different discussions throughout the evening. "First, Ricky, Tad, and Will had already met Ed. Then you meet Douglas and Thomas at church. Ricky named the babies home after me, after hearing about Charles' mother working at the   girls orphanage out here. John, I feel we're supposed to work with them somehow. I think this journey God has us on will be interesting." She yawned. "I do look forward to tomorrow."

"Don't forget about Charles and Bill meeting Falconer-Meade sixteen years ago when he first came looking for Matthew and then Tad. Now we're going to Bill's daughter's wedding." He bent and kissed her. "Night, love. Sleep well."

"Hmm, night…" she murmured sleepily. "And don't forget Amelia and Ned." She was nearly asleep.

~

In the next-door room, Martha said to Jack. "She won't see out the week, I bet. The baby has dropped. Did you see her rubbing her back? I bet she'll go tomorrow, just hopefully, not in the middle of everything. I'll talk to Maureen tomorrow morning."

Jack said. "Fire is nice, though, warms the entire room. Night, love." Not really interested in what she was saying.

~

Maureen and Finn's conversation was much the same as Martha and Jack's.

"I don't think she'll see the day through tomorrow. She says she has another month. I say twenty-four hours no more." Maureen said. "Baby has dropped already."

"The bed's too soft, love," Finn said. "Hmm, all right. Might have to move onto the floor."

"Just as soft as I am, Finny me darlin'," she turned to Finn and distracted him until he fell asleep exhausted in bed.

~

Colleen was only able to get a broken sleep. John had dozed off quickly following their earlier conversation. The baby was now very active and her back was hurting a lot. She got up and was walking around the room, then stood at the window and prayed. Since she heard about Sadie House, her heart went out to the orphan babies. She loved children, she always had. She had certainly had plenty of practice with her numerous siblings. Looking after Wills and Cathy's babies was a dream come true. She loved them all. Each time she thought her heart full when another one entered her realm, and it too soon found its place in her heart. Now she was having her own: hers and John's.

Her backache did not lessen; she was cold. She stretched then returned to bed. Hopefully, she would doze, if nothing else. She slept fitfully next to her husband. She would need him totally rested when the time came.

~

The two who did sleep well were Luke and Ellen. Both slept undisturbed all night. The next morning the happy couple each slept in. Their parents let them sleep until they woke naturally.

Luke woke and lay in his bed, smiling. "I'm getting married today."

Up the street and around the corner, Ellen had just woken, and the same thought when through her mind. She lifted her hand and looked at her beautiful emerald ring. Today it would be joined by a wedding band. Tonight she would become Luke's wife.

The morning passed without incident.

The wedding was at eleven. Charlie and his household readied the cart and a wagon. Tim had their gig harnessed to their horse, and it too was decorated in greenery. Eddie had Paddy prepared their carriage and Ed would drive a wagon. Colleen would be unable to walk any distance and the ladies could travel with her.

Cara was taken aside by Maureen and Martha both discussed the imminent birth. All the women thought that she would not make it through the day.

Cara was one step ahead of her. Everything was ready. She even planned to leave a large pot of water on the stove during the service, just in case. She had a stack of linen and towels in readiness.

All the households were soon up and getting ready for the wedding. The food was sitting covered and ready to transport. The post-party was again to be held at *The Jolly Sailor* at Charlie's inn, courtyard.

Charlie would enlisted the help of his visitors Ricky, Will, Stevie, and Phil, and his own twelve-year-old twins, Teddy and John. The bulk of the work had been completed well before the guests had arrived. By ten, everyone was dressing in their wedding finery. By half-past, most were on the way to church.

Ellen and Bill arrived at the church five minutes early.

Luke, Wills, and Ed were already in the vestry with Reverend Clarke and Reverend Gore, who would share the service. Reverend William Clarke had been given the honour of actually performing the ceremony. The bridal couple's eldest brothers, Charlie and Tim were to be the witnesses.

The music started. The clergy filed out of the vestry, and Eddie gently pushed Luke and Will ahead of him.

Charlie and Ed were so proud of their brothers. As the music started, the men had been standing in the vestry praying. Luke released a long, slow breath of contentment.

Ed looked at Luke; he was not as nervous as he had been. He was just anxious that they get it over and done with. He just wanted to be married. His face was beaming with joy.

The three brothers arrived in the central aisle. Luke in the centre and the other two off to his side. Charlie was in the front row with their parents and Gracie.

Wills poked Luke. "Luke, turn and look."

Luke turned, Ellen was standing at the church door, haloed in light. Her gown was shimmering white and she had a long veil; it added to the glow.

The congregation saw him turn and did likewise. They were astonished at the vision. Her gown was of pure white silk, pleated at the dropped waistline and fitted in panels at the bodice, dropping to a low point. A gathered ruffle of silk, trimmed with lace was at both neck and hem, finishing with tiny bunches of sparkling beads and silk flowers in minute bouquets topping the neckline. The short sleeves were also of the ruffled silk and had georgette ribbons flowing down each arm's back. The gown had a train trailing a yard behind her. Her netted veil covered her face to the neckline then fell behind her the entire length of the gown and a yard longer.

The morning sun shone through the windows and the coloured glass sent rainbows of colours throughout the church. Prisms of colour reflected off the crystal beads and shiny fabric, giving her an angelic aura.

Luke stood open-mouthed as she walked on her father's arm towards him. Her beatific smile entranced him. His eyes were fixed on her as she drew closer. She had taken her time, slowly walking down the long aisle.

Bill was enjoying every moment. It was the second and last time he had to perform this meaningful act. Gracie's wedding had been fifteen years earlier. With only six years between the girls, he expected Ellen's nuptials would have occurred sooner. However, she had waited for the only person to stir her heart. Today they would be made husband and wife.

In the eight months Luke had been away, Molly and Ellen had made the exquisite gown themselves. They had travelled to Sydney soon after Luke had departed and found a wonderful store to purchase the fabric.

The English Emporium was a lady's dream store and would be sure to be frequented by many women of the colony. The bolt of polished silk fabric they had purchased was slightly watermarked. They worked around the marks by making ruffles out of that section of the material. The effect was an outstanding success. The small packet of crystal beads was a gift from Bill to his youngest child. They had no idea where they came from. He had ordered them from India for her.

Before their return to Parramatta last week, Ellen and Molly had returned and bought more lengths of fabric for them to work on, including Ellen's favourite, a length of linen that was the lightest ice blue colour. It was made into a lovely day gown. It was so comfortable, but sadly, being linen, it creased.

Bill was thinking, now it was time to give his last child away. Only to someone like Luke would he have considered worthy of her. The lad was almost like a son to him anyway. Bill smiled at them both. When the time came, and Bill was asked: "Who gives this woman...?" He was able to reply confidently, "I do, with great love and affection for both."

The two ministers continued with the service, Reverend Gore, as an assistant.

Wills handed Reverend William the two rings. They were blessed and then, one by one, gave them to Luke and Ellen.

William took their hands and joined them. He wrapped his stole around them and said, "What God has bound, let no man tear asunder," and pronounced them husband and wife. After releasing their hands he said, "You may now kiss your wife."

Luke replied with a smile. He folded back her veil. He stood looking at Ellen for a moment before sweeping her into his arms. She wrapped one arm around his waist and the other around his neck. He initially brushed her lips with his before crushing her to him in a deep and passionate embrace. Finally raising his head. He murmured so only she could hear, "I love you, Mrs Luke Lockley."

William coughed. He knew this would take some time. He was about to ask them to come forward and sign the register when there was a cry from the congregation.

All eyes turned to Colleen.

She had sat through the service in silence, holding John's hand throughout. As they were seated, she grasped it and squeezed it hard. He thought it merely a gesture of love. When she did it again halfway through the service, he looked at her face to see it was contorted in pain. The third time, just now, she was unable to hold in the cry of pain.

Maureen and Cara both motioned for William to continue but hurry.

He did.

As the couple moved to the sanctuary to sign the register, Maureen escorted Colleen and John outside.

The contraction was over, and she could walk. Caro and Douglas were hard on their heels. Finn was already in the carriage seat.

Before the couple had finished the signatures, the small group had departed to Eddie's house. Cara and Maureen both laughed. "I knew it," said Cara. "You've had back pain for the last day or so. We were only talking this morning that we were sure you'd not see out the day."

"John, you'll be a father by tonight," Finn called from the front seat. Suddenly the prospect of impending fatherhood was frightening. John had not seen a woman in labour pain before. Her moan of pain tore through him. Finn had taken him aside the night before and given him some birthing hints.

John had no intention of being with her through it. Backing away from his father-in-law with his hands up, he said, "Oh no! No! No! I'll stay outside," That was something for hospitals. Just hand him a neatly wrapped babe, and he'd be content with that. Now that was not going to happen. The babe was coming like it or not.

As they reached the house, another contraction hit. John sat with her in the carriage until it passed. The ladies alighted and went to prepare the house.

Douglas and Finn tied the carriage to the rail and Finn offered to carry her inside. Caro had gone upstairs immediately to prepare the room.

"I can walk. I'm only having a baby, I'm not a cripple, Papa." She laughed.

John looked astounded. She showed no fear. Walking up the stairs to the verandah, he heard her gasp. Her waters had broken.

"Well, thank goodness that happened here," her mother said. "Things will hasten even quicker now."

Sure enough, before John got her to the front door, another contraction hit. John still had no intention of staying. He would get her upstairs and then wait outside.

Maureen had other ideas about John; she smiled knowingly. She showed him how to hold Colleen through a contraction and how to take her weight. Colleen's arms were wrapped around John's waist while he enfolded her.

"That was not long between them," Cara said. "The little one is not going to be long in coming."

"Coll, how long have you been having back pain?" her mother asked.

"Since we arrived, yesterday Mama. I didn't want to say anything. I didn't sleep much last night; the baby was moving all night. I had hoped I would at least make it through the wedding. I did manage most of it." Colleen looked at her husband guiltily, then grinned. "Sorry, love. I wanted to go. If I said anything, I knew I would be confined to the house."

Her mother chuckled, "John, she's been through this enough with me to not know the symptoms. How many of mine have you delivered? Three, four?" Maureen asked.

"Six, Mama. I've helped with six," Colleen said. They made it slowly to the top of the stairs before another contraction hit. John again took her in his arms and supported her through it.

Within ten minutes, she was in their room, in her nightgown.

John had been told to change into loose, comfortable clothing and join them. He was horrified but did what they told him to do. He dared not disobey any of the women who were now waiting for him.

The two prospective grandfathers, Finn and Douglas, took the carriage back to the church and said they would return later with the family. There was nothing they could do anyway.

The two Irish ladies had prepared well and within minutes had the room ready for birthing. Caro helped where she could. The crib was waiting, and bundles of towels and linens were prepared for the child. Basins of hot water were ready for washing and cleaning, and an empty basin was near the bed. John didn't dare ask what that was for.

John expected her to be put to bed and the birth covered up. He had no idea what to expect. There were basins, buckets, piles of towels, hot water and a chair. He listened to the instructions of the three women, but most of them went over his head. Perspiration beaded on his brow.

His mother had joined them again after bringing more hot water and basins. She was on hand to offer any assistance. She had birthed three sons herself. All had been born in the hospital. She did not have any family with her, as Douglas had been at sea. Tom and Margaret stayed for a while, but she had to give birth alone, just doctors and nurses, who were very strange and impersonal. These women were proficient at the job. Outside the room was a basin of hot water.

Maureen made both Caro and John scrub before entering. "And use the soap, please."

After a few more contractions, which were now really close, Cara prepared John. "Shoes off, kneeling behind Colleen, son." As he moved. Colleen vomited. The smell was nauseating. However, Colleen was soon resting against his chest with his arms around her. She could brace herself against him. He murmured encouraging things to her and prayed softly. Thankfully, he could not see much.

"It's coming, Mama. John, hold me," Colleen said. She was groaning in pain as she delivered their child.

As noises from down below signalled the families' return, a new person entered the world. He was a healthy 8lb 2oz and had an excellent set of lungs. The look of awe on John's face said it all. He had seen far more than he wanted to, and would not have missed any of it if asked.

Caro held the babe before the cord was cut. John sat mute.

Maureen and Cara were waiting for the afterbirth.

Colleen was relaxing on John's chest, exhausted. It was less than an hour from leaving the church; she reached up and stroked his cheek. "We're a family, love, what a gift from God he is." She looked up from the tiny babe. "He's a Jonathon, love."

"Yes! Jonathon Finn Douglas Evans it is, love. Our gift from God." John kissed the top of her head.

"Mama, Cara, ready?" Colleen said.

Cara merely nodded.

Maureen reached down and quickly tied twice, then cut the cord in the middle of the ties. Caro wrapped the baby and stood cuddling him.

"What's happening, Colly?" John enquired.

"Afterbirth, John, this bit is painful. Get ready, love. Hold her again." Maureen answered him.

John was stunned. If this was painful, what was the delivery?

Colleen emitted a bloodcurdling scream. "Cor, Mama, you didn't tell me it hurt that much." She fell back against John's chest again. "Having the baby was easy compared to that," she said.

"Different sort of pain, love. Sharper and well, a bit harder to cope with," her mother explained.

"How did you do this sixteen times?" her daughter asked her laughingly.

"Well, let's put it this way, it's not all that difficult getting them in there; it only hurts getting them out." She grinned and winked at John. "Give it a week, and I bet you'll be wanting more. It may not even be that long." As they talked, Cara had removed the afterbirth, placing it in an empty basin, and covered it with a cloth. They cleaned up the area.

Colleen was washed and changed into another one of her nightgowns and was soon sitting up in bed, cuddling her newborn son with her husband beside her. "Mama is right, you know, John. I want more, lots more." She snuggled into his shoulder as they sat against the bedhead.

Caro had wiped the baby gently and swaddled it before handing her grandson to his parents. "Jonathon, I like that." He had the same jet black hair as his mother and his father's blue eyes. One day, he would be a handsome young man, but today he was just a bonny baby.

After some fifteen minutes, Maureen suggested that he be fed for the first time. Caro and Maureen helped Colleen feed her son, showing her how to hold him to achieve the best results.

"Ouch! He bit." Colleen grimaced. She pulled him off her breast. She rubbed her finger in his mouth. "He's got a tooth. No wonder it hurt."

"Ahh! Eion and Bren were both born with teeth. Emmy got her first at one week old; sorry, love should have warned you about that. Every time he nips, pull him off. He'll learn quick enough." Maureen looked sheepish.

Colleen put him back on the breast, and he tried it once more. She pulled him off again. Jonathon's eyes opened, looking at her. She waited a minute before allowing him back on. He didn't try it again.

John sat in awe, watching it all. He adored Colleen. He was in awe of what he had just experienced, but watching his son suckle was an experience he would remember for ages. The room was warm, so the child's wrappings were loose. The tiny hand emerged, and he laid it gently on his mother's breast. The infant had his eyes open and was watching his mother as he fed. Colleen reached for John's hand and held it.

He bent and kissed her cheek. John's eyes misted. He thought he had known what love was until that moment. His heart hurt; it was so full.

Caro was watching John's face. The emotions were clearly visible. She, too, teared up with love. She had been kept well away from the other girls. Not even being allowed to cuddle their children for over a week. Now they were to live with them, and she would be totally part of their lives. Caro was thrilled.

Jonathon fed, and finally, Colleen handed him to her husband, who was shown how to burp him. John was fearful of hurting the tiny man; the lad gave a grin, then one almighty burp. He fell asleep.

Caro took her grandson and placed him in the crib.

It was only then that Colleen and John were left alone. She turned to him and wrapped her arms around him. "Sorry, I didn't tell you, love. I was really hoping I was wrong, but as it happened, I'm glad we were here and not in Sydney. They would not have let you into the hospital."

John bent and kissed her. He was still overwhelmed with what he'd just experienced.

"I think I'll grab a nap, love. You go and tell all the others our good news." She shooed him from the bed. "You'd better change back before you go, sweeting."

He looked down at his clothing. He was in a pair of clean but tatty old trousers he had thrown in his bag, just in case he had to do some dirty work. He had worn them on their trip, but they indeed were not suitable for a wedding. He changed back into his wedding finery. He returned, then bent and kissed his wife, stroked his son's cheek and left them alone. He stood at the door, looking at them both. His heart had never been so full. He quietly closed the door behind him. Colleen was already asleep.

Douglas greeted him at the bottom of the stairs. "Congratulations, John! A boy, I believe. The ladies would not tell us his name." Douglas led his son into the crowded sitting room.

As the door opened, the room hushed. Eddie walked over and congratulated him first. Then they hushed everyone again. "We're waiting for you; what have you named him?" Ed asked.

"Well, he's a gift from God, so we've named him Jonathon Finn Douglas Evans." John was somewhat overwhelmed by all the people waiting for his news. His brothers and their families, Sal, Charles, Cathy, and Wills, along with all their brood; Harry and Vicky, with their children; Charlie and Gracie were all awaiting news. He looked at them all, and finally met a pair of blue eyes he knew well. Across the room, William and Maria were standing arm in arm.

"Congratulations, John, and to Colleen, too." William's smile was heartening.

Charles coughed and then said. "All right, everyone, we have a wedding party to attend." He held the door open for them, and soon John stood in the nearly empty room with only his parents remaining.

Caro had insisted that, as Cara was in charge of catering for the wedding, she must go. She would stay with Colleen, as would Maureen.

Cara nodded. Knowing that Colleen was in good hands with the child's grandparents, she hastened over to Charlie's inn and got on with the wedding party. Every fifteen minutes or so, one or other of them went upstairs to check on the sleeping pair.

Two hours after he had left the room, John gently opened the door to see Colleen awake. "Hello, love, are you all right?" he asked as he walked in.

"Hm, huh? Yes, fine, a bit sore, but better than I expected. Can you help me up? I need to use the commode." She swung her legs around and off the bed. "I'm as weak as a newborn kitten, love."

He helped her to the commode and went to the window to give her some privacy. "Done, love. I'll need some help back to bed, though."

John came and helped her back to bed. "Sorry, John, but it's going to be at least a month before we can be together, you know, that way," she said apologetically.

"Oh Colly, after what I saw today, I'm surprised that it will be that soon. Mother said at least six weeks. I lasted over thirty years without it. Six weeks won't hurt." He lay on the bed, cuddling her. She dozed on his chest. He just held her in awe at what he'd witnessed. A small whimper stirred them both; their son had awoken. John stood to attend to him but had no idea what to do.

There was a gentle knock on the door. Maureen was there. "Did I hear the babe? He'll need a change by now." John let her in, and she went and picked up the swaddled child. "As I thought, wet through. Come and learn how to do this and learn a few tricks. He'll need changing eight to ten times a day, so get used to it." She went to a pile of old flannel squares. "These are the napkins for the child. Thankfully, there are many here. Jenna said to use as many as you like. They won't be needing them until Christmas. Did you know they are expecting again? As is Vicky. Liza and Anna are both expecting as well, but about a month later." Maureen continued with her instructions. "Now, lay it on the table as a folded square, take the top corner and pull it over like a triangle. Flip the whole thing over and fold the other side into a roll in the middle. This creates multiple layers in the centre where it absorbs more moisture. Then take a muslin square and lay it over the top. This makes removing the solids easier. Do this before you remove the dirty one. With a boy, you need to have everything ready, or you will get showered. Watch." She gently pushed John to the side, and she stood on the other side. Sure enough, as soon as she released the covering, the baby released a stream. She chuckled. "Now you know, be warned." She covered him loosely until he'd finished.

John stood watching.

Colleen was sitting on the bed, giggling, "Did he get you?"

John shook his head. "No, love, I'm well warned, though. I must apologise to my mother. I gather all boys do this?"

Maureen nodded. She showed him how to grab the child's feet and lift him, changing him quickly and placing a clean napkin under him. Folding the bottom of the napkin up, then the sides of the triangle to the front, she deftly did it up with one large napkin pin. "It's more fiddly when it's a dirty one; it turns your stomach sometimes, but it has to be done. But with a boy, you nearly always get a shower when you take it off. You have to wash all the bits too when they're dirty. The next one may be a dirty one. When he starts on solid food in some four to six months, that's when the stomach really turns." She swaddled him again, then handed John his now-dry son.

He was still fearful of carrying such a small person. This child was now totally their responsibility. He took him to Colleen, the little boy's eyes trying to focus on his face; John stroked his son's cheek adoringly. He wasn't quite so red now. His thick dark hair was dry, and his skin had smoothed from the wet wrinkles he had when he was born. He lovingly handed him to his mother for another feed.

Colleen sent him away for a while. She said, "John, can you go and put in our apologies and then come back in about an hour or so? Mama will stay with me." He bent and kissed her as she fed the child, then departed, turning again at the door and looking back at her.

On his arrival at the wedding party, he was greeted by everyone. Being thoroughly congratulated, he was somewhat overwhelmed by how the day had turned out. The focus was supposed to be on Luke and Ellen, not them.

Everyone was talking about this name: Jonathon Finn Douglas Evans. A thick Scottish voice yelled out, "Jonty, it means little John." Hamish's voice carried across the momentarily hushed group.

So Jonty he became.

Hamish came over and congratulated John, nearly shaking his hand off. After some forty similar encounters, John took his leave and returned to his new family.

Chapter 15   Jigsaw Pieces

*T*he wedding party continued on until the wee hours of the morning. Knowing this would be the last wedding for some time, many of the younger ones did not wish to go home. The two Reverend gentlemen and their wives and families departed during the afternoon, The Clarkes on the four o'clock ferry, with many of Luke's university friends. Reverend Gore and his wife ambled home soon after the Clarks' departure. They had enjoyed their catch-up.

The ale, cider and ginger beer flowed freely. The younger children lasted until about nine o'clock, when they were put to bed. Charlie ushered a few of the more unsteady partygoers home. He and his brothers had, in the main, stayed off the heavy grog, drinking the apple cider instead. The last big wedding had been Sam and Belle some five years before, but they were not Lockleys and, therefore, did not draw the greater community. Nearly all the family had come to that. Luke, of course, had been in the middle of exams. It was only later that he'd heard about it. Before that was the double wedding of ten years ago. The family called it the Gaelic Wedding, where Maria Clarke's two nieces married Wills and Harry's friends, Aidan and Lewis. The Irish fiddlers, along with George and Bertie Ellis on their violins, and a Scottish bagpiper set the mood for that one. That had been a fun wedding.

Ellen and Luke were the last of the three Parramatta families to marry. The Lockleys, Millers and Ellis were now one large family. There were still two of the Turner boys to match up, and most of the Murphys.

During that afternoon, Ricky and Will English, Tim, Stevie, and Phil sat discussing the legalities of getting some birth certificates for orphans. It was something that Tim, Phil, and Steve had never thought about. Will English sat listening to the conversations. He said, "Rick's worried because I don't have a birth record. It makes a few things hard. Like, I can never work for the government or join the army, not like that's going to happen anyway," he said, patting his dud leg. "If I had been placed in an orphanage at birth, I would have had one, but being a foundling of some months old, I have nothing. I doubt I shall ever find out who I am now," Will had a note of sadness in his voice.

Ricky picked up the story, telling the three listeners of the work they were doing with other street waifs. Ricky did not realise the implications that this one conversation would have on many of the children they would help in the future.

Harry Harlow, Vicky's husband, walked over and joined their conversation. They each nodded a welcome to him.

Ricky thought Tim was just a nice young man, but discovered that he was married to Ed's sister. Ricky did not know that Tim was also the Parliamentary Member for the area, and the other two, John's brothers, were two of Sydney's top barristers.

Tim and Anna had come across this problem before with the girls in the Female Orphans' School. When Anna's grandmother, Elle, married the headmaster, the family did what they could to sort out the children's legalities. Back then, many of the girls in the Female Orphans' Home were children of the Female Factory, so at least one parent was usually known. Tim was brought in on the issue, and he had been the one who had individually applied for birth records for each child in the orphanage. Now he had another area to help. He had worked with Phil before on this.

Ricky didn't realise, but he'd spoken to the three perfect men to change this ruling. They would take on Will English's case and sort it out for him. They asked if they could use him as a 'test case'. He agreed with alacrity, so excited that he had even been considered.

As they circulated throughout the multitude during the afternoon, Ricky had eventually been introduced to Harry and Vicky. He knew Vicky was Jenna's sister, then discovered she was also the sister of Wills's wife, Cathy. He picked up that Harry was actually English, and when he found his brother was a Viscount, he wondered what he was doing out here in New South Wales.

Harry was equally intrigued by Ricky's innocent observation. Harry discovered that he had a fascinating history of once being a 'street rat.' After some time together, Harry laughed and said, "Rick, you have no idea, do you?"

Ricky looked puzzled, "At what, Harry?"

Harry continued to explain, "Vicky and I are at the bottom of the pecking order around here," Harry said with a smile.

Ricky and Will looked even more puzzled. They had been

overwhelmed by so many new people. At one point, they both wished they had not come.

Harry pointed to Charles, "That's Charles Lockley."

"Yes," said Ricky, "I met him and his wife; they are nice."

"Well, he's the Earl of Coxheath," Harry said.

Ricky and Will had each taken a mouthful of ale. Both choked, and both spat it out.

"... And Charlie... yes, the one you are staying with, is his oldest son and is, therefore, a Viscount and also the Viceroy for the western area. All the rest of their children are titled 'The Honourable', the same as me. Only they are one step higher on the pecking order, as they are children of an Earl, and I was the son and brother of a Viscount."

Ricky was stunned; he could not tear his eyes away from them. "But he's so nice; they all are. They are normal people, just like us," he stumbled over his words.

"And that's how they like it too, comfortable clothing and tattered hats. Warm hearts and loving too." Harry sat next to Ricky on the old cart. "Pity you never met their Uncle Ned. He turned out to be the Duke of Gracemere. He is one of God's true gentlemen. He was a Major at what is now the Police Barracks for over twenty years. It turned out Ned was Charles' cousin, and they didn't even know it. Charles became an Earl on his father's death when he was only five, but didn't find out for twenty more years. Ned became Duke in '39 or '40 but didn't know for over two years. He found out the week Eddie married. Ned got engaged the day he found out." Harry looked around at the young members of the family who'd now adopted him. "Oh, Ricky, this family is one to cling to if you can. The Evanses are also wonderful."

The heads of the young men nodded. "Mr Evans and Hamish have offered to help with the boys. I should accept their offer, then?" Ricky was still anxious about accepting assistance from strangers.

"Absolutely, Ricky, can't go wrong with either. Oh, and Hamish is another."

"Another what?" Ricky asked, fearful of what he'd hear.

"Why 'The Honourable,' of course, he's the second son of a Scottish Baron," Harry said. "Captain Evans is one of the most capable men I know, and Hamish's maternal great-grandfather was a Duke, I believe, the Duke of Cheatham. Despite Hamish working at Wills' house, Hamish is no servant but a friend paying his way the only way he can. If you can get them interested in your project, you will never regret it. What's more, they won't give charity; their offer of assistance will help them as much as you." Harry watched Rick's face.

The revelation dawning on his face, Ricky looked at these people with new eyes. He hated taking charity, but he had learned over the years that help was not always charity, for it often worked both ways.

John Landon caught Ricky's puzzled look across the courtyard. He smiled and came over. He nodded to Harry and then asked, "Everything all right, lad?" he asked Ricky. He had been introduced to Harry earlier.

Ricky was a little dazed, "A little overwhelmed, Mr Landon. Mr Harlow, here, told me that he, Hamish and all the Lockleys are titled folk. But they are so down to earth. I've been with them the best part of a day and have only just found out."

"It doesn't make a difference, does it, Harry?" John chuckled. As an importer, his business had brought Harry Harlow's name across his desk more than once over the past years. Never once did he mention his titled status. They had never met, though. When he was introduced to Wills and Harry, he discovered from Eddie that these two were the ones who ran the hardware emporiums. It was then that he realised why he and Sadie had been invited. Douglas was a sneaky one. He foresaw more discussions between them all.

Soon after Harry married, he realised that although he had married a convict's daughter, her two other sisters were married to sons of an Earl. He, being only the second son of a Viscount, was much lower in precedence. His ego was initially pricked; he had learned the hard way. Pride doesn't help at all.

Harry looked Ricky in the eye and said, "Ricky, in this amazing country, it's not what you're born with; it's what you do with what you have. It's about what you also do to help others. I know nothing about you, except that you helped Will and Tad. I bet that's not the end of the story, or you probably wouldn't have been invited here otherwise. We have learnt over the years to trust our friends. God has led us to unique finds through trust. Never underestimate how much He can open the doors you think firmly closed."He pointed Heavenwards. "God interweaves lives in a way that is far beyond our understanding." Harry looked at the surprise that flashed across Ricky's face. "If you have a need, take it to the Lord and then take your hands off the reins. I had to. I was turfed out of my home by my brother the week my parents were killed. It wasn't a good feeling. One day, I'll tell you my story. I've never told anyone else that much, except Wills and Vicks." Harry caught his wife's eye; she was beckoning him. "Have to go, Rick. Come to Emu and stay some time. I want to get to know you both. Can't miss us; ask at the Emporium out there. More than likely, I'll be there anyway." Harry bowed and turned to depart.

"Thanks, Harry, I will," Ricky said to the departing man.

John Landon sat talking with Ricky and Will. "I had no idea what was in front of us when Douglas invited us to come. Rick, I think that this family could be an answer to your prayers. It will be interesting to see where God leads us all."

Ricky was still astounded by who these people were. They knew his background: a street waif and an orphan, a nobody. The family really didn't care one iota; all were treated as equals.

Finn and Paddy later saw the two boys sitting alone. They went over and sat discussing their favourite topic, potatoes.

Ricky had never really thought about potatoes before. He had sold them from his fruit and vegetable barrow as a boy; therefore, he could tell a good one from a bad one. He then found out that Finn was 'Murphy's Spuds'. They were always the best quality and rarely had imperfections. He always tried to get them whenever possible.

"Mr Murphy..." Rick was about to continue when Finn interrupted.

"Just Finn lad, no Mr for me," Finn said, with a mischievous grin.

"Finn, I started out selling fruit and vegetables from a wheelbarrow in King Street. I was ten. It grew from there to a shop rented from Mr Landon. I always tried to buy your product; it was the best."

Finn grinned. "Tanks laddie. Dat's the best ting you can ever say to an Irishman. Nice to be appreciated. Even better if you loves a good spud." He chortled. Even after years, the colony, his Irish brogue was still thick.

Paddy butted in. "Ricky, I heard you talking about titles and the like. Our daughter, Maryanne, married Robert, Liza's brother-in-law. This family doesn't draw boundaries; they knocks 'em down faster than you can build 'em up. We'll never be free; we're both lifers. But the life we have here is far better than we ever had at home when we lived in our own house. Our children are free, but even more importantly, they are happy and healthy. Our two youngest boys run the Government Dairy herd here now. It was our faith that brought us here. We're not Catholic, and that was enough to get us locked up from where we both came from."

In the course of the conversation, Paddy had let drop about them being a lifer. It took Ricky some time, but Will leaned over and questioned, saying, "A convict?" his eyes were wide in astonishment.

"Yes, I know what a lifer is," he said to Will. "One saved me when I was a tacker." Ricky turned to Paddy and said, "Really? There is no way I would have known. Are they really as unbiased?"

"They are, lad. Your background does not stop you from anything in this amazing country. Look at William Wentworth. Illegitimate and born to a convict woman and a father who was also a bit of a highwayman. Doctor D'Arcy Wentworth, his pa, should have come here as a convict. Only he volunteered to come as a doctor. D'Arcy Wentworth became chief surgeon and later the head of police. Mr William is one of the wealthiest men in the colony, although I think our Wills is beginning to give him a run for his money. Mr Wentworth started 'The Australian' newspaper and helped found our university. Luke, our bridegroom, by the way, was at the University at Wentworth's suggestion the year it opened. Wills was named after Mr Wentworth, you know, and Luke even lived at Government House for over a year at Mr Wentworth's suggestion." He released a contented sigh. "Ricky, my boy, nothing stops that man. He has just stood down from the Legislative Assembly. I wonder what he'll do next?" Paddy looked around at the people surrounding him. "Finn, you are free; I'm not. But we be friends, good friends. Many in the colony do care. If you dig deep enough, you will find skeletons in most of their cupboards. Those who don't like the situation out here often go home. Harry has no skeletons, but he's staying. He had a fight with his brother; don't know any more. It was the best thing that ever happened to our Harry. He has a new life here, and it's made a man of him. I don't even know the story of most of them. I never heard why Bill or Jack got sent out. It doesn't matter. No one really cares, and no one asks. Being here is what counts. What does matter is who the person becomes and what he does with his life. Never forget that, lad. Whatever the start in your life, only you can change the ending. Few here would stay home if we got sent back. We would fight to return here. This is home." Paddy stood, looking around at his friends and family. "Ricky, it's a pity you can't meet the Major. It's what we all call him when he's here, but in reality, he is the tenth Duke of Gracemere. He's so down to earth. He's due out soon. Said he would bring the family for a year or so. Finish off the children here before they grow up and leave home. If you hear he's here, tell Doug you want to meet them. No fancy European finishing school for that family."

"Harry said the same," Ricky thought back to Tom. The convict who had befriended him as a child. He never knew his story, nor his full name; he never asked. "Paddy, I so agree. I'm just astounded that there are so many like-minded people. I knew Mr Landon was different; Major Hinds in Sydney was the same. Even Major Humphrey Downes, who is Major Hinds' friend."

"So are all these folk, Ricky. More than you know, lad. So much more than you know," Finn said.

Luke and Ellen were circulating around all their friends. Most of the people there had known this young pair all their lives. Luke looked around at who was there: mostly close friends, and some were mere acquaintances.

Mr Harry Moffatt and his wife Emily came as well. He was the Justice of the Peace at Parramatta Courthouse. He had become a close friend of his father, Charles, some sixteen years ago. The day of Eddie and Jenna's wedding was far more eventful than a mere birth. In the middle of their wedding service, Ed had been accused of horse theft. Of course, he was exonerated, and the accuser convicted of bush-ranging instead and sent to gaol. Eddie still owned James, the most amazing black stallion. The stallion had sired a swathe of startling colts and fillies around the area, all inky black, and all inherited his temperament.

Luke knew Mr Moffatt also worked with Wills and had become his confidante. He had smoothed the way for all the building and development around the gold rush. Wills had told Luke this in case something ever happened to him. Wills wanted someone in the family to know.

Luke looked around for one noticeable missing person. Old Tom, the remarkable identity who had almost taken up residence at Ed's Emporium, was absent. He bent and asked Ellen where he was. "Oh, Lukie, Tom died six months ago. Not long after you left, actually. He died peacefully, went to bed and didn't wake. Ed discovered him when he didn't turn up to work." Luke remembered the last conversation with the old man. He had been coming back from asking for Ellen's hand, and they met late at night. Old Tom had said farewell to him that night. Luke thought he was a bit mixed up, but now he was not so sure. The town would miss him.

At three o'clock, they had cut the cake and had the speeches, so that those who had to catch the ferry would not miss either.

Reverend William Clarke spoke to the assembled multitude. He was nervous, which was unusual considering he did sermons most weeks and was also a teacher. "Dear friends, many of you are far more than that, especially my own dear family. I wish to tell you about the last few months. No, do not fear that I shall waffle on too much. I shall instead tell you of Luke. You all know my connections with young William over there. Ahh! Where to start?" He rubbed his nose as he was wont to do. "Right, oh well…um, oh, all right, it has to start with Wills after all, for that is how I came to know this lad. I was teaching at The King's School. That is old news for most, but I took some time off and went to Hartley after one Easter. On my return, I reported certain finds to Governor Gipps. I was told to keep them quiet. Of course, I couldn't. I was too excited, and young Wills was a good listener. He and I had many long discussions about the mineral formations of gold, among other minerals. That, though, is another story; I won't go into it. Suffice it to say, it made me notice his younger brother, Luke. He had previously slipped my notice, as he was exceptionally studious and would rather sit in the library studying than exploring with me in the bushland and creeks as Wills did. While at the Museum one day, my associate, Entomologist and Taxonomist, John Evans, and I discussed the upcoming mineral survey and Luke's name came up on a list of possible assistants. I'm not one to make friends too quickly, but I already knew this lad, as did my friend John. Long story short, the three of us, with John's lovely new wife Colleen, who, by the way, is a brilliant cook. We did another leg of my long-drawn-out mineral survey for the government. There are more areas to investigate, but they may have to be left to someone else." He chuckled. "I'm getting off the track. Luke taught an old dog like me many new tricks. Who knew ducks and scrub turkeys could be cooked in balls of mud? Colleen taught me that camp cooking was not just beans and damper. Harry and Wills, I believe you taught him about emu egg, French bread made from damper? Am I correct? Yes, it was also delicious. However, I was introduced to something delicious called 'Doughboys and Cockies Joy' by Colleen. Now, my friends, if you have not tried this delicacy, you must. I think it would be delicious with clotted cream. Ask me about it later. Again, I digress."

Chuckles, guffaws, and belly laughs rippled through the crowd.

William continued with his story. He brushed his nose before continuing. Luke could see that William was nervous. "Luke, as a travelling partner on a scientific expedition, was wonderful. His skills with the pen were lightning speed. His ability to capture a mineral formation, a headland, an outcrop and a creek was astounding. His journal entries are exceptional. However, it was his ability to sniff out forms and ways of posting letters to his sweetheart that endeared me most; from chasing a dust cloud on the horizon, to even offering to carry homing pigeons. Ellen, you were never forgotten, even for a day, for he would not sleep at night without penning some part of a letter to you. I had no idea that mail could be sent in so many forms. I estimate over fifty letters were posted in an eight-month period. At least, it seems he found some means about every four days. I'm guessing that not all have arrived."

"Fifty-three have already," Ellen voiced with a chuckle. "I replied to each and was unable to post any of them, as you had no direction, so he has a lot of reading to catch up on."

Laughs rippled through the listeners.

Luke was standing with his arm around her; she had not been more than an arm's length away from him all evening. He bent and kissed her neck.

William's chuckle was followed by, "Hmm, I surmised that." He continued. "Well, on our return here, I thought Luke would be on the next ferry to Parramatta, but his young lady here had beaten him to it. She had dragged her parents to the metropolis and intended to stay until he arrived. I might add that Luke had notified her of his pending arrival from Brisbane, so the wait was not too long. Sure enough, she was almost on the dock awaiting him. The joyous reunion was, shall I say, of an ardent nature. One would presume they did like one another and that it was most definitely not an arranged union," He chuckled as did the listening crowd.

William sighed lovingly and turned his attention to his beloved wife. "The other joy awaiting me on the dock was my own beloved Maria and our family. Having now been educated, they too have returned. Of this event, I am most joyful," he blew a kiss to Maria. "Ohh, I'll be in trouble for that later," he smiled and looked embarrassed.

Another ripple of giggling and laughter floated through the listeners. Maria joined them and nodded.

He continued, somewhat abashed. "I wanted to say a big thank you to Luke. His work on this survey. It will not go unacknowledged by me, although I know that in future years we shall be but a footnote in some journal somewhere. Something like 'he travelled with two assistants'. Sadly,

Science is like that. Our finds are astounding; the recording of such will be far-reaching for many years to come. Ed, we discovered some iron deposits, so your boundary may yet be a possibility."

William called Luke over. "Can I tell them about your new job?"

"Yes, sir, of course," Luke said.

Taking a deep breath, William said, "What I would like to announce tonight is that Luke is taking over my teaching position at The King's School. Sadly, he starts teaching on Wednesday, so he will not get a long honeymoon. Our time together on our trek has taught us both much. Luke will be able to teach with hands-on experience; many teachers, however, do not gain this knowledge. They teach from books, having never seen the real thing. If you teach a child to love learning, you have taught them all they *need* to know. The rest will follow. Help them understand *why* they should learn something, and the job is all but done. Luke, I congratulate you. I am proud to be part of your extended family, even if very distantly related by our nieces' marriage to your distant cousins. I, no…" He glanced at his wife, "…*we* claim you all. Luke, it's an honour knowing you. I hope I shall be asked as a guest teacher should the need arise." William bowed to Luke. "Now I propose a toast in two parts. To his wife, Ellen, may they work well together for the benefit of all, and to Luke and his new job."

Everyone cheered and drank deeply to the toast.

Wills and Luke lifted their mentor down from the makeshift stage on the cart.

Charles and Bill both gave speeches.

The time for their departure was drawing near, but the groom had yet to reply.

Luke cleared his throat, and silence fell again. His speech was short. "Some time ago, I prayed that the Lord would hear my pleas. He did, after a long and twisted saga. Ellen and I became engaged on the very day before I left on our expedition. We arranged our wedding the day afterwards. Then we were separated as the four of us departed for eight months. Thus, there are over sixty letters. I tried to complete one at least every few days. Thus, having one ready to dispatch should the opportunity arise. Which, thankfully, it did often!" He turned his attention to Ellen. "Never a day passed without my thoughts of you diverting or sustaining me in some way. My return to you could not be soon enough. Now I am here; you shall get very sick of me. From now on, wherever we go, we go together." Luke turned to everyone and said, "I propose a toast to my beautiful and blushing bride. Ellen, my love, my heart. I am forever yours."

Luke lifted her up on the cart with him. He crushed her to him, enveloping her in loving arms and covering her with kisses. His kisses were ardent and passionate. There were ooohs and aaahs emanating from the watching audience.

When he finally let her go, she nearly fell, as she was light-headed.

"Oh, Lukie." She rested her head on his chest and looked at him dreamily.

With the speeches complete, the bridal couple, along with many of the family, escorted the departing guests to the ferry.

The ferry captain had joined them for a short time and walked with them. The Clarkes and Hamish joined them as their children awaited. The jovial group of Luke's university friends could be heard shouting and singing as the ferry slid around the river's bend.

Hamish had refused to stay longer; he seemed eager to return. As so much was happening due to the wedding, no one questioned him. He left with a bounce in his step and a smile.

Douglas and Caroline were to have joined him, but with a new grandson to attend to, they were to stay with Colleen and John.

Hamish took a note back for the museum explaining John's absence. It also gave John time to get to know Finn and Maureen.

By five o'clock, the sun was setting.

Luke and Ellen were ready to depart. The majority of the older guests had retired either inside or gone home in the chill evening.

The young ones were starting to dance. The fiddlers were on the cart and taking turns to keep the party moving. Dancing was the only activity to keep everyone warm.

A bonfire was stoked again in the middle of the courtyard.

Luke and Ellen had hoped to slink away to their cottage, but this was not to be. His three brothers and Harry kidnapped them.

They carried the bridal couple on their shoulders to the cottage. They deposited the newlyweds at the gate.

Luke opened the door and carried Ellen inside, kicking the door shut behind them. He then locked it, just in case.

Ellen giggled. She clung to him as he took her into their bedroom and gently placed her on her feet.

"My wife, I do like the sound of that. So very much," Luke said against her lips.

"You had better like it, Lukie, because I'm not letting you go again. I've waited long enough for you," she giggled naughtily.

Luke kissed her passionately, then, holding her at arm's length, said, "Before we head to bed, though, darling one, I would like to say a quick prayer of thanks together. I want to hold you, sweetheart, so very close, so I will cuddle you while we pray."

They stood clasped in each other's arms and prayed. Dedicating their lives and marriage to God. He bent his head and said in unison, "Amen."

Kissing her on the top of her head. "Elle, Belle, you must admit, they do sound similar," he murmured.

"Yes, but you could have asked." She had, by now, undone his cravat and thrown it on the floor, and was working on his vest. "I'm holding you to a promise you made me last week in Sydney. Something about 'body changes' if I remember correctly." She divested him of his shirt.

He was preoccupied with the fastenings on the back of her gown as she was with his shirt. He couldn't see what he was doing. Minutes later, both items joined the trail of rapidly discarded raiments that reached from the door to the bed.

When Luke reached the gossamer-thin lawn undergarments, he gasped at her form. He lifted her onto the bed; he was only in his linen drawers, and they hid nothing of the very changes she mentioned.

Little of her was left to his imagination. She lay back on the bed with her arms thrown high above her head and let him admire his new view. A groan of desire emanated from deep within him. "Oh, Elle, you are so magnificent. I cannot believe you are mine, all mine. I have dreamt of you, and this, and well, us, for years. I was so angry I could never have you." He ran his hand gently over her stomach and under the lawn camisole. His fingers felt the warmth of her skin against his. His hand shook as he eased apart the ribbons holding the transparent fabric closed. It fell open. He could no longer just look; he touched. He removed his final garment. After gently removing her final wisps of fabric, he took her in his arms and made her his.

Their initial coupling was brief and somewhat painful for her as they both knew it would be. However, the evening was long and loving, as was each time together. They fell asleep in each other's arms, their desire temporarily sated.

In the evenings, there was a knock on the door, and Sal delivered two hot meals.

Luke threw on a dressing gown and answered the door. He thanked his mother and took them, smiling.

Then she whispered, "All good?"

Luke nodded and gave her a big, dimpled grin.

She blew him a kiss and left them alone.

The newlyweds ate at the kitchen bench, put on the kettle to make tea, then washed the dishes and went to the sitting room. The fire in there had not been lit but was set.

Luke struck the tinder box and lit it; he sat watching the flames while Ellen finished tidying the kitchen.

When she joined him, he pulled her onto his lap when she walked in. He was intending just to cuddle her, but she had other ideas. She straddled him, pulling her dressing gown around them both and settled herself comfortably on him.

Luke remembered his father's conversation about making things fun. "Oh, now this is nice." From this angle, they were on eye level, and he was free to touch and kiss her. "Oh, Elle, I didn't know marriage was this good."

How they ended up on the floor, neither remembered, but they woke some hours later when the fire had started to die down.

She woke with his fingers gently moving a strand of hair from her face. The flickering flames were dancing across her hair. She reached out and drew him back down to her.

~

Outside, the ice freezing on the water tub finally drew the party to a close about an hour after midnight.

The remaining young folk had been standing around the bonfire in the middle of the courtyard. They ran out of wood, and the fire died quickly.

Over in Eddie's house, *Bramblemere Close*, a tiny voice woke his parents in the middle of the night. Their fire had also died down, and the room was cool. The baby had kicked off his blankets and was cold. He was ready for a feed, so John rose, changed his son carefully and brought him to Colleen to feed. He stoked the fire and checked his watch, four o'clock. No wonder new parents looked tired. On his return from the party, he had told Colleen of Hamish's new name for the babe. "Do you know Hamish has given him a name? It's Jonty. Apparently, it means 'Little John'. I like it, love."

"So do I, sweeting. I like Jonty." She stroked his cheek and woke the babe to keep him feeding.

John waited until Colly had finished, burped the little chap and returned him to his bed. He wrapped him a little tighter and placed him back into his crib. He crawled back into his nice warm bed, took Colleen in his arms, and they went back to sleep. "I think our sleep will become precious, love," he whispered into her hair.

Chapter 16   Teaching

*S*unday morning came way too early for the young ones who had
stayed up until late or early in reality.

Charlie's youngest two children, Emily and Molly Grace, decided to
fight at dawn. As they had been put to bed at dusk, they were well-rested.

The screams of the small children woke Ricky and Will. They had
managed to sleep through the dawn chorus and the early morning rooster
call; they were used to hearing those, even in Sydney, but the howl of small
children was new to their ears. Both sat bolt upright in their beds,
wondering what on earth had occurred. They were lucky or unlucky enough
to stay in Charlie's house, *Willow Grove*.

They discovered that Wills had built it for his older brother as a
thank you for taking care of him whilst his parents travelled. It was a more
modern version of Eddie's beautiful home, but with a double-storey bay
window at the front. It was built with indoor bathroom facilities and every
possible modern convenience that was available. There were ten bedrooms,
and their room overlooked the river. Phil, Stevie, and their nine children
occupied many of the other rooms. Ricky was awake enough to voice a
comment. "Will, if we do take on these new children's homes, I will not be
living in." He flopped back on his pillow.

Will groaned, "Me neither, Rick. Are children always this noisy, or is
it just that my head is spinning?" Will clutched his aching temples. "Is
yours?"

"Yes, mine certainly is. What was in that stuff? I thought the cider
was too potent. I stayed away from the ale and the rum, and stuck to the
ginger beer. Bad choice, should have just had the cider." Ricky held his head
and groaned.

"What time is church, Rick?" Will really did not want to move; he could see the sun was already up.

"Some unearthly hour, like seven o'clock or some such. What time is it?" Ricky asked his friend.

"Cor Rick, it's six already. We'd better get up." Will was far more alert than Ricky. "Come on, sleepyhead."

With regret, Ricky finally managed to sit up again and swing his legs out of the nice warm bed. "I'll never drink again, Will. Horrible feeling! I've never been drunk, not fully drunk. I didn't think I was last night. No, I mean this morning. Oohhh! My head," he groaned, clutching at his pounding appendage.

The two men made it down to breakfast.

Gracie had a large pot of cracked barley porridge, huge pots of clotted cream and jugs of freshly juiced oranges. They were just the thing for the morning. Only the children were at all boisterous, and Gracie sent them outside to eat on the verandah.

"Oh, bliss," said Ricky quietly.

"Oh, Mrs Lockley, sorry, Viscountess Lockley, this is delicious. Is this barley porridge?" Will asked.

"Will, if you call me that, I'll have to call you Mr English. I'm Gracie, nothing more, nothing less," she said breezily. "And to answer your question, yes, it is."

Will grinned and nodded a little too quickly for his head. They all ate their breakfast in silence and then slowly walked up to the church. Many of the younger adults were in similar condition. On the way to church, Ricky heard Charlie say to Eddie, "Cor Ed, Dar's ginger beer has a roaring kick to it. He must have been brewing that for some time."

"It's the batch he made before he went to England. He just bottled it. I stuck to my cider. Got a bad head, eh?" Eddie answered. He'd turned and looked at Ricky, Will, Phil, and Stevie. "Did they all drink it too?"

Ricky gingerly nodded, "Yeah, and we sat talking way too long, so add tiredness to that too. Thought we were safe with simple ginger beer, not so." The service was a trial. The choir voices set off the heads of the suffering men. Each noticed the wincing of the others' faces.

By the time the one-hour service was finished, the younger folk were somewhat recovered.

They all meandered back to the *Willow Grove* and prepared to catch the afternoon ferry. Expecting it would leave at one o'clock, they were surprised to find that there was only one afternoon ferry departing that day at four o'clock.

They packed their bags and placed them on the verandah, ready to grab them later. The Evans boys and their families did the same, then all had been invited to Eddie's for luncheon.

Cara and her daughters had done their magic in the kitchen. It was all hands on deck, with over fifty expected for luncheon. Once again there were mountains of food.

It was a beautiful day, so long tables had been set up in the back yard. Ricky and Will were seconded to help with seating. Big hessian bags of feed grain or logs were the easiest to place. There was always plenty of these. They laid them in an open square. They were then covered with calico or old sheets. Trestle tables were set up and covered with more sheets.

Paddy made some bench seats from planks mounted on log bases. A section of the garden had previously been fenced off for the numerous children who often descended on the house. The log seating faced this area. The youngsters were herded into this area, with the older children instructed to watch over the little ones.

Eddie softly issued the order of no squealing.

Ricky lost count at thirty-two children under about fourteen. They just kept coming. Most were fair-haired with blue eyes. He had no hope of telling them apart. He noticed that Charlie and the other men were still talking noticeably quieter, well away from the children. Ricky found his head had nearly returned to normal, as had Will's. Even the bright sunshine no longer hurt his eyes. They both thought that rather than sitting alone, they would make themselves useful. They offered to assist with various jobs, and Cara soon had Ricky carrying platters of food out to the tables, and due to Will's injured leg, his job was to keep the flies off it and serve the punch.

The afternoon passed quickly, with many stopping to chat with them.

At three o'clock, the group started to prepare to leave. Farewells were said and Cara handed Ricky and Will a picnic pack, each with enough food in it for some time. She then offered more to Stevie and Phil; they said, "No thanks," so she handed their share to Ricky, too. "Give this to someone if you can't use it."

Paddy appeared with an empty wooden crate, and she loaded in their picnic packs and added even more food until it was overfilled.

Ricky knew that there were some pasties and small pies in it as he'd seen them being packed. He was already hungry. It took both of them to carry it. They would return home, laden. They collected their bags as they passed the verandah of the *Jolly Sailor Inn* and slung them over one shoulder and walked from the verandah down the hill to await the ferry.

Stevie, Phil, as well as their wives and children, joined them. They and their friends and the children would eat like kings for the next week. This was an extraordinary gift. The box seemed amazingly full. Neither was prepared to peek inside to see what else there was. Neither had ever had a gift that they could remember. They were astounded at the generosity of these people and the joy this would bring to so many.

~

For the newlyweds, Wednesday came all too fast. For the next two days, they did not plan to dress. Only moving from the bed to eat, drink, use the privy, or light and stoke the fires. Cara had stocked the kitchen well. When they did leave the cottage, it was before anyone else was up.

Luke and Ellen had emerged to go for a walk on Monday. They didn't go far. Just up to Ellen's parents to get her some clothing. She had two empty carpet bags and planned to gather the remainder of her clothing and personal belongings. They filled the bags, and Luke had them slung over his shoulder with a few more items resting on his arm. She had a few trinkets in her hands; they snuck out of the house without meeting anyone.

Molly had seen them arrive and made herself scarce. She could tell that they didn't wish to socialise with anyone. One of the things Ellen had to collect was her personal bundle. She was due for her menses the following week. She had talked about this to Luke when she said she needed to get some things from home. She hoped that she might not even need them. Only time would tell. They had undoubtedly given nature enough chance to conceive a child.

Luke was due at school in less than forty-eight hours. There was not much he could do to prepare, as he had no idea what years he would be teaching or even if Mr Armitage had changed the syllabus. He had to sort out a syllabus and a lesson outline of some description. Reverend Clarke had given him all his teaching notes, but until he met Mr Armitage again on Wednesday, these weren't much use either. Luke spent as much time as possible in various pleasurable activities with his new wife.

He walked into his first-class nine days after the wedding as the school was two weeks late in starting the second term. It was because of the entire reorganisation of the school by Mr Armitage that the term start was delayed.

Once Mr Armitage had met with him, Luke only had a week to prepare. Luke had heaved a sigh of relief.

There were seventy-three students with more due to enrol the following year. Luke found that fees for each day student were £4 per annum, and boarders paid anywhere from £8 to £25, depending on where they boarded. He presumed that the more expensive ones had better access to facilities. When he was there as a student, there were only about six students in each year. Now there were up to double that. Most boys were in the senior years, and from King's, they were now able to go directly to the university from school. Luke's first class was a senior geography one. When they discovered he'd only finished university the year before, they pumped him for information as many hoped to attend themselves.

At thirty-three, Luke didn't feel much older than the boys were. He used this initial class to get to know his students better. He remembered something William had told him as they were travelling north. "Luke, to be able to teach, you must teach the students why they need to learn. If you can only teach them that, you have succeeded. You have to start with their personal knowledge, interests and experience and work from there. Identify that in each student." An idea had come to him while travelling; a mineral sample board, and he had collected many samples along his journey for this purpose. He had finally had a chance to build it. He and Ellen had some fun drawing ideas until they came across the best design.

On the second teaching day, Luke arrived at school with a big wooden crate and a large board. No matter what class he was teaching, the trip had taught him one thing. Hands-on touching will beat a textbook any day. His box was full of his specifically collected rock and fossils samples from his trip. Each a unique teaching tool. He'd collected the three main types of rock, sedimentary rocks in various forms, metamorphic, and igneous. Paddy had helped him make the actual back board that he and Ellen had designed. The only difference with this particular board, and the one he'd seen at university, was that the specimens were not attached. Each of his classes had to study each of the numerous specimens and work out how they were formed. As there were excess specimens to places on the board, it wasn't as easy as it looked. He also added duplicates of sandstone, shale, schists, basalts, and granites in various colours and formation. This idea had been born from Luke's own lessons with Reverend Clarke when he was in his classes at The King's School. He sometimes still got some of the granites, and basalts confused. He decided to also make other boards with eras of rocks. Another one with different semi-precious gems. He also had ideas about drawing all sorts of charts. He had found it hard when a child to learn the difference between pinnacles, mesas, and buttes; a lake and a lagoon and other similar geographical formations. With the younger students, he turned these into games; with the older ones, tests. Each worked well.

By the end of the week, the students were all entering into the fun of learning. They had expected lectures as from most teachers. His lessons were very different. With the younger students, he also instigated a star and reward system. If they could each recite the chosen formations, the main rivers down the coast or whatever they had been set to learn, each student was given a star. Three stars earned either a humbug or a bullseye boiled lolly. He had also been able to buy some caramel toffees occasionally, and these rewards were kept for class tests. As these were a real treat, his classes became popular. It also kept the noisy ones quiet.

Luke used a different system with the older boys, but their little brothers told them what they were getting, and they complained. So soon, they too earned sweets. Spelling tests also were rewarded with stars and sweets, right up to the students' in the final year.

Ellen laughed and called it bribery.

Luke nodded. He agreed, but it worked a treat. He still liked lollies himself, so why not the students? Each week he would choose a student from each class to do some research, in whatever format they chose, which included time in the library or just talking to someone, from a sailor to a convict. They would have to tie it into the set Geography or Science theme somehow.

The more eclectic and eccentric the results, the more interesting they were for the class. It was great fun for everyone, including the teacher. Each week, he would guide the subject back to what they were supposed to be learning. His sketch of a syllabus fitted this new system of learning.

Reverend Clarke came and delivered a lecture to the entire senior school during the third week of term. He brought Maria for the night, and she joined Sal at the Orphanage School for reading time. The orphanage had moved next to the Female Factory, and the Catholic nuns now ran it. The old building sat empty. Maria had found a friend in Sal. Now every time William visited the area, she would accompany him. They were rarely seen apart. Maria looked happy and pleased to be at home. William's role as Commissary to the Bishop was expanding and giving her some kudos amongst her peers. William found that she was more interested in being with him than he expected. This in itself delighted him.

William liaised with Luke about what his lesson schedule was. They had already worked out a year's lesson plan on their trip. William's notes and his old class notes were now invaluable for Luke.

One of the other ideas that William suggested to Luke was creating small models for class, better still, having the students make them, from a volcano to a waterfall and showing the students how things worked. Each grade was creating a model. These, too, were popular.

Luke and Mr Armitage decided to have an entire school competition for 'A scale model of the Parramatta'. It must include the harbour area, river, and some of the more important buildings. Each class had one month to complete it. The only requirement is that it must be a geographical model and include a scale.

Mr Lock, the headmaster of the new Ladies' School, decided to have the female students also make a model as an informal competition entrant. Mr Lock suggested to Mr Armitage that they open the competition to other schools in town.

Luke took on the challenge.

Jenna, Ellen, and Sal decided they'd also enter the competition and get the girls at the orphanage to enter one. They ended up with two, one by the older girls and one by the little ones.

By the end of September, the models were nearly completed. Each of the now ten models was brought to The King's School for judging. The Governor, who happened to be in town, heard about the competition. He decided he would choose the winner. Mr Moffatt had been going to be the judge of the competition but willingly stepped aside in the spirit of fairness, as he was a known friend of Luke's family.

Came the day of the judging, Governor-General Denison arrived, and Lady Denison accompanied him.

William arrived with Maria. Mr Armitage had assembled as many dignitaries as possible. Charles and Sal dressed in their finery, as did Charlie and Gracie. The family all came too, including Harry and Vicky.

Luke was proud that a simple school project could inspire such enthusiasm. It had turned into a colossal fete and gala day, too, fundraising for the poor. It wasn't often that the Governor-General and Lady Denison visited the schools. The ladies' craft group set up craft stalls. The Church of England Ladies Guild had a cake stall. The Catholic ladies had a preserves stall. This was rivalled by a *Kitty's Kitchen* stall run by Guy and Martha Manning out at Orchard Hills. Proceeds from this were to be given to St John's church. A few enterprising shopkeepers had also set up stalls of their wares. Maryanne and Robert set up a tea stall with fresh scones, homemade jams, and clotted cream.

The September day dawned fine and crisp. Everyone was excited that the Governor and his Lady were coming, so care was taken in everyone's presentation. The students of the visiting schools were lined up at the King's School entry gates. They processed in a very orderly manner, taking their model into the largest classroom. Around the room were ten models from seven different schools or institutions. Assorted ages had obviously done them. Some were primitive, and some almost professional. Each model was easily identifiable at what the area looked like.

Once all the students had placed them down and then repaired any damage to their work, the room was emptied. There were no labels on who had made which one. The ten entries had been placed in the room; Mr Armitage had sorted them with the five marked as junior on one side of the classroom and the five senior ones on the other side.

The Governor-General and Lady Denison were escorted into the room by Charles and Mr Moffatt. The four judges surveyed the models. They eliminated four, two from each age group. Then Charles and Harry Moffatt left the Denisons to make the final decision.

The work was excellent; one in particular stood out. The scale, checked and proven accurate, had a superb definition. This senior entry had been painted in bright watercolours. Also, one of the junior ones was outstanding. These two models were given the first prizes. Two others in each group were given commendation awards and marked with either 'first runner up' or 'second runner up.' The reason for this would later become apparent.

A selection of five students from each class was brought into the classroom. When they were told to stand next to their work, they stood in silence.

Their teachers and judges were in the room awaiting them. Luke watched the faces of his third year class. The five fifteen-year-olds from Luke's younger King's class, including Neddie Lockley, had beaten the senior classes. They had won first prize. No less surprising was the winner of the junior model. Their effort was excellent. They, too, stood proudly at their work. The junior children at the Orphanage school had done it.

"Children, I wish to congratulate you all." The Governor addressed the hushed children. "The overall winning entry will be installed in the library in Sydney. The first runner-up in the senior category will be taken to the Police Barracks here in town. The winning junior model will be installed in the Post Office here, and the first runner-up junior model will be taken to the Library, again here in Parramatta and kept on permanent display there. Congratulations, children, you have all done brilliantly."

They were presented with calligraphed certificates. These were to be framed and then hung in their classrooms.

As the Governor made his announcement, the children of the four winning entries gasped. "We may also install one at Government House." The Governor looked at the second runner-up in the senior category and said, "Yes, this will be adequate." He discussed the transportation of the models.

They decided to participate in a community display at the library for a week, after which they would be transported to their various destinations.

He stood looking at them, then said, "And the second runner-up of the juniors is good enough for Hyde Park Barracks." The Governor then came over and congratulated Luke.

Mr Armitage had pointed him out and explained that this was his first term teaching. He realised they had met before and said on arrival at his side, "Trust a Lockley to have thought this up, good on you, Luke. I had no idea your nephew was on the winning team. I gather your time spent with Clarke was as useful as you thought?"

"Yes, sir, it certainly was." Luke was surprised that he should remember him.

The models were open for public exhibition after judging.

William and Maria Clarke arrived for a look. He sought out Luke. He was amazed at what he saw. Here was a lad inspiring students in a way he'd never thought of before. "Luke, when I suggested models, I never thought of something like this. What a wonderful idea!"

Wills and Cathy, with their brood, arrived from Emu Plains to view the work. They tied the journey to Parramatta with a work trip. Wills was in the process of rebuilding the small private staging post near Rooty Hill so he, or any of the family, could change horses there and make the Emu to Parramatta trip in five hours with a team of four. Wills was actually in discussions with Harry about enlarging it and turning it into a small but proper coaching inn, with food available and a place to change horses. Harry and Jim already had a team of horses there.

Luke and Ellen greeted him warmly, and Wills' children were vying for Luke's attention.

Luke soon had the youngest twins in his arms. Rick and Bette were nearly one. The two imps were adored by anyone who picked them up together. The last time Luke had seen them for any length of time was the week they were born.

Luke was surprised to see Harry, Vicky and their children come in with Wills and Cathy. With two small children already in his arms, he greeted them warmly but could not shake Harry's hand. Vicky was looking well in her advanced condition. Luke bent and kissed her cheek.

"Some of Colleen's brothers are minding the store. I saw your face, wondering how we were here." Harry chuckled, "Luke, congratulations." He exclaimed, "What a coup!"

"I didn't plan it this way, Harry. I was only trying to interest the children in learning. It started with just one class, then another, and soon the entire school. A few other schools heard about it, and they joined in, too. Mr Moffatt was to judge, but then he heard the Governor-General was coming. From there, it grew its own legs. Lady Denison heard about it, and she wanted to come too. Well, that brought in the rest, hence the fete. It sort of blew up into, well, this." He waved his hand over all the models.

The toddlers were wiggling to get down. Harry reached over and removed little Rick from his arms. The little boy sighed. Knowing all hope of release was now impossible, he wrapped his arm around 'Unca Harry's' neck, and with thumb in his mouth, he snuggled into his neck.

Bette, now content she had her other uncle's full attention, did likewise. She snuggled down on his neck and fell asleep.

All other lessons were abandoned for the day. The children had learnt more in making these models than they would learn in a month of class lessons. Luke stood, watching the crowd filing past the models.

Harry was standing, gazing at one of the rejected ones. "Hey, Luke, what's happening to these ones?"

"No idea, Harry. Why?"

"I have an idea. These two are of a much wider scale. They probably didn't get as much notice, but look, they go out to the foot of the mountains. They would be great to have at the Emporiums, one here and one at Emu. They actually show the road west really well."

Luke stood, peering at them; he had not noticed the difference in scale of these two models; one was by the oldest boys. All of the models were outstanding. The two that had been eliminated from the competition didn't conform to the rules. It was only supposed to be Parramatta. Luke had initially thought the details were wrong, but he'd not looked at them very hard. "Oh, Harry, you're right. These are a much wider area. No wonder they look different." Luke walked off and asked Mr Armitage what they were going to do with the non-winning models.

"Thrown out, I suppose. Why, Luke?" Mr Armitage said. Not much interested.

Luke explained, and the headmaster's brows lifted.

"I think they'd love that." Mr Armitage walked back to the two rejected models. "By Jove, you're correct. They are on a different scale from the others. They are excellent, but that will teach the boys to listen, won't it? They were rejected as they did not follow the model guidelines you gave. 'A scale model of Parramatta'. They didn't do that."

Charles and Eddie joined them at his desk. "Good job, Luke," his father said to him.

Harry and Eddie stood behind them. Luke could hear Harry discussing them with Ed. "What a grand idea, Harry. Yes, we'll certainly find somewhere to put them at the Emporiums. Many people ask what the road west is like; this will be an excellent answer. Actually, that is something we can all sell. Maps. Why have we never thought of that before? Folded portable maps rather than rolled ones."

Wills and Charlie joined their brothers and father. "I wish I had had this sort of education, Luke. You make learning so darned interesting." Charlie said.

"We learnt from one of the best, Charlie," Wills added. "Lessons with Reverend Clarke were never boring, but wow, never this good. These students will never forget this."

"That's what started it. I was trying to get them interested." Luke said to Wills. "I'm thinking of a mapping competition next, cartography." Luke grinned with mischief in his eyes.

"Well, my boy, you've exceeded my expectations, Luke," a voice came from behind him.

Luke spun around. "Hello, William, so you're happy about this?" he asked his mentor.

Wills still could not get used to his little brother calling Reverend Clarke by his Christian name.

Reverend William's mouth twitched with excitement. "Happy? Why, lad, you have instilled more love of learning in your first six weeks than I did in a year." Reverend Clarke patted him on the shoulder. "I knew you were the right man for the job." He grinned and waggled his mouth again in the funny way he had when he was happy. His moustache and whiskers twitched too. "You've started something. I foresee an inter-school competition every year now. You're going to have a hard time topping this, though."

"Actually, I already have an idea, William. You inspired that, too. When at school, I wondered how you used to get your hands on Major Michell's maps so quickly. When I learned on our trip that he was an old school friend, it all fell into place. I was thinking about teaching the students some cartography. All will need to be hand water-coloured; some can be copies of old maps. Of course, we have all Major Mitchell's ones, but there is Tallis' 1851 map that you had. His maps are beautifully decorated; Hughes

'54 and I hear Karl Flemming is about to release one from his last year's trip. I'm sure there will be more, but this will be a start. From there, they can learn much. We may even interest some to do it professionally."

"Grand idea, I'm sure Thomas would have loved that. Pity he died last year. I'll ask Mary, though, I'm sure she has more unpublished ones. I've been in contact with her since our return," William replied. He checked wh was nearby before adding, "Be careful, though, Denison and Mitchell were not friends. I'd stick to the other maps if I were you, at least while Denison is here."

Luke had totally forgotten Bette, now asleep on his shoulder. She murmured against his neck and clung to a lock of his hair at the back of his neck. In her sleep, she pulled it. "Ouch!" Luke exclaimed softly.

Wills smirked, "She does that often. Watch out when she dribbles. She'll get you right down the front." As he spoke, she released a long flow of dribble. Wills was ready with a cloth and dived for it before it landed. He carefully removed her from his little brother's arms. Wills had her lying almost flat in his arms.

Ellen had been watching him from across the room. The look of loss on Luke's face made her smile. They had been married for seven weeks. The week they were married, she had her menses, but had missed the next one. That look on her husband's face made her smile. Hopefully, soon they would have one of their own. It really was too soon to tell him, but she wanted him to know it was possible.

On competition day, when he returned home from school, Ellen greeted him, closed the door and opened her arms. She congratulated him, enfolded him in her arms. Lifting her lips to his, she drew his head to hers. "Luke, love, would you like to have one of our own? I saw you with Bette today. I saw the look of loss on your face when Wills took her from you."

"Oh, sweets, she was adorable. I so love the feeling of a sleeping child in my arms. Something in my heart just melts." He returned her kisses. Then he lifted his head. One eyebrow raised. "Is there something you're trying to tell me?" he murmured into her ear.

"Well, answer me this, Mr Teacher. What do you get if you add one and one?" she asked coyly.

"Two love, why?" He stood holding her at arms' length. "Ohh! You mean? Are you, well, you know, um, expecting?"

"Um, yes and no, the answer is actually three," she had a huge smile on her face. "I think so. I'm pretty sure anyway, it's a bit early, but I missed this month. Though knowing your family, the answer may not be three, it could well be four." She laughed as he swung her around in excitement.

"Oh, my Elle, you could not have given me a better ending to a wonderful day." He crushed her to him, kissing her excitedly.

"Pity about the 'ending' bit. I was hoping for a 'rest' before we go to Ed's for dinner. We've all been invited to celebrate." She drew away from him and walked saucily to their bedroom.

Luke abandoned his briefcases. He dropped them and followed her. Sweeping her off her feet before she reached their room, he carried her in and gently placed her on their bed.

They laughed like the carefree young couple they were. Their love for each other gave them a freedom that neither had imagined marriage could possibly entail. They were lying on their bed. Ellen was dozing in his arms. Their clothing was in a state of disarray, their desires temporarily sated.

As Luke lay with her curled up in his arms, he was thinking about their future. Their new house was nearly ready for them to move into. He had delayed the move until the long midterm weekend; he also wanted some improvements completed before moving. An internal privy and adjoining bathing room were being built. He had not told her yet. The new bathing room was to feature checked black and white tiling on the floor, with bare white walls. It was to have a large bath on legs; over this was to be a frame where a bucket of warm water could be hoisted on a chain, wound up with a handle, so it wasn't heavy. The bucket had a lever where, when you pulled a rope, a flap lifted off the inside bottom of the bucket, and a spray of water came from above in a shower so you could wash off the soapy bathwater. It was a design he had been fiddling with for ages. The shower bucket would be filled from inside. There was also a pedestal sink with running water. Both would be drained outside into the garden, and the privy would empty into an outside cesspit. The overflow would water the citrus trees in the backyard. Water would come into the room from an elevated outside tank. He had read about these in university and had hoped one day to have one. Never in his wildest dreams did he ever think he'd be able to afford it in his first house. Nor that the house was the first one his parents had lived in when they first married. He had yet to refurbish their old apartment above the stables, but that could wait. The house had been built by Uncle Ned's friend Perry White in Lachlan Macquarie's days of governorship. It had been at that house that the shared Sunday meals had started. The large dining room table had once been central to the study group. When Perry and Katy returned home, his parents continued the tradition for Ned, providing not only a home-cooked meal for the soldier but also fellowship. It was over these meals and that same table that their friendship had deepened. The table was now in Eddie's dining room.

Luke had also read about new things where the effluent drained into a divided underground tank, meaning there would be little water table seepage. But that could wait for another day, as he knew of no one who could build it. The construction of this new room and the updating of the house would take another month. By October, it should be ready, and they planned to move in then. Both families had offered to help. However, they didn't need much as the house was almost entirely furnished. Perry had sold it with all their furniture, and the previous owner had left it all in situ, also selling the home furnished. It would make it a quick move, and it would almost certainly mean a party afterwards.

Luke absentmindedly stroked Ellen's cheek. With a child now on the way, things would have to be completed a little sooner, so Ellen would be inconvenienced as little as possible. He had hoped to be in the house for some weeks before Molly and Bill would join them. The house was so large that they would not be under each other's feet. The Millers would be downstairs in their own apartment. He had installed an internal staircase for them to their flat. He would enjoy having them with them, especially after the birth of the child, or children, as Ellen pointed out. He smiled at that thought. The other thing that had occurred to Luke is that it would be nice to source some help to work in the house.

Cara had made many friends amongst the Irish families that Uncle Ned had sponsored to come here. Some of the orphaned girls now worked with Cathy at *Roseneath*. Three were with Gracie at the inn. And there was always the possibility of asking Colleen if any of her siblings needed work.

Luke was sure that there might be one or two who might be interested in employment. He decided to ask Ellen before dinner that night. He lay looking down at her asleep; she was so beautiful. Her dark lashes were on her soft, downy cheeks, her hair soft against his chin. He could hold her forever and be utterly content. She was now his life; he had loved her for so long, and he thought he had lost her, but she had never wavered in her affection for him. She had waited, never looking elsewhere. She was Luke's and no one else's. He remembered her following them around when he would be off on some adventure with their brothers, Sam and Wills. Ellen would be dressed in Sam's old clothes and insisted on being included. She had been fearless. The three boys had protected her, Luke especially. Even then, he loved her.

Now they started each day with a morning prayer. Each evening, the last thing before turning out the lamp, they again would pray together. If Luke had to sit up and mark papers, she would insist on them saying prayers before she slept. Being newly married, they both had a very healthy appetite for each other's bodies. They both delighted in their frequent physical unions. She had no qualms about stating her desires for him, particularly recently.

He looked down at her again and, this time, met her eyes.

She reached up and brushed her fingers over his lips. "Lukie, have I told you today that I love you?" She whispered lovingly as she once more pulled him to her.

~

Over the next week, the students settled back into regular classes. The bar, however, had been raised. The other teachers tried to instil the love of learning in their students.

Luke himself had never liked studying Latin. He could see no point in it until the trip with William and John. They would spiel off Latin names, and he actually understood what they were talking about or why things were named so. A ladybird with big spots was called *macro-punctata,* one with small spots was called *micro-punctata.* Once, William was trying to describe the geographical landscape to him, and the words failed him. In his frustration, he used the Latin names, and all became clear to Luke. Only then did Luke understand the descriptiveness of Latin. This is what he needed to make the students understand: the interrelation of subjects.

In the staff room, one of the teachers turned to him and said, "You astound me, Luke. You have helped the boys understand that there is an interconnection between each subject they are learning. I often wondered the relevance of geography, but I heard you explaining the need to understand the rock formations if you need to build a dam. Only then could you work out by mathematical equation, the volume of water that it would hold."

Luke was embarrassed at the accolade, but suggested that they put up a syllabus board in the staff room, so the others could see who was teaching what and how they interlaced with each class. Each teacher added the broad subjects they planned to teach.

Even though one of the newest teachers on the staff, Luke's work at school became a delight.

He and Ellen worked on various plans and ideas; they pored through William's class notes from his teaching days. Luke made notations and updates.

William came and helped them get organised into a new teaching plan and worked out what they'd need to know for the upcoming exams. Maria and Ellen also worked on more hands-on ideas.

Luke also knew what was required for university. One or two of the older students required additional coaching to bring them up to standard. The senior students showed him respect. Even more than that, they gave respect to the other teachers now, too. This had previously been lacking. Luke was closer to their age, and he could understand them. He could growl them out in a way that a much older teacher would get their backs up.

Mr Armitage spoke to Bishop Barker and told him how impressed he was with his new teacher. The entire year of seniors was showing improvement in both academic achievement and behaviour. The day students now rarely skipped classes. If they were absent and no note appeared, Luke would be on their parents' doorstep that afternoon.

Chapter 17   Visitors

*L*uke and Ellen moved into the new house the first weekend in October.

Ellen was sick most mornings and often in the afternoons as well. She was always tired and always complaining that she was hungry.

Molly and Bill didn't like her alone in the big house, so they moved in a week later. Sam was now to run the inn with Belle. Bill would head up there occasionally.

While Luke and Ellen lived in the cottage, Sal had been close to them, but here she was alone through the day. They settled into their new apartment with glee. Molly and Ellen loved the inside privy. Bill and Molly had expected the move to be stressful, but it wasn't. The luxuries of their new apartment were astounding. Luke had added two bathrooms, one upstairs and one in the flat downstairs. Both of which had running water and a flushing privy, as well as a bath with a plug, so there were no hip baths to empty. Molly loved this. It was like staying in Sydney. They had learned very quickly to be a careful with the water in the privy as the cesspit overflowed once. They kept a bucket inside and used a jug to 'flush' the privy for wee's. Ellen soon discovered how often she now needed to use this facility.

~

In November, Luke arrived home from school to find a letter from Mr Lamb, the Sydney jeweller. He had finally been notified that the buyers from Antwerp were due in December. He said he would let Douglas and John Evans, know as well as William.

Luke had also built a safe into his house. His jar of gems currently sat in there alone. Once he had shown Ellen and the stones he locked them away and had nearly forgotten about them.

William, John, Colleen, and he had not discussed the gems since their trip to the jeweller with Douglas Evans.

~

The next note from the jeweller came on a scorching hot Thursday, on the second last day of the school term; Luke was due to finish classes for the year the following day. The students were sitting their final exams all that week. Luke had to mark them that night and return the papers on the last day. He was exhausted and looking forward to a long break. There were only twelve papers that needed to be done from the final exam. Classes finished at noon, and he only had to return their marks and yearly reports. If he could get them done, then they would try to catch the afternoon ferry.

He sat up until just before midnight; he had finished them. He put the pen down with a thump, thankful that ink had not splattered on any of them. He left them on his desk and crawled into bed.

Ellen greeted him with a quick kiss, and they both slept. They had prayed before she had gone to bed. She was up, packed and ready to go early the next morning.

Luke had planned to spend the week in Sydney anyway, so the timing was perfect. She was over most of the morning sickness stage of her interesting condition. It had lasted longer than she expected. As yet, her condition was not too obvious, so they decided to take an extended break as a delayed honeymoon.

If the sale of the gems went well, Luke would buy her anything she wanted; however, a new maternity wardrobe was first on the list. He also wanted to treat her to some plays, live performances, and other town entertainments. They would stay at Wills' house with Hamish.

~

William, Douglas, John, Luke and the four ladies met at Wills' house the morning after their arrival. Douglas had arranged for the buyers at Mr Lamb's shop at ten o'clock on Saturday morning. They rearranged the packets and bundles, making a list of what the jeweller had mentioned previously.

Douglas and William were to do the talking.

Colleen had opted out of the sales talks, happy with whatever John decided on for them. She stayed with four-month-old Jonty and the three other ladies.

Ellen was dressed in a loose-fitting tea-gown, and Caro guessed immediately. "Are you 'interesting', my dear?"

"Yes, Mrs Evans, four months," she whispered.

"Caro, please, dear."

They all quietly congratulated her.

"I am already too big for my gowns, so I feel we may have the family condition too."

They all looked puzzled.

"Twins," she said. "I shouldn't be showing this early. I haven't been excessively ill, but I'm wondering. Jenna said that she was very sick when she was having the twins. I'm so tired, and my emotions are all over the place. It's just as well Luke hasn't been home during the day. I go from laughing to tears in a matter of moments, poor mama. And I'm tired, did I say that? I've been falling asleep four or five times a day. I can't concentrate either." She gently put her hands on the bump. "Mama said I should start feeling 'flutters' at four months, but I've been feeling them for a few weeks. Luke said he can even feel them now. So I'm pretty sure there will be two."

"Oh," Caro and Maria said in unison.

Colleen was excited. "Oh, Ellen, this is wonderful news, I think. Isn't it?" The news was double-edged. A twin confinement was always far more dangerous.

"Yes, Colleen, it's wonderful news. We talked about the high possibility of twins before we married. Thankfully, many of the family members have had twins, so I have lots of experienced help. Jenna and Gracie live nearby, so that will be useful." Ellen explained they had now moved into their new house. "Oh, one blessing of the new house is that Luke has had a bathroom built, and we have an indoor flushing privy and a bathroom with running water. Oh, ladies, it's luxury."

Colleen giggled. "Ellen, I had nothing but bushes and waterholes during my months on the road. The leeches loved me, so I had to be very careful. But I grew up with only the river to wash in, so I'm used to it."

Ellen looked horrified, "Oh, Coll, that's horrible."

"I know that feeling, Colleen," admitted Maria. "It's part of the reason I returned to England for so long, but I missed my William so much; life on the road was too hard."

Caro swallowed. Douglas had never made her cope with the discomforts of living rough. She did, however, say, "I was alone far too often. Single parenting is not fun with three boys. Douglas was away for some time, a year. With Stevie, poor Doug didn't even know I was with child before he left, and when he returned a year later, I had a three-month-old baby. Just as well Stevie looks just like him." She smiled, remembering, "Thomas and Margaret came often, and then when the two extra boys came, Major Ned dropped in when he was in town. His friends, Majors Tim and Humphrey, helped greatly. The three majors would ensure any repairs were done were sorted without any fuss. Otherwise, it was just Effy and me. These men really don't understand what we have to go through."

Caro took her grandson from Colleen and bounced him on her lap. They were sitting in the newly refurbished Hyde Park and waiting for their men. "Thankfully, we no longer have to dodge cricket balls while sitting here. I'm glad they have moved the cricket pitch to the Domain."

Jonty was enjoying the unadulterated attention of four doting ladies. He was able to sit up now and could poke out his tongue if you did it to him and give a big smile when they grinned at him. He had them all giggling at his antics. They had over half an hour to wait until they saw their menfolk coming to them. All were anxious as to the outcome of the day; they waited. Knowing the result would have a drastic change in all their lives.

Luke and John hurried to them, leaving the older men to meander more leisurely.

Ellen opened her mouth to ask how it went.

He bent and gave her a quick kiss. "Don't ask. Not saying until the others arrive," Luke said breezily.

"Oh, meanie," she said with a chuckle. His face gave nothing away.

Douglas and William finally joined the small group.

John had taken his son and was throwing him in the air. Jonty was squealing with joy.

The ladies settled back down on the grass again.

William and Douglas finally arrived.

"If I get down there, I won't get up again," Douglas said.

"We'll help, Father," said John

"I'll stand, thanks," replied William.

So the ladies stood and joined their husbands. "Well? How did it go?" Colleen asked.

William took a deep breath. "Thanks to Douglas here, and his little pile of gems, they were none the wiser. They have bought many of the smaller ones outright. We made the decision not to trust them with the very large ones. If they really want them, and they do, they can come back with a cash price. They came hunting for gold and sapphires. Colleen, your big one is almost priceless. The other two large ones, mine and one we found panning, are a small fortune each, and the remainder, we're looking at over £10,000. It could take some time to sell them unless we can trust someone to take them over to Europe." William looked at Luke. "Err, Luke, His Grace isn't planning a trip out again, is he?"

"Not that I know of. Oh, that would be nice if he could take them. It would still take years, though," Luke said. "Oh, I've just had a thought. Uncle Ned did say he might come out for a while to 'sort out his children'. He's always joked that they need to see both sides of life. They are the same age as Ed and Jenna's children, so the two oldest have just turned fifteen." He thought for a bit. "They could come soon if they are going to come at all. That would be perfect. Ed and Jenna are taking the children over soon, in '58 or '59, I think, to be presented. I'll ask Dar when I return home."

Douglas said, "Go on, William, tell them how much you sold the whole lot for. You've only said a few of the diamonds." He had dropped his voice when he mentioned those particular gemstones.

"Oh, all right. We got another £3,300 for the sapphires. Some individual ones also sold, but they don't become part of the group price we share. By the time we've paid commission to the jeweller, we have £15,300 to share, three ways, that's £5,100 each."

Douglas butted in, "And, love, I sold the rest of our diamonds too, so we don't miss out either. We get £3,200 for our tiny parcel," Douglas told Caro.

Each of the ladies gasped.

John was watching Colleen's face as Luke was watching Ellen's.

Both turned into their husbands' arms. Ellen was stunned, and Colleen was sobbing.

John took her aside at some distance. He was speaking gently to her. "Colly, it's only money. Think of the good we can do with it. We can now help your parents and all of your siblings." The more he spoke, the worse her crying became. For a girl who had grown up in a dirt-floor slab hut, she was overwhelmed. John knew he only needed to hold her. So he did. Stroking her back while she cried.

After some minutes, she finally hiccuped and then giggled. "Oh, John, they were just little rocks that we found in the dirt." She looked up at him with her wet, starry eyes. "Why has God blessed us with that much money? What are we expected to do with it?" she asked, "They were just rocks, diamonds in the dirt, John."

"We will help others, love. That's what we'll do, and remember, Colly, this doesn't include your big one. That's yet to sell. I wasn't going to say anything in front of the other ladies, but when we showed it to the buyers, they estimated a value of over £25,000 for that one stone alone."

It's just as well he was holding her tightly, as she would have collapsed. "Whaaaat? How much?" she asked again.

"You heard love, and it's all yours." He bent and brushed his lips on hers. "Sweetheart, he said it will cut at least a fifteen-carat flawless D grade stone or even bigger. That's top grade. He has only ever seen one before, and it went into a Royal crown for the crown jewels. I can't remember which country he mentioned, as I was just stunned."

She stood staring at him. A single tear slid down her cheek. "Oh, John," she said and fell against his chest. "When I think of all those years with nothing, the money means we can, and will, help so many people, including my parents and siblings."

"I've never known someone like you, Colly. No wonder I love you so very much. It's no wonder everyone loves you. Barefoot with one old gown, and you still gave your only cape away. Yes, I heard about that. And yes, we'll be able to help many, many people, sweetheart. I think we'll start with Mrs Yates, though. What do you think? Ricky and Will said she could do with some help."

She looked at him. He understood her. Through her joyous tears, she nodded. "Could we really?"

"Sweetheart, do you remember the small dark blue sapphire? I sold that too. He paid £1,800 for that one stone." He ran his thumb caressingly over her cheekbone. "Darling, remember, we have to sell that monster of yours before we get the money. So we have to be a bit careful, but we'll help where we can. Mind you, we have the £6,000 from the first sales."

"John, once it sells, do you think we can buy the house from your parents? So that they can pay out the boys, but then they can live with us forever? I love them so much, and it would give us all a sense of security. But the boys and their families would not miss out either." She looked absurdly adorable. Pleading with him to make his own family happy, when it was her family who was so in need. Of the two, he knew which one was on the whole happier.

He again drew her to him, laughing. "Oh, Colly, whatever you want, my sweet. As a token of our trip, I have these made up for you." He handed her two small jewellery boxes.

She opened the first one, and it was the yellow sapphire ring.

John took it from the box and put it on her right hand. "Just to remind you, I love you. You are my sunshine."

She opened the second box. It was the blue topaz in a heart with diamonds. It was set in a double heart with a single diamond on top. Simple and stunning.

He removed it from the box and clasped it around her neck. It was a stone he had found, and Mr Lamb had cut and set it for her. "To remember our trip, love." He gave her a kiss, and they strolled back to the group. She was fingering it as they arrived.

Colleen reached for her son.

Jonty reached out for her and then for her new sparkly necklace.

As she took him from Douglas' arms, he asked, "Are you all right, pet?"

"Yes, thank you, Papa Doug, just overwhelmed. So very overwhelmed in fact. Before I married John, I had never owned a pound note; now this. I just can't absorb it." She looked at her thoughtful father-in-law. Her eyes were still red and a bit glassy.

"Oh, pet. Really? I think I understand now. You know you can talk to us any time you wish to." He patted her shoulder.

The new jewellery flashed in the sunshine. "Oh, Colleen, they are beautiful." She had almost forgotten it already. "John found the topaz, and Luke and I swapped the yellow for your green, Ellen." She knew Ellen knew about the stone as they had just been talking about it.

Jonty wrapped his tiny arm around her neck and snuggled into her. He held the new necklace clutched in his baby hand. It's just what she needed. She knew his and John's love was the most precious gift of all; it's all she needed, her child and her husband. Those two alone made her rich. The rest were just extra blessings, blessings of love.

Luke and Ellen, too, were stunned by the amount of money they would have access to immediately. Having seen Colleen's yellow sapphire as a ring, Luke decided to ask Mr Lamb to cut and set the green sapphire into a ring for Ellen. He was sure it would cut to just under five carat stone and would make a spectacular ring. Something she could wear while doing any rough outside work she wished to do, rather than her emerald one. She was in the habit of removing her emerald when washing or gardening. This is what she could wear when she did that.

They all walked back slowly to Wills's house.

Hamish greeted them with, "Kettle's on. Go sit ye selves doon an' I'll bring ye all in a cuppa."

In the privacy of the sitting room, they sat discussing the money. The men were to head back later that afternoon and complete the transaction. Mr De Jong and Mr Cohen, the buyers, needed to sort out access to the monies. They were to meet the foreign jewellers at the bank at one o'clock and transfer the cash for the gems whilst there.

The transaction was completed amicably and to the satisfaction of all involved. Four bank accounts became very healthy.

Douglas was ecstatic with his funds. However, once this money was gone, the house would have to be sold, as there was no more income. It should last them, but he would have to discuss their future with Caro. He also wanted to leave something for the three boys. However, he had no need to worry about that for some time. God would sort it out. Of that, he was sure.

~

Two days later, Luke took Ellen to the beach. She had never had much time in the town and never without her parents hovering near her. She had spent the time waiting for Luke's return, nervous and anxious. She was looking forward to seeing all the sights and experiences that the town could offer her. Luke would certainly know where to take her. He'd been nearly everywhere possible in the years he'd lived there. While killing time in the town for four years, he had discovered many bays and beaches that he now wished to show Ellen.

John had shown him many haunts that he would never have known about otherwise. They had found a tiny beach where they could scramble down the rocks and swim. There were actually two beautiful beaches on South Head: Lady Bay Beach and Lady Jane Beach. One had waves; the other didn't. They visited both, but decided to swim at Lady Bay Beach. Luke had taken a towel with them, and Ellen quickly slipped off the new maternity dress and put on her swimming smock while Luke held up the towel. It was so hot that sitting in the cool seawater was beautiful. Her smock clung to her wet figure and revealed her slowly growing bump and curves. "I'm only four months along, love I shouldn't have a bump yet."

Luke said she looked delightful.

"Oh, Lukie, I'm wet and bedraggled but delightfully cool." She had been lying in his arms while floating on her back. Her wet smock stuck to her curves. He pulled her up and out of the water.

She sighed. "At least I was until we left the water. Can we go and sit under that ledge in the shade?"

They wandered, dripping wet, to the rock shelf. Once under the small overhang, they realised it was totally secluded. He sat down and pulled her onto his lap. "How's that, my love?"

She giggled in reply, "Perfect." She leaned down and kissed him.

After some time in the shade, enjoying the privacy this area provided, they decided to head in for another swim. They were standing on the water's edge when a school of large fish started jumping every which way.

Luke pulled her out of the ankle-deep water. A large fin broke the surface about two feet in front of where they were standing. Further plans for a swim were abandoned. They decided to head back to the house and rest through the heat of the afternoon. He held up the towel while she changed again. They were soon on their way back to Wills' townhouse.

The curtains were pulled closed, and the occupants in the room were sitting in stunned silence.

Susanna, Dowager Duchess of Gracemere, was gone.

A black mourning wreath of laurel was placed on the front doors of the castle, and the knocker was wrapped. The clocks were stopped and set approximately at the time of her passing, and the castle fell quiet. Deathly quiet.

Madeline sat with the Duchess's body. Suze still lay in her bed, covered with a sheet. Someone would soon replace Madeline, and this would continue for all the hours until her funeral.

The Dowager Duchess would be dressed and laid out for burial in the Chapel Crypt next to her beloved husband Charles.

Ned knew she had everything ready; she had mentioned it to him only last week. He refused to discuss it with her, but he knew she was organised. He now sat in dazed silence. She told him to look in her journal. Everything he needed was in there.

The day before, she had been sitting on the floor playing with the nine-year-old twins. She was well and enjoying life. She loved living back at the castle and being part of the family.

The last words Ned said were, "I love you, Mother, I'm so glad you came back here to live." He had given her a big hug and a kiss as she left them for her bed.

Susanna had put her hand on her son's cheek and thanked him, saying again what she had said in Parramatta some years before. "I've not been so happy since you were born, my boy. I should never play favourites, but David was your father's, and the two little ones were 'spares'-you were always mine." She had told Ned how proud she was of him and all he had done. She kissed Christina and said that she was just as she imagined Sarah Joy to be. Now his mother was gone. She had fallen asleep in prayer and never awoke.

Madeline, her maid, had brought in her morning chocolate. The Dowager Duchess was lying on her side. Her hands, as though in prayer, under her chin. She looked as though still sleeping, but she was cold.

The maid had run to Ned. She knocked and just stood in tears.

Ned knew without her saying a word. He had donned his dressing gown before opening the door and followed her. He knew his beloved mother had gone as soon as he touched her. He fell to his knees, grief-stricken and unable to catch a full breath.

Christina had followed and stood beside him with her hand on his shoulder. She, too, was stunned and silent. She turned and sent the sobbing maid to, "Go get Dr Gerry."

Madeline nodded and left immediately.

Gerry came and pronounced her death.

Gerry's wife, Annabella, collected all the children. She took them to the orangery and explained what had occurred. They were to stay quiet and out of sight until they were called. She comforted them in their loss. She would be there for them to talk to. They were as close to Aunty Bell as their parents.

The rest of the morning was a nightmare.

The children fully understood their loss. Nana Suze was gone.

Two footmen were dispatched to notify Paul and Douglas. Both came immediately.

Two grooms were sent for the minister and solicitor.

All the staff were functioning on automatic. Many had red eyes. Jobs were done, food was prepared, but the laughter and conversation were absent. The castle was eerily silent. Death had come and taken their beloved dowager duchess.

Christina left Ned alone for an hour or so, then went to him. In the privacy of his office, he walked into her arms and broke. His deep sobs showed the depth of his grief. Christina was crushed in his strong arms. "She's gone, my love. She's gone. Yesterday, she was so alive. She'd had a beautiful day with the children." Ned had always been the tough soldier; nothing phased him. His mother's passing almost crushed him.

Christina had never seen him like this. She pulled him onto the settee and sat cradling him in her arms. He was hurting like a little boy. Soothingly, she said, "Oh, love, what a wonderful day she had yesterday. She never suffered a day of illness, and she went to sleep peacefully. She was two days shy of seventy-eight and enjoyed every single day."

Ned nodded; he sat up and rubbed his eyes. He had just blown his nose and wiped his eyes when his two brothers arrived. He bent and kissed Christina. "Thank you, my beloved. I needed to hear that." He sucked in a ragged breath. He drew another deep breath and became the strong Duke again. His eyes were still red, but his brothers would understand. They would also be hurting. They each greeted their older brother with a warm hug. They had adored their fun-loving but awe-inspiring mother; she had filled the role of Duchess to perfection. Paul and Douglas came to the door of Ned's office. Christina greeted each with a silent hug and a kiss, then left the three alone.

Two hours later, Jamison, the butler, ushered the solicitor in to join the three brothers..

The Dowager's private secretary, Colin Fraser, had also been informed and stood waiting. The week before, he had worded the Mourning Card and the Death Notice for the newspaper. Duchess Suze approved both with a tearful nod; all that needed to be added was the date. Then they had written a list of people to be notified, which she also approved. She added the Australian family to the list with her own hand.

Colin now had to let His Grace know that Her Grace knew she was unwell and refused to talk to anyone but Colin. Not even to Dr Gerry. Colin had been called in by Her Grace last week to write to Her Majesty. The Duchess had dictated a list of grandchildren and their cousins, and the years expected they were to be presented either at a Drawing Room or Levée. She had done everything that she could in preparation for them all. She knew now she would not be there, but she could undoubtedly prepare and ease their paths. She had even chosen the hymns she wished sung at her funeral. They were joyful ones of praise.

Colin had shed his tears then. "Oh, Your Grace," was all he'd been able to say. Had that really only been last week? It had been the longest week of his life since she had sworn him to secrecy. Now he had to admit all to the duke and his brothers. He took a deep breath before he walked into the Duke's office. The duke's own private secretary, Joseph Carpenter, was hard on his heels.

~

The following week was horrific, exhausting, and draining. The children were exceptional. Their way of coping was to help in any way they could. Aunty Bell's shoulder was often used. Each had adored the Dowager Duchess. To many of them, she was "Grandmama Suze;" to Gerry and Annabella's children, she was lovingly known as "The Great Aunt." She would say to them all, "I know I'm great. Just don't you forget it." They'd chuckle, then be wrapped in her loving arms.

~

Less than a month after the funeral, Ned left his brothers in charge and packed up the Castle. Gerry and Annabella were to come too. They were going to Australia. Ned was coming "home" to the family he needed to be with. He needed Gerry with him to make sure he would eventually come back. Ned needed to get away. He sent Colin to book passage on the first available ship.

The *Lady Hodgkinson* was leaving London on December 26. As it was so close to Christmas, the cabins were all still available. Colin booked them all. When in London, Colin had sent a note to Charles Lockley to say they were coming. It caught a cargo ship that was in the dock when he was booking their berths. He hoped it would arrive before they did. He had not told His Grace he had sent it until shortly before they left. It was short and hastily written.

> London Docks
> 6 December 1856

> *Christina's Cottage*
> *Philip Street Parramatta*
> Dear Charles,
> *The Major is coming with Dr Gerry and both families. Expect March on 'The Lady Hodgkinson'.*
> *Colin Fraser,*
> *Secretary*

Colin had seen a ship in port while booking the tickets. He took the opportunity and sent the note; he would have to deal with any consequences later. He knew the Earl would hate formality, so he kept his note brief and without titles. He insisted that he be on first-name terms with the main upper staff. Colin liked him.

The deed was done and could not be undone. Colin was leaving for a six-month break in Scotland with his family. Ned had guaranteed him a position on his return, but he, too, needed a break to mourn alone.

Ned told him to enjoy his time, and they would work out a job on his return. Reg Hawkins, Ned's estate manager, and Joseph had already decided that they really needed a secretary both in town and at the castle. So hopefully, Colin would take up this role.

Ned only did the work he needed to do. All his responses were automatic. His mind refused to concentrate.

Christina did what she could for him. Only time could heal now, time and prayer; she would be there with him every step.

Christina said farewell to her parents and brother. She told them that it would be about two years before they returned. She turned and waved a final goodbye, wondering if they would still be there when she returned.

Her father had taken the Duchess's death very hard. Her mother walked to the door with her to say goodbye. She stood waving farewell to her only daughter. Her husband came and stood beside her. "I envy Ned. I wish I could run away sometimes, too, my dear. I was so unfair to both you and her for so long. I judged her and shunned you. I'm so sorry, my dear," he said to her quietly. He waited until Christina's carriage was out of sight, walked into his office and shut the door. The Earl planned not to be seen again that night. He had never told his wife that he had offered for Susanna and been refused; he still loved her.

Suze, however, had told Catherine many years before, so Catherine understood that she loved Edmund, whatever the circumstances. However, she realised he had never recovered from the rejection by his first love and now seemed the right time to tell him what she knew, and that she had known for a long time. When he discovered their children had married, Edmund knew he could not escape meeting Suze any longer. At the Baptism of their grand-twins, they had finally sat down and had a talk. Only then did he admit his feelings for her. Suze had remained silent for some time, then finally confessed to him that she had never returned his feelings. Her heart had always been for her husband, Charles, the Duke. Now twice rejected, Edmund was still hurting.

As the carriage vanished from sight, Catherine turned and went to the office door. She walked in without knocking. She was greeted by the warm, welcoming arms of her tearful husband. She had lost a friend, he had lost a dream.

Christina's next visit was to her brother, Edmund Junior, and his wife, Catriona. Christina explained everything to him and said her farewells. Catriona and their children hugged her farewell.

Ed promised he would keep an eye on their father. He hugged his sister, and they had a prayer together before she departed.

His sister said, "I'll need your prayers, Edmund. Edward is not himself at the moment. He is just not coping. He missed nearly two decades with her, and now she's gone. I've not seen him like this. He has always been the strong one. Getting away will be the best thing for him; he needs Charles. We were planning to go next year anyway. So, yes, I will need those prayers, Edmund." She kissed her brother.

~

Somehow, they managed to get through the weeks before departure.

A very quiet Christmas was spent in the *Gracemere House* in London. Gifts were exchanged, but there was little joy. That afternoon, they boarded the ship and settled into the cabins. The next morning, the ropes were cast off at dawn, and the vessel was towed into the river.

The journey ahead would be both trying and healing. The first time they had made the trip together was sixteen years before. Ned's friend, Gerry, had met and married Annabella on board. Then, eleven years ago, Ned and Christina went 'home' with Charles and Sal. They had stayed for nearly two years then, and Suze had accompanied them with Charles's mother, Elle. Elle had stayed and remarried, but she had been gone for over a year now. Suze had spent the return trip entertaining the baby twins. The girls had been born in Parramatta and were now nine. Now they were returning to New South Wales. Christian and Ned had left all the staff at home, wanting no one but their family, their chosen family, around them. Time was what was now needed for Ned.

Annabella and Gerry took charge of all nine children on board. Not that they needed much care. Their daughter, Susanna, or Sanna, was the youngest of them all; she was only eight. She was best friends with her twin cousins, Charl and Izzy.

Colin had booked every suite and cabin available, so the families had plenty of room to spread out. The older children had taken over the reading room. It was the ship's library, but they set it up with chessboards, tapestry frames, and other assorted passive activities.

Chip, Sarah, Liam, Charl, and Izzy, the children of Edward or Ned, and Christina, were joined by their 'cousins' Bella, Neddie, Matthew, and Sanna. The relationship was very distant, but they claimed it. Annabella's brother Matthew had married Charles Lockley's sister Lilabet. It was just easier to say, cousins. They settled into their cabins.

The first week of the trip down the Thames River was cold and rough. Sleet and ice covered the ship most days. Everyone stayed indoors except Ned and Christina, who rugged up in fur overcoats or oilskins. They would be found in a little nook out of the force of the wind. Ned stood with his arms around Christina. He still looked haunted, although he was beginning to talk about his mother.

Christina encouraged him in this, and it was indeed helping. He related stories from his childhood that he had never mentioned before.

By the end of the first week at sea, they joined Gerry and Annabella in the sitting room cabin after the meal. It was New Year's Day. During the day, they had all watched the north tip of the African coast slide past in the distance. It was as though the past was also rolling away. Each day, Ned stood a little straighter, and his mood lifted.

Their joint sitting room contained two double settees and assorted upright chairs. The ladies sat in the settees with their husbands' arms around them, much as they had so many years before when Gerry and Annabella had met.

Gerry had taken the opportunity earlier that day to take Ned aside and have an in-depth talk. They leaned on the ship's railing and talked. They were much closer than brothers.

This conversation prompted Ned to reflect on the past sixteen years he spent with his mother. The children called Gerry away, leaving Ned free to recall the past. Gerry was Ned's best friend; he had been since childhood. They were part of a group of four young men. Gerry had never planned to live permanently at the castle, but Ned made them their own quarters and found him a purpose. In a castle with over two hundred rooms, this had not been a chore. They even had their own entrance. By remaining, he could help people. Gerry had once been one of London's top Gynaecologists in Harley Street, but had left and gone to Sydney to find Ned. He never returned to the hospital. Instead, Ned set up a clinic for him in one of the estate cottages, and it became a Medical Centre for the area. They now employed six nurses who did community visits and two young doctors. He had brought a young doctor onto the staff. For the first time, Gerry felt he could leave and have the work continue. He had initially worked from the rear of the Gracemere Castle. They found it was too far for the villagers to walk, so Ned had *Hedgemere Cottage* converted to a mini-hospital. It was another of the 'grace and favour' cottages of the Estate and had recently become vacant with the passing of an old retainer.

This cottage was a twin to *Bramblemere* in Coxheath, where Charles had grown up. A gorgeous thatched-roof building. It was known as *Hedgemere Hospital*. This cottage had eight bedrooms. Two were set up for rooms for the staff residences. One was used for emergency accommodation, three were used as hospital rooms, and one was reserved for overnight occupation by family members caring for the patients. This had a selection of single beds and bunks. *Rosemere*, another of the cottages nearby, was recently vacated. This was in the process of being converted into a recovery cottage and nurses' accommodation.

Ned's brother, Paul, was overseeing the conversion. Although a lawyer, this work had given him some purpose. His older son had taken over his position in the law firm, and two of his younger sons were training as doctors and were hoping to take up residence and grow the 'family hospital.'

Douglas's younger sons, too, had taken an interest in the castle changes, and one had opened a branch law office in town, and the other had taken over as headmaster of the now much-enlarged school in Maidstone.

The staff from the castle kept them clean and tidy. The nurses were all local girls whom Gerry had trained. They ranged from widows to young girls. Most were capable, and they were able to live at home. They only stayed overnight if a patient required intensive nursing. More often than not, a family member would remain with them. Other helpers from the village were made welcome. No volunteer was turned away. Gerry took the opportunity to train as many as possible. The office, sitting, and lounge rooms were used as waiting rooms and doctors' rooms.

Ned thought back to the beginning of the change. The Dowager Duchess had started working at the school on her return from Sydney nine years ago. She had taught the village girls the importance of cleanliness and how it improved their health. The village was now a model of happiness. Death rates of the babies had dropped from three in ten to less than one in twenty. Gerry trained more midwives and showed them how to scrub themselves before, during, and after the births. Once the families realised how cleanliness impacted their lives, they threw themselves into cleaning and maintaining the general cleanliness of everything. Health picked up, and death rates dropped.

The castle children attended the village school rather than having governesses and tutors. The castle paid the teachers. These people had initially been employed as tutors and governesses, but they were quickly set up in a village school. No expense was spared in the education of all the children. Every child learnt everything from Latin to grooming and deportment. Dancing classes were always a favourite; the grooming did not sit so well with the older village boys until it was pointed out that the girls preferred the clean, neat and tidy boys. That understanding changed their attitude quickly.

Christina and Ned laughed that they would be the best-educated farmers in the country who could dance brilliantly. The village was a happy place. Ned would not have it any other way. Ned also stocked a library of farm practices in the village hall. He wanted to build a town library next.

Ned employed a military major friend of his, who lost a leg on active service. Ned had run into Reg in Maidstone on his return from visiting another of his friends. Ned and Gerry were two of a youthful foursome, Jimmy Westaweller was the third and Robbie Styles the last. Robbie was now married to Jimmy's sister Amelia. She has been in Sydney as a convict, and through her, he reconnected with his friends again. This had occurred soon after their arrival sixteen years earlier.

On his return from Robbie's house, Ned had recognised his old friend walking along the street on a pair of branch crutches. He stopped his phaeton and picked him up. Reg Hawkins thought he was unemployable. Ned, however, knew his organisational ability and employed him on the spot as his new Castle Estate Agent. He had been praying that God would lead him to the right man; Reg was that man. He didn't need to walk far, and he could ride like the wind, as well as have access to whatever vehicle he required. Reg was allocated quarters in the castle, though he could have been given a cottage if he wished. However, had he accepted one, he would have had to fend for himself, and he hated cooking, so Ned sorted an apartment for him on the ground floor of the castle. This had his office next door to his personal rooms. Reg only had to ascend the stairs if there was an issue that needed his personal attention. A prosthetic leg and a new walking stick helped him become more mobile.

The official estate office was also moved to the ground floor. This gave Ned a chance to sort all the ancient documentation kept there. Most of which would stay in the old office as it became the Archives room.

Ned's friends from Sydney, Sam and Danny Garney, now in Billingshurst, were assisting many more men like Reg.

Sam was as reluctant to be an Earl as Ned was to be a Duke. Through Reg, Ned had been able to find more wounded soldiers who needed assistance. If Reg needed any documentation, he would ring, and other staff members would soon do his running. As a castle agent, he was brilliant. Farmers took their gripes to him, and he worked through issues with the wisdom of Solomon. He and Ned thought the same way, both worked with their military exactness, and soon the castle was running smoothly.

It was Reg who had found Joseph Carpenter for Ned as his personal secretary. Both men were from Ned's old regiment, and Ned knew Joseph's skills with the pen, so Joseph, too, had been employed as his secretary. There weren't as many social outings held at the Castle other than the yearly Garden Party, and he coped in this new role brilliantly. Others, too, were employed where possible. Although thrown in the deep end, Joseph learned quickly from her ladyship's secretary, Colin Fraser. Many of the new under-gardeners were also disabled soldiers.

Another friend had been Perry White, as Ned called him. He had been in a silent partnership with Sam since their return from Australia. Perry's main estate was *Cheatham Castle* in Warwickshire. Although by preference, they lived not far from Jimmy Pittford's place in Aylesford most of the year. Perry had become the Duke of Cheatham, and his wife, Katy, specialised in helping the physically scarred soldiers and sailors, as Perry had been badly burned himself and knew the traumas associated with them. Their son Jem had taken over the work two years ago when Perry died. His death had knocked Ned hard, but Charles arrived just at the right time. He brought news of his mother's passing, and they grieved together. Charles had first been assigned to Perry, so he knew him well.

Jem's grandfather, Percy, had groomed him to step into his shoes as Duke of Cheatham, and he was filling those shoes well. Katy, aged seventy-three, lived at their small estate, *Blackberry House*, nestled between Jimmy's and Colm, Earl of Buckchester's estates.

Ned's thoughts returned closer to home again. Gerry brought a doctor friend from London and had Reg measured for a prosthetic limb. Within six months, Reg no longer needed his crutches but still didn't like stairs. Other amputees were employed on the various estates by Ned, Jimmy, and Sam. Sam was also supplied with new limbs and taught to walk before being given new jobs. A burns specialist was sent up to Perry's estate, and Gerry assisted with setting up a special burns clinic there.

Paul and Douglas had initially laughed at his plans for change until they saw the effects on the people in the area. Villagers were taking care of their properties. Rewards were given in practical gifts. Not just the traditional gifts of five yards of red flannel, but more often, it was a prize ram, a pair of stud lambs, a run of chickens or a sow. Christina quickly discarded the red flannel. She knew how the colour ran and ruined other items in the laundry. Sometimes, it could even be twenty labourers for a week or a new coup for the poultry or garden for their yard. Each was presented in acknowledgment of that family's effort in the village and their house's upkeep. It was not unknown for the smallest child to be given the best gift.

One lame little lad, Jake, had been given one of Ned's stud beagle puppies. It was said that the pup had an injured foot. He had actually been walked on by a horse in the stable when he was a tiny pup. Ned knew, however, that he would be an excellent sire. The pup's leg healed, but it was left with a limp. He would never make a hunting dog, but he was the most popular dog in the village to cover the bitches. Cross-beagle dogs were a common sight in the area, and all had their father's loyalty. The limping pair were a constant sight in town. The thought of this pair made Ned smile. Ned's head gardener had taken the lad on under an apprenticeship and taught him hedging, topiary and gardening. This was a job Jake excelled in, as it didn't involve much walking. The trusty beagle Sonny would be waiting for Jake under the ladder, often entirely covered by clippings. Everyone employed under Sam's disability scheme was interviewed and directed into a role that was not only to their liking but also their skillset. Sam told Ned to focus on their ability, not their disability. So Ned did just that.

Widows and orphans were taken in or cared for in a way never heard of before. The castle subsidised families taking in orphans. One other need Christina found was placing the illegitimate children of nobility. These children had often been hidden away or abandoned. Christina and a group of her friends would hide the expectant mothers in cottages until their children were born. More often than not, the father, once challenged privately by Ned, would take over care of the child themselves, but occasionally they would not, denying it was theirs. The child would be placed with a widow or family, and the estate would cover all costs. Usually, the mothers, often very young women, returned to society and got on with their lives. Some, however, stayed and became part of the village life as teachers or nurses at the hospital. The Gracemere Estate and the village surrounding it became the epitome of how a village should work; others followed.

Ned and Gerry knew that in their absence, Paul would take over and continue their work. Once Ned stated his wishes and instructed them on how everyone was to work together, he then, most importantly, explained the ultimate goal he wanted the estate to aim for; things just got done. Paul saw its worth and all reaped the benefits, pleased to follow Ned's lead.

Over the last fifteen years, Ned called six-monthly community meetings. These were held in the Great Hall at the castle. Everyone had equal speaking rights, but they must be orderly. No question or topic was to be ridiculed, but all must be respectful. At the first meeting, no one spoke up. It had taken some years before he broke through. It was only on the return from Sydney that things really started to change. His Mother had led that change. If she said it was all right to do, then everyone followed. Ned laughed when she referred to herself as an 'Ape leader', and she was. Where she went, everyone followed. She wanted children at the school, so she went and taught there herself. All the children came, including those from the castle. She wanted the village to learn how to be clean and healthy, so she educated them herself. They all followed her lead. Ned was not exempt from her cadging. During one major storm, the village required an organised effort to assist with rescue and cleanup. Ned was sent by his mother to organise the village workers. He would have gone anyway, but he let her think it was her idea. Ned's army training gave him the experience for such a job, and his authority as a duke sealed his position.

Paul and Douglas were also seconded to various positions. They both entered into it dubiously, and now both were realising they relished the roles to which they found themselves. As younger sons of a Duke, one at least would have been expected to have gone into the church. Neither had, both had chosen law. They worked together in their law firm, Lockleys Law Offices, in Maidstone. Their eldest sons had followed them in the family business. They lived in estate houses, *Lakemere* and *Forrestmere,* on the castle grounds; both his brothers had welcomed Ned's arrival. Neither wanted to take over the job themselves. Duke David, their eldest brother, had left the estate in a horrific state. He had sacked most of the elderly estate staff, and no one had wanted to work in the house with his wife, Elouise. Until Ned's return, everyone just stayed away.

On their return to England, Ned and Christina had walked into a dysfunctional household with few staff. They, therefore, had a clean slate. This void allowed Gerry and Ned to start afresh. Frederick Jamison, his father's butler, had bided his time with Duchess Suze and knew where to start. He, too, had served in the army and had resigned his commission when his father, the old butler, had died. Frederick left the castle when the old duke died and worked with Duchess Susanna at the Dower House. Ned hired a new butler for London, too, another old regimental Sgt Major, Percival Cutler. One of Sam's finds, he had only just recently started in his new role.

So on Ned's return from Sydney, it was to Jamison they turned. With military precision, Jamison employed new staff and removed others whom David and Elouise had employed. Jamison listed the jobs that needed to be filled and personally chose the staff to fill them. He had instructed each and oversaw everything. He interviewed the injured soldiers that Reg or Sam sent him and placed them in roles they were not only qualified for, but that they also enjoyed.

Ned was called "The new Duke" when he arrived, but was now 'Duke Ned. He was the third Duke in three years. Ned's father, Charles, was called 'the old duke' and had not been on top of the work when he died. Ned's eldest brother, Duke David, was supposed to be aiding him but spent most of his time in London socialising with his wife, Elouise. Consequently, when he inherited the title, David had no idea what to do.

Ned had joined the army when he was twenty. Just after Elouise had broken their engagement in 1819, she married his older brother instead. Ned had tried to warn his brother, but David would not listen and told him to leave. So Ned left. James, the Duke of Malvern, had overheard the entire argument with Elouise. Ned had initially been aghast, but in the end, he realised this had been a blessing as he had someone in whom he could confide. Duke James had been wonderful to a nineteen-year-old hurt heart. Ned told Duke James that he would enlist under the name of Grace and head to the other side of the world. And so Ned Grace was born, and Edward John Charles Lockley disappeared from society.

When Duke James heard of Ned's destination, he gasped; he then told Ned of his own dilemma. His son Sam was over there as a convict. He confessed to Ned that this child was, in essence, illegitimate, although acknowledged as the second son of the Earl of Meldon, and that Sam didn't know his own parentage. Duke James asked, "Would you seek him out and report in occasionally to me to let me know he's well?" Ned had. Sam Corbett was surprised when Ned arrived one day with another soldier friend, Tom Turner. Ned sighed. And then there was Perry White, who had been an Earl even while over there. In due course, he became the Duke of Cheatham, followed now by their son Jem. Ned thought Jem was doing a great job as a Duke.

They had all become friends. Perry and Sam were old school friends, and Tom's mother had been Sam's mother's maid. They had all become friends in Sydney. Ned was much the same age as Sam's son, Danny. Visits to him gave Ned a chance to report to Duke James how the family were doing. Tom later told Ned that Sam was now the Viscount as the elder son of the Earl had died. Perry had never let on who he was, but then titles were taboo in Sydney. However, Perry had also become good friends with Lachlan Macquarie.

Ned had chuckled when he found the new house Perry had built was named *Glenmere*. It was a nod to his friendship with Lachlan and the time he had spent living with Ned's family in Kent when Perry was looking for his wife Katy before he knew she had been transported for theft. That was an entirely different story, though.

Tom Turner had no idea about any of them. Or did he? Ned wasn't sure. Funny to think that Sam ended up back in England as the Earl of Meldon in a similar situation as Ned himself. He had been born as the second son. Never expecting to inherit, he had never been trained to run the estate, though he knew how the books were to be done. Sam had no idea of his convoluted parentage and had been confounded when it was finally uncovered. Even more so to find the convict wife, Annie, he'd married in Sydney, was the old Earl of Meldon's illegitimate daughter, and so their son Danny was, in fact, the true bloodline of the Earldom. Ned smiled to himself. He still saw Sam when he could and counted him and his son, Danny, as true friends. Sad that Sam would be gone soon. He would probably not see him again, as he was nearly ninety.

Danny Corbett Garney would make a grand Earl when that time came. At sixty, he was already a grandfather. Dan and Georgie often made the nearly sixty-mile trip from their estate in West Sussex to *Gracemere* for an extended visit. Georgie's brother Robbie married Amelia Westaweller, whom Ned had assisted so long ago in Australia. They would all often catch up during the season as their London houses were on the same street. Dan, too, had reluctantly grown into the role of Viscount Clarestow. Funny to think they, too, knew Charles from his Government Stores days. Ned's reverie made him thank God for how things had turned out for them all. He could see the threads of God's plan being woven, but until now, he had never put all the stories and friendships together.

Christina came and joined him at the rail. He drew her to him and kissed the back of her neck as he wrapped his arms around her.

Thinking back to everything that had happened, Ned realised that God *was* in control all the time and looking back now, Ned was relieved he had never married Elouise. He was brought up with a start. He gasped. The realisation finally flooded over him, how different his life would have been, and not for the better. His Christina was an angel, his sure foundation, his rock.

She stood locked in his arms, resting her back against him. She felt him tense and then relax.

He bent and kissed the top of her head. Yes, he had lost his beloved mother, but he still had Christina, and he still had his family and children and all his friends. If it had not been for Elouise Wickham rejecting him, he would have had none of those beloved people in his life. She was a pretty face, but she was also a shrew. His mother told him that she could not conceive, so he would not have even had children. Oh, how different it would have been; horribly different.

The emotion of relief flooded through him. He nuzzled Christina's neck and kissed it. He spoke softly so only she could hear. "Love, I just want to say thank you. You have been my rock. I could not have made it through the last month without you, let alone the last sixteen years. I never say thank you enough. My life would have been a disaster but for you."

She turned in his arms. "Oh, my dearest, darling Edward, it has been my joy and delight. You, too, are my everything."

He drew her close to him, and he bent and gently kissed her.

She wrapped her arms around his waist under his big fur coat and leaned against his warm and loving chest.

She had given him the time he needed to process his feelings and loss. She had been there when needed and left him alone at times, too.

She felt him release a deep breath and relax. She knew that now the healing could begin; no, it had begun already.

They stood relishing their closeness until the freezing sleet turned into rain; only then did they retreat inside.

She expected they would head into their cabin as usual, but no, Ned led her to the children.

Outside the cabin door, he quietly said, "Love, it's time I became the father they need, rather than wallowing in my own grief. I forgot for a while, sweetheart. I'm sorry." Again, he brushed his lips against hers. "Let's brave the young fry, eh? They always cheer us up."

He opened the door of the cabin. "Good morning, young ones, over the seasickness yet?" he asked breezily.

He was soon mobbed by nine children hugging and cuddling him.

Gerry looked a little surprised at his old friend's change of attitude, then smiled.

Christina, Annabella, and Gerry stood watching him. He was nearly back to the old Ned.

~

Over the following weeks, Ned spent a great deal of time with the children. They were so understanding and healing. They asked no awkward questions and were content with what he could give, his time and love. The little ones, especially, would be more sensitive to his moods. Izzy would often be sitting on his lap and stroking his cheek, just loving him. Christina looked at their youngest child. She had such a caring soul. Christina would smile and leave them alone.

A week out of Cape Town, Christina came across Chip and Ned in deep conversation. She left them alone and sought out Sarah. She was her grandmother's favourite. More for her name than anything else, for Suze had lost her only daughter, also named Sarah. Sarah had been her first granddaughter, and they had a special bond.

Christina now took the opportunity to let her daughter know that her grandmother's final letter had been to Queen Victoria to arrange her come-out.

Sarah gasped, a tear escaped and rolled down her cheek.

Christina hugged her daughter, easing her grief. She knew her daughter was hurting too, but had not shown it in public.

When she heard about this, she turned to her mother and let the tears flow. They had all needed time.

~

From leaving Cape Town, they had to tack all the way across the Indian Ocean as the prevailing winds were unusually from the Northeast. This, by necessity, slowed them down, delaying their arrival at Fremantle by nearly two weeks.

By the time they reached the Western Australian coast, the family were enjoying the trip. At least the frequent tacking gave the boys something to watch.

The anticipation of getting to Sydney was great.

The wind was now behind them, and Captain Wilson said they were about five days out of Fremantle, then another ten days to Melbourne and three until Sydney if the winds held good.

With a day in port at each, they were due in a month. He hoped to be there at the end of March.

~

By Melbourne, Ned knew the families would be ready never to step foot on the ship again, but they still had the last few days to travel.

Ned had thanked Colin in London when he confessed he had sent a note to Charles. He knew they were expected, knew they would be welcomed. He couldn't wait. There, he could be the man he wished he could be; just Ned – the Major; friend and family. He needed them now.

On 7 January 1857 in Parramatta, the newest Lockley family members entered the world. Liza presented her husband with identical twin girls, Amelia Suzanna and Charlotte Elizabeth.

That same afternoon, Tim and Anna had twin boys, Timothy Edward and Samuel Aidan.

Only weeks later, Charles received Colin's letter. His heart hurt for his friend. He shared the news with Sal and guessed the reason, though nothing had been written. Charles had done the same thing himself. He had arrived when Ned was grieving the loss of Parry White. Charles knew him well, as he and Sal had both been assigned to Perry as convicts. He thought it funny that Luke and Ellen now owned that house.

A message arrived from Melbourne that the ship was due to dock within the next day or so.

Downing tools and heading to Ned.

Charles waited until the ship was due before telling the rest of the family of his suspicions. He expected that Ned would come as soon as his mother died.

Charles and Sal intended to go alone to meet the ship. However, Ed and Jenna accompanied them.

Six weeks earlier

The months on board had eased the rawness of Ned's grief. The loss would never go away, but now he could cope. Something Christina said had helped him. He'd heard it before, but this time it sank in. "My dearest Edward, you grieve because you loved her, there would be no grief without that love." It finally had stuck with him; it was because he adored his mother that he grieved so deeply. That same love would now sustain him; it's what she would want.

Nearly thirteen-year-old Liam was the first to see a seagull. It perched in the rigging above him and dropped a visiting card beside him. "Ooh, yuck," he said. Then he looked up. "Papa, a bird, look."

They had all been hanging over the sides watching the dolphins.

A cheer went up from the crew as it meant land was not that far away. Sure enough, two days later, the land was seen on the horizon. Fremantle drew close, and they were soon entering the Swan River.

The two families descended as soon as the gangplank went down. They would stretch their legs and might do a bit of shopping. The three youngest girls, ten-year-old Matthew, eleven-year-old Neddie and Liam, could finally run and let off some energy.

The older children walked for some distance sedately, but once they were off the dockland area, they played hide and seek in the parkland with their younger siblings.

By the time they returned to the ship, they had all laughed and walked and laughed some more until they were exhausted. They had foregone the shopping for playtime. It was certainly time well spent. They needed nothing; anyway, worldly goods were fleeting.

Ned was finally looking like his old self, so Christina was happy. "Edward, look." The children were holding hands in a long row and skipping.

For the first time in a long time, she heard her husband's laugh. Ned's face lit up when he saw they were having fun.

~

For the final two weeks on board, they were within view of land for most of the time. The wind was cold and from the southwest, which meant that they did not have to tack all the way to Melbourne.

Melbourne was an overnight stop, then they departed for Sydney.

Ned sent word to Charles of their imminent arrival.

This leg of the journey could take up to three weeks, depending on winds, but *The Lady Hodgkinson* did it in days.

The final few days north from Melbourne were spent in a frenzy of watching the coastline and packing.

Chip and Sarah remembered the view of the heads in Sydney.

Just after dawn on 30th March, they all stood along the railings with their siblings and parents, not wanting to miss a moment.

Having finished their packing the night before, Christina and Ned stood together, her arm linked in his.

Neither could wipe the smiles from their faces.

Gerry and Annabella were next to them.

"We're home, Edward," Christina said softly.

Ned bent and gave her a quick kiss. "Yes, sweetheart, we are. It's where our hearts and souls are. It's certainly a homecoming for the girls." He gave a low chuckle. "My heart is racing. I'm so excited to be back." He said so quietly that only she could hear.

She leaned against him, and he placed his arm around her shoulders. "I do so wish we could stay," he whispered.

She whispered in reply, "No, we can't, Edward, we can enjoy it while we're here." The ship sailed down the harbour with the easterly wind propelling them; they dropped their sails and slowed to a drift. A small steam tugboat came and manoeuvred them into the dock.

There was a small group there waving.

A big dimpled grin broke Ned's stern look.

Charles, Sal, Ed, and Jenna were there waiting.

Sal was so excited that she was jumping on the spot, waving with both arms.

Chapter 18   Strength of Friends

$\mathcal{A}$s soon as the gangplank was down, Charles and Sal were up and in the arms of their cousins. Charles looked at Christina's black gown and asked, "Is she gone?"

Ned nodded, totally unable to say more. His eyes were glassy with unshed tears, and he bit his lip.

Charles greeted Ned with a handshake, then pulled Ned into his arms in a bear hug. Both men were unable to speak due to their grief-stricken emotions. Each understood the other's loss far too well. Once the initial greetings were over, they ushered the children from the ship, where Ned thanked the Captain, and they bade him farewell.

They were all booked in at the *King's Arms Hotel*. Mr Frederick Stewart had long since retired. However, his son, Herbert, had taken over his position. He had been a footman there while growing up, so the younger Mr Stewart knew this family well. He had sent down two carriages for the passengers and three for luggage. As usual, though, they walked up from the quay. The noise of their arrival preceded them. The young Mr Herbert Stewart greeted them warmly, showing them immediately to their suites. He had a feeling they would not stay. He awaited instructions. Charles quietly asked him not to unpack the luggage. The carriages moved away, but would stand ready.

Christina dragged Sal into their room, and they hugged again in private. Christina was telling Sal of their loss and comparing notes about their husbands' grief. Their loss was quite apparent as Christina was dressed in black. Ned had lost a lot of weight and looked haunted—something Sal had never seen in him before. His loss had hit him hard.

Charles had felt the loss of his mother, much as Ned had. He, too, had jumped on the first ship after the funeral and gone to tell his sister, his Aunt Emily, and Ned. They had only been able to stay a few months until they tore themselves away and came back home. Now it was Ned's turn.

They would spend their year of mourning in Australia. How long they would stay after that was unknown, but at least a year, possibly two. They had always planned to come for some time to show their children another side of life.

Christina and Sal went and found Jenna. "We have a surprise for you, Christina," Sal said. Jenna was leaving her room to find the ladies. She had four-month-old twins, Philip and Ruthie, in her arms.

"Oh, Jenna, I had forgotten to ask. I should have asked. They are so sweet."

Christina took Philip from her. "Vicky was expecting too, wasn't she?"

"Yes, she had a little boy the week after these two were born. They were born on 6th December, and James was born on the 13th. He is really James Anthony, but the children first called him Jimmy Ant, and it's stuck." Jenna cooed at her little girl.

Christina did the same to Pip in her arms. The little baby had curled up in her arms and snuggled into her. "Oh Jenna, I'm so pleased I'm here; I so wish I could have had more. I did manage five children in three confinements, though." She kissed the cherub in her arms. "I thought that was quite clever. I'll just have to enjoy these ones while we're here."

Christina and Jenna had married in December 1841, within three weeks of each other. Both couples had twins, and they were born less than nine months after their parents' marriages. They had been allocated a private sitting room upstairs and decided to remain in there. Ed joined them, and he rang for tea. Gerry and Annabella came in. They sat and chatted until Ned and Charles arrived.

Charles and Ned had been cloistered in Charles's room for some time. Their grief, once shared, had eased. Ned had been there for Charles; now it was reciprocated. The time ahead would be healing. Ned needed the support of his two best friends, as he knew they could and would help.

Two of the hotel maids had taken all the ambulant children into a park for a run. The eight adults sat catching up with the happenings of each family, while the ladies cradled the sleeping babies. They were sitting in peace, enjoying the stillness of the room. A knock on the door interrupted them all. A knock stilled the various conversations. John and Colleen asked if they could join them. They were welcomed warmly and sat down.

Colleen had seven-month-old Jonty in her arms, and he was wiggling to get down. John took him from her and stood him between his knees. Jonty was content with this for the moment.

Ned welcomed John, "Last time I saw you, John, you'd just finished school. Now you're married with a child. Ahh! Where has that time gone? And Colleen, you look, well, you've changed, wonderfully changed. You were only a young girl when I knew you and..." Ned said, smiled, leaving the sentence unfinished. "Oh, I'm so glad we're home again."

"I believe the word you're looking for, Major, was 'scrawny'," Colleen chuckled.

Ned found it hard not to laugh, but his eyes twinkled and he nodded. "That you were, my dear, but even then you were kind and loving."

The peace of the afternoon was soon shattered with the return of the children. The three older ones came in leading the little ones; the three boys, Liam, Neddie, and Matthew, had returned ravenous.

Charles rang for room service and called for a plate or two of sandwiches and some lemonade for the children.

When the three platters of food arrived, the hoard of children descended upon it as though they had not seen food for a week, rather than three hours. Jonty also reached for a sandwich and managed to persuade his father to have some. John slowly fed him some cheese. The sandwiches and cold boiled eggs were nearly finished when there was another knock on their door.

Caro and Douglas had come to welcome them.

More chairs were brought in from the surrounding rooms.

Christina looked at her husband to see a smile on his face. Even his eyes were now smiling. Most of the new arrivals did not know the reason they had come, but her black gown told them all they needed to know. They knew who was missing. No one asked the obvious. Ned knew his family was surrounded by love. Gerry and Charles were with him, and that's all Ned wanted; the rest were extra blessings.

Eddie, too, had guessed. His father had just nodded to him on his return to the room. He squeezed Jenna's hand and said quietly, "We guessed correctly."

She nodded, knowing the grief of loss too after Richard and Grandmother Elle's deaths.

"Right, friends, plans for the day," Charles said. "Ned, Tina, do you want to stay in town for a bit, or will we catch this afternoon's ferry and clear out?"

A plea from Christina settled it. "Edward, can we go? Please?" said Christina.

Ned turned to Gerry and gave him a questioning look.

"Let's go. Before the Governor finds out you're here," Gerry said.

"Unanimous, Charles; we're off," Ned said, grinning. The last thing he wanted to do was go to Government House. "Let's go home." Gerry caught Christina's eye and smiled.

Charles pulled out his fob. "We have an hour. The ferry is a bit late today as it's the low tide. It's leaving at half one. I had a feeling you'd say that. The luggage is still in the carriages on my instruction. I'll get it sent back down to the wharf. Let's go. If an invitation from Government House arrives, we'll have missed it.

"We've sorted rooms. Ned, Tina, you will, of course, be in your own rooms at Ed's. Caro, Doug, are you packed?"

They nodded.

"John, Colleen, are you all right at Charlie's this time?" They nodded

"No, actually, we're all staying at Tom and Maggie's," Douglas replied on their behalf.

Ned laughed, "Charles, you sound like me; military precision."

"It's rubbed off, Ned." Charles smiled and continued. "Gerry and Annabella, how about Luke's new house for you, as it's nearby, or you may wish to move up to *Roseneath* later. It's vacant most of the time. We can juggle rooms later if you wish, but you may be needed at Luke's for a short while, and they can tell you about that. There is also *Gracemere Close*, it's empty at the moment. Our spare room has turned into a day nursery room for babysitting. Everyone will be coming in on Sunday, so you'll have five days to get organised."

Christina looked at Ned. Her heart had leapt when they heard that Ned's old cottage was empty. He met her eyes, then said to Charles. "Charles, we'll stay at Ed's, but we're claiming my cottage too. We'll take some short child-free breaks there while we are here. We may even move back in ourselves and leave the children at Ed's. The smile that crept across Christina's face was his reward. He met her eyes and returned her smile.

"Thought you might/ It's ready for you," laughed Charles. "I'd suggest we get moving."

~

Everyone stood and returned to their rooms to collect their personal belongings.

Charles went and settled the account, then arranged for the luggage to be collected from the Evans' household and sent to Parramatta. It would all go by road. It would be halfway there before the ferry even departed.

By the time he returned to his room, the stewards were already loading their hand luggage into another carriage. The new arrivals had only their personal belongings, so all moved quickly and as surreptitiously as possible down the sweeping staircase and out of the hotel.

As they exited, Mr Stewart was the only person around to farewell them. He had banished all the rest of the staff, threatening them with dismissal if they showed their faces. The letter in his back pocket would have to be returned to Government House with an apology and explanation that it had missed them. It had arrived only moments before. He had half expected it and took delivery of it himself.

The large group walked sedately out the door and down the hill. They were heading to Doug and Caro's house to collect their personal belongings. Effy would have everything ready.

Caro hugged her as they left. "Effy, have a holiday while we're gone. We're staying until at least Monday this time. Go and see your friend." Effy had come to the family as an assigned convict aged just fourteen. She was supposed to stay only seven years, but she had never wanted to leave. Now she was a paid servant and almost part of their life, certainly treated as one of the family. Caro knew most days she would slip out for an hour or so. She had done so for some years. Indeed, she now also disappeared on her two half-days off. She guessed she was seeing someone. Maybe their time away would give Effy the time they needed to see her man. Caro had offered her more free time, but she didn't want it.

The look on Effy's face said it all. "You know?"

"I knew there was someone and has been for a while. Be happy, dear, that's all we ask. Is he a good man?"

"Oh yes, Mrs Evans, he's wonderful. I'm hoping he'll finally ask if I'll walk out with him." Effy blushed. She was just shy of forty-one, yet she was still the same quiet girl as she was at fourteen.

Caro loved her. She gave her a hug and a quick kiss on departure. They said their farewells and then meandered down the street towards the Cove via the gardens.

They walked through the Botanical Gardens for a while, then out into Bridge Street and back down Pitt Street to the Circular Quay. This allowed the children to run, laugh and stretch their legs. The gardens were an area where children were often heard squealing with joy at being allowed to run free.

Jenna and Ed had not brought their large twin baby carriage, so the babies were passed from one adult to another.

Jonty was asleep in his large wheeled perambulator, and his bag and the twins' change bag sat in a basket underneath it. He soon fell asleep, and Jenna placed the sleeping twins in with him.

The group passed a pleasant half-hour in the gardens before leaving for the trip home on the ferry. The paddle steamer, the *Black Swan*, was waiting for them. Their hand luggage was already being loaded as they headed on board. They settled the three sleeping babies in the small cabin and went to watch the loading. At half past one precisely, the ferry departed.

Once they pulled away from the wharf, Ned released a huge sigh. "We did it, love. Now we can relax." He threw his head back and drew in a deep breath.

Ned stood with one arm around his wife and holding a daughter in the other hand.

Christina did similarly, only with an arm around Ned's waist. "Nearly home, Edward. I can't wait." They had spent their honeymoon in Ned's cottage; it was where they really called home. It was a tiny two-bedroom sandstone and brick cottage on the side of the Parramatta River. They had courted from there and lived only two doors apart. After their marriage, they had lived there for the three happiest months of their lives. It was their 'heart' home. All the wealth and titles in the world could not equal that. Their over two hundred room castle had been more of a burden than a home.

Charles and Sal took the girls from their grasp and left them alone to reminisce.

Eddie was sitting at the bow with all the rest of the children seated around him. They sat away from the slosh and spray of the paddle wheels. He was pointing out all sorts of interesting things and answering their questions. Charles and Gerry both sat with them in case they were needed.

The three youngest girls were held tightly, and Sanna sat in Gerry's lap. Charlotte, or Charl, sat on Charles's lap, and John had Izzy. Matty, Gerry's son, was with Douglas. The four smaller children asked about birds and boats.

Ed smiled; he remembered his first trip aged just ten. He had been on his way to live with the Evans family. His mentor, Thomas Tindale, had arranged for him to live with his sister, Caro Evans and their boys. John was the youngest. Ed had seen whales for the first time and had looked for them every trip since, and never again saw any. Twenty-seven years later, they were now all one extended family of sorts. The Tindales and Evans were not related to them in any way, but John had married Colleen, who was considered as good as family. That was enough. In this country, where family was scarce, one claimed the most tenuous relationship, even if there was, in reality, no connection at all.

Eddie met Douglas' eyes and smiled.

Doug had been at sea when Eddie had moved in; he had arrived home about a month later. They had bonded on meeting, and the friendship had stayed as strong.

Charles, too, watched as Ed patiently answered each question. He was so proud of all of his sons. Each had far surpassed any possible expectations he had for them when born. Each had taken their own path in life. He sat deep in thought, the sloshing of the waves relaxing him. With no official education other than a few years at the charity school in Parramatta, Charlie was now the Governor's Viceroy to Parramatta and the west. Charles had handed that mantle to him mid-year as his own injured leg had never fully recovered from his accident some seventeen years previously. It had broken in three places, and although it had knitted, the pain never completely went away. He now walked with a pronounced limp. Charlie had picked up the reins of running the inn and kept it going. The family, of course, packed around him. Eddie had left school at fifteen and became his brother's backstop, as well as returning to the forge. Both lads had just been teenagers at the time. Charlie had had a rough start as a child, having been the subject of abuse at the hands of a soldier. Charles knew Ed had guarded his older brother as much as a young child could. However, Ed had never stopped protecting him. Charlie had minimal education; therefore, Eddie did all the paperwork for the inn, so his brother didn't have to worry. Charlie ran the inn, and Ed still did the books. Charles had managed the Government Stores, and that kept him occupied until transportation stopped. Charlie and Eddie married soon after that occurred. In addition to the paperwork, Sal used to have to cope with feeding everyone; now, Gracie did all that too. It had been a hectic time.

Nothing was ever too much trouble for Ed. He was the most humble of them all but also the strongest, both physically and in character. Charles had never understood the word 'meek' in the Bible until Ed grew up. He was the one all the others turned to in times of both good and bad. Yet he then willingly relinquished his roles to whomever stepped up. There was no guile in him. Yes, through him, Charles understood the difference between weakness and meekness. There was nothing weak about Ed, but there was a Godly meekness in him that made him stand out from the masses. He was wealthy from hard work as a blacksmith, but also from the Emporium that he'd built with his wedding gift money from Ned. He was as strong as an ox. Charles thought back to the day Ed met Jenna and smiled. Ahh, what a day that was. It took a year before Jack let them marry. Then, the week of the wedding came the attack by the highwaymen. He still shuddered at the memory of Eddie arriving home virtually unresponsive and covered in blood. He was brought home by Doctor Gerry Winslow-Smythe. Because of him and that incident, their lives changed forever. Ned discovered he was now the Duke, and because of that revelation, not only was their relationship as cousins revealed, but that he, Charles, was an Earl.

Ned had given Ed and Jenna a wedding gift of £1,000. That money had been put to excellent use. Ed could have spent it all on himself, but he didn't. The Emporium was now the meeting place of the farmers and tradesmen in the area, an important centre for the town. It was both new goods and produce; a central hub where you could buy almost anything. All the craftsmen in town now sought to sell their goods from there. Only the best quality was obtainable. The small produce store next door also grew and started a trend in other towns. It was like a farmer's emporium but for fresh food. Ed had built his house near the family's *Jolly Sailor Inn*. He had helped financially with the Female Orphans' School when it was open and did so much more for the town that only God knew about.

Charles smiled as he met Ed's eyes. He really shouldn't have a favourite, but this lad of his also reminded him of his best friend and cousin, Ned. He had named him after him. Funny that their name Edward means 'prosperous or fortune'.

Charles thought of Liza, named Elizabeth after both his mother and sister. She married Bertie Ellis, who was now the Colony's most acclaimed saddler and leather goods manufacturer. He, too, was wealthy in his own right. He had worked hard and had earned the warrant for Government saddles and leather goods, even making saddles for Queen

Victoria, at the Governor's suggestion. Ned had given Her Majesty one of Bertie's saddles as a gift from the colony. She loved it, and it was now her preferred choice of mount.

Charles smiled when he heard both his daughters were expecting again. Still smiling, he thought of Anna, named Susanna after the beautiful Duchess who lived near him when he was a child. He had seen her but once, but he had never forgotten her. Her youthful beauty was astounding. Little did he realise she was Ned's mother. The same Suzanna, or Suze, who had recently passed away. He realised it was something he had never actually told Ned. Anna married Tim Miller. He was a Member of the Legislative Assembly and a top lawyer in town, and Eddie's best friend.

Charles thought back to when Ned and Thomas Tindale sent Eddie and Tim to Cape's Academy in Sydney so many years ago. Charles only found out the night before Eddie's wedding. Ned had kept that quiet. That education had changed life for them all and for the better. All the family had benefited. They were going from strength to strength. Their two oldest sons had their feet planted on the ground, and they were still best friends, as were the youngest boys.

Every family had their dreamer; Wills was theirs. Always wanting to know what was around the next corner before he had turned the last one. He had run away after he left school and found himself on a grand adventure that changed the colony. Charles laughed as he had also returned as one of the wealthiest men in the colony, next to his friend, William C. Wentworth, whom Charles had named his son after. Wills was now beginning even to give W.C. a run for his money. He had also returned from his adventure with six Englishmen in tow. Unbeknownst to them all, they were all related in some way. They had not even known of the connection between themselves. Wills had been their lynchpin. Oh, what a difference Wills had made to each of their lives. Both Christina's brother and Annabella's cousin, Philip, were two more of them, his own nephew, John, a third; Harry, now Vicky's husband, a fourth and Ned's and Sal's cousins, Lewis and Aidan, were the last two—the last two married Reverend William Clarke's wife's nieces. However, the group had discovered gold, a great deal of it. Rather than keep the information to themselves, they prepared for the boom time. Wills built Parramatta's Warehouse and two more Emporiums, one at Emu Plains and one in Bathurst. Two of the Englishmen, Harry and Phil, ran them. The other four had returned home. Harry married Vicky, Jenna's sister, and Phil was Annabella's cousin; he too married, and they ran the Bathurst store. The threads of the family pulled closer. Phil and Lucy were also arriving soon from Bathurst. They would stay with Wills again.

Charles, still deep in thought, was watching the foam on the waves. His mind fell to his last child, Luke, the studious one. He had spent his thirty years with his nose in a book. He seemed to forget about life, or so Charles thought; apparently, not so. He had fallen in love early and bottled it up. He studied to keep his mind from her, thinking she had married elsewhere. Only when he was leaving with Reverend Clarke's Government mineral survey was the truth revealed. He smiled fondly. They had been married in August last year, the week Sal and he had returned from England. Luke was now teaching at The King's School. He, too, had gone from strength to strength there. Luke had only recently revealed to him the value of the stones they found on their travels. One bundle of sapphires alone had sold on their return and had made £600, allowing him to buy a house not far from them. Ellen was now expecting a child, or possibly twins, and life was settled for them, at last.

Charles caught movement to his right. Sal, his beloved Sally, had come to join him, his Countess. When they married, thirty-seven years ago, they were both convicts under Ned's authority. Ned had saved her from the assignment auction by claiming her as a housekeeper. She had been freed with a Ticket of Leave on her marriage to Charles, although she had still agreed to work out the year with Ned. She had never stopped, always kept cooking for him and never stopped mending his clothing until he married. Ned arranged a Ticket of Leave for Charles on arrival in 1820 and later had both his conviction quashed. She had been given a Full Pardon.

Charles smiled. Over twenty years later, he discovered he was an Earl, and the revelation was earth-shattering for him. He had been happier as a convict innkeeper. Then Ned revealed their relationship as third cousins. Charles's reverie continued.

Sal was now sitting next to him.

Gerry had been the one to start that particular ball rolling. He'd come across Ed after highwaymen had attacked him. On bringing him home, Ned was there, and they reunited after some twenty-five years apart. Gerry had come to Australia to find his boyhood friend, Ned Grace or Edward Lockley, as was his real name, although he did not let on that bit of news for some time. In reality, he had been sent to find and bring Ned home to England as the tenth Duke of Gracemere. Instead, he found Major Edward Grace, a retired Major and lonely bachelor, adopted by a convict family. Charles's family had adopted him, and Ned was visiting their inn for Sunday dinner as usual. They were sitting around the table Perry had given them. It was now at Eddie's house. During the meal, Gerry told Ned who he now was. After recovering from nearly choking, they departed for his cottage. After showing Gerry where to sleep, Ned left him and went two doors up. He proposed to Christina. Charles smiled. Ned didn't even tell her who he now was; he did that the next day, again in front of them rather than privately. She was surprised, but had shocks of her own; she was a Lady in her own right. Her father was the Earl of Riverdell, and they lived quite close to each other in England. Both Ned and Gerry had met her when she was an eight-year-old child whom they knew as Tiny Tina. Even then, she was a beauty. Ned and Christina married three weeks later on

Christina's thirty-third birthday, Christmas Day 1841.

Sal watched the emotions playing on her husband's face. Ned's visit had stirred memories in them both; mostly happy ones. She sat next to him on the elevated section of the deck. He pulled her close, and she leaned against him. He was her life, all she needed or desired. Through Ned and Charles, she had found faith. Belief in God had been sorely tested more often than she wished to admit. When Charles fell from the loft and broke his leg, she only had God to rely on, or so she thought. Ned arranged help with both the inn and the family.

Charlotte, or Charl as she preferred, was snuggled to him. She had looked at him when they first met, head tilted on the side, then looked to her father. Ned had nodded to her, and she took Charles' hand. Totally trusting her father to know she would be kept safe. She remembered Charles from his visit last year to her home. "Uncle Chas, are we going to be home soon?" she asked him quietly.

"Not long, Poppet, see that row of trees?" he pointed out the mangroves on the river mouth. "We go between two rows of them, and round a few bends, then we're there. Did your father tell you that you were born there?"

"Yes, Uncle Chas, but we don't remember it. He's always calling us his little Aust-raa-leeans," she chuckled.

He laughed too. He had heard how Ned said it, and it was a perfect mimic of him. It had been known as New South Wales until Lachlan Macquarie used the new name in his reports. It stuck.

Sal pointed out some white herons in the mangroves.

Charl called to her twin, "Izzy, look," she pointed them out to her sister. "They look like skinny chickens."

"Funny you should say that. Eddie's girls call them garbage bin chickens. Well, ones that look a bit like that but with black beaks."

John had been listening. "Those white ones are called herons, and the ones with black beaks are called ibis. There are other colours too. Look, there's a grey heron." He pointed to a bird wading in the shallows.

Izzy was all eyes, asking about everything.

John had answered her patiently. He was astounded by the depth of her questions. Most he could answer, but some, like "Why does a bird's wing twist when it lands," or "How does a bird know when to take a breath when its head goes underwater?" He knew the answers but was astounded at how observant she was about these things. They were the sort of questions he used to ask his mother when he was a child.

As the ferry rounded the last corner, a cheer rose from the jetty. There was a sea of friendly faces awaiting them. Charlie was there with the dray. He had brought it right down to the wharf and was standing holding the horses. Luke and Ellen were there.

Wills and Cathy had arrived unexpectedly and came down too.

Harry and Vicky had already been in town and had their six children at foot. Some of Ned's retired army buddies had heard he was coming back; they stood there waiting as well.

Christina was delighted to see Elizabeth Bobart waiting for her. Other than the family, she was the one person Christina wanted to see. She was saddened to hear of her husband's shock passing and could now give personal condolences. What a wonderful welcome home.

Chip and Sarah were searching through the crowd. Young Ned and Tina were there, waving both arms each. They raced down to where the gangplank would be placed. Eager to renew their acquaintances with their twin cousins. Being only two weeks apart in age, the four look-alike cousins were close. They had formed firm friendships nine years ago and, at their parents' suggestion, regularly corresponded.

Chip was anxiously waiting to see Tina again. It seemed she, too, was looking forward to seeing him. Sarah and Tina wrote monthly. He knew she had no beau and was hoping that the year or so out here might change that. He was naturally shy like his father, but had never felt that way with her. Time would tell.

While all the others were hugging and kissing, Chip greeted her quietly with a "Hello, Tina. I'm so glad we're back to stay for some time."

She bent to kiss her cousin on the cheek, but he moved, and she caught him on the mouth. "Oh, sorry!" She blushed delightfully.

"Don't give it another thought, anyway, I liked it," he said so only she could hear.

She smiled at him sweetly. It reflected in her eyes. Her heart was pounding. "It was an accident, Chip."

"I know, but the next one may not be," he said softly.

Her dimples showed as she smiled at him and blushed again. "Oh! Okay," she replied quietly. Her heart still hammering, now with anticipation.

His heart was as well. He thought to himself, "Wow, I didn't expect that reaction." Accident or not, he certainly enjoyed it. It was the first time he had kissed a girl. Hopefully, she would be the only girl he would ever want to kiss, he thought. He stumbled, shocking himself at that thought. Where did that idea come from? Puzzled at his own reaction, he looked towards her again.

She was walking with his twin, Sarah. She skipped with happiness and glanced back at him shyly. She smiled.

Was it because they were so alike, or did he really feel something special? He would need to ask his father for advice and even his approval. He knew one day he would become the Duke. It was not something he looked forward to. His father told him about duty and he is role in caring for the community. However, he knew his choice of bride would need to be vetted by his father. He had to know that if Tina were suitable before he started anything they couldn't stop. Before their hearts became too involved.

Yes, he would ask his father soon.

Ned was watching his son as he walked up the grassy hill alone. Something was obviously concerning him. And that was 'something' ahead of him in a lovely blue gown by the look of it. Ned noticed that Chip had not taken his eyes from her since he arrived. Ned had missed the kiss but saw the quick conversation and blush afterwards; however, he did see the quick nod of her head. He caught up with Chip. "Hello, son, is everything all right?" he said softly.

Chip welcomed his company, "Fine, Father, but I would like a moment of your time, soonish if possible, and alone."

As father and son, they were close and good companions. They had had the obligatory father-son talk when Chip's voice was starting to break. Being a future Duke brought far more responsibility for the young man. Their one discussion had led to many. Particularly about 'girls, urges and man stuff'. Chip had listened, and the advice from his father was absorbed. He had many freedoms, but Ned had been very strict about respecting women of all walks of life. He reminded him that Aunt Sal had been a convict when they met. Women were not chattels for his use. That included maids, school friends and village girls.

Ned knew that many other soldiers had taken women like Sal as 'comfort women,' but that was why they were still close. He had never laid a finger on her; Sal was like a sister to him. His respect for all women was one of the reasons Christina loved him. He'd be as happy to sit and talk to the old toothless ladies from the village or the little children in school. There was never a breath of scandal about him. Even his soldiers claimed he was the ultimate gentleman, just and fair. Chip was often seen on rounds of the estate with him. They usually went on horseback, visiting every hamlet and cottage; no one was deemed unimportant. Chip was taught to respect every one of their tenants.

Ned and Gerry had gone through the estate record book with a fine-tooth comb. His father had been too old to notice, and David didn't care. Every relative was visited, income was adjusted, and repairs were ordered for every cottage. Chip was encouraged to tag along and learn. As Liam grew, he would also need to familiarise himself with the estate.

Ned had seen the importance of being able to hand the estate to Gerry or his brothers. If Liam, too, knew how things were run, it would ease the burden on Chip. Thankfully, they were close. Ned had explained to both boys that they had a responsibility to the family and each other. Reg was training Chip to know the estate manager's job; Liam, in turn, would learn and take over that position when Reg retired, if he wished to. Ned would not force him. God may well call him to do something different. He explained that he had never been taught about the estate, as his father only had David in mind. No one had expected David to die a mere two years after inheriting the title. Nor that he would have no heirs, so Ned said both his sons had to learn everything. The more Liam helped, the larger his allowance would be, too. If he became the estate steward or the agent, they could work together. However, he would give Liam a choice, as there was nothing worse than being forced to do one thing when he had his heart on another. If Liam chose to stay on the estate, it would benefit both, as it would mean each could travel as desired, knowing the Estate was left in safe hands.

Now, Ned was pleased that Chip wanted his advice. He may have to have a quick chat with Ed first. If what he thought was to happen, a discussion would immediately be needed. "Come to my room once you're settled, son." He dropped back and watched Chip walk on. His son's gaze was still fixed on Tina.

Eddie was carrying both the young twins. Jenna had handed him their son as he was wiggling too much for her.

Ned stepped in and rescued Ed. "Come on, my fine young man." He grabbed Pip and lifted him as though flying. "Ed, fall back with me," he said quietly. They were playing with the babies and carefully fell behind the group. "Ed, I have a feeling we may have the possibility of a budding romance brewing. Chip has asked to see me alone. He's not taken his eyes off your daughter since our arrival," Ned said softly.

"I think it's already started if the kiss was anything to go by," Ed replied, smiling.

Ned groaned. "Oh, I missed that. Not a passionate one, I hope."

"No, a brush, by accident, but certainly one I expect to be repeated reasonably soon if their body language is anything to go by. The gentle hand on his chest was a dead giveaway. Uncle Ned, I could not imagine anyone better for her, but how do you feel?"

"Ed, I'd be delighted. At least then you could drop the Uncle bit. Do it anyway," he smiled in reply.

"So we both approve then. I never expected to be having this conversation this early, nor with you." Ed chuckled. "Let's see what happens. Might be expecting a bit too much too early."

"Eddie, at home, it's not been unknown for girls to have their come-out ball or debut at fifteen. We could agree that if things proceed, they can have an understanding but not an engagement for some years. That's if a relationship moves that way. What's more, they both have to be presented first." Ned was staggered.

"Good idea, yes, they are far too young for an engagement. But we might come back with you and present her early. I hope that won't be for a year at least, though." Eddie looked at Ned.

"Possibly two, lad, I'm sad I actually have to leave at all, but as we actually have not yet arrived at your house, we'll not talk of that yet. Reg and Paul are running things, so it's in good hands. I'm just glad we're here."

"Me too, very glad." Ed gave his other mentor a huge grin.

Luke and John were so in deep conversation and nearly missed the path into the house. John and Colleen had changed their minds and decided to stay at Charlie's home; John's parents would go to Caro's brother Thomas.

Ellen was waddling on Luke's arm. She had met the duke before, but he was only a Major then; now she was expected to call him 'Uncle Ned'. She was still adjusting to being an Earl's daughter-in-law. She had totally forgotten Luke was an Earl's son. It had only sunk in when she was introduced as 'The Honourable' at the wedding.

"We were wondering how we were going to get your goodies to Antwerp. I think we just found our trusted path. Uncle Ned can take them when he goes back," Luke said as they wandered along the dusty road.

"We'll sound him out later. I'm guessing he'll be here for a while, so there is no hurry," Colleen said so softly that even Charles and Gerry behind them couldn't hear what they were talking about. The finding of the diamonds had not yet been officially reported. Until it was, no word was to leak out.

The Governor knew, but until William Clarke submitted his written report and completed the mineral survey, it was unofficial. They had mentioned finding sapphire and rubies, but everyone knew about them anyway. They had sold some of those, with more to come. "You know we can't say anything to any of them until William's reports are submitted. So I hope he'll stay long enough for that," she added.

The four agreed. Nothing could be said until William's official report had been submitted to the governor.

The large group dawdled in through the back door of the house.

Everyone settled in quickly.

Luke and Ellen said their farewells to John; they would talk later.

They caught up with Gerry and Annabella and their brood, who were slowly dawdling along Philip Street.

"Hello, Doctor, Mrs Winslow-Smythe, I hope you won't mind a bit of a walk. It's another couple of blocks away." Luke said.

"The walk is fine," Gerry said, "The names, however, are a mouthful. Just Gerry or Uncle Gerry if you wish, and my dear wife here is Annabella, or as Ned's children call her, Aunty Bell."

"I'd like Aunty Bell, is that all right?" Annabella said warmly.

"Aunt and Uncle, it is then. Now, who are these little angels?" Luke asked.

Gerry introduced his brood. Bella was fourteen, Neddie was eleven, Matty was ten, and Sanna was eight.

On arrival, Luke introduced them to Ellen's parents, Molly and Bill Miller. The guests had settled into their new suite in Luke's house. Sam and Isabelle now ran the inn, and Bill would still lend a hand if they were busy, or more often when he was bored.

They were greeted by brother and sister, Connor and Kerry Murphy. Colleen had let Luke know that her siblings were looking for work and whether they would be interested in any staff. They had moved in the week before Molly and Bill, and were now settled. Connor had rooms above the stable and became the groundsman, stablehand and general hand. Charles had chuckled, as it was his first job. Kerry had the maid's room off the pantry and could not believe she had a room to herself. Sal had once shared this room. Kerry laughingly complained to Ellen that she was lonely, though. "Maybe another of my sisters could come too? Especially with the extra people coming."

Ellen had taken her seriously. Twelve-year-old Siobhan had arrived with Wills and Cathy. She was excited to be staying, even if only for a little while. She would be with Kerry, and her parents were pleased she would be trained and employed somewhere safe. Ellen had heard her name but asked how to spell it. The young girl explained, "In Irish, sometimes the b's sound like v's. So it is pronounced as 'She-von'." Then she giggled. Considering she had never been there, she had an Irish accent. Ellen had learned to love her dearly.

Luke had welcomed her, but said she must go to school while there. She would be going to Mr Lock's Ladies School during the day. Luke had a bunk built for her in Kerry's room, and like Kerry, she couldn't believe that she had a bed, let alone one to herself. It was a treat. Neither could believe they actually had a proper room to share. Both usually slept on the hard dirt floor.

Gerry, Annabella, and their children settled in quickly. Everyone, including the three Murphys, headed to Ed's for dinner.

Wills and Cathy had arrived with Immi and Deidre Murphy. They were considered family; they, too, were coming to the welcome party. Colleen was the first one in the family to have a baby, and they all loved children. Any excuse to see her was a good one.

Ed planned that they would all meet at his house for dinner at seven. It was a fine evening, and Cara and Paddy had set up the tables in the backyard. The last time they had a large gathering, Ricky and Will English had been there to help with Luke's wedding. They had pitched in and served.

Colleen, Caro, Doug, Hamish, and Effy now spent a considerable amount of time working with both Landon Homes and Sadie House for the orphan babies. They had all become friends with all these needy folk. Every week, they had found some other poor child who needed help. Ricky and Will were still the ones to whom these waifs preferred to turn to. Their reputation around town was good. All they needed were the facilities to do their work. The family helped with Mrs Yates, now a fixture at the home as house-mother, as she had taken on some new girls in the shop.

Colleen and Caro had taken it upon themselves to help teach them cleanliness, grooming, and deportment. The spoken language was a work in progress, but they were making headway. Reading and writing were a trial, but at least the older children could write their names. Two new assistants were helping Ricky. Mr and Mrs Fishbon were incredible.

Mr Fishbon recognised Luke when he visited one day. "Weren't you at The King's School?" he asked soon after meeting him.

"Yes, sir, you taught me mathematics, amongst other things. You helped me with the bookkeeping system I was working on," Luke replied.

"Ah, yes, I remember now. You created a new system based on what I taught you. I use yours now, you know. Works much better. It's how I set up Ricky's books. " Mr Fishbon had never worked out why the lad needed to know something that intricate. "Luke, I have to ask. Why did you need a bookkeeping system while at school?"

"I was developing it for the Emporiums, sir. First Eddie's, then for Wills. They are all still using it. They had no head for figures. Neither did I, until I understood how it worked. Once I put it to practical use, it made sense. I had to streamline it so everyone could use it. Do you know that I'm now a teacher at King's, and I use the same principle?"

"Huh?" his old teacher didn't understand.

"I teach the boys 'why' they need to learn, then 'what' they need to learn. Once they understand the 'why,' the 'what' follows. Reverend Clarke taught me that."

"Oh, that! Yes, most teachers wish they could get that across, but you meant you actually teach it?"

"Yes, sir, I teach it. I ask a little about each student, including their interests and likes, as well as their goals in life. Then I tell them what they would need to know for that work, why, and how they can learn it. Then I provide examples of how a particular subject can be important in each of their lives. We then do a physical project on it. Something tangible, then the rest falls into place," Luke said

"Well, I never. And it's working?" he was asked.

"Yes, sir, it seems to be. I've only done six months so far, but if last year's final exams are anything to go by, it certainly is. 100% passed and passed well."

The family assembled in the cool of the evening. The five members of the Murphy family pitched in and offered their help on arrival.

Moira and Shauna were so relieved. Most notably, Moira; she had met Connor Murphy a few times and liked what she saw, as did he.

Throughout the evening, Connor also took every chance he could to offer her aid, carrying, lifting, and finally packing away. He was by her side. Paddy kept his eye on him and noted that he did not take advantage of opportunities. He just showed he cared by helping her.

Paddy took him aside later in the day and said, "Connor Murphy, if you are serious, lad, you can walk out with her, but if you are foolin', then you can go home now and not return."

"You meant that, Mr Connor? I can walk out with her? Sir, I'd love to. I've got a good job now and could support her," Connor replied.

"Don't get ahead of yourself, laddie, I said, 'walk-out', that's all. Let's see how that goes first." Paddy turned and walked off.

Connor took the opportunity as soon as he could.

Moira was alone in the kitchen after all the food had been served. She was putting on the water for after-dinner tea.

Connor walked in as she was trying to move a large pan of water. "I'll get that, Moira. Don't strain yourself. I'll move that for you." He shifted the pot for her. "I wanted to catch you alone. Moira, your father, has just permitted me to ask you to walk-out with me. I was wondering if you may possibly be interested." He was somewhat tongue-tied with his request.

"Oh, Connor, really? He said yes? I would love to. Ohh, I shouldn't be so keen, should I?" she giggled as she clapped her hands with delight.

"I'm glad you are, though, so that's a yes," he bent and gave her a quick peck on the cheek. "I'll bide by his rules, Moira. Just walking out for the moment." He held the door for her as they rejoined the party outside.

Their hands touched on the door; she turned and smiled at him. They were the same age and had known of each other for years. Their parents had been friends much longer. Moira had not been to Emu Plains, and he had only recently moved to Parramatta.

At twenty-nine, Moira had never been allowed to walk out with anyone before. Her father had never before given permission, considering the convict men unworthy of his daughters. Moira was ecstatic, as this meant her papa approved of him.

Connor had never been in a position where he had money, and so had never asked anyone before. Both were from Irish Protestant families; both were born free.

"Connor, I'm free tomorrow afternoon," she whispered. "It's my afternoon off."

"I'll ask Luke, but I'll get to see you somehow." He had never expected to be on first-name terms with his employer. Luke, however, was different. He was as good as family.

Connor saw that Luke was standing by himself for a moment and approached him. "Hello, Luke, I was wondering if I could ask you something."

"Sure, Connor, how can I help?" Luke and Connor had spent many years playing on the Nepean River together. They were the same age and had many adventures. For Luke to be in a position to now employ him worked well for them both.

"Paddy has just permitted me to walk out with Moira, and she's off tomorrow afternoon. Did you need me?" Connor said to his friend.

"That's fabulous, Connor. Of course, you can take her. Work your time around her. She might be a bit busy for the next year, mind you. So take the time when she's free. Come and help here if needs be." Luke slapped his friend on the back. "I hope it works out, Con. I really do. You have my blessings. Hey, and just in case, we can turn your rooms into a nice apartment. How about we get on to doing that anyway? Just in case." Luke watched the smile spread on Connor's face.

"Serious? You'd do that." Connor grinned.

"We are going to do it, Connor. You need a wife, and she's a beauty. Grab her while you can. Oh, and she cooks eggs perfectly. Don't mess around. But wait until we get your apartment done before you propose."

They sat, watching their friends and family.

Connor's gaze followed Moira. "You know, you should introduce Brodie to Shauna. They are of an age. We need to get him a job. Wills needs a caretaker for *Roseneath*. Or would you rather that?"

"I'll stay with you if that's all right, Luke. Brodie would need more than just Shauna to help him up there. Brennan or Shamus could help, but Marc would miss them; the little ones could help him now and still live at home. But doesn't Wills have maids up there anyway?"

"Did! He had three Irish girls, but they are all now married. He's looking for more, preferably someone trustworthy, and preferably a couple."

"I'll ask him, Luke. I can't do more. Might be better if Wills did, though. He'll see Wills before I mention anything to Brodie."

Connor was still watching Moira, and she looked at him and mouthed, "Help."

"Gotta go, Luke, see you at home; hey, and thanks."

Luke watched him flee to her side. He was thrilled for his friend.

Ellen had been waiting for Connor to go. "Lukie, is everything all right?" She put her hand in his outstretched hand.

"Yes, fine, love. Paddy had just permitted Connor to walk out with Moira. I told him we'd redo his room into an apartment like when my parents lived there."

"Ahh! That's all right then." She leaned on his chest. "Lukie, do you think we could ask Dr Gerry about the baby? I'm due soon, sooner if it is twins. I don't want to see a stranger. If Aunt Bell is there, I'll feel happier, and Mama." She lay her head on his chest; she could hear his heart beating.

He wrapped his arms around her. "I love you so much, Ellen Lockley. We'll certainly ask him. It's actually nice that he's staying with us. Do you know he's a specialist baby doctor?"

"Yes, I heard, that is why I asked," she said quietly.

He bent and kissed her gently. "Whatever you want, my lovely one."

"Whatever? Can we go home? I want you alone," she whispered.

"Well, almost anything." He said apologetically, "I can't really leave our guests alone on their first night. If I say you're not well, Dr Gerry will come and investigate, but later, I promise you. I'm all yours." He cupped her face in his hands. "And I'm looking forward to that rendezvous so much." He gently kissed her again. "In the meantime, we'd better behave."

"Spoilsport, all right. You'll keep," she giggled and gently pulled away. Her distended belly came between them. It was hard to overlook. She could sit a mug of tea on her stomach.

The children were occupying themselves in the yard. The three babies were asleep again in the nursery upstairs. Both Ned and Eddie had watched their teenage children surreptitiously throughout the evening. Chip did not overstep the bounds of propriety; however, he was always close to Tina. Not too close, but close enough to be of any assistance should she require it. Ned laughed to Ed, "I'd hate to be going through that heartache again."

"At least when I saw Jenna, I got permission to pay court to her the week I met her. But Uncle Ned, you had to wait, how long? Nearly two years? It's going to be hard for them if this is the case."

"Yes, we'll have to protect them from themselves," Ned added. "We might, of course, be jumping the gun. I doubt it, but if they do wish to proceed, I think we should lay down the ground rules for them. Can I use your office, Ed?"

"Of course, whenever you need to. If the door is closed, the house rule is a 'NO ENTRY' zone, though. So that you know."

"Thanks, Ed," Ned said.

Later on that evening, Chip finally had a chance to talk to his father. He'd tried earlier, but his mother was resting, and they couldn't be private. Ned took him into Eddie's office after most had retired to bed and shut the door. "Now, son, how can I help?"

"Sir, I know I'm only fifteen, but how do you... Oh, well... Um. How do you know you're in love?" His son looked to him as though he had all the answers. This is one question he didn't have a definitive answer for.

"Ahh! Son, some questions have no answer. All I can say is, you do not marry a girl you can live with. You marry one whom you cannot live without. It's a bit of sage advice your grandmother told me when I was about your age. Chip, if you're prepared to do anything to be with her. If you feel life is destroyed if she's not part of it, then you know you're in love. It's how I felt with your mother. I resigned my commission so I could be near her. I love her more than life itself. That is love. Once before, I thought I was in love; on reflection, I was merely attracted to her pretty face. I later found her nature was, shall I say, not as attractive as her face."

"Mmm, thank you, Father." Chip sat, thinking. "Father, what do you think of Tina?"

"I wondered when we would get around to her." Ned smiled at Chip's shocked expression.

"But how, huh?" Chip looked wonderingly.

"I was your age once, Chip, my boy. And she's beautiful, and so is her nature. Chip, her father, and I had a little chat this afternoon. I'll make this a little easier for you. He will talk to her tomorrow sometime, and if she is interested, which by the way I think she might be, so don't stress over that; but if you are both in agreement, you have our blessing to walk out with her, no more, no less. Remember, Chip, you are both only fifteen. Son, you will *never* be alone with her. She is a lady, well, the daughter of an 'Honourable' anyway, and the granddaughter of an Earl. You must treat her as you would a princess. Do you so understand? You will *not* compromise her in any way. Your reputation will escape; you're a Duke's son. For some reason, there would be few repercussions for your actions. For her, her reputation would be destroyed, even if you then married her. It is not the right way to start a marriage. So it is better not to allow it to happen in the first place. It is *why* we have the rules of etiquette. If you love her, you will protect her any way you can."

"I would not hurt a hair on her head, Father," he swallowed. "Father, you mean I can woo her? Really?" His eyes were fixed on his.

"Err, I don't think she'll need much wooing. It's more like you may eventually have an understanding. You are both too young to become engaged. But an understanding is the step before that. Sadly, it means you would have to wait until you are eighteen before you marry. That's over two years away, a bit more actually, as she's a little older than you. I'm sure you know how old you both are." He grinned.

"Over two years!" Chip sighed with a touch of a groan. He was somewhat horrified. "Can I hold her hand? Or kiss her? Or anything?"

"This is where it gets hard. A stolen kiss here or there could compromise her irreparably if seen by the wrong person, and it only takes one slip. Once you reach that stage…" He shook his head. "But until then, you treat her as a queen. Nothing but friendship until you're both sixteen anyway. Chip, this is your cousin Tina we're talking about. You will be living in the same house as her for the next year at least. This will be both hard and easier. You will get to see each other in good and bad. Become her friend first and foremost. If you fight with her, make up quickly. We will still be living here with her even if you have a big argument, so be sure, be very sure before you make a move." Chip nodded, but did not reply.

"Chip, become friends first, good friends. This way, you can often be together with others present. You can escort her to dances as her partner; you can even kiss her on the cheek or hand. Take it slowly, very slowly."

"All right, Father. I'm just over the moon. I have your blessing. That was my first hurdle." Chip gave his father a huge grin.

"Respect, Chip," his father said lovingly but firmly.

"Yes, Father," he said, suitably chastised. Six months until he could kiss her again, but he would be able to be with her every day. To see her and get to know her properly. He felt like cheering.

Chapter 19   Walking Out

*T*he next morning, Ed took his daughter into his office before breakfast. "Tina, please sit." He pointed to the settee. Ed took a deep breath. "Love, don't look like that. You're not in trouble. I need to talk to you about Chip."

Her face relaxed. "Oh!" She brightened.

"He spoke to Uncle Ned last night, and then Uncle Ned spoke to me. Tina, I have given permission for him to ask you to walk out with him. I presume this is your wish, if that kiss yesterday is anything to go by." Ed smiled.

"Oh, Papa, it was an accident," she blushed. "But oh, such a nice one," she said, dimpling as she grinned.

"I know. But you will be sixteen in only a few months. What you could get away with as a child could now ruin you." Ed swallowed; how can parenting be this hard? "Love, I could imagine no one better for you than Chip. I love him like another son. Having said that, you must be circumspect. Uncle Ned and I have worked out that your friendship may progress. The ground rules are that you are never to be alone with him. You do not want him to be forced to marry you. If you want this to work, you must not tempt him. You must not allow either of you to be compromised. Remember, he is a duke's son; his reputation would recover. Yours, however, would be ruined forever even if you married him."

She looked horrified. "But Papa…"

He put his finger up to silence her. "Tina, teenage love is hard. Your brain is saying one thing and your body another. Without discipline, your body will win. Later on this morning, the four of us will have a talk." She was looking distracted. Ed wondered if she was fully listening. "It will be hard for you to live in the same house with each other for at least the next year. Uncle Ned has suggested that, at least until you are sixteen, you will be no more than good friends. Stay with your twins. You and Sarah are already good friends. Always be in foursomes, never be alone. Once you are sixteen, we will allow you to walk out with him properly. That means you can be a little closer. Tina, love, become his friend; be his confidante. The romantic side of a relationship waxes and wanes; the friendship will always remain. Encourage that now, and it will see you in good standing for the future. Do you understand what I mean?"

"Yes, Papa, thank you, Papa. Do you think he'll ask today?" she asked.

"Ahh, Tina, no; he will not. Not until you're sixteen, but that's why we're meeting after breakfast. I didn't think you were listening. Your heart is already running away with you. If you are not careful, it could ruin you both." Ed saw her blush. "You could kill any possible future for you both."

The look of shock on her face showed that what he said was true. "Sorry, Papa, I've not felt like this before. He keeps coming to my mind. I just want to be near him."

"I know, sweetheart, but that's the heart talking. When you're sixteen, we may occasionally let you snatch a kiss or hold his arm on a walk. Be guided by us. When the time is right, we will make allowances. Until then, get to know his likes and interests. Learn to love what he likes. To do the things he likes to do. He will be doing likewise, Tina, in all things, be honest with him. Granny Sal gave me some good advice. 'Start as you mean to go on.' Learn to discuss things that interest you both, and don't harp on about things you know will bore him, like the fribbles and furbelows of fashion. Be honest in all things. If you set the ground rules for your relationship now, they will be easier to follow later. Each milestone, therefore, becomes more critical. Remember, until he turns eighteen, you are legally unable to marry, and he's two weeks younger than you. So, my darling girl, make it easy for you both. A girl's passions are a lot easier to stop than a boy's. Do not push him, do not make suggestions of illicit liaisons or secret assignations. I do not think he will suggest such things; I hope not anyway." Ed sat, looking at his daughter with new eyes. She had grown up, and he had not realised how very lovely she was. She had a slightly darker colouring than her twin brother and her cousins. Her eyes were somewhere between his sky blue and a stormy sea. Her dimples and pale, honey-gold hair softly rippled around her head and shoulders. No wonder Chip had fallen in love with her. When she turned sixteen, she would be allowed to wear her hair up. By then, she would be 'taken' and safe from the pariahs of the social world. He sighed with relief. Yes, she would be secure with Chip. They would live with Ned after they married, and she would be safe.

She returned her father's intent gaze, wondering about the deep scrutiny. "Papa?"

"I'm just wondering where my baby girl has gone. She grew up, and I had not noticed. We'll enjoy this time ahead, sweetheart. If Chip is half the man his father is, you have done well. Now give your Papa a hug, and let's have breakfast."

She ran into his arms with the joy of a child. "I love you, Papa, you know that. I won't do anything to hurt either you or Chip."

She kissed him on the cheek and hooked her arm through his like a child; they left the room for breakfast. Ed looked at her in wonderment that he could possibly have a child, already contemplating marriage. Where had those years gone?

Chip was walking down the stairs as they emerged. Accidental or not, the timing was perfect.

"Office, after breakfast with your father, okay?" Eddie said quietly to him as they walked into the dining room.

"Yes, sir," Chip said.

~

A mere six weeks after the arrival of the family from England, they were all together celebrating Connor and Moira's engagement. All the Connors, Murphys, Evans, Lockleys, Millers, and Ellis families gathered for the celebration. Saturday had been festive, with every room filled to the brim with family. Caro and Douglas stayed with the Tindales again.

The following day, Ellen was so uncomfortable that Luke did not even want her to go to church, but she refused to stay at home.

Dr Gerry had carefully examined her the day before and had watched the confinement progress. As he was on hand and he had checked out of the hospital, he decided that she did not need to make a trip to Sydney to give birth. He had recommended that she walk daily and never be alone. Twin births could be complicated.

Gerry watched her intently; something didn't sit right with him.

Ellen took his words to heart. While Luke was teaching, someone was always with her. Be it Annabella, Kerry, or even little Siobhan. All she needed was a runner to get help if required.

~

It was 26 April 1857, two weeks after Easter; the church was packed with many extra family members and the many Murphys.

Luke was anxious. Ellen had not slept much, commenting about being unable to get comfortable.

Gerry had given her the all-clear to attend service, but insisted that they sit with him to watch her. Their pony trap was kept in readiness, and Connor sat near the door in case. Molly and Bill were behind them.

Molly was the first to notice that Ellen would grasp Luke's hand every twenty minutes or so. After Communion, she tapped Gerry on the shoulder and just said, "It's time."

He nodded, and they left the church as quietly as possible. Luke escorted his wife outside. They had just made it to the gig when the first significant contraction hit. Ellen leaned against the gig in agony. "Oh, Luke," she felt a flood and knew her waters had broken.

He lifted her into the gig, and Connor drove them home as quickly as he could. Her parents, plus Gerry and Cara, followed in Ed's carriage with Paddy driving. Luke carried her onto the verandah and was going to carry her upstairs, but Gerry suggested it would be better for her to walk. Luke looked horrified but placed her down. Cara and Molly hastened to prepare for the birth; most was in readiness.

Kerry had left a large pot of water on the stove, just in case. It was already hot. She had seen her mother in labour often enough to know when things were close. She had been ready for three days.

The effort of walking up the stairs hastened things, and three hours later, at noon, William Edward Lockley entered the world. He was five pounds but had strong lungs. Soon after, Mary May was born, 4lb 10oz, followed by Sally Elizabeth, 4lb 9oz. All were perfect. No wonder Ellen had been uncomfortable.

Molly had called in Maureen as she had come from church to assist if required. She certainly was needed.

Sal had followed in the second carriage and attended the birth as well. She was handed her grandson after his cord was cut.

"Well, I never. Three! Aren't we clever, love?" Luke said after she had delivered the third one. "You don't think there's a fourth in there, Dr Gerry?"

"No, that's it, but the afterbirths will tell an interesting story. William will obviously be a single, but I have a feeling the girls could be identical." He explained the difference. "They'll have trouble explaining that the girls are both twins and triplets all at once."

"Oh!" they all said in unison. Ellen was exhausted, and no wonder.

The sitting room downstairs was crowded. A few of the family had remained at church. Jenna, Christina, Cathy, and Gracie were in prayer in a huddle. Knowing that for each of their lay-ins, this was how their family had supported them. The assembled group heard the cries of the first birth with joy and relief. They awaited the second and sighed with relief, but were stunned when they heard a distinctly different third cry later. "Three?"

Cathy giggled. "Trust Luke to better us all, but poor Ellen. She's going to need a lot of help. How is she even going to feed them?"

Luke had no intention of being in the room for the birth, but Wills, Ed, and Uncle Ned had all said he would never regret it. Gerry didn't give him an option. So Luke had stayed with Ellen. He followed Molly's instructions on how to hold her to give her strength. He whispered prayers and words of love all through. He was in absolute awe of how she coped.

She relaxed against him until the first of the afterbirths came. The agony of this made her emit a scream. Luke looked horrified. He felt ill himself.

"Don't stress, lad," Gerry said. "These are a different sort of pain, often far sharper and therefore hurts more. The birth pain is not 'attached to the body'; therefore, it's a pressure pain of delivery; the afterbirth is the placenta coming away from the womb wall and it hurts more. It's like a cut or skin tearing, so I'm told." The women around him all nodded. To Ellen, he said encouragingly, "One down. How are you doing?"

"Tired and sore, Gerry. So very tired," she replied weakly.

"Rest if you can, it could take a while," Gerry said gently.

Ellen relaxed back against Luke and was soon asleep. Some fifteen minutes later, Gerry woke her. "Ellen, it's not coming away as it should. You will have to feed a baby. That can trigger its release." She struggled to sit up.

Gerry gave her a bit of privacy by turning his back to her.

Molly brought William to her and showed her how to nurse and get him to latch on. He fed for some minutes.

Luke was still holding her. He felt her stiffen. "Love. Are you all right?"

"No," she gasped. "Pain again," she said, grasping his arm painfully.

Molly removed the baby, and a side-splitting agony hit Ellen. The bloodcurdling scream that emanated from her reverberated around the room. Molly had a hot towel and placed it on her stomach. This eased it a little. There was not much else they could do. Ellen relaxed and was prepared for the second contraction. It wasn't so bad. The afterbirth finally came away, and Gerry and Molly carefully examined it. "Two cords. They are definitely identical." He chuckled. "Well, that's a first for me. I've never had a fraternal and identical in one hit before," Gerry said, smiling. "The pain should be gone by now. If you can give the girls a feed too, then sleep for a bit."

Luke moved so she could rest against the bed head. He was sitting on the side of the bed, in shock; they had three babies.

Molly shooed him out while they cleaned Ellen up.

Gerry had already gone but was still hovering close by if they required him. Gerry said Luke should have the honour of breaking the news. Luke walked downstairs slowly, still in shock and very pale. They had prepared for twins, but three. He was still shaking when he walked into the sitting room. A hush descended. "Three, we've got three: a boy and identical girls." His legs could carry him no longer; they buckled, and he sank into a chair.

His father was the first to reach him. "Luke, son, are you all right?" he said in loving concern.

"I don't really know, Dar, I'm still in shock." He looked dazed.

Ed handed him a steaming mug of tea and a slice of cake. "Get this into you."

Luke ate and drank automatically. "How can she feed three?" he finally mumbled.

The thought had obviously not occurred to any of them.

Gerry entered and answered. "Luke, you may need a wet nurse if she can't cope, but let her try. Her mother is here with you, and you've got many other helpers too. Give her the option, but let her try. You will be surprised at how the body does cope. Support her in whatever she decides. If the babies are not thriving, only then will I step in, but I'll watch them all." Gerry looked at Jenna and the other ladies present. "She'll need help and lots of it. You know all know what twins are like. Add another one into the mix, and it's twice as bad. She'll need sleep and help. Don't ask, just be there for her. Thankfully, we are staying here, so we'll be on hand with Molly and Bill."

Jenna, Christina, and Cathy all nodded in agreement. Each being the parent of twins, they knew what he meant.

By mid-afternoon, the babies had been viewed and were finally all fed and asleep. Gerry would not let anyone touch them, as none had washed their hands. Ellen was left to rest. He absolutely forbade anyone from kissing any of them until they were six weeks old.

Luke hovered, staring in awe at his ready-made family. "Three, Molly, how are we going to cope?" The babies were all perfect.

"I'm here, lad," she said. "I'm glad we moved in now. And Dr Gerry is wonderful too. Annabella can change a nappy at lightning speed. She was a hands-on mother at home, so she knows her way around the nursery, and with Kerry and Siobhan, too. We'll be fine."

Cara's special Sunday engagement lunch for her daughter at Eddie's turned into an early dinner, or was it a late lunch? The meal was served at three o'clock. No one was concerned.

Although she called them 'flapjacks,' Shauna had made pikelets for the children after church at Eddie's place. This had been planned the day before, and the batter had been made at dawn and was sitting ready for their return after church. They would be cooked on a griddle plate on the stovetop.

The children each helped and also assisted with the cleanup afterwards. Chip and Sarah learned how to do the dishes.

Liam watched a cake of yellow soap be swished in hot water and suds up. Shauna burnt her fingers in the boiling water. He had never done the dishes before and was intrigued by the process. He had an idea and thought he would discuss it with Uncle Eddie. If Uncle Ed could make a little wire basket with a handle on it, maybe even a pair of them and clip them together, the soap could be swished in hot water without their hands getting near the boiling water. In due course, Ed made a prototype and tried it out. It worked. It actually worked so well that he started making them for the three Emporiums.

Liam earned a cut of the profits. Ed took Liam to the forge and showed him how to make other things. He enjoyed the dirt and noise. Life for him here was so different to the sedate and staid life at home. This dirt satisfied the boy in him. Liam began searching for other things to create that would make life a little easier. Chip and Ned Jnr also joined them. Ed knew exactly what he meant and encouraged the others to join in as well.

Ed's son, young Neddie, had started working at the forge when only a child. He and his younger brother Kit would come after school. They were always encouraged to try out their own ideas and designs. The prototypes from over the years hung on a pegboard, and they worked on them, modifying their designs. Once in a while, a new idea took off. If not, it would often be reworked into something different. Liam's idea took some fiddling. The mesh for the basket was initially woven, but Neddie tried a new welding method, laying out lengths of wire into a large sheet, making welds at each join. Once done, this could be cut into the required sizes and turned into small baskets. Eddie realised that they could now make their own sieves for gold panning and for sapphires too. They had previously had to buy them ready-made from England. Eddie tried some sheet welding of fine wire mesh; this was even quicker. And they could make many sheets of mesh quickly. It involved just laying the rows of thin wire on top of each other, then placing the sheets in the hot forge and partially melting it together. The boys enjoyed this hard-working time. Their friendship grew, as did their muscles. Three months saw Chip borrowing Neddie's work shirt, and by the end of the year, he was in his father's.

~

The last Sunday in May saw the Baptism of the triplets. William and Maria Clarke came and stayed with Wills and Cathy at *Roseneath*. He performed the triplets' Baptism, and he was ecstatic that Luke had chosen William for his son's name. A nod to both himself and his brother.

After the service, at the post-Baptism party, William Clarke took Doug, John, Luke, and Colleen aside. "I've finally submitted my mineral survey report. It's official. We have diamonds in Australia. Now what? Have you asked His Grace?"

"No, William, we've not said a thing. I think today is as good as any," John added.

Luke said, "We can use Eddie's office. No one interrupts when the door is closed. It's an unwritten family rule. Can Dar, Charlie, Ed, and Wills be included, too, please?"

"Of course, Luke," William said.

They spoke to Ned, Charles, Doug, Wills, Ellen and Colleen. "Eleven o'clock in Ed's office, please."

At the prearranged time, they assembled in Eddie's office.

"I've asked the Duke, Charles, Charlie, and Eddie here as well. The rest of you are already involved." William had been in deep conversation with Eddie. He had discovered that the Duke was returning to England with the family and would be a means of returning the funds safely, so he, too, was included. It was his find, so his call.

Wills and Charles already knew about most of the gems. Charlie was to be included out of etiquette.

William got the ball rolling. "You may wonder why you are gathered here. Doug is involved, as he has been our cover until now, more of that later. Your Grace …"

Ned interrupted, "No, just Ned, please."

"Fine… Ned, Eddie, we need your help. Charles, Charlie, Wills, you have to know what's going on, as this may turn into another rush. We've not been able to say anything until my official mineral survey report was handed to the Governor this week." He looked at the faces of his friends. "Gentlemen, we found diamonds; the most wonderful, amazing diamonds, sapphires, rubies, garnets, amethysts, beryls, and other gems. The diamonds, though, are superb. Colleen found a corker. Some of the little ones we were able to sell through Mr Richard Lamb. Douglas here had brought some back from China. He has been slowly eking out his hoard. We added some of our little ones to his pile, but Lamb recognised the difference. He is good and honest; he introduced us to some buyers from Antwerp last December. They bought the bulk of the poorer quality sapphires and all but one blue star sapphire. There were some three pounds of them. Some other stones were included in that lot, I think. It seems so long ago. Douglas presented them with the diamonds in various parcels and caused them no surprise. They recognised them for what they were. However, when they saw the big ones, they baulked. The small packets of second-grade sapphires cleaned them out. When they saw the big one, oh gentlemen, you should have seen their faces. Colleen found what I think is one of the largest diamonds ever found. It's top-grade and perfect. Lamb said he could see no flaws. He said it could be over £20,000 alone. And there are others." He paused, watching for a reaction. He was not disappointed.

Ed's eyes flew to Luke and then to John. "Oh!"

Ned looked intently at William. "How do we fit in?"

"Well, sir, we need someone to sell them for us in Antwerp. That's where you and Eddie come in. We were hoping that you might do this for us. We have a parcel of ten large diamonds from ten to twenty carats or more, all either top-grade or near. The value of them all could be as high as £50,000, possibly more, depending on the buyer. We can't trust just anyone with that sort of money. Initially, I thought we would be lucky to get £1,000 or so for them all. Then we showed them to Mr Lamb."

"Ahh!" said Ned. "That's a lot of money; I can understand your concern. You would trust us with these pebbles?"

Charles had sat listening; he started laughing. He had been worried about Luke, living on his small teaching salary. He shared the humour.

Luke stood embarrassed. "Dar, we did well out of the stones we already sold in December. Those ones we sold first in July paid for the house with money left over. This will mean so much more. We still have three years' wages already in the bank." He had been careful not to mention any numbers.

William wasn't that secretive. "Charles, we each had a private package that we found alone. The rest we found together and sold as a group, then divided the spoils. The first sale netted us £600 each, the second over £5,000 each."

Those who were not involved gasped.

"How much did you say?" Charles added.

"You heard, Dar. Hence, the house, improvements, and staff." Luke was sitting on Ed's desk, swinging his legs in amusement. He was enjoying this. "Dar, we brought back over two flour bags full of stones."

William gave them a rough round-up of what they had found. "We only had flour bags to store the stones in. The two bags were three-quarters full on our return. We had sixty-one good diamonds, all cuttable, and some small ones, including a yellow one. Three large mugs full of large, good, cuttable sapphires, overflowing actually; a handful of rubies, a mug of topaz, and a smattering of amethyst, garnet, spinel, and quartz. Did I leave any out? Oh yes, beryl, and red jaspers for seals; probably others too. Well, there were a lot of stones. Then, on top of those, we each had our own jars. Colleen's diamond is one such stone. Luke and John have each had some stones cut for their wives. She was alone when she found it, as was Luke with his blue sapphire, so they don't get counted in the group lots. We each have up to ten more diamonds in our jars."

Ned looked stunned. "You mean full camp mugs? Not dainty teacups? Flour bags. Are you kidding? That's some haul."

William chortled. "Yes, big tin mugs. It was all we had to measure things with. Do you know, we all forgot about the jar in my boot?" He pulled the small jar from his pocket and handed it to Ned. "It's gold dust. I found the jar last week when I had to do some gardening. There are about fourteen ounces of gold in there. Every creek we panned, we would pool the gold. We also have those to sell. Should bring about £140 at £10/ ounce"

Ned had not seen alluvial gold before, as the others had. Wills had shown him some of the quartz gold he had previously found. "This mineral game is a good lark, William," Ned said while passing it on to Charles. "That is such a small amount but so heavy."

William chuckled. "Yes, sir. Will you be our agent? Ed, will you bring the money home? That's what we need to ask you. We have a valuation for each parcel and hope you can get as near to it as possible. We're quite happy to pay 10% commission plus costs. What do you say?" He stood twitching his beard, awaiting a reply.

"Of course, we'll do it, won't we, Ed. What a challenge. I wouldn't miss this for the world." Ned grinned. "And you can forget the commission and costs. I'll cover that. This is a once-in-a-lifetime adventure."

Luke invited Ned over to his house to see their finds, and John did likewise, for when they were in Sydney next.

Ned willingly accepted, as did Charles. They had an invitation to meet Governor-General Denison the following week. So they would call to see John, Colleen, Douglas, and Caro then.

~

In Sydney

In the Evans family's absence, another romance had bloomed. More than bloomed, it had blossomed and was in full flower.

As soon as the Evans family departed, Will English received a visitor. Hamish wanted a haircut. He had shaved off his beard and appeared fashionably dressed at the Landon Homes for work. Will did the deed and sent his friend home without seeing anyone.

On arriving at the house the following morning, Ricky did not recognise him.

Will and Ricky walked around him approvingly. "See, I told you it would look good."

"You're responsible for this?" Ricky asked.

"Why not? If his wooing is serious, he needs to show change. This should be change enough. Why Hamish, you're handsome enough for Government House!" Will chuckled.

"Och aye, the noo, ma silly brother o' mine wrote to the Governor and told him I was here. I thought I cud hide oot here. Not so, haven't told Effy yet." Hamish grinned.

"Told her what, Hamish? That you are brother to a Baron? You would have to explain what a Baron is. Hamish, I'm not sure she would worry. She's just happy she's got you. That is, unless you take her back with you?" Ricky said.

"Back? I'm nowt going back. This is home now. I have nowt there but Fergus. I'll keep in contact with him, though. I do hope he marries one day, as I have no wish to be the heir. He would love it here, too. If things get any tougher over there, I'll suggest to him to come oot too. Wot's more, it's warmer here." He thought for a bit, then said, "I want you two to stand up with me for my wedding tomorrow. We want it all over and done with before anyone makes any fuss."

Ricky and Will looked at each other, then shrugged. "Why not?" asked Will.

"Love to, when?" said Ricky.

Hamish gave them the details and returned home. He was a different man, and he was happy. Hamish and Douglas had become good friends since starting work at Landon Home. Ricky, Will, and Tad were thrilled that they had lots of adult male help. Their store was growing, and the clientele was more upmarket than they could have ever dreamed. Even Lady Denison came occasionally. The cheap fabric was one of the main draw-cards.

~

On the return to Sydney, Douglas and Caro were met by a beaming Effy. She had been exceptionally happy since their earlier trip.

Caro knew she was walking out with someone, but had not enquired who it was. That was her business.

The man who met them on arrival home surprised them, though. It was none other than Hamish, but no one recognised him. After four years, he had finally proposed to Effy when she had made him realise she really didn't care a hoot about his missing leg. He was even more astonishing because he was now clean-shaven and not dressed in his regular scruffy clothing but in very tidy new trews and a jacket.

Her engagement ring was a large blue sapphire. Set as a solitaire. It sat next to a wedding band. Hamish had received his back allowance from his brother, Fergus, who had arrived in Scotland and received Hamish's letters. He was now 'flush for funds.'

Effie had not wanted any other stone than a sapphire. Ellen had one, and it was beautiful. "Our Lord sits on a sapphire throne, and so that's why I chose that. Ellen doesn't wear hers often, but when she does, it looks lovely. I like it better than her emerald."

Hamish grinned lovingly at her. "We have a bigger surprise for ye both. We were married by the Reverend Archibald Fullerton two days ago. Neither of us wanted a fuss. So we kept it quiet. Ricky and Will English stood as witnesses."

Effy slid her hand into his. "Sorry, Mrs Evans, but you know I don't like crowds."

The newly polished Hamish slid his arm around her and drew her close. Their biggest problem was where to live. Effy wanted to stay at the Evans'; however, Hamish had enough to buy them a house. No one had any idea of how old Hamish was, but he certainly looked younger than before. Wills had thought about forty.

Unbeknownst to everyone, when Effy had found Hamish at the back of the church, she had been in daily contact with him once he moved into Wills' house—helping him settle in the town and answering any questions he had. She even taught him to cook.

Not one of the family had even realised, as there was no breath of a relationship between them.

The Evanses knew that she would disappear for a walk every day, but sometimes even twice a day, and no one knew where.

~

Three months after they were married, Effy realised she was with child; they were stunned. She also seemed ageless. However, Eddie knew her to be forty-one, as she was fourteen when he had gone to live with the family, and he was ten. Hamish turned out to be only forty-two. Once shaved and tidily dressed, the years shed from him. They never expected to become parents at their age.

Douglas and the family had come running when, one evening, they had heard Hamish's roaring laugh. Followed by, "By jinks, that's bonny news, my lass." Douglas knocked and asked if all was well.

"It seems the guid Lord is having a guid laugh with us. We're having a.bairn." He swung Effy around in his arms and then kissed her soundly, regardless of the visitors.

Doug, Caro, John, and Colleen were all delighted. Life again would change for them all.

Effy was fearful. "Having a child so late in life is not good, Hamish."

By the time she was five months along, the surprised newlyweds had moved back into Wills' empty house as her room was needed for the new maid. The small room at the Evans' house was too awkward for her to get around. She knew that once she had the child, she could no longer work. So, at four months into the confinement, she had told Caro she would need to leave.

Doug and Caro knew this already, for Hamish had spoken to them. They had employed a girl from Mrs Yates, and for the last month, she had come to help Effy in the house. She did all the cleaning and most of the cooking. Her name was Carly.

About four years earlier, Mrs Yates had found her asleep on her doorstep one day and had taken her in. Carly looked about ten. With food, warm clothing and security, Carly settled in and learned quickly. Effy had come to the Evans' at about the same age. Carly loved children; she had been helping at Sadie House with the babies. When she found out there was a baby in the house already, she was ecstatic about having another one arrive soon, a few doors away. "Babies, a paid job and a loving Christian family. Oh, coo, Mrs Evans, can I live here forever?" she pleaded.

Hamish had not yet told Effy that he had purchased the house next door to the Evans family. It was a small cottage with four rooms, but large enough for them. They would have room to extend if they wished to. It would be done up while they lived at Wills' house. Effy would be none the wiser until it was ready for them. The Evanses were the only family she had, and she wanted to stay close to them. She had never known her own, as she was born in a workhouse, and her mother died at birth, just like Ricky's foster brother, Will. Hamish had no family at all in this country unless he counted Wills and Luke. He called them brothers. Though now, Douglas was even closer. Now Hamish had Effy, and she wanted to stay close to them, so that's what she would be—right next door.

Sometime earlier, Hamish spoke to Douglas on the way to work. "Douggie boy, did I tell ye that I wrote to ma brother as ye said I should? Well, I finally received the reply back. He's finally back from the wars as well, with three years' back allowance and an ongoing allowance for life. Fergus had thought I had died. As I did to him, but I wrote to Lord Colin on the off chance he had returned. He is thrilled I'm alive and well, so there ye are. You told me I should do it, arn I did. The noo I'm married and with a bairn on the way. Ain't life grand? A new Macdonald on the way. Who'd a thunk?" He grinned mischievously.

Doug and Caro had warmly welcomed the lonely man into their extended family. He certainly loved children, and they were sure he would make a wonderful father.

"We ha' been thinkin' aboot names. Fergus Douglas James Macdonald for a boy and Elizabeth Caroline for a girl after her mother." Hamish grinned, "There's a reason for the James instead of the Hamish. But I'll noo go inta that too much except to say Fergus told me that our grandmother had remarried."

Douglas looked puzzled. "Elizabeth?"

"Dinna ya ken, Effy is Greek for Elizabeth? I learned that at Edinburgh University, where I studied Classics. Caroline, after your guid lady. That's what my Effy wants, so that's what it will be. What's more, my own mother was Elspeth, which is Scottish for Elizabeth; her full name was actually Amelia Elizabeth Broome-Hall, and she came from West Sussex. My Papa called her Elspeth. My grandmother remarried at eighty-five, to James, Duke of Malvern." Hamish grinned mischievously.

"Ahh! Well, I think it's wonderful either way, Hamish. Classics, eh, Hamish? You're a dark horse," Douglas said. The more he learned about his Scottish friend, the more astonished he was. A Classics scholar. He really liked this not-so-dour Scotsman. They had grown even closer since working with him at Ricky English's house for orphan boys and street waifs.

~

John Landon's business, which imported fabric, amongst other products, was also growing. Now that he had a direct outlet rather than just a wholesaler, he could shift stock that had previously been dead stock. Even the water-damaged items were now making a small profit. Sadly, one of the problems with importing all stock by sea is that every shipment inevitably suffers some water damage. Ricky's shop solved the problem. John sold it to him at cost, so he wasn't even out of pocket. Ricky then on-sold it for a small profit. Most of the bolts were only damp on one end and could be cut around. Some Ricky realised that he could wash and restore. They dyed and ironed other bolts and then sold them. Ricky also bought a small selection of top-quality fabrics, particularly lawn, poplin, and linen.

Mrs Yates, the girls at the house, Sadie Landon, her daughter Amabel, who was married to Tad, Caro, Colleen, and now Effy were able to take the many damaged bolts and make clothing from them, then sell those. Ivy Vine, whom Sadie Landon knew, was an emancipated convict seamstress and now had her own store. She called it *De'Vine Couture*. Ivy employed about ten ladies who sewed gowns for 'off the rack' sales. Any fabric that was too badly stained was used to make clothing for the orphan babies or toys. They also made bags, buttons, and mob caps from the offcuts. Various lichens and other vegetation were used to dye the worst bolts.

Doug and Hamish's work with the boys had given them direction in life. The skill of rope splicing meant that they could offer their services to many of the dockland boats. Doug had taught Hamish first, so they could both teach the boys. Douglas and Stephen Roberts, although he was now having a bit of trouble walking, had honed this skill. He'd donated his set of fids and other rope repair items to Ricky so he could keep the skills being taught. If the boys could start a business fixing ropes, they would all be able to support themselves. Every ship needed ropes and lots of them. They could even supply the ship's chandlery. They were already receiving orders from the Government for the ferries. The first order was for six fifteen-foot lengths with eighteen-inch eyes on either end.

They had these completed within a week. Hamish was teaching woodwork, carving and whittling. They were also teaching the boys the importance of reading, how to manage money, and how to start a business using the skills they were learning. Hamish even taught them a smattering of Latin, Greek, and French. From ages six to twelve, the boys were given a roof over their heads and food in their bellies; after that, they were expected to either get an apprenticeship or find a job. Unless they had some basic education, that would not be enough.

Mr Iles, the boot-maker, had already taken on some boys as junior apprentices. He couldn't pay them, but they didn't need money; they needed skills. He needed help.

Once word had spread through the church that both Douglas and Hamish were volunteering at the Landon Homes, others joined in. Sadie and John Landon were frequently seen with Douglas or Hamish, as were others, and many businesses offered positions for the free apprentices.

~

In Parramatta

Chip and Tina's relationship progressed; on her sixteenth birthday in August, they had come to an amicable understanding. They slipped around the side of the stables. "Sweetheart, I want to wish you a happy sweet sixteen in a way only I can. I want to kiss you. May I?"

"Yes, but that's all, Chippy. I don't want us to get into trouble." She looked so different with her hair now allowed to be put up. Christina had dressed it for her, rolled down the side of her head and ended in two long ringlets trailing down her back.

Chip drew her into his arms and was about to kiss her. He saw movement out of the corner of her eye. Their fathers were both standing watching, one with hands-on-hips the other with arms folded. Both were looking exasperated.

Ned cleared his throat. "Ah, hum, exactly what is going on here, young man?" his father said.

"Tina?" Ed's eyebrows were raised.

"Oh, Papa, nothing happened. Oh well, it may have... we were going to kiss, but you came. A first real kiss. It is my birthday. You said on my birthday I could." She melted into her father's arms.

Chip looked guilty. "Sir, it was my fault. I'm sorry. I'm so sorry, Uncle Ed, and Tina, I shouldn't have asked you here. I'm truly sorry."

Ned looked at Ed. "We did say they could have their first kiss at sixteen, didn't we?" He looked at Ed with a glint in his eyes.

"Um, well, yes, we did. Didn't we? Even though he's not actually sixteen." Ed's mirth nearly overtook him. "We could just turn our backs."

"Or walk around the corner." Ned was nearly in stitches himself.

"Or just stand over here in the sunshine talking. We won't be long, mind." Ed and Ned walked into a patch of sun, just out of their sight and earshot. "Oh, I would hate to be a teen again, Uncle Ned," Ed smiled. "Jenna was the first girl I kissed."

Chip was allowed to kiss her properly for the first time that day.

"Ed, will you kindly drop the Uncle? I'm pretty sure we're going to be in-laws," Ned said, smiling.

Eddie nodded.

They were soon joined by two errant children who looked like they'd just been given a cream cake. Both were starry-eyed and walking hand in hand.

Ed and Ned's eyes both dropped to the joined hands.

"Two weeks yet," Ned said.

They dropped hands.

Ed lost it; he broke out laughing. "Oh, children, we're not angry. But you really have to be careful. It's just as well it was us." Tina went into her father's arms.

"Oh, Papa, you scared me. I thought you had changed your mind."

Ed chuckled. "No, sweetheart, but can you see how quickly this can turn?"

Tina nodded.

"Chip, you are not sixteen for two weeks yet. Be careful, extra careful. No sneaking off again. We'll give you a chance to have the occasional kiss, maybe even a daily one, but please, my dear ones, don't ruin it for each other. Believe it or not, we all want this to work out for you." Ned looked at the guilt on his son's face.

"What? You do?" Chip said.

"Of course, my boy. Ed and I are thrilled. We're over the moon, actually. It's why we're so protective," Ned said in earnest.

"Ohh!" Chip and Tina said in unison. Looking at each other with smiles on their faces. New understanding finally soaked in. "Oh," Chip said again, this time understanding. He took her hand. And caressed it. "I'm sorry, Tina."

"So am I, Chippy." She didn't intentionally flutter her eyelashes and send his heart swirling. Ned noticed that she was just naturally shy.

"Oh, give her a hug, will you please? You can while I'm here. Just make it look sisterly," Ned said laughingly.

Chip swept her into his arms. He whispered, "I love you, you know, happy birthday, sweeting." He kissed her on the cheek. He had heard his Uncle Luke call Aunt Ellen 'sweeting,' and he liked it.

Ned and Ed walked to the kitchen door. Ned was holding it open for them to follow.

Chip dropped a kiss on her forehead, then they walked indoors.

~

On Chip and Sarah's birthday two weeks later, two fathers opened the office door, ushered in the two sixteen-year-olds and closed them in the office. "You have five minutes, no more," Ned said sternly, then closed them inside.

Wasting no time, Chip drew her into his arms. This time, it was more than a peck on the lips for them both. Two weeks ago, they knew their fathers were listening only an arm's length away. Chip had given her a quick kiss on the lips. This time, they had permission. Their first kiss was awkward. They banged teeth. Both giggled. Then tried again.

"Oh, Chip," she reached up and pulled his head down to hers. Their lips met in an innocent and loving touch.

The time passed too fast. They broke apart when they heard a gentle knock on the door. They exited hand in hand and rejoined the birthday party. They blushed on leaving, both meeting their fathers' eyes.

Later, Ned caught Ed's eye across the room and both their faces dimpled in broad smiles.

Charles watched on, delighted. As did all the women.

Sal leaned over to Christina and said, "This will mess up the family tree somewhat."

Christina chuckled. "Yes, but I'm over the moon, Sal. Have you been watching Charlie's Teddy? He can't tear his eyes off Bella. He's only thirteen, isn't he?"

"Oh, um, yes, but he's fourteen next month, and she's sixteen in December, isn't she?" Sal replied. "A bit young, but one to watch. An eighteen-month difference will make it hard for them."

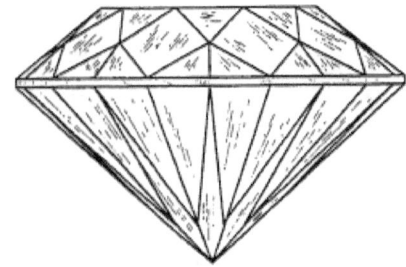

Chapter 20   Diamonds are a...

$\mathcal{M}$r Lamb wrote to the three explorers. The same letter was sent to each man.

Luke's read his note:-

Lamb's Jewellers,
Sydney
13 November 1857

Attn: Mr Luke Lockley
Phillip Street,
Parramatta,

Luke,
  Hold off selling.
  Buyers want your product. I don't trust them. Wait.

Richard Lamb

Sure enough, the buyers from Antwerp were trying to find them. After a chance comment, they found John at the museum. They recognised him as owning the massive diamond. They had come well prepared and loaded with funds. They offered cash, but knowing Colleen's diamond was worth a fortune, they offered a mere £10,000.

John politely refused, saying they had a better offer.

The buyers were not impressed, so they upped the offer to £15,000.

John laughed. He still said, "No." He was now pleased that William had not shown them all of the stones. He still had the fancy yellow diamond and also the group bag of big ones. Once they had said no to one of the larger ones, they had not revealed the remainder of their collection.

After the third offer to John was frefused, they finally departed, seeking out the other two men.

William and Luke gave them short shift as well. Both were ridiculing their offer. "Thank you, but we've had a better offer." Each said the same in turn. That all three had said almost exactly the same words was worrying for the buyers, as they felt that perhaps they had another purchaser for their diamonds. They purchased gold and sapphires from different sources and returned home without the desired diamonds.

~

September 1858

A year passed in a flash.

Ned knew his time in the colony was drawing to a close. At least they would not be returning alone.

The two sets of twins were about to celebrate their seventeenth birthday, with Neddie and Tina's in less than a month. Plans were discussed for Eddie, Jenna, and all ten of their children, plus Teddy, Charlie's oldest son, to go to England with them. They had yet to talk to Charlie and they knew he would object.

"Father, I've had an idea," Chip said to him one day about a month before their birthdays. "I'd like to give Tina a ring. I know it can't be an engagement ring, but what about a friendship ring for her other hand? Something with a few smaller stones set in the band? No one would think twice about her wearing that, would they?"

"I don't know, Chip. It's a bit risky," Ned finally said to his son. "I suppose it would be all right if she told people it was her seventeenth birthday present from her family."

A month later, Chip had taken her aside in the sitting room. The room was packed with family. Young Neddie and Tina cut their cake, and all enjoyed the party.

Chip and Tina were standing in the corner. He had his back to the crowd. "Tina, I have something special I want to give you—a personal birthday gift. You know I can't ask you to marry me until I'm eighteen. I also have to be presented at a 'Levee' before I can even propose. I hope you also know that I will, as soon as possible, after my birthday. In the meantime, I can give you a friendship ring." He heard her gasp as she opened the box.

She had no idea what a Levee was, but said, "Oh, Chippy, it's beautiful."

He took it from the box and slipped it on her right hand. "This time next year, there will be one to put on the other hand."

She stood on tiptoes and kissed him on the lips. "Thank you, Chip. I love it."

"There's a catch, though, my Tina. If someone asks you, you have to say you received it for your birthday from 'my family'. Which, of course, I am. You see, to be presented at home, you must be unattached. If anyone thinks you may not be, well, it would not be right for you."

"Oh, I love my birthday present, Chippy, and the sentiment in which it was given," she said with a twinkle in her eyes.

"That's my girl," he said as he crushed her in a big hug, surrounded by family. He lovingly kissed the top of her head. "Tina, the stones are diamond, emerald, amethyst, ruby, emerald again, sapphire, and the yellow is topaz. It spells 'Dearest', but you are never to tell anyone."

Her twinkling eyes said it all. She kissed her fingers and placed them gently on his lips. "Thank you, my dearest love, for my rainbow of happiness ring."

"When I kiss your ring, I'll be kissing you," he said softly. He took her hand, turned it palm upwards and kissed her ring.

During the afternoon, family members came and went. The last ferry was due in at half-past two, and Douglas had sent a note that they were coming for the night.

Cara came and told them, "I can see the ferry smoke. If you are going to meet it, you had better hurry."

Within minutes, everyone was on the way to the ferry. The ferry was sloshing its way around the final bend as they arrived.

Douglas and Caroline were standing holding a child.

John and Colleen emerged from the cabin with Hamish and Effy following them. Each had another child in arms.

Effy and Hamish's red-haired Fergus was wiggling to get down from his father's arms. He was now nearly seven months old.

Jonty was in John's arms, itching for a run. He had turned two a week before.

Caro held little Maureen; she was her mother's image, with jet black curls and huge, piercing blue eyes. She was only a small baby, a mere three months old. She had won the hearts of the six adults who cared for her.

John wanted to call her Mary, as she was the image of Colleen's little sister.

Colleen had said a flat, "No!"

John was somewhat disappointed; however, he insisted that they call her Maureen instead. Maureen Caroline Evans was born on 8 August 1858.

Hamish was the first to start calling her Reenie. He had given Jonty his name on the day he was born. His own son, Fergus, he called Ferdie. "Hooch, laddie, if you give someone a special name, it shows you love them, that's all. I love you all, so you have special names from me. When you have a name like Hamish, it's hard to shorten. My Fergus calls me Hame or Hammer. I'm not minding it from him, but it's not what I would like to be known as. I won't let ye ken what my Effy calls me. That for her an' me alone," he smiled.

John loved it when he fell back into using his Scottish brogue. He knew his English was perfect, but he fell back into using his native brogue when he was passionate about something. Since they had moved in next door just after their son was born in February, they had become even closer friends.

John had become involved with the work at the children's homes along with the three older men. He had taken one of the lads from Ricky's boys' home to work at the museum. John showed him the work that a scientist had done. Then he showed the lad some drawings, how to record finds, how to relax a dried butterfly, and then pin it out. The boy, Lance, had talked of Hamish and Douglas as they worked together.

John was still sorting through the specimens collected on the trip with William and Luke. He started attending Saturday workshops with Stephen Roberts, his father and Hamish. He, too, loved assisting the orphan boys.

On Friday morning, knowing he would not fit in a full day, he was racing to get through his work before leaving for Parramatta. The governor's aide visited him at work that morning, somehow knowing of his prospective visit to Parramatta. He had presented John with an interesting situation.

The aide said, "Mr Evans, I am charged with asking you to deliver two envelopes on behalf of the governor. I could send them via the usual channels, but the Governor requested that I not do that in this instance. I believe you are attending a particular birthday celebration this weekend. I would appreciate it if these could be presented in private." The aide handed him two thick embossed official letters. One addressed to *His Grace the Duke of Gracemere, K.G.,* and the other to *The Honourable Edward Lockley.*

They were an interesting pair of invitations and were safely in his pocket. John had taken a large manilla envelope from his desk and carefully placed both inside, then tucked them in his coat pocket. The aide's timing was perfect as he was about to depart, and the family was to catch the afternoon ferry. Somehow, the Governor always knew when and where to contact the Lockleys and if anyone was visiting.

John had smiled and had shaken his head in wonderment.

He made it in time to join the family on the ferry.

As they stepped off the ferry in Parramatta, John touched his pocket to make sure the letters were still there. He was itching to know what was in them. Yes, they were safe. As he alighted, he said to both Ned and Eddie, "Hang back." They nodded in reply.

Charles relieved John of Jonty, and everyone set off for Eddie's house. The three men ambled along, allowing everyone to leave them behind. They were obviously deep in conversation. By the time they were entering the grounds, they were alone.

John stopped walking. "Gentlemen, earlier today, I had a visitor at work. He hand-delivered these to me and asked that I personally deliver them privately. I have no idea what they contain, but he did not want them to go via regular post." He handed each gentleman their respective letter.

They took them, looked at each other, and then each tucked their letter in their pockets.

John sighed. He did hope they would tell him what they contained, but he'd not ask. He left them talking as he walked inside. Their bags were taken to his aunt and uncle's house, as they would be staying with them, as were his parents.

Hamish and Effy were to stay with Luke.

Once inside, John joined the revelry of the family group. His ears were listening for Ed and Ned's arrival. They didn't come.

Ned and Eddie walked inside quietly and went directly to Eddie's office. Both were eager to read the enclosed letters.

Ned gasped.

Ed looked puzzled. "Ned, what's a 'Levee'?" Eddie asked.

"It's the young man's presentation to the court. Out here, he can be presented to the Governor, who's the reigning Monarch's representative. I've not heard of it being done much. However, in India, it's common. Kudos to Denison for thinking this up. It could solve our problem with Chip."

Ed still looked puzzled. "Chip is two weeks younger than Tina. Therefore, there is a window when she will be open to the predators at court: the fortune hunters and slippery characters who are out for a title or money. Some may even try to compromise her. Once Tina is presented, and that can be early now, as she doesn't have to be eighteen, we can declare an understanding very soon afterwards, and she be safe. Chip can be presented there, too, but if that is done anywhere in the Empire, it's official. Oh, Ed, this will solve much."

Eddie mused, "Ned, I still can't quite get my head around that they are to be married. Neddie and Sarah are nowhere near ready. Funny, isn't it?"

Ned nodded. "Denison just says to choose a date, and he'll arrange a semi-private ceremony for the boys. He says in my letter to also include Liza's Albie as he's of age too." Ned continued reading. "Ed, he wants us to set a precedent with this. Looks like we're having a Levée. Ed, something has just occurred to me. If you don't know what it is, then you haven't been presented to it either. All of you should be. I should have presented your father in London when we were there. Your mother and Elle were presented by Mother and Christina."

Ed finally read his letter. "Ned, mine says to invite other family members who would benefit and to consult you as to who else would benefit."

~

Later that afternoon, Ned and Eddie called Liza and Bertie aside.

Before they made the decision, they had to talk to them. Ned said he was covering all costs, so they were not to regard that in their decision.

Liza looked to Ed, who nodded, then at Bertie. After a brief negotiation, they accepted with thanks.

Ed called in their three sons and told them what would occur. Young Neddie and Albie had, of course, never heard of a 'Levée'. Once they explained what this entailed, they understood that it was a formal presentation to the Governor, demonstrating that they were considered mature.

Ed walked to his bookshelf and selected a book of court etiquette. "It's from 'The Ladies and Gentlemen's Etiquette': This is what it says in here …

Levées are conducted somewhat on the same plan as that of the Drawing Room but are confined exclusively to men who wear uniform or Court dress. Hosted by the Monarch, those entitled to be presented to H.R.H./ H.M. are members of the aristocracy and gentry, the members of the diplomatic courts, the Cabinet and all leading Government officials, Members of Parliament, leading members of the legal profession, the naval and military professions, the leading members of the clerical profession, the leading members of the medical and artistic professions, the leading bankers, merchants, and members of the Stock Exchange, and persons engaged in commerce on a large scale. An exception to the rule as regards retail trade was made in favour of any person receiving Knighthood, or when holding the office of Mayor, or being made a Justice of the Peace, or on receiving a Commission in the Territorial forces."

Ned looked at the young men standing around him. "Boys, this will open doors for you. Albie, you do not have a title, but you are still the grandson of an Earl, just like Neddie. Chip, as my oldest son and soon you are a Marquess, but you have no authority until you turn twenty-one, you will, of course, be presented first, Neddie, you next, as your father takes Precedence over your cousin, being a son of a son, and Albie is the son of a daughter of the Earl. It doesn't matter as much in the colony, but this will be vastly important in your futures. It's called Precedence. You are all expected to know where your rightful precedence position is; Chip and Neddie in particular. Teddy will need to be presented in future, as should Charlie, as you will one day both be Earl's; so maybe we will add Teddy to the list as well. Ed, can you get him, please? He can certainly learn what it's all about. I should have thought of him before his twin, John, could join him. Bring both Teddy and John too, Anna's boy, umm, Billy, they can listen in. Oh, Cripes. Their father hasn't even been presented, Tim either, and we'll sneak in Bertie too, as he already has a royal warrant from The Queen. Wills and Luke as well. Ed, it looks like we'll be doing the lot of them," Ned said. He leaned over to Ed and whispered something to him as he left. "We'll have to rope in both Harry's and Hamish as well to do the presentation. It's supposed to be one each, but we'll have to do two each. Pity Phil isn't around."

Ed nodded, then left to find his father, brother, and nephews. The five returned and joined the others.

"Ted, John, and Billy are only fifteen, so they'll have to wait a while, but I want you to listen well. Lads, sorry, I should have thought of this before, but you all need to do this. Now we have the opportunity."

They looked at Ned, somewhat confused.

"Denison is offering to have a Levée at Government House. It's a presentation for men, like a Drawing Room is for women. It's never been done out here before, but Denison is offering to host one for us while I'm here. Charles, as a Duke, I should have sponsored you in England, and not being in the swing of things, I totally forgot; sorry. Now we can do it less formally, just *en-family*. I made my presentation just before I enlisted."

A wave of embarrassment swept across Ned's face as he remembered. With a groan, he recounted what he wore. "My outfit was a blue velvet and brocade coat, blue silk breeches, stockings, an embroidered waistcoat, and oh, you should have seen the shoes. The buckles jingled when I walked. Oh, and of course, a sword. I looked like a doll. Fair hair and blue eyes. All was mother's idea, as you can imagine. I wished for black, like my friends Rob, Jim and Gerry had." Ned chuckled. "I lost that battle against her will; you all knew what Mother was like. Well, Mother liked Gainsborough's painting, 'Little Boy Blue'. She even had me painted like that when I was a six-year-old." He groaned. "Mother got her way as you can imagine, but it was the last time she did." He smiled, then groaned again at the memory.

Charles laughed; he remembered just what Ned looked like at that age as he had seen that painting. He only had to look in the mirror and imagine himself dressed in light blue silks and velvets. Yes, he understood Ned's groan.

Ned continued, "At least here, the etiquette will be much less official, but your presentation will be equally acceptable. Charlie, Chip, and Teddy, this will be especially vital for you three. You will be Peers of the Realm. Chip with your title as Marquess of Allingmere, as it's a hereditary peerage, you will have a court position when you are of age."

To Teddy, John, and Billy, Ned said, "Ted, you may one day decide to return to live in England or even just to visit. You three are too young to be presented this time, but listen well, as I won't be here to explain when it comes time for you."

Ned turned to Charlie. "I was wondering if you would allow Teddy to return with us so he can see what England is like. He can finish school there too. As a fifteen-year-old, he will have far more freedom than a child, but none of an adult's responsibility. As he's at The King's School here, they should be able to slot him in with Gerry's boys. He can learn the possibilities of what's in front of him. He will also meet the sons of other Peers. He can stay and finish school there and even university if he wishes. He can see what it's like living in England, or he can return with Ed and Jenna when they return, or stay and finish his education with us." He saw the look of horror cross Charlie's face. Ned lifted his hand. "No, don't answer. Have a talk to Gracie."

Charlie caught his father's eye. His heart sank as his father said, "Charlie, I'm sorry, but I agree with Ned; this is really something you all need to do. Ted, you especially. You will have the biggest change in your life. John, the invitation is open for you, but whatever you do, you will not inherit the title. John, inn will be yours, should Ted choose to remain there." Charles looked at his grandsons and eldest son.

Ted nodded, he was keen to see England. His grandfather had told him what it was like.

"Thank you, Grandfather, but I'll stay here," John said, relieved. The fearful look passed across his face as they discussed this more.

A date was chosen from the list the Governor had offered. October 6th at 8 pm was chosen. This would give them all ample time to select clothing for the presentation. It would be evening dress rather than court dress, as that wasn't worn in the colony. There was much to be done in the following weeks.

They were still deep in discussion when there was a knock on the office door. Ned opened it for Gerry.

Some weeks earlier, they had put their heads together and spoken to Gerry's friend Harry Moffatt, Justice of the Peace and Magistrate.

Ned nodded to him, and Gerry joined the group.

"Hello, all. I'm not butting in, I've been invited," Gerry said, smiling at them all. "I've got a birthday present for Chip and others," Gerry said. "You know I'm friends with Harry Moffatt?"

They all nodded.

"Well, we've been busy, Ned, Harry and I as a birthday gift for some of you boys, and you too, Charlie and Teddy too. Harry has made an age exception for him. Harry and I worked out something for you all." He took a deep breath. "You are all going to be made JPs."

They looked puzzled. Charlie voiced their query, "Do you mean a Justice of the Peace?"

"Yes, all of you, you included, Charles, Charlie, and Ed. Oh, Wills and Luke too," Ned smiled.

To Charles and Charlie, Gerry said, "You two especially have the prestige of titles, but this will give the rest of you a step up in the official society. JPs have an authority attached to them as they are 'Officials'. This also gives you some minor authority in the Courthouse should a magistrate not be available. There are other requirements. Harry will teach you all. He's expecting you this coming week."

Ed knew Tim was already one, and it meant that he often had to take documents to authorise or witness legal forms.

Luke exclaimed with delight. "Wow, Uncle Gerry, that's amazing. Thank you so much. I've just been reading about them. I've just found out that the boys can also be presented in court. Oh, there's so much to learn."

~

The following month saw many visits to the courthouse for various lessons. Harry Moffatt was considering retirement and had wanted to install more Justices of the Peace before he did. They could deal with petty incidents and witness documents. The Lockleys needed no vetting.

Chip also joined them for lessons, as the documentation was legal in England. Ned explained that both he and Gerry were already JPs in England. Chip would need to be registered here and receive additional instruction once home, as there were extra rules at home.

John and Billy would be sworn in when they turned eighteen. Bertie, however, was stunned that his son was to be included.

Harry conducted the swearing-in ceremony for the large family group the week before the Levée and handed them their documentation.

~

October saw all the men *en route* to Sydney for an evening at Government House. The ladies were not invited, so they stayed at home. Harry Moffatt, Harry Harlow, Ned, Chip, Gerry, Charles, Charlie, Eddie, Neddie, Albie, Tim, Bertie, Wills, and Luke caught the ferry together.

Hamish Macdonald was to attend too, as they discovered he had been presented when of age. He arrived in his formal Highland dress. He wore his red Macdonald dress kilt, a crisp, clean white shirt with lace cuffs and had an exquisite hand-made thistle-patterned lace cravat around his neck. There was a cairngorm thistle-shaped pin in the cravat. His dark double-breasted black velvet jacket had black corded braid edging and brightly polished square silver buttons in two rows of five. He wore red and green diamond-patterned knitted hose, which were complete with *Sgian-dubh*, a small knife, tucked in the side of his good leg and a satin flash holding them up. His shiny buckled brogues were laced up his hose. His wooden leg was hardly noticeable. His sporran was a long six-tasselled horsehair one, in black and white, and it hung from a thick braided gold chain from his hips and covered half the front of his kilt. It was all held in place by a wide leather belt with a square buckle. The Macdonald motto was clearly visible: *Per Mare per Terras*. A fly-plaid topped off his formal ensemble, flung carelessly but artfully over his shoulder and held in place by a substantial, round, polished Macdonald buckle over his heart. His fiery red hair was tied pristinely back in a black velvet ribbon. He was now clean-shaven, and this showed his pearly white, straight teeth and a broad smile.

Charles and Ed walked around him and whistled.

"Oh, Hamish, you are going to steal the show," Ned said as he stood and watched with his arms folded.

"Hooch, man; It's just me. Effy said the same." He grinned. "Fergus finally sent me out some real clothes. He put this in, too. I only had my regimental kit and some stuff of Colin's. It's nice to get back into a Great Kilt or '*Filleadh mòr*,' though. I haven't worn one for a while. Think the Governor will mind?"

"No way! You look fabulous, Hamish," Luke said. "And you have a new leg too. Did Michael Lenehan make it?"

"No, not this wee stick. We made it down at the Landon Home workshop. I've been teaching them woodwork and whittling. They decided to try to make something useful, other than fids. So I have a fully shapely leg with a hinged foot and knee. It's Western Red Cedar, so it's lovely and light too. It even moves as I walk. Look, the knee and foot both bend." He demonstrated, "Good, eh? I told the boys we might have to go into business. Legs and ropes."

"What's the motto mean, Hamish?" John asked.

"It means *By Land and By Sea,* I'd have ta give ye the history of Scotland to explain why. In essence, we defend all avenues of attack." He chuckled. "Canny Scots, ye ken." His joyous nature set the theme for the outing. It was a sensational evening.

Governor-General Denison greeted them in the Red Drawing Room. His eyebrow raised when he saw Hamish, but he smiled. The ceremony included some of the Top Brass, as Ned called them. The leading military personnel in the town, the Governor's aide, and the local magistrates and judges all attended. Some were presenting themselves. "So much for keeping it small and quiet," Ned whispered to Charles.

Hamish was welcomed and introduced as "The Honourable Hamish Macdonald". Most had not known of his exalted family connections. The Governor had, as Fergus and he had corresponded on various topics, mostly of work for returned soldiers.

Ned, as Duke of Gracemere; there was also Gerry Winslow-Smythe, now Viscount Fanshaw, heir to the Earl of Winslow; Hamish; The Honourable Henry Harlow and finally Mr Harry Moffatt, JP, as all had been presented previously, they each introduced some of the gentlemen to the Governor. Ned presented Charles and Chip; Harry Harlow presented Charlie and Bertie Ellis; Gerry presented Eddie and Tim Miller; Sir Harry Moffatt presented Wills and Luke, and Hamish presented Neddie and Albie. The official ceremony was not that long. Other dignitaries' sons were also presented.

The family group were both officially presented at Court and acknowledged as Justices of the Peace. All of those presented today would both be able to enter society anywhere in the Empire and now be able to do the same for the other boys in future years. Tim decided to ask if Phil and Stevie could be 'done' next year, as both were aiming to be barristers. The Governor agreed that they, too, needed to be presented, and he may even hold another ceremony later that year.

Ted had stayed at home with Douglas, as he had only come to buy some clothes for his trip to England. His father had relented and permitted Ted to travel with Eddie and Ned.

The day after their presentation, the group visited Morris Jacob's Gentleman's Dresser Outfitter and ordered clothing for their trip to London. Ted, in particular, needed full attire, as he had never required more than church clothing. They then visited Webb and Co., and each bought something special for the ladies in their lives. Even the boys bought gifts, primarily for their mothers.

Chip also purchased an exquisite silk scarf with butterflies on it for Tina. He would give it to her on their evening assignation, which they were now allowed to have, to say good night. It was an arrangement their fathers had agreed to when they turned seventeen. They were given five minutes alone every evening. Every day could not pass fast enough for them both.

Ned had explained that this would not be permitted at home. In England, rules were a lot more strict. However, they would manage somehow. He would have to be in the room with them.

Ned thought about erecting a screen in the sitting room. He chuckled to himself. By the time they arrived home, it would only be months before they could officially announce their engagement. Such an announcement was now only a formality as the family knew the relationship was only two birthdays and her presentation away from formalising it. Tina's presentation had already been booked with Sarah's. Easter was on 4th April, and their presentation was the second one after Easter. The presentation was booked for Saturday, 22nd May.

Colin had seen to this in their absence. He was still following Duchess Suze's instructions. They would not be able to be there for the two pre-Easter presentations. They would be cutting it fine for the first one after Easter, so the girls were booked in for the second and last presentation. It would be only three months before Tina turned eighteen. Hopefully, there would be no delay on their passage as they would be cutting the dates close as it was.

Chip would turn eighteen two weeks later in September. This would allow the girls a few months for their Season without raising an eyebrow due to a previous 'understanding.'

It would, however, be known that there was something in place. It also meant Ed could refuse other offers as he could say she was taken. The family were preparing for their return home.

~

November, December, and Christmas came and went.

They had booked passage on *Vimeira,* which was due to sail towards the end of January.

Christmas passed with the knowledge that they had been absent for two years and must return to England. Gerry, Ned, Eddie, and their families, including the twenty children ranging from seventeen to three, including Teddy, were packed and ready for an extended tour of England with a side trip to Antwerp.

Douglas had all the diamonds and other gems from everyone, along with an itemised list, and each one was in separate bags.

They had been there since the trip to Government House in October. The list from William Clarke included each gem, what was hoped to be gained from their sale and who owned it. John, Luke, and William Clarke each had a copy. Ed and Ned had reviewed it with John and Luke twice.

John explained in detail who owned which stones.

Ned was then entrusted with the gems for the journey.

William and Luke had both given a letter of written authority for their sale. John's letter was in the bag with the gems.

Ned locked them in his portable jewellery safe, along with Christina's jewels. This had actually been her Christmas-cum-50th birthday gift given the day before they sailed from London. He had purchased it some months before and had seen it sitting in his dressing room as they packed to leave for London. He had actually remembered it in his numbing grief. It also contained a set of exquisite Ceylonese blue sapphires, the colour of her eyes and an intricate diamond necklace set as well.

Ned paused as he opened it. Coming out here was the correct decision. The compassion and understanding of his closest friends and family were what he needed. He smiled. He ran his hand over the exquisite box. It was impeccably made from polished walnut with polished brass embossed corners and a marquetry insert on the top of a floral panel of various timbers, and it had tiny blossoms in mother-of-pearl. Christina loved it. The minute ornate key Christina wore around her neck on a gold chain was craftily hidden in a locket. Yes, the gems would be safe.

Chapter 21   Success

$\mathcal{A}$ tearful farewell was inevitable. The parting was made a little easier as Charles and Sal promised they would accompany Gracie, Charlie, and Emma over the next year with Harry and the other family members who wished to attend. They would only stay for the Season and then return home.

The *Vimeira* was known for speed and comfort. They had hoped to book on the *Blue Jacket*, but she was departing too late in the year for the Drawing Rooms.

The group had managed to book many of the cabins, but they had missed three of them. The McKay family were already booked in. Others booked smaller second-class cabins, but the master suite and other first-class cabins were reserved for the extended Lockley family.

Ned and Christina were allocated the master suite. It already had its own sitting room. The remainder of the cabins were distributed amongst Gerry and Ed's families, with the children sorting themselves into the available cabins. Ned and Eddie kept their eye on Tina and Chip; they had set ground rules for them on board. Their evening rendezvous would be conducted in Ned's dressing room. They could be given ten minutes for their nocturnal farewells or have five in the mornings and five at night. They chose the latter, as they knew they could be together with their siblings all day, but it meant a kiss morning and evening. They were delighted. They had obeyed the rules and been rewarded.

There was no room on the ship where the entire group could fit at the same time. Even the small dining room meant they needed two sittings. As the children needed supervision, they alternated their meals as well. With twenty under eighteen in their group, the six adults had their hands full.

The Captain introduced the McKay family to Ned. They volunteered to supervise the older children with their own children for the second dinner sitting. They had joined the ship in Melbourne before it came north to Sydney and were returning to London for their daughter Catriona's presentation. She was nineteen, and Andrew, her brother, was eighteen. They were thrilled to find some passengers their own age on board. Sarah and Tina liked her immediately. It turned out they were all booked in for the same Drawing Room presentation.

Sarah suggested to her mother that they spend the time taking dancing and deportment lessons, including the older boys. Ed and Jenna knew they also had to know how to dance, so they cleared Ned and Christina's sitting room daily and had dancing lessons. Andrew was included as he, too, needed to know how to act correctly. He had yet to be presented at a levée. He was partnered with Sarah, Neddie with Catriona, and Tina with Chip; they especially rejoiced in this. Ed and Jenna fitted in where and when they could, as they too needed to practise the various rules and dances.

Gerry and Annabella, or the McKays, looked after the younger children during these lessons. At two, Pip and Ruthie were the hardest to occupy, as they were both at the tantrum stage. They settled the younger children and had them complete some lessons. It also relieved the boredom.

The McKays were let into the secret of Chip and Tina's understanding. They had been seen emerging from Ned's sitting-room one morning. They were holding hands, and the McKays saw them. Although Ned emerged moments later, the damage was done. Ned, Christina, Ed, and Jenna decided to let them in on the secret. They were asked to help keep an eye on the pair, although it would probably be unnecessary.

Ed and Ned took the pair aside and pointed out how fast the single, simple act of holding hands can cause problems. They now had to rely on the McKays to stay quiet. After that incident, the pair were far more circumspect. By the time they had rounded Cape Horn and were travelling up the South American coast, the six teenagers were thoroughly versed in what the requirements were for the Drawing Room. The date of their presentation at the end of May would give them only two weeks to ready themselves on arrival. They had to be in London at least the week before the presentation and then wait until their cards had been sent in. This was a necessary formality.

~

The first month at sea passed in peace.

Ned said, "Christina, I'm thankful that Mother now sent in that list. I hope Her Majesty will allow the girls to be presented this year. I'm thankful also that Easter is late this year. The only thing I'm sad about is that she left Bella off the list."

They docked in London on May 2, to find that their Presentation

Cards had been sent a month earlier by Colin Fraser; they now only had to arrive on time. Colin and Reg Hawkins met the large family group on the dock. The McKays were farewelled, and they would head to his father, the Earl of Yardboard's, home.

Ned supervised the loading of the children, distributing an adult in each carriage. Christina was in the carriage with Tina and Chip, who refused to be parted. They took all the littlest children with them. Ed and Jenna wished they could travel with someone who could tell them what they were looking at. Jenna was in the second, with Annabella. They arrived moments apart at Gracemere House in Piccadilly.

Jenna thought they had arrived at the Queen's palace.

The children poured out of each carriage as they arrived. Jenna walked into the foyer and stopped in her tracks, her eyes fixed on the portrait on the stairs. She had never been in such a huge room. She had stood frozen in the foyer until Christina had led her into the larger room. It was even more awe-inspiring. Her jaw dropped open.

Sarah, Neddie, Chip, and Tina were holding the small children's hands. Compared to the Government House's Red Drawing Room, this was huge in comparison. Jenna stood in the middle of the room, mouth open. Her children all stood near her, gaping. There could be no other word for it. Each group that joined them stood in a similar stance.

Liam, Chip, and Sarah were eager to take their cousins upstairs to see their rooms, but needed to wait until they were given permission to leave.

"Ed, go inside," Ned said on his arrival.

"No way, Ned! I would get lost at the front door. I'll follow you." He could see the vast size of the foyer through the open door. He was carrying Ruthie, who was asleep in his arms.

Ned had Pip in his arms, and far from being asleep, he was all eyes, with thumb in mouth. The very small boy looked up, and his eyes kept lifting. He had never seen a four-story building before; neither had Eddie, not one like this.

Colin and Reg were standing as ushers, waiting to show their visitors the direction they should take. Both were grinning at the looks on the faces of the young couple.

Ed entered and stood frozen, as Jenna had, and totally in awe of what he beheld. The staircase alone was breathtaking. A single eight-foot-wide sweeping staircase led up to a landing where it split in either direction. His eyes were drawn to the ornate gilded ceiling. The wall at the top of the first stairs on the landing showed a battle scene. His eyes stopped abruptly when they rested on a portrait of a fair-haired gentleman. "Ned, is that the 6th Duke? Our mutual relation?" His eyes slid across the other fair-haired portraits. He would ask about them later. Ed could see more than a family resemblance in the man in the painting, he could see Charlie's likeness in it.

Ned merely said, "Yes, my great-grandfather, and your great-great-grandfather. Looks familiar, doesn't he?"

Teddy had walked up beside his uncle and stood staring at it. It was like staring in a mirror. It could have been himself or even his father. He blanched, then uttered a soft, "Cor!"

Ned, merely catching his eye and smiling.

Ted and Eddie stood gazing around them; there were carved marble busts of varying shapes and sizes along the side of the railings on the ground floor. On closer inspection later, each was discovered to be a Lockley or Duke of Gracemere ancestor. Ed's eyes were drawn to the most spectacular chandelier above his head. The bannister railings were also ornately carved. "Cripes, Ned, I thought my house was big."

Ned, standing beside him, chuckled. "Ed, wait until you see the castle. This is small in comparison to *Gracemere*. This only has fifteen bedroom suites and numerous standard rooms. The castle has 200 bedrooms, and it also features crenellated walls and battlements. The boys love it. Hence, my concern about the love birds. They will have far too much opportunity there." He gave Eddie time to gather his wits. "Come on, you two, we have to get you all settled."

Colin and Reg followed them into the drawing room.

Ned pulled a velvet bell pull twice as he entered. He left the door open.

Within moments, a bevy of staff appeared in the lobby. Ned called in Mrs Mathieson, the housekeeper, and introduced her to Ed and his family.

She curtseyed.

Ed bowed his head in return, and then Jenna and the children followed his example.

Gerry asked if they were in the same rooms.

"Yes, Doctor," she replied. "I was wondering if the children had made friends and wished to share, or if they each wished their own rooms? All are ready."

There was a babble of voices, and soon all the boys had their rooms sorted out. Christina made suggestions for the girls, "Sarah and Tina, you will share, Lily and Bella too, unless you wish to use your own room near your parents, Bella. Then Lily can be in the nursery with the rest of the children. How about that?"

Mrs Mathieson and Annabella approved the arrangements. She waved her hand, and maids in black and white came and collected the eight younger children.

Ruthie teared up until Pip called her a baby. "I'se not," she said stubbornly, "I'se a big girl, mummy says so," but turned to Mrs Mathieson with a beaming angelic smile and said, "Up please." Lifting her arms to be carried. How could she refuse such an angelic child? She lifted her and caressed the little girl's cheek.

Ned smiled; another conquest had been made.

Everyone followed Mrs Mathieson and Ruthie up the staircase. Neddie still carried Pip but moved him onto his back.

Gerry and Annabella turned into their room on the second floor.

Ned and Christina opened the door to an extraordinary space for Ed and Jenna. It was larger than their drawing room. They had no time to investigate as Ned said he wanted to show them something.

"We're next door," Ned said, "So this will be convenient. Don't linger; I want you to see the nursery."

The noises were receding from the older children's excitement. The little ones were silent as the four maids took them from their parents.

Jenna was anxious. As they followed Ned, she whispered to Eddie, "I'm not sure I like not being with the children."

Ed squeezed her hand. "I think it's why we're heading there first. So you'll know where to go."

They climbed to the third floor. This staircase was nowhere near as impressive, but it was still better than Eddie's one in Parramatta.

Ned walked to a door along the corridor. He stood aside and waited for them before opening the door.

Jenna gasped in awe.

The nursery stretched across a vast space. It was every child's dream room. Toys as far as you could see, rocking horses, doll houses, farm sets, and blocks. Henry and Philip were already trying to climb onto the rocking horses. Jenna giggled. "I don't think we'll actually get our children out of here to go anywhere."

Ed looked from the windows over the battlements. "Was this once some sort of war room?"

"Yes," replied Ned. "I thought you would be worried, Jenna. I used to love this place. Wait until the others arrive. I bet Chip will round them up, and they will be here in a few minutes." As he finished speaking, they heard the sounds of many running feet. The nine older boys arrived and skidded to a halt on entry.

Kit's comment equalled Eddie's. "Cor, I've died and gone to heaven, Papa."

From then on, worry about the children was obliterated. Jenna was continually kept informed of what they were all doing. She learned the maid's names were Judy, Florence, Wendy, and Janette. These four were to have oversight of the children. Other girls worked in the house. Christina introduced them to the children, and each gave a slight bow or curtsy in reply.

An hour later, Mrs Mathieson said that the dressmaker would be calling at two o'clock.

Jenna's eyes caught Christina's with raised eyebrows.

On the housekeeper's departure, Christina replied, "One of the benefits of being a Duchess is that they come to us. Madam Genevieve is a discovery of mine of sorts; she came here after the last war and was impoverished. We came across her in a tiny store in the Soho making costumes for Drury Lane Theatre at Covent Gardens. Edward first heard about her skills because of John Landon and the damaged fabric and their work at the Female Factory. His friend Amelia introduced him to Ivy Vine at the prison, and they started sewing for the Benevolent Society. I believe she now has a sewing business in Sydney."

"Yes, it's called *De'Vine Couture*," Jenna said.

Christian laughed, "Oh, I love it. Anyway, I needed a dressmaker and I sought out Madam Genevieve on Ivy's recommendation and discovered her skills are way beyond the normal ability of a dressmaker. Her designs are astounding. Since my patronage, she has moved into a new, big store and is very sought after by the nobility. Jenna, through her, Colin has obtained tickets for us all for *Les Huguenots'* Opening night on the 15th, so we also have to all have gowns for that. So, we need three gowns each as a starting point. We won't take the children to that, it's an Italian opera. I don't like it, by the way, and you won't either, but it's just 'done' to be seen there. Madam Genevieve's gowns are divine and are perfect for what we're after. Wait until you see what she brings."

~

At two o'clock, Jenna, Tina, Christina, and Sarah were in the Dowager Duchesses' old bedchamber. Ned had suggested this as it was something that would have happened if she were alive. Once used, it would become alive again. It was as though she were watching. He smiled. Yes, she would like that.

Annabella had discussed her daughter Bella's presentation, but as the older girls were nearly eighteen and she was only seventeen, they decided to wait the extra year for her. In reality, they had no choice as they had missed out on submitting her card for this year anyway. For some reason, the Dowager Duchess had left her off the list of Presentations. Bella was quite pleased as she was not one to enjoy the limelight.

Sarah teared up on entering the room. She looked at her mother with her eyes filled and glassy.

Christina said quietly, "Grandmama would want this, love. This is where we would have had the fittings had she been here, so let's do it for her," her mother said. "Choose what you think she would like."

Sarah nodded and took a deep breath. "Let's do this," Sarah said, grabbing Tina's arm, and they went in to investigate what was available.

Inside was a petite Frenchwoman with four assistants. Lying on the bed were bolt after bolt of white fabric and many more on the floor.

Tina gasped, "I had no idea there were so many shades of white." She was gently fingering a pure silk fabric in the middle of the row that had taken her eye.

Sarah's eyes had gone to this same fabric. "Oh, Mother, this is divine." The fabric was heavy silk with a sheen rather than a shine.

"*Bien!* That was easy," said the tiny French woman. "You both have good taste. It's what I would have chosen." She waved for her assistants as she waved the two rows of the other fabrics away. "Now, you have to decide whether you would like to dress alike or very differently? You are hmm… how you say… aah, spectacular and together, oh together, *trés magnifique*. But it is up to you. Mama Duchess, you have the final say; what do you think?" The girls were gently pushed to stand together.

Christina and Jenna knew what Susanna wanted. In unison, they said, "The same."

Madam Genevieve continued, "*Trés bien.* You know there are many, many rules for dis. De men, dey are to wear de knee breeches and buckle shoes and wield a sword. De ladies have to wear feathers in their hair, two for a girl, three for a married lady, high enough for de Queen to see, and the train on their dress needed to measure two and *trois quarts* meters, dat's how you say three yards long; exactly. Your dress for presentation must show a lady's neck and much of her shoulders bare, but, non, you must not show your ankles." Madame spieled off the requirements of the gown, while acting the words with her hands. "You must carry your trains on your left arm while waiting in their place for their presentations. Several lords-in-waiting will be at hand to lay out your train and pass along your card to announce you to her Majesty. After entering, you kiss de Queen's hand, or the Queen kisses your forehead if you are a peeress or daughter of a peer. Serrah, she will kiss your forehead, ahh but petit Christina, for you shall not be 'Tina' this night; she will kiss your hand, as you are merely the daughter of the second son of an Earl." Genevieve had acted out each movement. She stood as though she were dressed for the presentation with an arm holding her train. "You then need to wait for a page to place your train on your left arm again before you somehow manage to elegantly exit the room without turning your back to de Queen. Eet is hard, very hard, but with practice, it is very do-able, oh, and so worth it. *Por amour*," she gave a long sigh, "It is worth it all. So again, I ask, the same or different?"

In unison, the girls said, "We are to be the same, exactly the same."

Tina and Sarah hugged each other. They had talked about this. They were so alike they could be twins themselves. Tina's eyes and hair were a shade darker, but they had the same physique, same hairstyle and looked similar. They would be a sensation.

Madam Genevieve was excited. "Two identical dresses with minute differences. Mademoiselle Tina's to have tiny white rosebuds, and Mademoiselle Serrah's to have pearls." She stood smiling. "You must choose some lace, wide, some twenty *centimètre*. Err, how you say? About nine inches or more. And then there are the veils."

The assistants showed the four of them some laces.

Jenna saw one that made her gasp. It was pure white. "Is that *Guipure* lace? I've heard about it but never seen it before."

"*Oui,* Madame and dis one is *Levers Lace,* it would be perfect for the gowns. The veils should be in *Venetian point de lace*, see like dis one trim de edges with this *Guipure* trim." The veil she held was exquisite. It was made of *Venetian Point de Lace*. At the top, a few tiny stars were scattered behind the head section. Then explosions of stars in clusters scattered over the edges to the foot, which looked like handfuls of stars caught in a net. The effect was glorious.

Jenna turned to Christina. "I like it, it's sensational, but they have to wear them."

Sarah was fingering one with minute flowers. "I like this, but I don't suppose it's wide enough. I love that, though, Jenna."

"Mama, that's a beautiful combination, but it will cost so much," Tina said with a sigh.

"Ah! A *jeune fille* with a heart, exquisite, *ma belle*. Now to try on some designs? *Bien*." Madam was bustling around the room, achieving much with the minimum of fuss.

From a colossal standing portable wardrobe, the assistants drew out some nearly finished gowns. "These are to give me an idea of styles." She umm'd and ahh'd and finally chose a beautiful gown that each girl, in turn, tried on.

Once selected, the girls were then excused. They left skipping with joy.

Christina turned to Jenna and said, "Now, Jenna, it's your turn. There are some differences to your gown requirements."

"My gown?" the fear that shot across her face "Christina, no. I can't." She took a step backwards as if to ward off the evil idea.

Christina knew she would feel this way. "If you don't, then Tina can't, and you know what that means. She can't be married. I'll be with you every step of the way." She gave her a comforting hug. "You can do this, Jen. My mother will present you. Annabella is presenting Tina."

Jenna nodded. Her eyes were glassy, but she agreed, knowing that if she didn't do this, then her daughter could not marry her love. "All right, Christina, for them."

Madame walked around her and said, "Ah *magnifique*, you are, how you say? Lovely, very lovely, like sweet honey. Hmm, white silk velvet, Madame, and simple, no lace, the only decoration will be gathering and bows. Of those, there will be many. The neckline is to be ruched in a, umm, *cœur*, um, a heart. On each hip a bow of velvet, hmm, no georgette; with an enormous velvet bow on the back."

"Ahh! *Madame*. You are correct, perfection," Christina said.

"*C'est magnifique*, err, non on the hips. *Bouffant* instead. Like so," She had a swathe of velvet draped around Jenna. Madame gathered it up in two big handfuls, so it fell in a folded flounce across the front. Eh, *"Bien,"* she said to Christina.

"Oh yes, Madame, you are right." Christina was delighted.

"The bows, though, are to be tied in satin ribbon. Eet shall also be used on the ruching, like so. *Voilà!"* Genevieve showed how the velvet ruching would be held in place with the ribbon, each with a bow.

Jenna had no idea what they were talking about. Ruching? Bouffant? The white velvet was lovely, though. She sighed; she was hoping for some of that lace.

Christina saw her eyeing it off with a sigh. "It is all about the initial impression, Jenna. You are so beautiful that the velvet will be all you need. Your honey gold skin will make it glow. Trust me, my dear."

Jenna just nodded. "So, no lace?" She looked disappointed.

Christina took her hand. "Jenna, the ballgown can have all the lace you want, so can the one for the opera. Trust me in this. I have the perfect colour for your gown for the ball; I'll show you later. It's not until next month. Now, for the opera on the 15th, we will choose blue, a light sapphire blue taffeta with sheer rushing as an overskirt of Venetian lace, tied around her waist by a wide satin ribbon; the whole to be trimmed with the fine *Guipure* lace, again, simple but regal. We shall leave the design to you, Madame. Can it be so, please? Matching hooded cape and all the trimmings, with swansdown around the hood. Again, you can choose what will work best."

"Oui, Madame la Duchesse," Christina could see that the French lady's mind was ticking over what the gown would look like. Her creative juices were flowing. She gazed at Jenna, then nodded.

Down the hall, Eddie was being prepared to be dressed in full court clothing. The tailor was measuring him for a velvet coat of deep navy so dark it was almost black. The tailor was in rapture with his physique. "What arms, what legs. Oh, you will be the envy of all the gentlemen at court. No padding needed for this gentleman, sir." The tall, blonde Adonis of a male stood and blushed. It was bad enough from women, but this was just too personal. The man was currently measuring his inner leg.

Ned was watching his young protégé and finding it hard to suppress his laughter.

The tailor measured and wrote, and measured again. "Breathe in," measure… "Breathe out," measure again.

Ned ordered a list of extra items, including over thirty of the fine white shirts, most with lace cuffs. "A dozen vests in various colours and designs, please. Classic style, no dandification for this one and all the matching accoutrements."

"Oh, Ned, I do like this vest. I think it would look all right with that coat too." Eddie was fingering a black damask vest with gold embroidery. "I think that gold one would look good with that, too." He pointed to the coat.

"I think you're getting the hang of it, Ed. Taking a leaf out of Wills' book." Ned chortled. He was impressed by how absolutely understated Wills was. His wealth alone could buy him a duchy if such a thing were for sale. Yet the only jewellery he wore was his wedding ring, a fob watch, and a single diamond pin.

"I do like how Wills stands out with his simplicity. A touch of colour and a simple fob. But the fabrics are all top quality. I've watched him and learned a bit." Ed grinned at Ned. "He does stand out somewhat, doesn't he?" He was proud of his little brother, of all of his brothers, actually, but Wills took his breath away sometimes.

"Ned, must I really wear a sword for the evening? Are you serious?" Eddie was astounded when he heard about this addition.

"You can use one of mine. I know the maker." Ned chuckled. Eddie had made him a sword for a wedding gift many years ago. Ned only ever wore it to court as it was so magnificent. "I have Father's, so would you honour me by wearing that one?"

Ed grinned and nodded. To wear one of his own making was like having a bit of home with him.

Chip and Neddie came in; they, too, had to be measured for court clothes. Both were to be dressed in severe black velvet with a hint of gold braid, with identical gold waistcoats. Like their sisters, they were to be dressed identically. Because of Neddie's work as a blacksmith, his physique was more muscular than Chip's. The four would make a stunning statement. As the boys had already been presented, this was one hurdle they could sidestep. They could therefore accompany their sisters to their Drawing Room presentations.

The tailor took more measurements, unable to believe his good fortune at dressing such men. His name would be mentioned along with those of Weston and Schultz. He made a movement as if to flick off an invisible speck from Neddie's shoulders. "Oh, what a marvellous specimen of manhood too," he muttered a little too loudly. He ran his hands over the young blacksmith's arms. No padding would be needed to set off the physiques of these two men. He released a long sigh of contentment.

The first letter Colin had posted when he heard they were returning was to send in the required information for the Drawing Room. He had already added Jenna's name to the presentation list; he so wished he had remembered Bella's, but had totally forgotten her in his grief.

He had also asked Christina's mother to present Jenna. The Earl and Countess of Riverdell had arrived in London at *Rivers House* the week before. He had not yet had a chance to let the Duke know, although he had managed to tell Her Grace. All was arranged for 22nd May.

The following weeks were filled with more dressmakers' and tailors' fittings, and sedate walks in the park.

As promised, Ned had indeed installed a tall screen in the drawing room. He escorted the lovebirds into the room each morning and evening, and they disappeared behind the screen for their good-morning kiss.

~

The day of the presentation arrived. Everyone gathered in the drawing room at Gracemere House. Christina's parents were there waiting with Ned. He greeted them warmly and thanked them for coming. The Earl's valet, Frank Bates, and Gerry were finishing Ed's dressing. Ned wished to be in the room when Eddie appeared. He was not disappointed. Ed was superb. His carriage and pretended aloofness were perfect. "Brilliant Ed, now hold it for some hours."

Eddie chuckled. Ned had long ago given him hints about his carriage and deportment.

The Earl Edmund and Countess Catherine Riverdell escorted Jenna and Eddie. Christina was surprised to see her father's arm around her mother. Her mother returned her gaze, and she beamed.

Christina saw happiness on her parents' faces for the first time. She greeted her brother and his wife, Catriona, then pointed them out to him.

Her brother whispered, "Apparently, Mama told him she knew about his love for Duchess Suze. I can't believe the change in them. Father has really changed, Christina, radically. He has even allowed me to help on the Estate."

Christina was amazed.

Soon, all were on their way to the palace.

The adults not involved stood near Ned as the presentations started.

Jenna was presented first, and the Queen extended her hand for Jenna to kiss. She was a commoner married to a Peer's son. After ten children curtsying so low and holding it for so long took effort. However, the Queen kept her talking for some time. The simplicity of Jenna's gown made her stand out in the right way. Her only adornment was the compulsory three white feathers in her hair and her pearl necklace, which the Tindales had given her before her wedding. She needed nothing else; she glowed. Her shyness presented a dignified stateliness.

After half an hour of watching some matrons being presented, Christina escorted Sarah to the Queen. The two girls had waited together in the foyer. Their brothers had initially stood beside them until they were ready. The girls knew they were all within view of the Queen. The four young folk looked stunning; they had all rehearsed similar movements in their bedrooms.

All heads turned to them as the four had initially entered.

Once the girls were settled, the boys returned to their fathers and stood waiting. As the girls would not have shawls or other accoutrements, their long bouquets and fans were the only accessories they would hold. These, too, were identical. Sarah and Tina practised how to use a fan. A flip open, a simper behind the fan, flick closed, then drop it. All done in perfect unison. Many eyes were drawn to them both.

The boys had obviously been practising in their room. They stood in the same stance, and if one moved their position, the other copied.

As Sarah reached Her Majesty, she curtseyed so low her knee was on the ground. She knew that as the daughter of a Duke, she would be kissed on the forehead rather than kiss Her Majesty's hand. As expected, this is what occurred.

Queen Victoria then did something unexpected; she told Sarah to wait and called Tina, by-passing the next girl. Annabella escorted her and presented her. Tina also curtseyed low and stayed there. The Queen drew her close and kissed her forehead too. She then called Sarah back and spoke to them both together. There was a gasp from all watching. The Queen had never done this before. All saw Sarah wipe away a tear, and then both were nodding.

On being questioned later, they admitted that Her Majesty was asking them about their relationship. Admitting they were cousins and both on Duchess Susanna's list. The Queen finally released them and continued with the other presentations.

They were returned to their parents and brothers. At the end of the presentations, they expected to leave when a courtier came and called the two boys and Eddie to the Queen, who was standing waiting for them. Ned escorted them and presented them officially, Ed first, then Chip as Charles, followed by Neddie as Edward. She then did something extraordinary: she called the two girls back.

Christina quickly told them to stand next to their brothers, which they did.

The Queen smiled and stood talking to the group for some time, thus ensuring their success. She finally dismissed them graciously. They bowed and curtsied, then returned to their places.

Tina was smiling. She had caught Chip's eye, and he returned her grin.

Sarah was white, but not with nerves; she was also shaking and knowing that with that reception from Her Majesty, she was made. Grandmama would have been so proud. A single tear slid down her cheek. Swallowing, Sarah glanced over the men in the room. Maybe one of those would be her husband one day. Her eyes locked onto a vaguely familiar face in the crowd. He, too, was gaping at her with his mouth partially open in a very ungentlemanly manner. He was gazing at her in adoration.

Her father was watching and followed the direction of her gaze. He caught his breath. Returning her gaze was a young version of Harry Harlow.

Christina had heard the slight sound and followed his eyes too. She, too, gasped. "Who's that, Edward?"

Ned had felt his beloved take his arm. "That, I believe, is the Viscount of Winchester's son, Anthony Henry Harlow. He is our Harry Harlow's nephew," Ned said quietly. "They live not far from us."

Christian gasped, "It seems he shows some interest, my dear," she said quietly.

Ned kept his eye on the young man. "To be here, he must be of age. Leave it with me, my love," he whispered gently so only she could hear. She gave his arm a gentle, loving squeeze.

Her Majesty singled out no other debutantes. She stood, and her courtiers invited various members of the nobility to her side.

Ned, Christina, Jenna, and Ed were amongst them. Each made their low bow as she stood. She conversed with them all.

After she withdrew, Jenna said, "Oh, Christina, no wonder she is so loved. She's wonderful."

"Thank you, my dear," a gentle voice said from behind her.

Jenna spun around to find the young Queen standing behind her. Jenna fell again into a deep curtsy, as did Christina.

The Queen had quietly returned without fanfare. "We wished to say something to you all. Gracemere, my sincerest condolences on the passing of your beloved mother. She was a wonderful friend when one was needed. Her grace and wisdom were appreciated. Although she was unable to be at court often, she came when she was needed most, often by personal invitation. You may not know that. She was counted as a friend, and we trusted her counsel."

Ned bowed in thanks, but remained silent. He was still choked with emotion. He had no idea of his mother's closeness to the young Queen.

"Duke, we received her letter with a list of grandchildren and other relations the week she passed. We shall watch for them all. Now, please introduce this lady to these amazing four young people. You certainly caught the attention with dressing them so."

Chip and Sarah were introduced, then Ed, Jenna, Neddie and Tina.

"We look forward to watching their progress in society. We feel there may already be more than a bond between two of them if the glance we caught was anything to go by. Announce it quickly, or you shall be inundated. And the other two?"

Ned smiled, "No, Your Majesty." Nothing had escaped her. Ned had watched them all evening; two glances, that was all.

"Pity that would have been too convenient, would it not?" she said with a smile.

"Yes, Your Majesty, but it is not so." He smiled.

Jenna and Ed had stepped back, trying to be invisible. Nothing escaped her.

"You Lockley, we believe you are a blacksmith."

"Yes, Your Majesty," Ed bowed low in acknowledgement.

"Why?" she asked abruptly

"Why, Your Majesty? Because I enjoy working with the material and making something out of nothing. The raw mineral that our good Lord has provided us with is refined by fire, as the Bible explains, and then purified. Like us in times of adversity, it is then beaten and moulded into something pure, beautiful and usable," Eddie spoke from his heart. His hand rested on his sword.

There were gasps of astonishment from those around him. No one spoke to the Monarch like that.

"So, you think we all need refining?" She asked.

"If I may be so bold, Your Majesty. We are all but human, none made perfect but our Saviour. Only He needs no refinement." He met her eyes. His simple honesty was refreshing.

Astounded by the simplicity and yet truth of his statement, she replied, "True. If only others believed so, the world would be a far better place." She put her hand out and patted his. Then reached for Jenna's. "My dear, we will not eat you. Your story, we believe, is interesting too. However, we will only say your fathers are both heroes. Your Papa's story is known to me." She tapped Jenna's hand gently with her fan, "Although we believe your husband has had his own share of that, too. That alone makes them all worthy. Hold your head high, my dear; you are worthy in the Lord's eyes, and therefore in mine too. Forsaking their own safety for the lives of others is honourable. Are they also men of faith?"

Jenna was speechless. She merely nodded. She could not have spoken had he life depended on it.

"Good! They have taught you both well. We believe you do much good out there. Continue with our blessing, for what it's worth, as you have higher work to be done. We believe you both lead by example. We like that." She turned and moved on.

As she left their group, each bowed or curtseyed low.

On standing, Ned saw Anthony, Viscount of Winchester, was seen to be making his way across the room. In tow was his son, Anthony Harlow Junior.

Sarah grasped her mother's hand.

Christina's eyes met her husband's in an understanding smile. Other Peers soon surrounded the small group.

Gerry and Annabella had not been ignored as Her Majesty was currently in conversation with them. She had heard he had been named as his brother's heir, and she was congratulating him. She complimented him on the work they were doing at Maidstone with the clinics and loudly encouraged other Peers to follow their example. Unbeknownst to many, Dr Gerald Winslow-Smythe had attended the birth of her first two children. He was one of the few trusted with her health. "Doctor Gerald, I look forward to having your daughter presented next year."

"Of course, Your Majesty," Gerry said with a smile.

The crush around the group was almost suffocating. White feathers bounced on the heads of those recently presented. Trains were thrown over the arms again due to the crush of bodies.

After standing in the group of Peers waiting to be introduced to the Duke and his family, Ned finally acknowledged Anthony. "You, I believe, are Harry Harlow's brother? And this must be your son?" Ned asked. "The likeness is astounding, although our Harry has grown browner and stronger."

The Viscount was shocked that the Duke was on nickname terms with his younger brother. He nodded and made the introductions.

Anthony had aspired to meet the previous Duke of Gracemere, but David, this duke's older brother, had cut him to the point of turning his back on him. Anthony was crushed and still somewhat hurt. He was their neighbour. But this duke, such was his gaze, it was as though Duke Edward looked through him and read his soul. Since this duke inherited the title, no opportunity had occurred to meet him. The Gracemeres rarely attended any Society functions. They may well live within riding distance of each other, but the duke was a private person. He was therefore shocked when the duke was so familiar with his brother. Anthony listened intently as Duke Edward spoke.

Ned continued, "Harry is one of the finest young men I have ever met or worked with. Do you know of his work in the colony? Have you visited yet? You should, you know. It will astound you what he has been doing." Ned dearly wished he could cut the man for his treatment of his brother. Instead, by exalting Harry, it would have the same effect. Harry had told him that he had written. He supposed that was a start.

"No, Your Grace, I have not yet visited." Anthony looked embarrassed. "I was not sure I would be welcomed."

"You would be. Harry has changed." Ned saw raw honesty in the admission; he was surprised, but it was a start. Ned looked at the man before him. Staring deep into the man's face. He saw emptiness. If the two young people's looks were anything to go by, he needed to build bridges, not walls. "Winchester, I would go over sooner than later. They will be coming soon for Sarah Joy's presentation. I would go before that and return with them. You will be astounded and you will be changed."

Anthony turned to go. He felt he'd been chastised and verbally shredded like he had tangled with a ferocious lion.

Ned felt sorry for him. He could tell he was a shrivelled man inside. "Winchester, bring your family for a visit when we return home. I shall tell you more about what they do, for I think you should know." Ned looked at young Anthony. "Bring the lad. I believe you are near enough to ride. Your boy shares an uncle with these two, you know?" Waving his hand to Tina and Neddie. "Harry married Eddie's sister-in-law."

"I didn't know, Your Grace. Thank you, Your Grace, we'd be honoured." The two Harlow men bowed and departed.

"Ned, that was naughty of you. Harry would be in stitches, though," Eddie said quietly.

"Papa, did you mean it? They are invited over?" Sarah said. Her eyes were starry.

"Yes, my sweet, although I would love to cut the floor out from under the man, due to his treatment of Harry, I won't, all because of a few looks I saw you give his son."

Sarah blushed, then beamed at her father.

"We may have our work cut out to mend that bridge, though. I believe they used to be close. I may send them both to the colony with Ed and Jenna. He has some repenting and reforming to do. If things work out, you may wish to go with them and return with Harry and Vicky later, but let's not get ahead of ourselves."

Sarah was delighted. Her hands were clasped over her heart. "Oh, Papa, thank you."

"Now, my poppet, enjoy your success, as you have both succeeded where many have failed. Stay close to Tina all night." He turned to his son. "Chip, a word." The word skirting around his head was "Incomparable", not one he thought would be associated with his daughter and her cousin, but together they were a sensation. He smiled and thought how pleased his mother would have been at their success. In a way, it was because of her passing that this had occurred.

Chip and Ned stood with heads together for a few minutes. Chip nodded occasionally and then gave a big grin. There was to be no dancing tonight. However, he would be allowed two dances with her until their engagement was announced. They now had the Queen's blessing.

Ned turned to find Ed deep in conversation with a gentleman. He could not see who it was, but thought he recognised the outfit. He could hear snippets of their discussion… horseshoes… types of steel, and, interestingly, farm equipment. Ed showed him the sword that he had made for Ned. Then, they moved on to new designs and techniques of equipment in the colony. The conversation then moved on to child labour. Eddie enthusiastically told the avid listener about their family's work with both the Female Orphanage and the Landon Homes and Sadie House with Ricky English.

The man said, "I wish to hear more of this; come to the concert with us on Friday." The speaker turned to Ned. "Gracemere, Friday evening?" Then he turned to circulate. Turning back, he said, "Better still, Duke, are you both free tomorrow at ten? Come to the concert too. Actually, both come tomorrow."

Ned gasped, bowed, then nodded, saying, "Honoured, Your Royal

Highness."

Eddie froze. Watching the man depart, Eddie turned to Ned. "Ned, why didn't you tell me that was the Prince?" Ed turned and looked at the Prince. "Nice bloke, though!"

Ned laughed, "Oh, Eddie," slapping him gently on the back. "In a room full of the most powerful Peers of the Realm, you chose the two most interesting topics of conversation with the most powerful man in the country and have absolutely no idea who he is."

"Well, he heard I did some smithing. He did ask first." Ed looked embarrassed. "I showed him your sword."

A young lady with two giant bouncing feathers eventually made it to the girls' side. She was overdressed and glittered like a star.

Christina nearly laughed out loud, but held her chortle in. Mrs McKay must have attached every sequin and diamanté she could find to the gown. The feathers were undoubtedly not as subtle as the girls' ones, as they fluttered high over everyone else's heads.

All the girls greeted each other warmly.

"Oh, Sarah, Tina, you are made. You both look stunning. Mother made me out to look like a gaudy jewel box. I had no say at all," Catriona said mournfully, looking down at her gaudy, glittering, over-fluffed gown.

Sarah called her mother over. "Mother, would we be able to take Catriona shopping for her first ball gown? Or even better, still, have Madam Genevieve make her one. Can she debut at our ball? Please? I do not believe they have had time to arrange anything." Looking at her mother pleadingly with one eyebrow raised.

Catriona was stunned.

Picking up not so subtle enquiry from her daughter, Christina answered, "I would be delighted." Christina said, "Hmm, A lovely sea green tinge on the ruffles, simple but stunning." Christina said gently, "…And matching our girls, but different."

"Oh, Your Grace, you would do that for me?" She teared up.

"Tush love, leave your mother to me." Christina left the three girls talking with Jenna and Annabella, supervising them. She sought out Mrs McKay, and after circulating through the crowd, she slowly made her way to her. "My dear Mrs McKay, your daughter looks delightful. She is such a friend with our two girls that I have persuaded her to accompany them to their coming out ball next week. I do hope you will agree, as they are such dear friends. You can leave all the arrangements in my hands. We have a French *haute couturier*, Madame Genevieve, who will dress her." Christina was not taking a chance of her refusal.

Mrs McKay was overwhelmed. "Thank you, Your Grace. We would be honoured. We have not had time yet to think further ahead than tonight."

"Wonderful, the girls will be thrilled. I shall send information." She nodded and slowly made her way back to Ned and the girls by continuing to circulate. She was greeted and congratulated by many.

Catriona was still standing with her daughter. She looked around for Tina. Catriona said, "Your Grace, look." She pointed with her head.

Queen Victoria was talking to both Chip and Tina. She took Tina's hand and placed it on Chip's.

Christina gasped.

Sarah spoke. "Her Majesty came back and spoke to Jenna. Apparently, she had been watching them. Honestly, they did nothing wrong, mother, nothing. We've been standing here the entire time. She must have caught a look or two."

Christina smiled. "No, Sarah, she already had asked your father. She loves a good romance; this will protect them both. Chip is already a target of every mama around, as he's a Duke's son. For him to be safely 'taken' is for his own benefit."

The royal couple finally departed, and the crowd dispersed soon afterwards.

Sarah's eye caught young Anthony Harlow's a few times throughout the evening. He made sure he was near the door for their departure. His father was nowhere in sight.

Ned was watching. Groaning inwardly, he knew he had much work ahead with that family. He would do it for Sarah and Harry.

~

The two invitations from Buckingham Palace arrived the following day, as did over three hundred other cards for parties, balls, and soirées. More poured in throughout the afternoon. Colin would be earning his pay this week. A thought occurred to Ned. "Colin, do you need more help? Second, who do you require? Joseph Carpenter can come from the castle."

"Thank you, Your Grace. I think I may need him and others. I must say it's nice to see the young people so appreciated."

"Any suggestions as to whom to ask for assistance?" the Duke asked him.

"I was wondering if Reg and two of the junior footmen, Ford and Young, could assist?" Colin said, "Err, I've been sort of training them." He saw a wave of fear flash across the Duke's face. "No, sir, I have no intention of leaving unless you don't need me. However, they are both clever, so I thought they could look for similar work if trained properly. This would be a good experience for them."

Relief flooded Ned's face. He would be lost without Colin. Joseph was a good secretary, but Colin was quasi-family. His mother had trusted him absolutely and relied on him heavily. "Ask them all, with my blessing, Colin. Trust you to be thinking of others." Ned smiled. "I would be lost without you, my friend. Just because Mother is gone doesn't mean you will be leaving us. Name your job, and it's yours. I have a feeling that the next three months will be extremely busy ones. I have had the term 'Twin Incomparable's' already thrown about for them. Get Reg to hire more footmen and take these two on as assistant secretaries if you like." He smiled to himself as he left the huge pile of mail to his capable secretary. "And Colin, train whom you like to, for whatever positions you see fit. I will write whatever references you ask me to. Be assured of that. Please don't leave. Please!" He looked pleadingly at his secretary.

"Thank you, Your Grace. I won't leave, sir. I have a few more people who may be able to assist us. Even if it's just for occasions like this." Colin grinned at Ned. They were the same age, and Ned had already trusted him implicitly. Joseph could handle the regular stuff, but Colin was... well, he could not think of the castle without him.

~

On their visit to Buckingham Palace the next morning, the Prince questioned them about gold, gems and finally about a document that he'd recently read about. "Gracemere, did you hear anything about the newest finds while you were there?" The Prince asked him.

Ned's eyes flew to Eddie. "Yes, sir, we did."

The Prince turned to Ed, "You obviously know more. Please elaborate if you're able."

"May we have a moment, sir?" Ed asked.

The Prince graciously nodded and walked to the end of the room. Smiling at the audacity of the young man.

"How much can we say?" Ed asked. "Do we tell him all?"

"The Governor has obviously sent some information through, if not Reverend William's entire report. The fact that he knows this much means he's privy to the State Correspondence. I'd say let's tell him everything," Ned said softly.

Ned cleared his throat to let the Prince know he could return. "Your Royal Highness, may we ask what you have heard about? I gather you have read the despatches from Denison that may mention Reverend Clarke?"

The Prince merely bowed in acknowledgment. "Yes, read them all."

Ned continued. "Ahh! We have been charged to be the carriers of... um, certain items." He stopped and looked at the aides in the room.

The Prince dismissed them with a wave of his hand, leaving the three alone.

As soon as the door closed, Ned spoke. "Sir, we have brought the diamonds back with us to sell in Antwerp, Amsterdam, or wherever we can get the best price. Lockley's brother Luke, a friend John Evans and his wife, and Reverend William Clarke found these in the New England area. Dealers from Antwerp bought a few of the smaller, lower-grade ones, but the large sapphires and most of the diamonds were too valuable to sell for the pittance they were offering. Hence, our planned trip to Antwerp after the

Season. We do not own them. We have been commissioned to sell them on their behalf. The money from their sale is all the owners will ever get."

The Prince understood the innuendo, "Hmm, I thought as much. It is one of the reasons why I asked you to come," He looked at Ed. "I recognised your name; it was too much of a coincidence. I would like to see them before you sell them. Might buy one, for you know who." He smiled. "Come see me with them." Before they departed, the Prince's secretary made an appointment with them to return that afternoon.

They decided to show Prince Albert the entire collection. They returned that afternoon and brought the stones. After showing the Prince the volume of gems, he settled on just the three he mentioned. The enormous blue sapphire tempted him, but she had a lot of those already. On seeing Colleen's huge diamond, the Prince told them, "I shall give you £35,000 for the big one. I know it to be exceptional. Is that in the price range you were looking at?"

Behind the Prince's back, Eddie nearly choked.

Ned ignored him and said, "Yes, Your Royal Highness, it is what we were hoping to get in Antwerp for that one. Ten to fifteen for the next largest and five each for the two perfect half-inch ones," Ned said.

"That's reasonable; I'll take the two smaller ones as well. £45,000 for the three. Not much you can give the Queen she doesn't already have. Well, she won't have these, as they've never been found there before. Australian diamonds, eh? It's my money, not public coffers, so I can spend it how I want. Not much else to buy here," he said, waving his hand around the palace. "She likes gems. Pretty baubles."

"Thank you, sir," Ed stammered.

"Bring them back tomorrow, and I'll have a bank draft for you. Not yours, so won't ask you to leave them," he said. "Birthday tomorrow, you know, hence the hurry, May 24. Always forget to buy her anything. Well, not exactly forget, more like I can't really go to a shop, can I? No secret if I get a jeweller to come here. These will be perfect." He smiled at the two stunned men.

~

On Friday, they joined the royals, and they sat at the back of their box; Prince Albert and Eddie were deep in conversation for much of the interval.

Finally, the Prince joined Ned. "Proud of that boy, aren't you, Duke?"

"Yes, Your Royal Highness, I am. And I have been since he was a tiny babe. His father placed him in my arms just hours after he was born, and they told me they were naming him after me as he was born on my twenty-second birthday. At the age of just six, he took himself off and found an apprenticeship with the blacksmith. He had just learned his elder brother was to inherit the family inn, and he realised he would need a trade.

He could barely hold a small hammer." Ned said, smiling at his protégé. Ed had succeeded where few others had, and without any, well, not much anyway, help from him. He chuckled. If word got out of this family's worth, they would be swamped. Wills' and Luke's children will undoubtedly be attractive as catches to the many pariahs in society. Eddie stood head and shoulders above most of the rest in the country. Nearly every female's eyes followed him whenever he walked into any room. He hated it.

~

The ball the following week was another resounding success. There, Chip and Tina also officially announced their engagement. The Queen had made it possible, if not compulsory, by publicly endorsing their relationship. They had not planned to do this until October, as both were still under eighteen. As her endorsement occurred so publicly, everyone had already guessed.

Viscount Winchester and his wife, Maud, and son were invited to the ball.

Catriona and the two girls were led out to start the ball. Each danced with their brothers. Sarah in a white gown with blue trim, Tina, with pink trim and Catriona with soft mint green trim. Madam Genevieve had dressed them in similar colours but different styles, and together, the three looked remarkable.

Andrew, Catriona's brother, had been presented at a Levée the week before. Ned had been able to have him added to the list at the last minute. He was now able to be included with the boys.

Ned officially introduced Anthony Harlow junior to Sarah. It was the first time they had been officially allowed to talk to each other. He was allowed only the two dances with her, and neither was allowed to be a waltz.

So far, Ned liked what he saw. He was more like Harry than his father in behaviour. Ned encouraged the boys to make friends with him so he could be invited over often. He smiled to himself. Neddie could break down that barrier by talking to him about their Uncle Harry. They had that in common.

Ned caught Neddie's eye and called him over. "Make friends with Ant Harlow, will you? You share an uncle in Harry; build on that. Invite him to stay sometimes, especially when we return to the castle."

"Okay, Uncle Ned, will do. Sarah eh? Good on her; if he's like Uncle Harry, then he'll be nice. I want to get to know him as a cousin anyway," Neddie said, quickly grasping the situation. "Convenient to have her nearby, too." He grinned knowingly.

Ned smiled and gave him a slight bow in reply. "Thanks, lad," he said softly.

Sure enough, some minutes later, Ned watched him find his way subtly across the room with Chip in tow. They were stopped many times and congratulated. Catriona's brother Andrew had joined them by the time they approached young Ant.

Ned watched them cleverly draw him into the conversation. He laughed to himself and turned to seek some friends if he could find any. He cast his eyes quickly around the room; Ned could see a few who wished to talk to him; he shivered, cringing and turned to seek Gerry or Ed. He hated socialising. He would rather speak to Winchester; anything was better than being buttonholed by an undesirable statesman or politician. He felt like a snob but was in no mood for politics. He didn't like politicians at the best of times, and tonight especially.

Eventually, Ned saw Eddie standing alone in the corner and diplomatically made his way towards him. Nodding at acquaintances as he moved nonchalantly past them, ignoring their hails. Finally reaching Ed, they stood in a secluded spot, deep in conversation about their children. With their fair heads together, they spent time discussing their proposed trip to Europe.

Ned referred to this as a 'leaning on a pillar and looking bored'. He had been told by his friend Sam Garney, a reluctant Earl himself, how to achieve the nonchalant look. No one ever bothered him. Ned discovered it worked.

Chapter 22   Changes

*T*he next three months in London passed in a whirl. Even though Tina was now officially engaged, she enjoyed the Season as much as her cousins.

Catriona McKay had met the Duchess Christina's brother, Edmund, Viscount Eames and his wife, another Catriona, who was Scottish. The Viscountess introduced her to some of the Bland cousins from Edinburgh. Then Edmund's friend Lewis Bland and his wife Fiona arrived from Scotland halfway through the Season. Viscountess Catriona was Lewis's sister.

Mr and Mrs McKay claimed a distant connection with the Moretons, Fiona's family, and therefore allowed Catriona McKay to socialise with them. When they found they were cousins to His Grace the Duke, they willingly accepted the invitation to visit Scotland in late August. Their planned visit to *Gracemere Castle* was not until September. Scotland would be too cold by then. Catriona had formed no attachment in London, which disappointed her mother, but she had been a success, partially because Christina took over her dressing. The Duchess had praised the simple taste of her ball gown over that of her mother's selection at her presentation. As Christina had chosen it, it was of a simple design by Madam Genevieve; Mrs McKay took the hint and allowed Catriona to select her own gowns from then onwards. Catriona often went shopping with the girls and Christina.

Andrew McKay was looking forward to some shooting and salmon fishing in Scotland. He teased Catriona that she might catch a Baron or Scottish Lord while she was there.

As it came to pass, she did just that. On arrival at Moreton House in Edinburgh, she met Baron Fergus Macdonald.

Fergus had not long returned from the Crimea. He had nearly died when his face had been sliced open by a sword. He had a scar running the diagonal length of his cheek. His otherwise handsome face was unmarked.

Before his departure, he passed the Clan lands into the care of Lord Macdonald as they were now unviable. Sadly, in his absence, the family home had caught alight. It now lay in ruins after a fire. Little had been saved. His Clan-sept soldiers who joined him on the battlefields had all either died or emigrated. Fergus and Lord Macdonald had come to an amicable agreement, and he would buy all the remaining property. However, although Fergus had lost everything he owned, the sale left him very flush with cash. He had a title, but nowhere to call home. He spent some time recovering on Skye with Lord Macdonald. Then he travelled, visiting various family members throughout Scotland. The Moretons were one such visit. He also planned to visit his cousin Robert Styles, now Baron Broome-Hall and his family at Broome-Hall Manor in West Sussex. While there, Fergus planned to visit Kent to meet the Lockleys. His brother's friends were out from Australia, and Hamish wished Fergus to meet them. Hamish had written that they were visiting, and he was sure that if he could possibly get there, they would welcome a visit from him.

On meeting Fergus, Catriona gasped with compassion and could not resist placing a hand on his arm. "Oh, sir, you fought for us? Thank you for keeping us safe." A single tear escaped and rolled down her cheek.

Her reaction was not the usual one he received from a lassie. On discovering she was from Melbourne in the Colonies, he realised she was not a regular English lassie. Maybe this one would not be scared off by the ugly wound. They usually turned away in disgust; this lass had teared up in compassion. He caught her eyes on him often throughout the meal, but in friendship, not in pity. She shyly looked away, but he saw admiration reflected in her glances. He met her eyes with a smile, and it was returned with unabashed admiration.

The next day, he offered his arm and suggested they take a turn in the garden. She went willingly. He even permitted her to touch the ugly wound, something he had never allowed anyone ever to do before. It was not that it hurt; it was just darned ugly.

Less than a week later, he sought permission to pay his addresses to her. Mr McKay willingly gave them, and Fergus proposed. He was twenty-three years older than her, but that seemed not to be of concern to her.

Catriona had fallen in love, as had Fergus.

She said yes, and they announced their engagement before their return to London.

Fergus travelled with them. His only concern was where they would live. He explained that he had received an official invitation to spend some time with his brother's friends in Kent. He asked if she'd be interested in visiting with him. They were visiting from Australia, too.

She sought permission from her parents, and they agreed. On the sea voyage from Edinburgh to London, she was surprised to discover that his brother lived in Sydney. Even more so, to find that the "friends" were none other than Ed and Jenna. They were heading to the same venue, *Gracemere Castle* in Kent. Of course, her parents and brother joined Fergus and Catriona on their September sojourn to the castle.

The Duke and family had returned from London when the Season officially finished in August.

Fergus knew that Eddie was friends with Hamish and found that the McKays travelled to England with the Lockleys. Also, the girls were all presented together. "Hooch man, what a wee world we live in. Ain't God grand?" Fergus laughed. "That you already know them is *braw*. But my Katy is grand too," he said to Eddie on arrival.

Eddie laughed and agreed with him. He had heard Hamish say precisely the same thing.

"Fergus, why don't you return with the McKays and visit Hamish and Effy? Meet your namesake. You might like it enough to stay. At least you have a family in Sydney," Eddie suggested gently after a long conversation about where they would live.

"Ooch, that's *braw*. I might just do that; I ha'e no ties here the noo. Bar Robbie, but I know them not. I might just do that. At least none I ken well. I have the Broome-Halls in West Sussex and must see them before I leave."

"Ned introduced me to them, Fergus, and their cousin, Daniel, is the Earl of Meldon and his family." Eddie explained, "My Dar told me to catch up with him as his father was a convict like Dar, and they both became Earl's. He was Dar's friend; sadly, the old Earl, Sam, died last December, so the family skipped the Season this year. Dan is actually Dar's age, and I'm about the same age as his son Edmund and his wife Essie. They introduced me to Robert when we visited them last month. Do make sure you see them before you leave, Fergus. They are doing much the same on their estates as Ned is doing here. It's where Ned got the idea, actually. Sam started it by taking in the illegitimate Peer's children. It grew from there."

"Ooch, that sounds *braw*, laddie, I ken what you mean. They do guid work there. Taking in wounded soldiers like me and giving them hope and worth. Then they have filled the place with wee bairns who their Peer parents abandon. Robbie writes often with his antics, as does my cousin, Jem. So yes, I would like to visit them, but as to Sydney…" Fergus grinned at Catriona. "Katy, love, we could settle in Sydney; what do you think?"

She nodded. "I'd love that, Fergie," she whispered to him. She was still in awe of this amazing Scotsman who had stolen her heart.

Ed laughed. Like Hamish, Fergus also lapsed back into his Scottish brogue when excited. Both had attended Edinburgh University.

To Ned, Fergus asked, "Dook, what's the marrying rules here? At home, I can 'church' a lassie or say in front of witnesses we be husband and wife. I believe that doesn't hold guid here?" he asked.

"No, Fergus, the minister has to read the Banns, and you can marry three or four weeks later. Or you get a Special Licence from a Bishop, and then you can marry quicker, but I wouldn't do that if you don't have to. Do the Banns," Ned explained with a smile.

~

So the Banns were read, and in the middle of October, Fergus and Catriona married at All Saints in Maidstone and left for a short honeymoon. Fergus took Katy to meet his cousins in West Sussex, and they then returned to the castle, having had a wonderful time with Robbie and Amelia and their family. Amelia's brother lived near the castle, and they visited him whilst there.

Fergus filled Ned in on the West Sussex family's well-being. Some eight years before, Amelia's daughter, Essie, had married Robbie's step-nephew, Edmund Garney, who was now Viscount Clarestow, and they had just had their sixth child. Edmund was the oldest grandson of Ned's friend Sam Garney, who had recently died. Esther, or Essie, was Ned's goddaughter. Robbie's brother Tim had married another friend's daughter, Mia Harrington. She was his friend Perry White's step-daughter. Ned was thrilled when he heard about those weddings years ago. "God pulling more threads," he had remarked to Christina.

Fergus was thrilled to finally meet his mother's half sister, the Dowager Countess, or Anne Garney, as she still introduced herself nowadays. She had remarried in her eighties to Duke James, Sam's father. She was ninety-one but still active and, as Fergus said, a 'knowing' one. Fergus adored her.

Rather than wait for Eddie's family to return, Fergus and Katy returned to Australia in November with her parents and brother.

~

Sarah and Anthony Harlow, or Ant as she called him, had an understanding, but as they were young, they were planning on taking things slowly. Ned wanted more time getting to know the lad's father. Since their return from London in mid-August, Ant would ride over from his father's house thrice weekly, and they were allowed to walk out with Chip and Tina, Neddie, and sometimes Ted when he was home from school. Others often accompanied them, so they were not tempted to pair off.

Initially, Ant was surprised that the family walks were not dainty garden strolls as he had expected, but rigorous tramps along various village and estate pathways. After the first visit, he dressed down into much more sensible clothes, sometimes even in a work outfit. The loss of a pair of dress shoes was worth the outing, though. They would often join the local school children, helping with the class reading and then escorting the younger castle children home from classes. He found himself sometimes even helping in the village vegetable gardens. Whatever their outing, it was always accompanied by much laughter and often many of the other villagers from the *Gracemere Estate*. He was learning by example how Chip, the future duke, was loved by his people. He craved the same for his estate but didn't know where to start. The villagers greeted Chip respectfully by title, Lord Charles, but more often just as M'Lord or Sir, and none were afraid to come and chat freely with him.

Ant said to Sarah one day, "I don't even know any of the villagers in our towns, not a single one."

"Oh, Ant! How come? Can we come and meet them one day?" Sarah asked.

Stunned, Ant realised he had said yes before he asked his father's permission. He knew there would be repercussions.

~

They were not, however, the ones he expected. Over the next month, Sarah, Chip, Neddie, Tina, and Andrew McKay would more often ride to *Chester Castle* in Nettlestead, where Ant would meet them. Soon they were making twice-weekly visits to every village, hamlet, and house on the estate. The ugly stares soon turned to waves of pleasure.

Ned and Eddie came with them a few times. Finally, they encouraged Anthony to join the young folk for a ride, when they did a ride around Chester Estate.

Then Ned invited Anthony to reciprocate.

Anthony came with Ant on his next visit; Eddie made his excuses and left the two alone. The experience was eye-opening for the Viscount. There were waves from every person as they shouted joyous blessings on Ned.

This was all the lesson Anthony needed. "Your Grace, I need help. My eyes are opened to the possibilities of, well, this." He waved his hand around the immaculate villages. "I had heard this village was different, but this... Why this is amazing." Anthony, Viscount Winchester, was humbled.

"Yes, Winchester, of course, and very different from what I inherited, too." Ned knew where his children were as they saw their horses tied up outside the classroom with a groom in attendance. They had dismounted and had gone inside by the time Ned and Anthony arrived some minutes later. "Here is the best place to start. Let's go in." Ned dismounted, as did Anthony.

The groom took their horses, and they, too, walked inside. The groom was more there as security for the Castle children.

Ned knocked. On seeing who was there, the children quietly stood behind their desks. There was no fidgeting or surprise.

The teacher welcomed him as if this were a regular occurrence. Anthony was even more surprised to find that it was just that, routine.

"Good morning, Mr Morris; all well?" Ned enquired.

"Yes, Your Grace, no complaints."

"Please continue." The class resumed as the two men stood taking in their activities. Ned watched as their young people soon entered from the other classroom. He knew this signalled reading time.

Anthony watched his son take a small girl to the shelves as she chose a book. Another girl, who looked amazingly similar to the first, walked to the Duke. "Papa, George's chicken was killed last night. Can I send him one of mine?"

The Duke bent and picked her up. "Yes, Izzy, we can." He kissed the top of her head. Without putting her down, he walked over to a little boy and squatted at his desk. "Hello, George. I believe the foxes got in again last night?"

"Yes, sir, they killed my prize chicken," the boy said.

"Ahh! Well, before I send you a replacement, how about a new chicken coop? One that will keep out the foxes?" Ned was squatting next to the small boy, Izzy still in his arms.

"Thank you, sir. Izzy said you might do that. Mama will be happy. Thank you again, sir." The boy went back to his reading.

Ned stood and kissed his daughter again. "Happy, pet?"

"Yes, thank you, Papa." She stroked his cheek, then kissed it. She gently hugged him, then asked to be put down.

Anthony had stood watching. "You know them all. Every one of them?"

Ned nodded. "They are my people, Winchester. They are all like family."

The men left the classroom and went outside to find a place to talk. "Yes, I know every one of them, and our children attend here too, as you saw. Why pay a tutor to teach one or two children when they can teach a class full? The staff live at the castle in the rooms provided, but don't have to." He pointed to the teacher. "Mr Morris married one of the local girls, so he lives in town now. Another teacher is a lady, Miss Lanham, who lives at the castle. She normally walks down with the younger children in the mornings with the groom. He stays around in case someone needs to send a message, and also as a precautionary measure. Not that he's needed for that. Our children and their cousins see life from both sides and make friends in town and vice versa. We no longer have village children skipping classes. Behaviour is good; the results are excellent. Those who do not wish to stay in school are apprenticed out to whatever calling they choose." He fell to watching Anthony's face.

Ned could see the idea was not being rejected, so he continued. "Not all the cottages have yards with good soil, so we also built a community garden. The children tend it, and then the village has preserving days when the excess crop is bottled, jammed, or pickled for use throughout the year. We all join in. It's great fun too. It is fenced from invading animals like rabbits and deer."

"Harry was right, you know." Anthony was rubbing his forehead as though it hurt. "I thought I knew better. I thought being a peer was lauding it over everyone. I'm wrong, aren't I?"

Ned shrugged but didn't nod. He did tip his head sideways and twisted his mouth in agreement. He replied with a story. "David was the same, Anthony. Do you mind if I call you that? Having permitted our children to court, we shall soon be closer than just neighbours. If we can set an example for other peers to change their estates, well, things can change. It's what Sam Corbett, over at *Meldon Hall*, did. Daniel, his son, is following in his footsteps. Edmund, Viscount Eames, Christina's brother, is doing the same on their Estate; John Saunders on his, as well. Perry White, Duke of Cheatham and his son Jem have vastly changed their estate as well. Even Viscount Ellison has finally seen the light. He was a tough nut to crack, but Matthew stepped in and took over some areas of the Estate. Matthew is Ed's uncle, by the way. For your place, start bit by bit, Anthony. We started with the school. Sam started by bringing in abandoned peers' children, illegitimate ones and then staffing the estate with both them and disabled soldiers. Sam's, or I should now say Daniel's, place has a prestigious school in one wing of their enormous house, *Meldon Hall*. Anyway, if you can win the education battle, then the rest will follow. Just don't push too hard." He sat in silence for a minute, then said, "Allow Sarah and Ant some freedom, Chip and Tina too. Tina and Neddie both have experience with teaching, and as you saw, they have already taught the others. If you allow them to do it, it will just flow. It will also allow you to ease into the change. God will open the first door, so be waiting. He knows where the greatest need is. Let the rest happen. Just wait for that opening. It will come. The good Lord knows what is most important. All you have to do is say 'yes'."

Anthony was soaking up the information. He fell silent. "Your Grace, I...,"

"If you're Anthony, at least call me Ned or Edward if you can't get your mouth around that. We shall be in-laws. So get used to it."

He nodded. "Edward, tell me about Harry." He gave a half-laugh. "He calls me Tony, you know. I miss him. I never thought I would, but I do, greatly. We used to be so close. Then I opened my mouth and cast him out."

Ned then told him of Wills and the trip of discovery with the six intrepid Englishmen in search of dangerous adventure. He mentioned the simple question from Wills that changed all their lives, his own included. "Anthony, Wills is Ed's younger brother and was only seventeen when he ran away from home. Little did he know that the six he chose to run away with were not strangers as he thought them to be. Wills was, in one way or another, related to them all. Christina's brother, Viscount Edmund, was one of them; John Saunders, yes, your cousin, is another. He, by the way, is also Eddie's second cousin. Annabella's cousin Phil was another; he has stayed over there too; he married Lucy Norfolk from the other side of your estate. He works with Harry and Wills. However, you need to talk to Edmund and John about Harry. Lewis Bland and Aidan O'Keefe were the final two of the group. They are related to my mother and Ed's grandmother."

Ned paused, looking at Anthony and let the information soak in. "Anthony, I will tell you of Wills and 'the question'. I have heard this from each of them." He took a deep breath. "Soon after they met, they were all sitting around a campfire. Each was telling Wills about their lives here in England. Of hunting, fishing, racing, gambling, balls, dances, drinking, women, and socialising. All the things that rich young men do here. They looked to Wills to see if he was impressed. He wasn't. Wills is one of the most amazing and impressive young men that I've ever met. He's also Harry's business partner, by the way. Together they can buy you and me out ten times over."

Anthony gasped. He knew Harry had left with limited funds and had an allowance that he no longer drew on.

Ned continued. "Wills simply asked them all, 'But what do you do to help others?' Each fell quiet, convicted and ashamed. They refused to answer him. It was a challenge that God had issued to each before, and they had chosen to ignore it. They all ran away to Australia. Harry too. So, Wills' question was met with silence, for none could answer honestly."

Ned saw that he had Anthony's interest and attention. "This way of life for Wills was just part of his everyday living." Ned again glanced at Anthony. "I must return to the beginning of the story before I tell more. Five months or so before, the six had met at White's in London. All had gone there to get drunk except Harry and John, who had arranged to meet. It was the week you spoke to him. Our Lord brought the others. Harry had planned an adventure trip to Australia and wanted to ask John to come along. He intended to find some other country to live in, far away from you and the memories here. Australia fitted the bill. However, God wanted the others along on the journey. As you know, they had all served in India together and were friends. After not seeing each other for over a year, they were in the same place simultaneously. That was not just a chance. White's, as you know, is not very conducive to a Godly lifestyle. Anyway, they all sat discussing their future and Harry's proposed trip. Within weeks, they were on board a ship; none can even remember its name. With no plan other than to leave behind their lives for some time." Ned glanced at him; he was still listening intently. "So… after Wills asked his question the first time and received no answer, he did not push them for some weeks. But some time later, he repeated it. Over the months of the trip, God peeled away the greed, lust, selfishness, idleness, and self-centredness of each. Each realised they had not had a drop of alcohol for months, and none had missed it. The trip had changed their lives completely. The other thing is that in the entire trip, the seven had not had a cross word. You really need to hear their story from one of them."

Anthony sat listening in fascination with his head bowed.

"On the return to Emu Plains, Harry then met Vicky, who is Jenna's sister. If you think Jenna is beautiful, oh, Anthony, she is equal in beauty to my own Christina and equally beautiful as your Maud. Anyway, their parents were convicts. Times served, and Certificates of Freedom earned. As you can imagine, Harry balked. He later told me, 'I am a Viscount's son, a brother to another. How could I, Harry Harlow, marry a convict's daughter?' John challenged him, 'Could he live without her?' When he realised that, no, he couldn't. Harry said that his feeling of relief was almost overwhelming. So he wouldn't be able to live in England, but did he wish to anyway? Some months after their wedding, just after they lost their first child, actually," he heard Anthony gasp but continued, "Harry realised that his own importance was as nothing. You see, Vicky's other two sisters married Lockleys, that's Ed and Wills. They are, of course, all my cousins. So he and Vicky were actually of lower Precedence than his in-laws. That realisation was the final burden for him to cast off. Anthony, Harry is a different man. To meet him on equal footing, you must be different too. You have to rethink your life and your role as Viscount. I ask you one question: Will you continue to be a taker or start to be a giver?"

Anthony didn't have to think; he answered quickly. "Edward, I have been a 'taker' all my life, but it has not brought me happiness. I married Maud for what she would bring me, not because I loved her. I do now, but I have no idea how to tell her. I've always just taken what is rightfully mine, just as my father taught me. I snatched it as soon as I could and told Harry he could go to blazes. He had nothing and nowhere to call home, and I didn't care. I have never given back a thing. To anyone, I don't know how to say sorry. I don't like what I've become, Edward. I don't like what I said to Harry."

"Then let's sort that first," Ned said gently. "Write to him."

Anthony was unable to reply for some time. Ned's gentleness had broken through where Harry's anger had failed. He looked at Ned and nodded. "Teach me," he finally mumbled. He was very close to tears.

Ned nodded. "Enough for today." They walked together to their horses. "Come and see me. We'll talk about a plan. As I said, get the children involved and encourage them. They will have ideas, and they all see things better than us, but I would start with the schools unless God directs you otherwise, and by that, I mean physically. Rebuild the thing. Yours is falling down. Build them a new one, with a big hall and include a piano and a stage. Singing is wonderful. Put on plays and encourage a village concert. Bring back the market days, and build a village green again. Does Maud play an instrument, or can she paint?"

Anthony replied that she did.

"Get her teaching there. It's what my mother did. It's how we broke through, but we let God lead. He will know what's more important in your village. Then we involved the castle staff. Teach grooming, cleanliness, cooking, and build a medical centre in the village. Gerry can help with that. Look after the people's basics, fix their cottages and repair the buildings, don't wait for them to ask. Build a healthy environment, and the rest follows. If you give first, then you will reap the rewards. Not just financially, although that will come too, but with loyalty and love. It's worth far more than money. God may have a different path for your estate, but it's how we changed. Admittedly, I had a blank slate."

They rode back to the castle via the medical centre at *Hedgemere*. Gerry greeted them and showed Anthony through the tiny hospital. He introduced him to one of the junior doctors; it was Ned's nephew. "Pity you don't have a clinic, Winchester. Our people are so well here now; we don't have the work for two full-time doctors and me, too."

"Hold that thought, Doctor, give me a week. I have a cottage in mind." Anthony said, grinning at Ned.

Gerry was stunned.

Ned smiled. It seemed the Clinic would come before the school on Chester Estate, but maybe that is what was needed most. "I told you God would open a door," Ned said as they were leaving.

Anthony nodded. He had taken the first step, and it hadn't been that hard.

He came the next day, and they started work on a plan with Ned. The next meeting was two days later at Chester Castle in Nettlestead. Gerry came to inspect the new cottage. They rode out to inspect the various vacant buildings and possible parcels of land for a new school.

Mr Davis, the current teacher, was overwhelmed.

~

Over time, Edward became Ned, and Anthony became Tony. Ned encouraged Ant to work with his father and discuss plans for the future. He also suggested they involve Chip and Neddie.

~

A few weeks later, Anthony arrived excitedly to see Ned. He had just received a much-delayed letter from Harry. It had somehow been lost and took ten months to reach him. "Ned, if this had arrived when it should have done, I may not even have read it. Now… well, now I may even accept his invitation."

"Tony, I will merely say that if you go, you will never regret it," Ned said with care.

~

September saw Teddy, Liam, Kit, and young Neddie Winslow-Smythe all enrolled at The King's School in Canterbury for the new school year, and they loved it. The teaching was similar in most things, but the teaching style was, as Teddy said, "It's learning by rote." Everything had to be memorised and chanted in unison. When they found out that Kit and Nick's uncle was a teacher at The King's School in Parramatta, they had a very different welcome.

By the end of November, Sarah and Ant announced their engagement. However, to achieve the changes required on the estate, they needed to marry as they needed to be hands-on in the school, and they could not be there unattended. Chip and Tina had the same problem. Although they were only eighteen, the three sets of parents agreed that they could have a double wedding in March the following year. All would be nearly nineteen or a bit older. They chose the church closest to *Gracemere Castle* as the castle chapel was too small. All Saints in Maidstone would see a second wedding from the castle. They had claimed Fergus and Catriona's as theirs. Neither girl wanted a huge Society wedding, just family. That, of course, meant a small society wedding as a Duke's, Earl's and Viscount's families were never small. Ned may not have extended family, except the Lockleys. However, Christina's and the Harlow families were enormous. There was the extended family as well, John and Edmund and their wives and children. The venue was close to the prominent family, and that's what mattered. The girls had decided on very different wedding gowns. Chip and Tina were to marry first, Sarah and Ant second. Neddie and Ted stood as best men for them both, as did Lily and Bella for the girls. Each chose to witness the others' signatures in the register. Tina would have to sign as a bride as Christina Lockley, then as a witness as Christina Allingmere, as Chip used his title of Marquess of Allingmere.

Sydney

Hamish was walking along the foreshore in Sydney, watching the latest ship come in; it was a big one from England by its look. Effy was carrying Elspeth, and Ferdie ran up and down the grassy banks of the hills outside Government House.

"Hooch, what does a man need to do to find a wee dram around here?" he heard called out to him.

Hamish spun around; he could not believe his ears. "Hold the bairns love." He took off as fast as he could walk down the hill.

Effy looked up to see him embrace a clone of himself.

"Ferg, what are you doing here? Ooch man, 'tis *braw*." Hamish hugged his brother again, "Now I have family here too. Oh, this is *braw*," Hamish repeated.

An attractive young lady was approaching them. "Katy, my love, come up and meet my brother." The lady wandered along the foreshore towards them.

Hamish turned and beckoned Effy to join them.

The girls arrived at the same time. They were looking from one man to the other; they were very alike. Both were clean-shaven, red-haired, with perfect teeth. Same height, eyes, and laugh.

Catriona was with child, about five months along and showing slightly on her slim figure. This brought a round of congratulations from Hamish and Effy.

They returned to the ship to collect their luggage. "Why dinna ye write and tell me ye were coming?" Hamish asked as they walked behind their wives.

Once over their excitement, their accents dropped.

"I wrote, but I ken the letter is on the same ship as us. We made the decision and only had three weeks until we married. We were married by Banns, Hame; I did it the English way. I wrote, but we caught the next ship. Katy's parents and brother are from Melbourne. We left them there and came on to Sydney." He laughed. "Oh, Hammer, you are a delight to my eyes. Now tell me about the leg."

"Crimea, Ferg. Darn thing still itches, been gone for years, now, but it still blooming well itches. A friend made me my first leg, but it didn't have a knee. We made this shapely specimen at the Home. I'll tell you all about that later, but it bends in all the right places. Now, what about your face? Same?"

"Yes, Hame, sabre swipe. I suppose I'm lucky it didn't kill me. My Katy is the first one who didn't turn away from it. Hame she wept, but touched it in such a way it was compassion, not pity. She's amazing."

"My Effy is the same. She found me in church three days after I arrived. I was filthy and smelled. Aww, the memory. I had nothing, Ferg, Nothing but what I stood up in and Colin's clothes, which were too small for me. I kept his plaid and kilt, swapped the rest for what I could wear. They were but tatty rags. Colin loaded me on board as he said there was nothing left at home. He knew about the lands and the house fire. You were gone, and I was unconscious. He died on board from fever; I was with him to the end, Ferg. But by then, my leg had gone. Originally a sabre wound too, but it infected and had to go."

Hamish looked lovingly at his wife. "Ferg, my Effy taught me to cook and how to run a house. I still look out for our Wills' house a bit. I care for their garden and teach the boys from the Home what to do, but we have our own, as you know. Will you stay with us? We do have room."

Fergus turned to his wife with a raised eyebrow. "Katy?"

She nodded in assent.

"We would love to Hame." Fergus slapped him lovingly on his back. "Oh, but it's good to see you."

A town carriage was waiting at the wharf. Hamish asked the driver, "If you'd take the luggage and deliver it to my home, please." He then turned to Fergus and asked, "Are ye fine to walk, or would you like to ride?"

Fergus looked lovingly at his young wife. "Katy, it's up to you, love."

"Walk, please, Hamish. My legs are swollen from inactivity," Catriona said.

"Then walk it is. 'Tis not far, but 'tis uphill. 'Twill give us a fair stretch, though. Thankfully, it's not too hot. January here takes some getting used to, Ferg."

Catriona and Effy were getting on well.

Halfway up the hill, Effy turned to Hamish. "Hammy, I have a sister now. I'm so excited."

Each woman had taken a child in her arms. Ferdie wiggled to get down, and Hamish took him from Effy. At nearly three, he was very active. They had forgotten to bring his walking lead.

"May I Hame?" Fergus took his nephew from his arms. His namesake went to him willingly; he pulled back in his uncle's arms, looking from one man to the other. Liking what he saw, he then gently ran his tiny fingers over Fergus' scar.

"Ouchie, Papa," he said, looking from his uncle to his father.

"Not any more, lad, it just looks bad," his uncle said.

"I might be able to help with that, Fergus," Effy said. "I have some special Rose-hip and Geranium Oil I've been using on Hamish's leg. It's helped."

"Sounds good, Effy. I'll give it a try. Nice if it works. Pity I don't have a cure to grow a new leg for Hame."

Ferdie touched it again and then snuggled to wrap his arms around his neck. "You smell nice, like Papa," the small boy murmured and nestled his red head on the new neck.

Fergus' heart did something unusual as he cuddled the small child. "Hame, I can't wait for us to have our own. Ain't God just grand?"

Both men laughed. Their mother used to say that often.

Caro heard the not-so-quiet Scottish voices approaching and appeared at the window next door.

Hamish waved and beckoned them over. "Caro, bring Dougie. My brother has arrived unannounced, and he's brought a wife."

Caro and Doug went next door with Carly in tow. She went straight to the kitchen and soon had tea on the boil.

Caro took the children while the others settled in the guest room.

When they entered the Macdonald's cottage, they found that the luggage was already there. "That's good service, Hame," Fergus chortled.

"Mr Stewart from *The Kings' Arms* often sends a carriage to the wharf to see if they could persuade any passengers to stay with them. I saw no one needed it. We have the use of it when required. Long explanation," Hamish said. "Also, I know the coachman, Cedric Tideman, hence I was able to use the vehicle for the luggage."

Fergus roared with laughter.

Caro and Doug had heard a great deal about Fergus, and it was a delight to meet him finally.

England

February saw the new Chesterfield Health Clinic open in the village near Chester Castle. The doctor was a presentable young man named Felix Johnson. He was employed full-time with one of the Gracemere doctors, attending every other day, except Sundays. There was a free clinic twice a week with both doctors available for appointments. It soon became known that the castle staff availed themselves of the clinic and had even seen the "Young Sir" there, having a wound stitched. Ant had cut himself while attempting to fix a fence. News spread, and soon the village residents began to trust the doctors.

Sarah and Maud travelled in the gig to the new school as they had been doing since soon after the wedding. Tony had opened their new school buildings the week after the clinic. Sarah had persuaded her mother-in-law to come with her to help teach singing and grooming. They were starting with hymns.

Ant and his father joined them after their rounds of the estate. The men had been to the new clinic and called in to see how the ladies were coping. As it was a lovely April day, they all decided to walk back a little before heading home. Ant led the horse and gig, and Anthony had the two riding horses.

Sarah and Ant were laughing as they walked. They were so very happy.

Anthony took Maud's hand as they walked. "Maudie, I don't know how to go on, but I look at these two and see how happy they are. It's what I wanted for us, but I don't know how to get there. I still don't. Can I ask your forgiveness, my dear?"

He heard her draw a sharp breath.

In twenty years of marriage, she had never heard him like this. It was as close as she had ever heard to an apology. "Tony, in the last few months, you have become the man I knew you to be, under everything." She did not want to use the word 'insecure', but that's what it was. "I don't know what changed, but I like it." She squeezed his fingers hard, but lovingly; she now clasped his hand, and she interwove her fingers with his. She had fallen in love with Anthony long ago, but only realised after their marriage that he had married her for her wealth and title. Her father was a Duke, and her dowry was splendid.

He asked, "Is it too late to start again? You see, I fell in love with you many years ago, though I didn't know what to do about it. I started off on the wrong foot and didn't know how to change things." Although he'd been holding her hand, he was now caressing it lovingly.

"How about this?" She stopped and reached up and kissed him. "I'm not too embarrassed to tell you I have always loved you; it's just taken you a long time to let me know. I would see you were looking at me, and I would wonder."

"Oh, Maudie, I'm so sorry. I've been such a stupid fool." He didn't kiss her but enfolded her in his arms. "We'll start again, love."

She pulled back in his arms. "No, we won't. We'll change the ending, Tony. Nothing can erase the past, but we can learn from it." She tucked her arm through his, and they kept walking.

"Let's hope the ending is a long way away." He fell silent, looking down at this lovely woman who had put up with his moods and tempers for the past nearly twenty years. "I was thinking about a honeymoon, love. We never really had one, you know, as we came here after the wedding and never really left. Would you come with me to see Harry? I understand if you won't, but I would really love you to come." He asked, hopefully. This trip had been on his mind since last year's letter. It still remained unanswered; he didn't know what to say.

"Not come? Tony, you would have to tie me down not to come. Of course, I will." She skipped with joy. "Really? We're going?"

He gave a long laugh, something he had not done for many a year. It felt good. "Yes, love, we're going, and it's going to be fun. Our lives will be different from what our old life was here." He slid his arm along her shoulders and drew her close. This time, he bent his head and kissed her with all his pent-up passion and desire. This was no passing kiss but a release of twenty years of bottled emotions.

Ant turned and looked back at his parents, open-mouthed. They not only sounded happy but looked happy. In all his years, he had never seen them even touch each other, let alone his mother in his father's arms, and them both laughing. As he watched, he saw his father bend and passionately kiss his mother.

Sarah grabbed his hand and kept walking. She was smiling. "Leave them alone. We may have your castle to ourselves soon, Ant," she whispered to her new husband.

Ant looked at her, puzzled.

"Ant, your father was asking me about the trip over to Australia, what it was like and if your mother could cope with Emu Plains. I think they may go to Harry," she explained.

"Oh!" he said, still in shock. "Sweeting, I think that finally, he's finding Mother's worth. It's taken him long enough, but do you know what? I like the new 'him'. I think he does too."

"Ant, I think he's found his own worth, too," she said adoringly, gazing at her own young, handsome Harlow.

Europe

The long-awaited trip to Antwerp finally occurred. Gerry and Annabella stayed home with all the younger children.

Ned, Christina, Ed, Jenna, and Neddie Lockley were all going. With both his friends and twin now married, Neddie thought he would enjoy some free travel with his parents. He liked London, but couldn't wait to get home. Like his father, his heart was working on an anvil. The trip to Antwerp may extend to a few other countries. Ned offered Chip and Ant and their girls the opportunity to come, but both preferred to stay home with their new wives. Teddy chose to remain in school. He loved England.

The Prince had been in contact with Ned and given him the names of three jewellers in London. They had sold the most significant sapphires to one of them, including John's large blue one, for £4,000: the fancy yellow diamond and a small packet of good sapphires sold for £12,000. Ned insisted on individual prices, not group prices for the remainder, but they were out of their price range.

These jewellers had given Ned the names of more reputable dealers, but far more importantly, who to avoid. They discovered that the buyers in Sydney were from any of the named companies.

They still had ten of the larger group diamonds and the thirty medium-sized good ones that they had not shown the Antwerp buyers when in Sydney.

William's large diamond also needed to be sold. He had put £10,000 on that, but Mr Lamb had told them to ask for more, £12,000 at least. Ned was going to ask for £15,000.

So armed with the thirty-one diamonds sewn into his pocket, they left the country for Amsterdam first. They were hoping that they could get over £2,000 per stone. Ned was happy to sell individually.

Jenna and Christina left the sale to the men as they shopped. Neddie stayed with the ladies, escorting them on their various excursions.

The Amsterdam buyers were excited to see the quality of the stones, but only bought six of the smaller gem specimens, two from each of the individual packs, as it happened. They could not cut the large one and reluctantly had to let it pass. They directed them to another firm in Antwerp.

The family group toured for a time through various countries, then moved on to Antwerp. Their first call was to Henry Morse and Co.

Of the remaining diamonds, they purchased ten of the medium-sized stones. They paid £3,000 for each one, exclaiming that the size and quality were exceptional, each a D-grade stone. They lusted over the large one of William's, but they valued it at a minimum of £12,000.

It was out of their budget.

~

Neddie accompanied Ned and his father on their final stop. He wanted to see how they negotiated. This stop was to CM Field and Co., known in Antwerp as *Tiffany's*. Hopefully, here they would purchase the final fifteen diamonds. On entering the building, Ned introduced himself, then asked to see the owner.

Within moments, they heard bolts being drawn back, the rear door opened, and a bearded gentleman entered. He had a strange apparatus attached to his head and looked at them with magnified eyes. He squinted, then realised he had not removed his headgear.

Ned introduced himself again and extended the Prince's greetings. Although he had not sent an introduction, the Prince had mentioned this jeweller at their initial meeting.

"Ahh, how is he? I have not seen him for many a year," the gentleman inquired.

"His Royal Highness is well. He has sent us to you on a quest." Ned thought he would get straight to the point. "Are you aware of a new source of diamonds from Australia?"

Mr Field said, "I have heard rumours, but had none that I can confirm were from there. Why do you ask, Your Grace?"

"I was wondering if you may be interested in possibly purchasing some. The provenance is guaranteed by me and my friend here, Edward Lockley, and his son, also Edward. The finder of the stones, Luke Lockley, is Edward Senior's brother; their father is the Earl of Coxheath. Luke and two friends mined these themselves. You can get no more guarantee than that. I have letters from each of the three finders as to their permission to sell."

Mr Field ripped off his headset. "Are you serious? Of course, I want to see them. With that provenance, well, show me." He clapped his hands twice, and one staff member opened the door to the back rooms. Another went to get tea, and a third locked the front door and put up the closed sign.

The man said, "I never do business with the door unlocked. Old habit, sorry! Can't be too careful in my business." He smiled and suggested they follow him. He took them through a solid, metal-lined door. Once inside, he drew it closed and slid back the three long bolts on another door.

They entered, and the room was well lit but airtight and almost breathless. It was obviously the cutting room. From there, he kept walking down a short corridor to another door. It was also steel-lined with more bolts. After entering this door, he locked it after them.

They were now in a small office. Its lighting was from small street-level windows and a large lamp. "Now we're in my inner sanctum. What have you got for me?" He stood, rubbing his hands together.

Ned reached under his overcoat and removed a bag from his inside pocket. The bag contained four smaller bags; he held back the blue bag and passed over the other three. The first bag contained most of William's personal diamonds, the second John's and the third Luke's.

"Ohh! They are beautiful. Far better than I expected. 'D' clarity, no flaws visible and excellent shape. Individual or price of parcel?"

"Both," Ned said, confusing the older man, "They belong to three separate persons, and they want individual prices. Some belong to the group."

"Ahh, now I understand." He undid the second bag. "My, my, they are all as good," then the third. "These too, I shall give you £2000 each for these nineteen stones, and that one has a chip, so only £1800 for it, even though it's slightly larger. I should be able to cut around it. If I cleave properly, I could get two stones from each. Work that out how you will. Now, what have you got in that bag?" Again, he was rubbing his hands together, his excitement tangible.

Ned held the bag by the string and let him grab it almost greedily. It had the remaining large diamond in it.

Ned explained, "This was the very first diamond Reverend William Clarke found. No other gem can ever claim that title. He sent a letter to establish its authenticity," Ned explained this before Mr Field opened the bag.

Mr Field tipped the contents into his hand.

The single half-inch stone rolled the length of his hand.

"Oh, Oh! OH! I have never seen such perfection. Such beauty, oh, such a gem! Oh, sir, I mean Your Grace. I am overwhelmed." He plopped himself on his swivel seat with a bang.

He took up his eyeglass and a mirror. Catching extra light and checking it. The sunlight caught the stone in the mirror and reflected rainbows on the ceiling. "It's also perfect. Absolutely perfect." He mopped his brow, stood thinking, then mopped it again. The room was stuffy but chilly, so it was not from the heat that he did this.

"I suppose you want £20,000 for this, but I can only offer £17,000; that is all I have on hand after I have purchased the others."

Ned and Eddie retired to the back of the room. It wasn't far away, but they both gave the thumbs up for the sale.

"We agree," said Ned, "But I have something to ask you. How much does it cost to cut a stone?"

"For my time to cut it, over £500 per stone if they are like this; less for the smaller ones."

"Then we shall accept the £17,000 conditionally. Trust me; you will not regret this."

Mr Field looked puzzled.

Ned went on to tell him of the diamond the Prince had purchased for Queen Victoria. "It is uncut and needs both cutting and setting. Would you do this for her? Mr Field, the stone is an inch point to point and is perfect. This is a once-in-a-lifetime stone. You would be forever recorded as the cutter; it weighs at least twenty-five carats. They did not have scales large enough. The Prince also purchased two smaller ones as well. They were larger than the £2,000 but smaller than that one."

Eddie felt very sorry for poor Mr Field. "How big? An inch?" He mopped his brow three more times. "Of course, of course; Oh, what an opportunity. Perfect, you say? One inch. Oh my!"

"So that's 'yes'?" Ned asked, intrigued by his enthusiasm.

He nodded. "Of course, it's a yes. Now to work out payment." He jotted down some figures. "£56,800, is this what you get?"

Ned agreed, having done the addition in his head.

"Are £1,000 notes suitable?"

Ned said yes.

Mr Field went through another door and locked them in.

A few minutes later, he returned with a bundle of paper. He counted out the £56,000 in £1,000 notes and then smaller amounts until he reached £800. Neddie had watched the transaction and was astounded by the wad of money the two men now carried.

On departure, Ned divided the notes and gave a third to Eddie and a third to Neddie, "Just in case."

They were then let out of the unique store and went immediately to find a bank—any bank, but one that he could draw out the money in London.

Thus done, they went to join the ladies at a tea house.

~

The group spent another two weeks touring Europe and then returned home.

Jenna enjoyed seeing a different side of the world. She worked out that France or Spain would be the closest land to the opposite side of the world from Sydney.

Everything was so vastly different and so very old. The buildings were so positively ancient compared to what both Ed and Jenna were used to.

In Parramatta, the oldest building would not have been even one hundred years old. Many were still made of timber, and most were still primitive. Lachlan Macquarie was responsible for most of the new sandstone buildings. Though beautiful, they were less than fifty years old.

The family group enjoyed their travel, and Ned pointed out many interesting places. He'd had to make a few trips over to Europe in the last few years. He also purchased a beautiful blue topaz necklace for Christina. He told her that as her birthday was on Christmas Day and she missed it every year, he made up for it with giving her a gift for her six month's celebration each year.

England

On arrival in London, Ned sent word to the Palace and asked for a moment of the Prince's time.

Word returned for a meeting at ten o'clock the following day.

Ned and Eddie planned to go alone, but Neddie pleaded and they permitted him to join them. Neddie knew he would never again have the chance to see inside the palace.

The following day, the three went along to the Palace and delivered the news of Mr Field's proposed visit. "Your Royal Highness, when he saw the quality of the other large stone we had, he was in raptures. I suggested that he might cut your pebbles for free, and once he knew the details, he acquiesced. He said he would send word."

The Prince had stood virtually silently. His hands clasped behind his back. "Ahh, so that is what that was about; yes, I had a letter from him yesterday. He is coming to collect them personally," the Prince explained. "Splendid, well done! And thank you. She did like them, but wondered how we were going to use them. Not much I can give her as a surprise, you know. This solves that problem. Again, thanks. It's Christmas soon. I hope they will be done by then." The Prince did not look well, and he was not inclined to talk much.

Ned knew the meeting was at an end, so they left. Only the three men had travelled to London for this meeting. They returned to the castle the following day.

~

On their return from London, Ned, Ed, and Neddie had fallen silent. Neddie had seen enough; he wanted to go home. "Papa, I've seen London. Can we go home? I will miss Tina, but she would have married sometime, and I know I can always return. I just want to get home and back to the forge. I didn't realise how much I miss it. This *la de dar* life is all well and good for a holiday, but it's not for me."

Ed looked at his oldest son. He knew the feeling so well. He remembered when his school years had finished; he, too, wished to return to the forge. "Yes, Neddie, we're going home."

Ned explained that the extended family planned to have a few weeks at the Castle after Christmas, before heading to London for the next Season. They would attend one Drawing Room before Ed, Jenna, and the family had to leave.

Bella Winslow-Smythe was being presented.

Ed and Jenna were sad to be leaving, but they knew on arrival that their daughter would be staying now that she had married Chip.

On arrival back at the castle, they were greeted warmly. None more so than by Anthony, who was awaiting their return.

Gerry had sent a note to Tony that morning telling of their imminent arrival. The change in the man was remarkable. Ned now typically saw him in riding clothes, but on this day, he had arrived in a gig, and Maud accompanied him.

As the London carriage drew up to the front door, Gerry and Annabella were surrounded by numerous small children and standing behind them was Anthony with his arm around Maud. They were smiling like honeymooners. On either side of them were the two newly married couples.

Chip and Tina had recently returned from a month on the Isle of White. Sarah and Ant had ridden over to welcome the family home.

The numerous small children took all their attention to keep them from under the horses' hoofs. Once the adults had alighted, the children were let loose to welcome them home. After many hugs and kisses, Neddie took them to play outside. The adults were finally alone. Ned looked at Anthony and smiled. Maud greeted Christina and blushed. They sat huddled on a settee in a sunny spot near a window.

Jenna and the two young brides sat on another settee.

Anthony and Ned stood watching the others. "Ned, we're going back with Ed and Jenna. I've written to Harry, but I'm not awaiting a reply. I'm taking your advice and we're going. I have to mend this bridge I built, no, I mean, destroy it. Can you help Ant continue what we've started?"

"Of course, Tony. It's my thing. Sticking my oar in where it's not wanted," Ned chuckled. "I see you've finally told her, eh?"

"Yes, oh, why did I wait so long?" He smiled across the room to his wife. His heart was thumping. She met his smile and returned it. He just wished to be alone with her. They were like young lovers. Three months on a boat would suit him perfectly. Though they never had a first one, this would be a second honeymoon.

"Tony, it was worth waiting for. Be the man she needs you to be, and she'll be happy. I think you have discovered that already." Ned smiled at his new friend. For that is what he had become.

"Yes, the children, no, I should not call them that any more; the young people have taught me much in a short time," Anthony said respectfully.

"…But you listened, Tony," Ned said gently.

Ned called Eddie to them. "Looks like you might have some company on the return trip, Ed."

"We're thinking of leaving in about June, Ned. How would that fit?" Eddie said.

"June, eh? Yes, June sounds fine. I'll talk to Maudie." Anthony said.

~

Only a few weeks later, the caravan of carriages left for London. After Bella's presentation, they had decided to forgo the rest of the Season of Balls.

Jenna was sorrowful as Tina had just discovered she was expecting. She would not get to see her first grandchild, but she knew this was always going to be the case. That did not stop the many tears on Eddie's shoulder once alone in their room. "We'll return, my love," was all he could say to comfort her. He, too, felt sad, but leaving a new babe would be no easier. They had to return home. He had responsibilities there.

Passage for everyone was booked on the *Cairngorm* on June 12th, 1859, from London. It was hard to believe they had been here for over a year; now they were going home.

Anthony and Maud were quiet. The unknown was ahead of them.

Jenna assured them the passage would be quick. Travelling in June would catch the best winds.

Two doctors were in other cabins; one, Dr Forest, was with his wife. The other was a family, Dr and Mrs May, with five small children.

This would be interesting with twelve children under thirteen and two older ones. Teddy had elected to stay in England and finish his schooling there. He was enjoying the new life and realised what could be ahead for him. He knew that one day he would be an Earl and needed to learn what that entailed. It also meant that his friendship with Bella Winslow-Smythe could continue. He was now seventeen, she nearly nineteen. They, too, had reached an understanding. Gerry was over the moon that eventually Bella would be one of the 'family' and even a Countess in time. Although she was now "out," she decided to forgo any further social activities. She wanted to wait for Teddy.

Ned was doing up *Bramblemere* for them. This was the house where his grandfather, Charles, grew up. It was in Coxheath, some thirty minutes' ride away.

Teddy's biggest problem was what to do to earn some income. He would be an Earl without lands or income. He decided to look around for an orchard for sale or some land to plant one, hopefully somewhere near Coxheath. This was the next village on the list to see change, and this time, he would be the one in charge. Thankfully, Ned, Gerry and Tony would be there to support and advise him.

Ed did not think that Ted would return home for long after school, if he ever returned to Australia at all. Ned knew he would have some explaining to do to Charlie, but it would be a good experience for them to visit England. They could return with Harry next year. He still worried about Charlie. His confidence had taken a severe battering at the hands of an abusive soldier named Simmonds when he was a lad. Charlie had never seemed to be fully confident in himself from the day that man had come into his life. The man's abuse of Charlie had scarred him deeply. Eddie always had his back and helped where he could. Their father knew, as did Uncle Thomas and Ned, but no one ever spoke about it. Simmons was dead and he could harm no other little boys.

Australia

The trip home was uneventful; however, Eddie and Anthony spent much time in deep discussion. Each day was revealing more of the real Anthony. Harry was often the topic of conversation. Ed told Anthony of the work in the Emporiums and their importance to the colony. He also told them of Harry's orchard and the new packing house they had built, of the egg business that ran in conjunction with the orchard.

~

Anthony was fearful of the reunion. However, he need not have worried.

Harry was on the wharf to meet them on September 13th when they docked. Ned had sent word they were coming. He had been in town for a week, waiting anxiously; they had been close as boys, and he wished for that closeness to be renewed. Yet, Harry knew he would always be the spare, but he hoped that he could have had some role on the estate one day. When that didn't happen, he felt lost, and he ended up on a ship heading to New South Wales with his five best friends.

Anthony was at the railing with Maud as they sailed down the harbour. His eyes lit on Harry as they were pulling into the Circular Quay. Standing beside Harry was one of the most beautiful women he had ever seen, the Duchess and his Maud aside. Even from a distance, he could see that her carriage was regal. He drew his breath. "Oh, she's unbelievable," he thought to himself. Ed had warned him, but Victoria was breathtaking.

The gangplank was barely in place before Harry was up and in his brother's arms. They were as boys again, with the barriers stripped away with a single hug. Then they introduced their wives.

Vicky was even more astounding up close. She was quietly surveying the man in front of her. He was the man who had caused her beloved Harry so much grief and anguish. They greeted Ed and Jenna, and soon all were ready to leave. As they left the dockland, Vicky was gently holding Harry's arm; she lovingly squeezed it to tell him of her love.

Maud was on Anthony's arm, and she did much the same; they walked up the street to Wills' house.

Vicky greeted Jenna and the family and said they would catch them that evening for dinner at the hotel. It was a joyous event with much news passed back and forth.

Harry's forgiveness was absolute, as were Anthony's apologies. Anthony explained that Harry's letter had taken nearly a year to arrive. Then when it had… Anthony didn't know how to reply, so he came instead. All was well. They planned to leave by carriage to Emu Plains the next day, while Ed, Jenna, and the family would head back to Parramatta by ferry in a few days. As it happened, it took three days before the trip was cool enough to happen.

Harry made them all stay at the hotel until the heatwave of summer passed, as it was cooler than Wills' Parramatta house. Also, Wills' house had no staff.

The heat climaxed with one almighty thunderstorm.

The day after the storm, they packed up and headed west.

Ed had something to do in town first. He had sent word back on the eleven o'clock ferry on their arrival for Luke to join them as soon as he could. He also sent notes to William Clarke, as well as to John and Colleen Evans. He had three Bank of London drafts on him. Once he handed them to their owners, he could relax.

At half past four that afternoon, three men and their wives entered the hotel and asked to see Eddie.

The manager escorted them upstairs into the private sitting room.

Ed had requested the Duke's suite if it were available. It was. They would not have any interruptions there.

Knowing what this would be about, Maria and Ellen joined their husbands. Ellen and Luke had left the now three-year-old triplets with their grandparents. She was once again with-child; this was a delightful surprise for both Eddie and Jenna. Colleen had their third babe with her arms. Billy was only a few months old, too small as yet to be left, so Jenna could coo over this child instead of her own grandchild, who was yet to be born.

Once settled and afternoon tea delivered, Ed locked the door.

The hotel maids and Neddie took all the children out to run and play, and told them not to return for about two hours.

Jenna sat with Vicky and Maud and spent some quality time together.

Ed smiled. "Now, to the sales, you are all anxiously awaiting the results so that I won't keep you any longer." Eddie said, "Luke, you sadly get the least as you didn't have a giant diamond, but we did manage to get £4,000 for your blue sapphire in London. Along with the rest of the sales, your share is £31,399."

Luke and Ellen gasped as the others sat stunned.

"How much? What? You mean to share?" Luke said.

"No, Luke, that's your share; I have it all itemised; we can look at the list later. Ned and I worked through them thoroughly. There was a £200 difference on one stone, I think, that may have been originally in Luke's lot, but I wasn't sure who owned that, so we added it to the group lot and swapped it for a good one. I could adjust the total if you tell me who owned it. I know it was written down, but I must admit there were so many stones, we took what we could get. And the jewellers did mess up some of them as they checked them. I hope that was all right. Now, Reverend Clarke, you're next. We took your big stone to Antwerp and sold it for…" He paused, watching the anxious emotions flash on their faces. "… For £17,000. With the division of the group stones, your tally is £55,533."

All gasped again.

Maria turned to her very own reverend and melted into tears in his arms. William's jaw dropped open.

"Now, John and Colleen, I have, of course, added your collection together, but I want you to know, we did not have to take your stone to a jeweller. The Prince Consort, Prince Albert, had been reading the 'Colonial Returns', Denning's papers and the like, and knew of our link to the finds. He had read a full copy of your survey, sir," Ed said to William. "He called us in for an interview the day we met him at the Presentation and asked if we, by any chance, had any diamonds with us. As we did, and we told him so. Knowing the royals, Uncle Ned also said, 'We are unable to give them away as we have been commissioned to sell them on behalf of others.' The Prince still wanted to see them, and he fell in love with yours, Colleen. Without asking how much he offered us…" he drew a breath, "He offered us £35,000, and we grabbed it, of course. We were only going to say £20,000. He also bought two of the group diamonds for £5,000 each. He gave them to Her Majesty as a birthday present from him. As we speak, they are being cut in Antwerp. Anyway, with the remainder of the group gems, your share adds up to £77,533."

Colleen was already in tears at the mention of the Prince. She gasped when she heard her stone was to belong to the Queen. She had cried at the few hundred pounds from the first sale; now this.

Like Maria, she turned into her husband's shoulder and sobbed.

The men were all sitting in silence, digesting the information.

Ed continued. "William, your big stone will be cut into two. We sold the large ones, including the one with a chip, in Antwerp. The buyers who travel here were not from either of the companies recommended to us. So if you find more, we know where to take them, and those two won't get a look in."

Each couple laughed as he said that.

"Not likely," said Luke, knowing that travelling with small children required a lot more than a pack horse and cart. His salary from teaching was £40 per year, and even with an incremental wage rise each year, it would never be much more. They already owned their home and had made various donations to the needy from the second round of sales. More would follow. Luke smiled and reclined in his chair.

Ellen took his hand as smiled at him.

Eddie handed each of them their bank drafts. "I am assured that these are cashable at any of our banks. I would not draw it all out at once, as it might cause a run on the bank, but they will be honoured." Finally relieved of the nearly £165,000 that had been sitting in the pocket of every jacket he had worn for the last three months, Ed relaxed.

John and Colleen had made a list of what they wanted to do.

Poor Andrew Lenehan was selling all his property, as he was having financial issues since the extra work he had done for Mrs Denison on Government House work had not been honoured. Andrew was seriously out of pocket and on the verge of bankruptcy.

John and Colleen would buy the three properties from him, allowing him to live in one himself rent-free. They discussed offering to buy his home in Hunters Hill. Thus, helping him and using the property as accommodation for older homeless children, as well as group homes for adults, which Ricky, Tad, and Will English founded. They needed rooms rather than dormitories, and houses, rather than just a roof over their head. They also needed to learn to run an establishment before they could be employed in one. The joined cottages would become a training school. With no rents to pay, the costs would be minimal. The couple had also discussed other plans and buildings.

Reverend William relaxed. "If it had not been for your family, Luke, our little diamonds from the dirt may have been sold for only about £1,000 collectively. How can I ever thank you for what you have done for me? But this…" waving the draft for over £55,000 in the air, "…This is nothing to how I value my Maria coming home to me. She is worth so much more than any diamond. Cut or uncut." He leaned over and kissed her, then handed her the bank draft. "For you, my dearest, darling, are my diamond beyond price. This is yours."

Chapter 23   Pay it Forward

*I*t was nearly Christmas and three months since Ed arrived home.

Luke stood looking out the window of his house on Church Street in Parramatta, thinking back over the last five years. A smile slowly spread across his face; he remembered doing the same in Sydney, looking at life passing by him. That was on the day after he had finished his exams; he was depressed; he had no job, no money, or not much of it, and no girl in his life. He was lonely. At twenty-seven, he pined for the love he thought lost. He felt desperately alone; he did the only thing he could: he turned to God in prayer, pouring out his hurts and sadness. He had still been praying when Wills pulled up to the house with Cathy. He was downstairs and in his brother's arms in moments. Within the week, he had a job and just weeks after that was engaged to the love he thought lost four years before. Now they had five children.

When the triplets arrived three years ago, he had laughed. They were so adorable; all were typical Lockleys with fair hair and bright blue eyes. Now they had just had twin siblings. They were four weeks old today. Charles Luke (Carlo) and Charlotte (Lottie) Elizabeth were perfect. Both fair-haired and blue-eyed, although Carlo looked like his eyes may already be a little darker than his sister's. Wills' son, Pip, had nicknamed him Carlo, and it had stuck. There were not many nicknames from Charles, and no one else in the family used this one.

Ellen was amazing. He hoped she was asleep, as well as all the children. He laughed softly to himself. God certainly had heard him. Deep down, Luke always knew he would; he had just doubted for a while, oh, how his life had changed.

As he stood watching the world pass by down busy Church Street, a carriage pulled up at his front door. He laughed. Once again, it was Wills arriving when he was needed. At thirty-two, Luke now had a wonderful, loving wife, five adorable children under three, and they had more money than he knew what to do with, so he was sharing it, at least he wanted to…

but how? This was causing him much concern. A loving, Godly family surrounded him. Work was good. The school had grown, and he enjoyed teaching. His heart was full. Yet, he was troubled.

Luke turned and walked outside to meet his brother. Connor took the carriage around the back to the stables. Wills always appeared at just the right time. He needed to sit with Wills and work out what to do with their money. As his brother lived at Emu Plains, he thought he'd have to make a trip out there. God, once again, had that sorted too. Luke opened the door quietly before Wills woke the children by knocking.

"Hi, Luke, can I doss here for the night? I'm knackered and I don't want to open *Roseneath* for just one night. Shauna is nearly due, and so they have enough on their plates. I had a meeting and didn't feel like driving home. We'll all be back for Christmas on Tuesday, though."

"Sure, Wills, everyone is asleep, though. The little ones had a night, last night. All five of them were awake. So everyone is having an afternoon nap. I need to talk to you, Wills." Luke opened the door wide. "Come in."

Rather than risk going upstairs then down again, Wills quietly left his bag at the bottom of the stairs and then went to the inside bathroom and washed his face. He would like a nap as well. He sighed; he could see Luke needed him. On his return, he went into Luke's office.

With hardly a pause, Luke said, "Wills, I was just standing at the window thinking. Seems to be a habit of mine, eh? Do you remember me starting a conversation like that before?"

Wills nodded, "A lot changed quickly back then."

"Well, um, I… it happened again today." Luke was falling over his words.

"What's wrong, Luke?" Last time, he was so depressed.

"Wrong? Ahh, err, um, well, not exactly wrong, but Wills, what the hell do I do with so much money? Those were just pebbles, little diamonds sitting in the dirt, and we collected them. It's not even why we went." Luke looked at his older brother anxiously.

Wills threw his head back and laughed, then clamped his hand over his mouth, forgetting that everyone was asleep. "Oh, Lukie, is that all? I thought something was wrong with you and Ellen. Oh, I'm so relieved."

"Not likely! She's blooming brilliant. No, I'm serious, Wills. How do I use it? You have done so much already, but I don't know what to do with it. I'm not going to sit on it. But like your gold, it won't replenish unless I do something useful with it. Wills, I originally thought of some transport company, but with the railways coming, that won't be needed. I was then thinking of a carrier company, delivering to and from the railways. That way, it could also work with all your businesses. Transporting oversize goods to and from the rail yards." Luke stood with his back to Wills while still looking out the window.

"Woah! Lukie, what do you need me for? You've got it all figured out." Wills said laughingly.

Luke spun around. "That's where you are wrong, Wills. You see, soon all goods will be transported by rail, including those for your business. I don't want to tread on your toes or your business either. Both could be affected by the railways. Yet how can I tie my idea in with yours so we can help each other..." he paused and then almost whispered, "... as well as helping others?"

"Ahh, now I get where you're coming from. It's fine to have the business plan, but it's the 'helping' bit that has you stuck." Wills smiled at his young brother.

Luke nodded like a keen schoolboy. "How is making money for myself helping others?" His blue eyes were piercing Wills' own, seeking answers.

"I think Hamish and Fergus might help you there," Wills stated.

Luke looked puzzled. He frowned.

Wills continued, "Have you never wondered why these two amazing Scotsmen have been brought into our lives? Now that they are both living here, they have found a way to help some disabled sailors. Hamish's leg started it. One of their cousins, Robbie, is helping Dar's friend, Daniel, Earl of Meldon, in West Sussex. When looking for staff, his father, Sam, decided to hire a group of disabled ex-army men; however, it was Uncle Ned's friend Perry White, who Dar was first assigned to, who started it. Remember his hearing of his burned face? Remember, he is the one who built this house."

Luke remembered the story of Perry, Uncle Ned's friend and how Dar and Mama had been assigned as soon as they arrived. He nodded.

Wills continued, "Well, Perry decided to help men like himself, scarred and wounded ones who couldn't get other jobs. Then, Governor Darling's mother-in-law, Ann Dumaresq, helped them get started in England. Perry and Sam trained them, then gave them references. As such, the trained staff are still in much demand all over England. Sam's son, Dan, has kept it going after his father died. He also takes in reformed 'street women' and trains them as maids. And primarily, they have taken in many, many peer orphans. They are the illegitimate children of the nobility that they hear about. They, too, are trained and placed in suitable positions, like Ricky English's homes, only on a much bigger scale. The boys in Landon Home made a leg for Hamish. Well, it was noticed, well, actually it was *not* noticed, and that did it. Hamish should have been limping, but no longer does. His new leg was so good that it worked like a leg, not a chunk of wood; that's now a business in itself. But Luke, what they have found is many sailors and soldiers who have lost an eye, hand, or a leg; they can no longer sail, but they can drive and work; if you hired them, that's a win-win for everyone, and then there is Jem's scarred warriors."

"Seriously? Do they want to work?" Luke looked stunned.

"Of course, they want to work. They have no desire to live on the Parish charity, but that's their only other option. Driving is a good job. You would have to employ some able-bodied men to do the lifting. Scarred ones like Fergus could do that. The driving, they could do, no worries. If you needed two drivers, you could have two different sorts, one missing a hand and one a leg. Together, they would make one fit worker. Giving them both purpose and friendship. I could certainly use a reliable courier service. Our wagons are, well and good, but we don't have enough to keep all the Emporiums stocked. Remember that even when the railway goes through, it can't leave the tracks. It will need transport to and from each station. Luke, even Ricky's boys from the Landon House, can also be trained and accompany the older drivers. Again, that's a win-win; Ricky is always looking for jobs for them."

Luke sat, looking at Wills. It's precisely what he wanted to do but didn't know where to start.

Wills sat and waited. He knew Luke. When the wheels started turning, they turned quickly.

"I'll talk to Hamish over Christmas, Wills. If I can make some good income, then the money can self-generate," Luke said while still deep in thought.

"Luke, I'm knackered. I'll leave you thinking, I need to sleep. Same room?" Wills asked.

"Huh? Oh yes, sorry, Wills, yes, it's always ready for you." Luke sat at his desk and started writing. He did not even hear Wills leave.

Hamish and Fergus, with their wives and children, were arriving the next day. They were staying for Christmas—plenty of time to discuss the future plans. A big, slow smile crept across Luke's face. The Evans family were joining them all this year as well. John and Colleen were staying with him. Phil and Stevie and their families were staying at Charlie's place, and Aunt Caro and Uncle Douglas were to stay with her brother. Thomas and Margaret Tindale had gone to them in Sydney for Christmas for decades, and they thought it was time to return the favour.

Luke had noticed a distinct interest from his nephew Neddie when news of their staying so close was mentioned. Luke had wondered which of the Evans girls had sparked his interest. He soon found out that it was Miriam, Stevie's eldest child. He wondered if Ed had realised yet.

After all these years, Tom Tindale would soon be one of the family.

Luke laughed softly when he thought over the conversation with Wills. Luke hadn't had time to mention to Wills that both Hamish and Fergus were actually coming to stay with him. Thankfully, he was on school holidays and so could give them all his full attention. He sat and racked his brain, trying to think what a hand amputee could do. Paperwork is something they could undoubtedly do; if they could read and write, yes, they could work. Each centre would need a record keeper and caretaker.

Oh, and a caretaker for a warehouse, a 'Carriers' Depot Co-ordinator', yes, there were plenty of jobs, and he could expand into more outlying centres. That's something else they could do.

He walked back to the window and continued to look outside at the world passing by. He didn't hear the door open. Ellen had come in and quietly walked to him. His back was to her as he stood deep in thought. He sensed her presence rather than heard her, turning and stretching out welcoming arms to her. She walked into them and lay her head on his chest, and lovingly slid her arms around his waist.

"Lukie, have I told you just how much I love you?" She pulled back in his arms and gazed adoringly into his handsome face. He bent down and kissed her face all over, then gently brushed his lips over hers.

She giggled and stopped his wandering lips with her own. She deepened it into a kiss that would eliminate all other thoughts from his mind.

With all his plans now formed, the following days were a breeze.

~

They greeted the two Scotsmen, their wives, and their three children. Eight children in the house for a few weeks would be fun. Luke put his arms out and took six-month-old Colin from Katy. He was a clone of his older cousin Ferdie.

Luke was able to talk to both Hamish and Fergus later that night. Both were so excited. They had both felt at a loose end and needed to do more with their time than just volunteer help. This idea would be perfect. It would also provide them with a regular income. Not that their funds weren't flush, but they could always do with a top-up.

Luke would do all the building and financial outlay and would own 100% of the physical structures, but Hamish and Fergus would help by organising the staff, running things and interviewing personnel.

Now they all had a way to help. Luke also insisted on a salary for them.

Fergus glanced at his brother's lack of a leg. "Luke, what you need is soldiers, lots of injured soldiers. Know where we can find any? And scarred ones too, like me, even one-eyed ones," Fergus said. "Emotionally maimed, too. Some will jump at a shadow and aren't good with crowds. Some wounds are not always visible. Luke, if we could assist those who are rejected." The smile on his face almost lit up the room.

A slow smile spread over Luke's face, too. He knew just who to ask. His next plan was a letter to Uncle Ned.

~

Luke's letter to Ned was written by the time the Macdonalds arrived. The Macdonald men would each have a ten per cent profit stake, but this would be negotiable once the business was up and running, and would grow with time, depending on their level of involvement. Their initial input was to source, train, and help the new staff. Some of the older lads at the Landon Home would also like to learn horsemanship skills. They could also be the runners for the disabled drivers.

Douglas would arrange for prosthetic limbs to be made by the boy's home for the disabled men. He and Hamish had varied the design for his leg and made various sorts depending on where the limbs had been amputated. Each group would be assisting the other. The boys making limbs at Landon House would gain more experience, and the drivers would gain some freedom, as Hamish had done.

Luke added 'get more cedar' to his 'to-do' list. This was the timber used for limb making. Now all he had to do was wait. That thought brought him up with a start, no, not wait, he had to get started and now. He had to build and plan.

Luke thought he only had until June or maybe a bit later to have everything ready and waiting. That included posters and advertising, even a few advance bookings. Accommodation would be required, even for building some married quarters.

The depots needed to be built with some basic housing attached. Once established, the staff could find their own places if they wished. Initially, they would need to share a room. Bunks were out of the question, as were steps. Hammocks were possible, but it would be better to have proper beds and a nice place to encourage them to stay and make their lives a little easier. Individual rooms were even better still.

Luke would start with timber buildings for depots. These could be erected quickly and flat-packed, then transported on carts and wagons, and then assembled on various sites. His mind was now running with the possibilities in front of him. He would buy the block of land next to Wills' warehouse and erect a roof on poles. Under the roof, a team of builders could construct the various panels required for the prefabricated buildings.

These timber depots would become locations where people could drop off their items for the next carrier. Permanent buildings would follow as the need required. He would specialise in bulky items that the post offices couldn't carry, such as crops, building products, bulk supplies and the like. Windsor, Camden, Parramatta, Emu Plains, and Castle Hill would be central depots. Sydney, Gosford, and Bathurst could be added if required.

Luke also thought that a new warehouse down near the docks would be needed. Loading bays at the depots would have ramps, allowing wheeled trolleys to be used and thereby reducing the need for lifting. A pulley system, like in Wills' Parramatta warehouse, would be required for heavy loads.

His mind now had much to occupy it. Luke thought he would enquire about initially leasing some space near Campbell's Store; so yes, Sydney too. Then he would need horses and stables. He would get Bertie involved in making the harnesses and all the tack required for heavy horse teams.

Luke's mind was still in a whirl when he finally slept.

Tomorrow was Christmas.

~

Over Christmas lunch at Eddie's house, Charles excitedly let everyone know that he had received a letter from a protégé, James Leslie.

They all knew about him as Jim regularly wrote to Charles from Melbourne.

Charles often read bits about the diggings and incidents Jim wrote about. They could hear the excitement in their father's voice.

"Listen to what Jim writes. Charlie, Ed, Wills and especially you , Luke; this will help you all. I knew he was to be part of our future. Luke, this will assist your new project, too." Charles's voice positively bubbled with excitement.

Cobb & Co stables
Melbourne
6 December 1861

Christina's Cottage
Philip Street
Parramatta

"Dear Lord Charles,
I do hope this letter finds you well. I thought I would write to tell you that the two American owners we met have sold the business, and Mr James Rutherford, another American, has purchased it as a whole. He is a much younger man, much the same age as me. He's keeping the name of the Company as it's now well known..."

Charles looked up, "Jim goes on with some of what he's doing in Melbourne. About the diggings and such, so I won't read that. You can, if you wish too, but listen to the last bit. This affects you all, so listen..."

"...Finally, Cobb and Co are coming to Bathurst next year. And, sir, Mr Rutherford has chosen me to drive the lead coach when we finally cross the mountains to Parramatta. To say I'm excited is an understatement. We are due to arrive about June.
Many years ago, I promised to let you know if I were to come your way, now we are. We will need accommodation and

stabling for many animals, initially a hundred or so horses and some forty staff, for a few weeks. Mr Rutherford will be starting in Bathurst and eventually heading towards the coast.

I was wondering if you could direct us to who could possibly help?

I look forward to hearing from you. Father sends his regards.

Your protégé

James Leslie

PS. I can never thank you enough for your assistance. I am forever in your debt.

Jim"

Charles looked up and smiled, "This will be a game changer for us all."

Luke frowned. Then realised. "Dar, he will need coaching houses and places to change horses. He can use my depots. I had better get cracking with my buildings. At least I know that I will need buildings every ten miles, as that's the distance between changes of coach teams. They will need to be close over more hilly terrain."

The family's eyes turned to him. This was the first time they had heard about his new project.

Luke met Hamish's eye, and they both grinned.

~

By the time the Macdonalds returned to Sydney a week later, their joint scheme was well underway. Luke still had no name for his new business, but he was sure God would provide that.

From London

Gracemere Castle,
Maidstone England
30 March 1862

Glenmere
Church Street
Parramatta
My Dear Luke,

    Greetings from over here.

    Congratulations on the birth of Charles and Charlotte! I think it's so funny that even across the miles, the birth of twins and naming is similar. Tina and Chip's twins were born only two weeks after yours on December 5. They named them Charles John Edward, called CJ, and Christina Susanna, called Christie.

    Sarah and Ant have just had their first child. Henry Anthony, but he was soon followed by Edward Charles. Yes, more twins. They were born on March 3 at 11.30 pm and on March 4 at 12.05 am. At least they have something different to every other set of twins in the family, different birthdates. Oh, please tell your father I eventually checked the Baptism book at church, our Grandfathers were indeed twins, born on August 15, 1740. One hundred and two years to the day from Eddie's oldest twins.

    Now to your request… Your family does set me some delightful challenges, don't you? This is one I am thrilled to assist with. I wondered what you would do with your share, as I knew you would not just sit on it. This is a fabulous idea.

    Luke, my only question is, how many can you use? The plight of wounded soldiers here is dismal. There is no work for them at all, and no pensions that they can live off. I like this idea so much that I may even start something here for those who do not wish to emigrate. You're inspiring me. With ease, I can find at least twenty leg amputees. Danny Garney (I should call him the Earl, but he is still Danny to me) and Jimmy Westaweller have many such men who need placements. Jem White, aka Duke of Cheatham, is absorbing the burns soldiers and sailors, and they rarely leave. I only need to determine if the injured people will relocate to Sydney. If not, I may hire them myself. I shall endeavour to select those who can drive a heavy wagon. Many are friends of Reg (you have not met him, but he's my Estate Manager and is an amputee as well). Some of them here also served with Hamish and Fergus. Most soldiers had basic training in driving heavy wagons, as this was needed for hauling cannons. As to literate hand amputees, I know a few.

    Luke, I shall also send some severely scarred soldiers who can't get work here. They have burns, cuts and horrific injuries like that. They have physically healthy bodies, but their souls are often crushed due to rejection. Others are so emotionally affected by the war that they can no longer assimilate into a community. Driving would be perfect employment for them.

If I understand you correctly, you have purchased or will be buying twenty wagons. Then I believe you need strong-bodied men to load and unload. These men will be brilliant and will give them purpose.

Luke, I believe 'Lockleys Logistics' will be a boon to the Colony. It's also a perfect fit to support your brothers. (I'm not sure if you have a name for your business, but this is what I'm calling it.) I also think it's incredible that both the Macdonalds can assist. God could not have sent two better men. I was wondering how they would fit into His plan.

Do you know the story of the Broome-Halls and Meldons? If not, your father knows the whole, and it's a story similar to his own, Convict to Earl. I had been asked to keep an eye on Sam Corbett as he was then. His natural father was not able to do much, but I knew he loved him. I wrote every time I heard anything about Sam, then I notified him that he was coming back. That was about 1830.

It took another twelve years before I returned. Sam was by then well-established as the Earl. We called on them as soon as Christina could travel after the birth of our first twins. My Mother and your Grandmother came with us a month later to meet them.

We have finally sorted out their story. Lady Broome-Hall's older daughter, Amelia Elizabeth, married Baron John Macdonald, and Fergus and Hamish were born. Amelia (or Elspeth as she was known in Scotland) was a half-sister to Anne White, Sam's wife. Anne became his Countess. Not many know the whole story.

I miss Sam; he became a good friend. As his father, Duke James, was too. Danny is much of an age to me, and we are friends. However, we do not see much of each other.

Anyway, back to Fergus and Hamish; God had them there before we even knew we needed them.

Luke, others will be thinking about similar ideas for transport; I suggest you obtain a letter from Governor-General Denison, almost like a Government Warrant or a Charter. I have a feeling many will jump on this idea. Better to be safe than sorry. Just a thought!

(Next day)

I have had Colin Fraser check the ships. I shall endeavour to send some men on 'Mary Bradford' departing in May, so they should be there by the end of July.

I pray that this venture will be as successful as the rest of the family's endeavours. The arrival of this letter should give you a month or so to arrange accommodation and employment for them all. Their passage is my gift to them, as a thank you to you, knowing that you can ask this of me. I am delighted to assist wherever possible.

Danny said he has some trained staff he can send when required. Many now wish to emigrate, particularly those wives with children. There are no jobs for them here.

To be able to give these men a new start is marvellous. I congratulate you, Luke. These men have no future at all but for this scheme.

We found that many are not willing to emigrate but are willing to work, so we will start a similar venture here. Do you mind if I call it the same name and tie it in with your company? Otherwise, I might tie this branch to the Earldom over here. So 'Lockleys Logistics' is going global before it even starts.

Remember this verse; it's appropriate that it comes from the book of Luke.

"Give, and it will be given to you. A good measure, pressed down, shaken together and running over, will be poured into your lap. For with the measure you use, it will be measured to you." *Luke 6 v 38*

We will continue to pray for you in this endeavour.
With love to all,
Uncle Ned
Gracemere

When Luke received Ned's letter, he chuckled. He had not thought of that name, but it was perfect. So, *Lockleys Logistics* was born. Luke wrote to the governor and obtained the warrant, as this meant that many of the government wagons needing replacement could be retired. Luke purchased many of them and had them refurbished. He had his fleet, the buildings were up, and the horses were being trained. All he needed now was staff.

Although this is the end of Luke's story, it is also the beginning of another.

"The Earl's Shadow" continues the family saga, with Charlie's story and how James Leslie fits in.

A Cobb and Co. Australian tale that transports you back to the days of tough men, tougher women, and bushrangers.

https://mybook.to/TheEarlsShadow

Emancipated convicts often had a very hard time in the colony
after their time had been served.
They may have had their 'Certificates of Freedom',
or 'Tickets of Leave' but little else, as jobs were not guaranteed.

Convict labour was free, and 'assigned convicts' needs were mostly
supplied by the Government from 'Stores', but only until the 1840s.
However, once freed, the ex-convicts had to fend for themselves, finding
work and accommodation. Life was hard.
Most had no possibility of returning to England and so had
to make do with what they could achieve in the Colony.
If some received 'Pardons', they were usually 'Conditional',
not allowing them to leave the shores.
An 'Absolute Pardon' was like gold or diamonds.

Many put their heart and soul into it and succeeded.
Those who were willing laboured hard and prospered.
Many assisted the community in which they lived.

My own family, the Ellisons, Hunters, and McLeans
from Parramatta and Emu Plains, were such people, although none were
of the upper class.
Four of them came as convicts, and within two generations, they were
wealthy landowners and farmers on
The Nepean River area and later the Northern Rivers of NSW.

Having been torn from their families, they turned their lives around and
'made good'. They put their blood, sweat and tears into making
Australia, known as 'The Lucky Country', home.

Historical notes
Author's Note & Real People

Jolly Sailor Inn, Henry Ellison, 1830s. Nth George St near Gasworks Bridge.

My own Great-Great-Grandfather, Thomas Ellison, inspired the original story in the series. He was the son of convict John Ellison and Sarah Watkins. Thomas was born at *The Jolly Sailor Inn* in George Street, Parramatta. John had helped 'put down a mutiny' on the *Albermarle* in 1791. He was given a 'Ticket of Leave' as a reward. He did indeed become the innkeeper of *The Jolly Sailor* and also ran the Government Stores Keeper in Parramatta. However, from there, the story becomes fiction. John Ellison's second biological son was Thomas. Thomas was educated at Cape's Academy in Sydney and attended the School with **Sir James Martin and Hon George Thornton**. Thomas's father, John, often took the boys to school in his boat, but according to oral family history and also James Martin, they sometimes stayed in town (probably during the week); however, the location is unknown. We have no more details. Sir James Martin mentions that they had to walk home occasionally. They may have occasionally walked home on weekends, as he claims. We do know that John Ellison or one of the other boat owners could have collected them, or they may have travelled on the ferry. The witnesses at John and Sara's wedding were John and Martha Bishop. They inspired Jack and Martha Turner, although I have never looked into the Bishop's story. Martha Bishop was actually a convict on the *Neptune* in 1789.

John and Thomas married sisters, Amelia and Betsy Huff (daughters of Joseph Huff, a convict who 'stole' a sheep, after it wandered into his yard). While John took over the inn, Thomas trained as a blacksmith in Parramatta from a very young age. Betsy's parents, Joseph and Mary <u>Amelia</u> Huff, ran one of the other inns in town. **Thomas and Betsy Ellison** later owned and ran the *Arms of Australia Inn* in Emu Plains as well as *Ellison's Pinch* at Linden. Both were Cobb & Co staging posts. They are not related to any peers in the UK.

Sir James Martin -(Martin Place), politician and Chief Justice. (inspired Tim).

Hon George Thornton – politician in the NSW Legislative Council (also Tim).

Reverend William Branwhite Clarke's find of gold at Hartley was indeed true; *however*, only a few specks were found in the creek in April 1844. He reported his findings to Gov Gipps and told him to stay silent.

Wills Lockley's find of an escarpment in Hartley is totally from my imagination. I have not even been to Hartley. The gold finds at Ophir were also genuine, but certainly not in the quantities that I have here. Miss Amelia Stather and Miss Fiona Moreton are fictitious nieces of Reverend William Clarke's wife, Maria Moreton. Maria did leave William for 15 years before returning.

<u>Andrew Lenehan</u> and his brother, **Michael,** were cabinetmakers and upholsterers in Sydney. Andrew's work was so good that he was employed to furnish the Government house in Sydney. The work was completed, then extra work was requested by the Governor-General and Lady Denison, which he also completed. However, since it was not included in the original order, he was not paid for this. Ultimately, this led to the failure of Andrew's business. Eventually, he was declared bankrupt and his properties were sold. Some of his furniture is still in Government House, Sydney, today. Michael married one of the Ellison girls, (there were ten Ellison children). Andrew declared bankrupt owing nearly £300 to his brother. He was a Tea merchant.

https://trove.nla.gov.au/newspaper/article/60520095?searchTerm=andrew%20lenehan%2C%20government%20house

James Hunter (he inspired Jim Leslie in the story) came out on the ***Red Jacket*** in 1856 aged just 20. When aged thirteen he drove a carriage from Durham to Newcastle, and later another one from Newcastle to Liverpool. He became a Cobb and Co coach driver within weeks of arriving in Melbourne in 1856 on the Red Jacket. A few years later, Rutherford bought Cobb & Co. and kept James (known as Geordie Jim) on as one of his top drivers. James was the first Cobb and Co coach driver to cross the Blue Mountains in 1862 (West to East). Newspapers report four holdups but family history only knew one, so he probably stopped telling them. He married Sara Ellison (daughter of Tom and Betsy Ellison) in 1865 (see photo) and moved to Ipswich, Qld, where their first child was born, Susanna Elizabeth Ellison Hunter. Their 3rd child, Eva, died aged two in Bathurst. James and Sara Hunter lived at T*he Arms of Australia Inn,* in Emu Plains, where my grandfather was later born (Norman A Hunter). Today, it is a Museum.

Red Jacket departed Liverpool in 1856 on May 20 and arrived in Melbourne on August 13. (83 days) Due to this being a novel, I have shortened the trip, with them arriving at the end of July, so they can make it back for the wedding.

The Mineral Survey

Reverend William Branwhite Clarke was accompanied by two assigned servants only. His wife had been absent for fifteen years before she finally returned to him. She never left again. He was eighty at his death, and she died some years after him.

I have not been able to find out his actual route of this journey (many of his notes were destroyed in a fire, but I'm sure he did not return to Sydney by boat trip. It is known that he was a school friend of Major Mitchell's and is reputed to have often used his maps. (Artistic licence.) I have also attributed to him the finding of diamonds. He did, but not in the quantity in this story His finds were some small lemon coloured ones in the town now known as Bingara, NSW(named Bingera until 1880).

The story of the enormous gems is just that, a story. (They were all lemon coloured and small. These can still be found up there.)

The value I had also inflated, but the publicly first recorded ones were some 15 to 20 years later. William Clarke was brought in to verify the finds. If he had not already found some, he would not have known what they were. There is a newspaper report on his sapphire finds.

sapphires https://trove.nla.gov.au/newspaper/article/2504984? searchTerm=sapphires%20for%20sale

diamonds https://trove.nla.gov.au/newspaper/article/166807237? searchTerm=REv%20WB%20Clarke%2C%20diamond

Bingara was originally named Bingara.
Inverell was called Green Swamp.
Toowoomba was called Drayton Swamp.

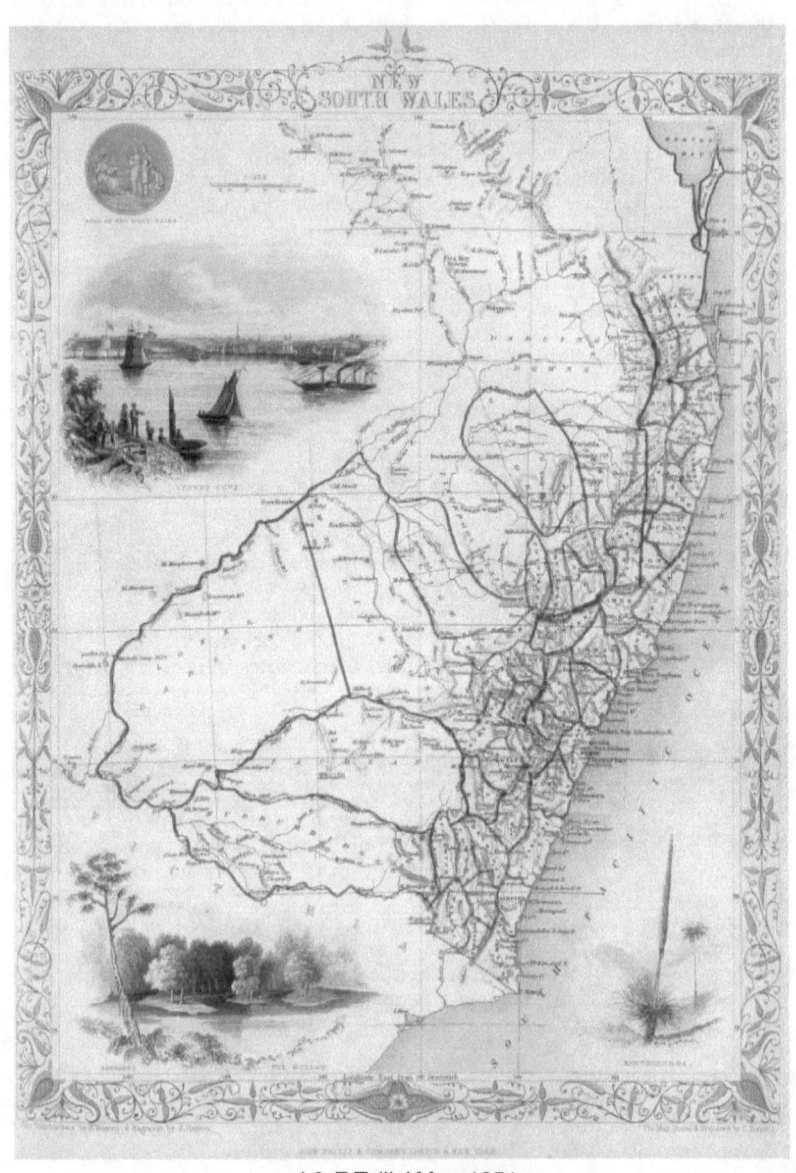

J & F Tallis' Map 1851

Characters

Lockley Family

Charles b 1800 *Dad John d 1805 & Mum, Elle d 1855 (Elle remarried Richard Childs)*
Sarah(**Sally**) Shannon **Lockley** (Dar and Mama) '*Jolly Sailor*' Sally's mother-Shannon
    McCarthy *parents Eamon (Edward) and Nioiclín(Nicola) O'Shane, Ireland*
#1Charles **(Charlie)** b 1820   m **Gracie** Miller m Nov 1842
    #1 Edward (**Teddie**), twin 26/9/44
    #2 **John** 26 Sept 44;
    #3 Emily(**Emma**) b 25 Aug 46
    #4 **Molly Grace** b 1850
#2Edward **(Eddie)** b 1821   m Jennifer (**Jenna**) Turner m Dec 4 1841
    #1 Edward (**Ned**) twin 15/8/42 m Jan 1864 **Miriam** Evans
    #2 Christina (**Tina**) Sarah Martha b 15 /8/1842
    #3 Jennifer (**Lily**) 13/4/45
    #4 Christopher (**Kit**) 26 Jan 1847
    #5 Nicholas (**Nick**) Calum 2/3/49
    #6 **Shannon** Mary 1/10/50
    #7 Victoria (**Toria**) b 1852
    #8 **Henry** b 1853
    #9 Philip (**Pip**) b 6th Dec 1856
    #10 Ruth (**Ruthie)** b 6th Dec 1856
#3Elizabeth (**Liza**) b 1823   m Nov 1841 **Bertie Ellis**;
    #1Albert George-called **Albie** 15/8/1842 Parramatta #2 b 1846 Edward
    #3 twin Feb 57 **Amelia** #4 Feb 57 **Charlotte** twin
#4Susanna (**Anna**) b 1824   m 1842 **Tim** Miller
    #1 William (**Billy**) b 6/9/43;   #2 b 1845 **Amelia** Grace
    #3 twin Feb 57 **Timothy** Edward #4 **Samuel** Aidan b Feb 57
#5William (**Wills**) Lockley 20/4 /1826   m 14/2/1845 **Cathy** Turner
#1 Luke (**Lukie**), b14 Jan 47
#2 **Philip** ; Sept 48,
#3 Catherine Matilda(**Tilda**) 3/Mar/50
#4 Aurelia (**Goldie**) 6 July 51
#5 Richard(**Rick**) Edward & 26 Oct 1855
#6 Elizabeth(**Bette**) Martha b 26 Oct 1855
#6 **Luke** b 3/1828 m 2/8/1856   m Aug 56 **Ellen Miller**, b 4/10/1830
    #1 26/4/1857 William (**Willy**), #2 **Mary May** #3 Sarah(**Sally**), triplets
    #4 20 Nov 60 Charles (**Carlo**) and #5 Charlotte (**Lottie**) - twins

John (**Jack**) **Turner** b 1800 Transported with Charles 1820
M **Martha** Turner (Pa and Maa) – *'Arms of Australia Inn' Emu Plains,*
#1 Marcus (called **Marc**), m Milly Ellis Dec 1843 baby Sept 4 1844 Charlotte Amelia
#2 Alexander (**Alex**) works for saddler Mr Ben Parker -daug **Mary** Parker),
#3 Jennifer Martha (**Jenna**) b1822 (met in 1840)
#4 Victoria (**Vicky**) b 1825 ,20 in July, Harry's girl
#5 Catherine (**Cathy**), b 1827 in June 24 Wills' girl
#6 Nicholas (**Nick**) b 1830
#7 Malcolm (**Calum**) b 1832

Caroline (**Caro**) **Evans** – Tom Tindale's sister
Captain **Douglas Evans**- supply ship captain Pitt Street
Phillip b 1819 Phil ; Law married to Alice 4 children (baby Mary Louise)
Stephen b 1821 Stevie; Law married to May 5 children -oldest – **Miriam** Evans
John b 1822 – John – loved bugs etc m 5/10/55 **Colleen** Murphy;
    #1 Jonathon Finn Douglas Evans (**Jonty**), b 2/8/56
    #2 **Maureen** Caroline Evans (**Reenie**) b 8 Aug 1858
    #3 William Luke John (**Billy**) b June 1860

Effy – convict maid – a convict b 1816 – m Hamish
Hamish Macdonald b 1815 m **Effy** 57
    #1Fergus (**Ferdie**) in Jan 1858
    #2 Elizabeth (**Elspeth)** b 59

bro **Fergus** Macdonald b 1813
m Mid Oct 1858 Catriona McKay (**Katy**)
    #1 b 59 **Colin** Hamish

William (**Bill**) **Miller** m
Molly Miller (Par and Ma) *'Rear Admiral Duncan Inn'* George St, Parramatta
    #1 **Timmy**   b 1822 (Lawyer)-   m **Anna**
    #2 **Gracie**   b 1824 (Anna's best friend) m **Charlie**
    #3 **Samuel**   b 1828 (Sammy) m 51 Isabella '**Belle**' Ellis 2 children in 56
    #4 **Ellen**   b 1830   m **Luke** Aug 1856

Finn & Maureen Murphy family 18 of them daug Colleen- b 1825
Eion, b 23 **Colleen** b25, Deidre b 26 (W&C), **Connor**(b 28 L&E), **Brodie**, b 30 (W& c
    Parra); Brennan, b 32 Shamus b 34, **Imogen** b 36(W&C), **Kerry** b 38 (L&E), Eamon b
    40 Fiona b 43 Siobhan(L&E)b45, Liam b 47 Aidan, b 50, Declan b 52, Mary b 54
    (*W&C = Wills & Cathy; L&E = Luke & Ellen*)
Major Edward (Ned) Grace b 1798 – Parramatta -His Grace the 10th Duke of Gracemere.
    Edward John Charles Lockley of Gracemere, at Maidstone 48th Battalion
Mother Susanna – dowager duchess- D Nov 1856 Father Charles
m Dec 25 1841 Mrs **Christina Meadows;** Lady Christina Catherine Meadows, née Hunt
b 1808 (daug of Edmund William & Catherine, Earl of Riverdell at Tunbridge Wells)
    #1 Charles (**Chip**)Edward John, Marquess Allingmere &
    #2 **Sarah** Christina, The Lady Sarah Lockley b 1 Sept 1842 m Ant
    #3 William Edmund (**Liam**) April 1854
    #4 Charlotte (**Charl**) Jennifer Victoria Jan 26/1/47
    #5 Isabella (**Izzy**) Catherine Grace 26/1/47

Duke of Gracemere
Brother 9th Duke **David** of Gracemere and wife **Elouise Wickham**
Paul Paul's twin died at 1 day old – **Charles** (same age as Charles Lockley, Earl)
Douglas
Sarah Joy – still born
Dr **Gerald Winslow-Smythe (Gerry)** b 1802 the Dr who helps Eddie (Emily dead wife)
    daug Charlotte. Winslow-Smythe's of Winslow Hall, Father Earl of Winslow, Older bro
    George 3 daughters; Gerry is 'The Hon Gerald Winslow-Smythe' (The Viscount Farlaw)
m March 1842 Hon. **Annabella Watkins-Harlow** b 1813 Papa is Viscount Ellison
    #1 Annabella Jennifer – **Bella** b Dec 42 m m **Teddy** Lockley
    #2 Edward Gerald Charles – **Neddie** July 46 m **Izzy** Gracemere
        #3 Matthew **Matty** Henry Dec 47
    #4 Susanna (**Sanna**) Elizabeth Sarah Joy b 49
Paddy and Cara Connor (Maryanne's parents)
    Maryanne   m **Robert** Ellis- 3 children Emporium Manager, Parramatta
    Moira 16 b 1828   m **Connor** Murphy -lives with Luke
    Shauna 14 b 1830 m **Brodie** Murphy lives at *Roseneath* for Wills
    2 little brothers working at the government Dairy,. **Shamus** and **Liam** Connor

From – DANCING TO HER OWN TUNE – prequel #1 to Lockley Series
by Sheila Hunter & Sara Powter
Sam and **Annie** Corbett aka Earl of Meldon Hall and son **Danny**
James, The Duke of Malvern (Sam's natural Father)
Lady **Mari** Broome-Hall; (Annie's natural mother) is Fergus and Hamish's Grandmother.
Cecil Broome-Hall LadyMari Husb, Annie's boss/lover, Tim's Uncle
Tim Broome-Hall – inherits title

From – **AMELIA'S TEARS** – prequel #2 to Lockley Series *by Sara Powter*
Robbie Styles (later Broome-Hall) Lady Mari's husband's nephew
Amelia Westaveller/Black (bro Jimmy) ViscountPittford
    -daug **Essie** (Ned's Goddaughter) m **Edmund** Garney- Danny 's son
Four friends – Ned, Gerry, Jimmy and Robbie from 1819 London
From - Once a Jolly Swagman
Paul, Douglas (Ned's bros) Jack Princhester and Jimmy Westaveller

From A LADY IN IRONS
Percy White - b 1750 cousin to Katy; inherited the 14th **Duke of Cheatham** (Perry's father)
    Cheatham Castle d 1835 (**Lady Mari**'s cousin from Dancing to her own tune)
m Margaret (**Meg**) Hamilton b 1753 d 1845
    #1 Peregrin (**Perry**) b 1772 d 1854 aged 82 (fire 1798)
    m **Katy** 1808 (Blackberry House in Aylesford (Between Jimmy and Mary)
    (as above) (15th Duke)

The Lockley Ducal Family Tree

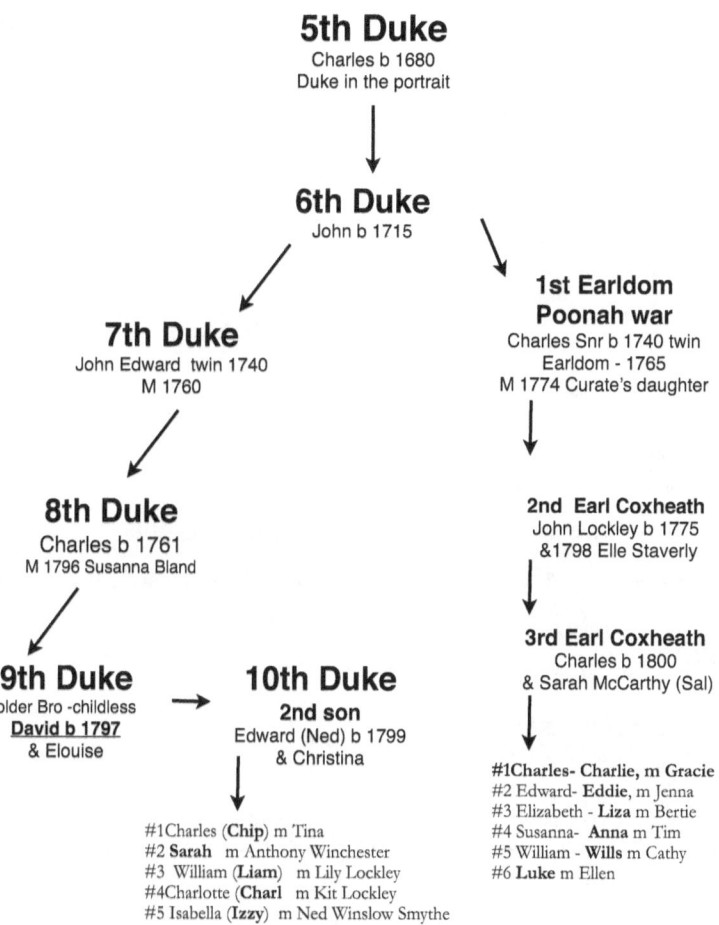

5th Duke
Charles b 1680
Duke in the portrait

6th Duke
John b 1715

**1st Earldom
Poonah war**
Charles Snr b 1740 twin
Earldom - 1765
M 1774 Curate's daughter

7th Duke
John Edward twin 1740
M 1760

8th Duke
Charles b 1761
M 1796 Susanna Bland

2nd Earl Coxheath
John Lockley b 1775
&1798 Elle Staverly

9th Duke
older Bro -childless
David b 1797
& Elouise

10th Duke
2nd son
Edward (Ned) b 1799
& Christina

3rd Earl Coxheath
Charles b 1800
& Sarah McCarthy (Sal)

#1Charles (**Chip**) m Tina
#2 **Sarah** m Anthony Winchester
#3 William (**Liam**) m Lily Lockley
#4Charlotte (**Charl** m Kit Lockley
#5 Isabella (**Izzy**) m Ned Winslow Smythe

#1Charles- **Charlie**, m Gracie
#2 Edward- **Eddie**, m Jenna
#3 Elizabeth - **Liza** m Bertie
#4 Susanna- **Anna** m Tim
#5 William - **Wills** m Cathy
#6 **Luke** m Ellen

Bibliography

Lenehan Furniture
http://www.polishbangalow.com.au/andrew-lenehan-brief-history

WB Clarke Travels
https://royalsoc.org.au/images/pdf/journal/138_Moyal.pdf

https://trove.nla.gov.au/newspaper/article/12933975?
    searchTerm=REv%20WB%20Clarke

https://trove.nla.gov.au/newspaper/article/65763682?
    searchTerm=REv%20WB%20Clarke

https://trove.nla.gov.au/newspaper/article/168844767?
    searchTerm=REv%20WB%20Clarke

diamonds https://trove.nla.gov.au/newspaper/article/166815709?
    searchTerm=REv%20WB%20Clarke%2C%20diamond

https://trove.nla.gov.au/newspaper/article/188988495?
    searchTerm=Reverend%20Clarke%2C%20diamonds

sapphires https://trove.nla.gov.au/newspaper/article/2504984?
    searchTerm=sapphires%20for%20sale

The King's School
https://en.wikipedia.org/wiki/The_King%27s_School,_Parramatta

Female Orphans school
https://www.discoverparramatta.com/history-heritage/female-orphan-school

John Tallis 1851 map
https://www.oldmapsonline.org/map/rumsey/0466.052

House sale – Parramatta Cnr Church St and Phillip St – August 1856
https://trove.nla.gov.au/newspaper/article/12985748?
    searchTerm=house%20for%20sale%20Parramatta%2C%20corner%20of%20philip%
    20and%20church%20streets

Populations stats
https://trove.nla.gov.au/newspaper/article/12997429

Parramatta ferry timetable
https://trove.nla.gov.au/newspaper/article/12985238?searchTerm=parramatta%20ferry

London Presentations
http://www.katetattersall.com/coming-out-during-the-early-victorian-era-debutantes/
https://people.howstuffworks.com/10-ridiculous-victorian-etiquette-rules.htm#pt7

If you loved this book, you may also enjoy these similar titles.
(*All are stand-alone stories*)

First Fleet Convict Era Trilogy 1788-1800

Gentle Annie Soames
Her dreams lead to unexpected outcomes. An Australian First Fleet story.

A First Fleet story with the descriptions taken directly from the Journal of Doctor Arthur Bowes Smith was the doctor on board the Lady Penrhyn.

Annie Soames is a girl beloved by the community but not afraid to voice her desires. That leads to trouble, illicit love, and a world turned upside down.

Oliver Quilpie, the newly married Marquess, finds his arranged marriage unsatisfactory; he is irresistibly drawn to his wife's companion. Unfortunately, he can't keep his hands off her. In retaliation, Annie copies his every move while riding, dressed as a highwayman. However, she has now fallen in love with him. This ultimately leads to her arrest and banishment to a distant land.

After some years, Oliver's wife dies, and his thoughts turn to Annie. He seeks to find her, but she has vanished. He is horrified to discover she was transported to New South Wales as a convict on the *Lady Penrhyn.* Will Annie want to see him?

ISBN 9780645441574   ISBN ebook 9781923097063   LP ISBN 978-1923097346
Long-listed in the Historical Fiction Company Competition 2024

The Emancipated Potter
Sydney Cove 1788 to Parramatta 1795
Not all felons are convicts, and not all convicts are felons.

Colin Osborne's serene life as a talented potter is crushed by a self-important peer. A single punch sends Colin across to the other side of the globe.

Aggie Gibbs is a young convict girl being hunted by a wayward soldier. The two find themselves in a town of criminals and lecherous men.

Captain John Hunter is Colin's mentor, and he paves the way for a new life for his young friends. Then disaster strikes, and he must leave.

Can Colin keep Aggie safe? Will they fulfil Captain Hunter's wishes to build a decent life for the convicts destined to live out their lives in the penal town? Will John ever return to New South Wales? Paperback ISBN 9781923097476   ISBN ebook 9781923097483

Paternity Unknown
Sydney 1788 - 1800 The Aftermath of the First Fleet landing.
Can forgiveness be that easy?

Connie Waterson is traumatised after she became one of the victims of the attack when the convict women were landed on February 6th, 1788. She finds herself expecting an unwanted child. Along with her friends, she must learn to cope with the challenges of their new environment while protecting the life growing within her.

Nigel Bray is a young convict who almost instantly regrets his carnal actions on the day the prisoners from the *Lady Penrhyn* landed. Knowing that Connie is the unwilling recipient of his base desires, Nigel does what he can to ease her path. He is racked with questions: is the child his? Will she ever forgive him? What must Nigel do to win Connie's trust?

ISBN 9781923097438   ISBN ebook 9781923097445   LP ISBN 978-1923097452

The Hunter to Macquarie Collection 1795-1822

When Upon Life's Billows
Sydney 1795-1821 - Governor John Hunter
Keep your friends close, and your enemies closer.

John Hunter loved his life at sea. The wind blows where no man knows, and John is caught in a storm. His ship, the *HMS Sirius,* was wrecked in 1790. Five years later, he became the second governor of the rough and filthy penal settlement of New South Wales. From a place he once loved, he now seems to be in the wrong place at the wrong time, trusting the wrong people.

Helena Rosedale is not your typical female convict. She fiercely battles to prevent the men from abusing her, earning her the nickname *"Helena the Hellcat."*

Crispin Milroy, alone in the world, serves on the new governor's security detail. Can he win the fair lady's heart? Life in 1795 in Sydney Cove was harsh at best. Food is scarce, and disease often ravages the settlement. Life throws everything at these three, yet somehow, they manage to survive. Why does John trust this young couple when others betray him? What trials must Helena and Crispin endure to make their new lives in this unforgiving town bearable? How can John ease their path?

ISBN: 9780645783339   ebook ISBN: 9780645783346

The Saddler's Song
London 1790s to Parramatta 1840s
The Strains of Starting Again.

George Ellis is the son of a tanner, living on the outskirts of London. Alone and hurting after a disease takes his family, he seeks a new life, setting up a business in New South Wales. His beloved violin is his most treasured possession, and his talent for making music is hidden from all but a select few.

Ben Parker, a saddler, is also heading to the colony. Combining their skills to start afresh in a new world, the young men find accommodation with a family. Two of the daughters steal their hearts — but how will the business survive in a stock-starved land where access to leather is limited? What is the saddler's song, and why is it so special?

ISBN: 9780645783353   eISBN: 9780645783360

Tuppence to Pass
London 1800s to Parramatta 1820s
An Unlikely Partnership

Josh Callan is a London lad making the best of the life dealt to him. Stealing from the man who killed his father, Josh gets arrested. The judge belittles him, saying he is not worth tuppence. Transported to the penal colony of Sydney, Josh arrives at the commencement of **Governor Lachlan Macquarie's** term.

Life in the Colonial town opens opportunities Josh could never have dreamed about and soon proves his worth to the Governor, becoming his confidante.

Can Josh find his niche? Where will this strange friendship take Josh and his family?

ISBN : 9781923097070   eISBN: 9781923097087

His Majesty's Pageboy
London to Emu Plains, Australia, in the 1800s

Jack Turner was born into a life of pomp and privilege that was not rightfully his. He was brought to the royal court for his protection. By the age of ten, he served as King George III's pageboy and was known as Lord John. For years, he struggled against society's immorality and people's shallowness; then, he met an unspoiled young girl whose purity stood out amidst the mire of humanity. He is unable to pursue her before his life hits a wall.

Martha Alexander is the daughter of a wealthy shipping merchant. She has been presented to London's second tier of society, where she meets the young man of her dreams. She is expected to marry well, and Lord John sets her heart fluttering. However, her father's drinking shatters her future. He was made to sign all his possessions away while drunk, unknowingly including his daughter. Refusing a forced marriage changes her life. How did these two young people end up as convicts in Australia?

Paperback ISBN 9781923097308   eISBN 978192309792

Coming 2026

A Fist Full of Holey Dollars
Sydney Cove 1810+

Captain **Rudi Greenwood** is a solitary man trapped in a job without a purpose in a land where alcohol is the currency and rules are frequently ignored in the pursuit of wealth.

Bethany Edwards is a grieving widow expecting her late husband's child. Rudi's attraction to the lovely widow compels him to reassess his views and contemplate someone new. She seeks Rudi's help and support, but is that all she truly feels?

When **Governor Lachlan Macquarie** asks Rudi for help improving the roads, a casual remark alters Rudi's life and affects the entire colony. To tackle the alcohol issue, he proposes creating a new currency. With Bethany by his side, will he rise to the governor's challenges? What actions led to him being despised by the exclusives and free settlers in the colony?

Paperback ISBN 9781923097407   eISBN 9781923097414

Coming 2026

Far From the Whispering Sheoaks
Set in Australia in 1817+

Fanny Little was in the wrong place doing something she thought was legal. Her actions led to her arrest, trial, and banishment. She was assigned from the female prison to ex-soldier Gordon McKenzie and soon found herself in the despicable and humiliating situation of being sold in the public marketplace.

Phil Bentley is a man running from his jealous uncle. He is seeking safety on a secluded farm a world away. With the community backing them, can Phil save Fanny from Gordon's vile abuse? Why is their relationship destined to spark controversy? And who is Jas? Why does Gordon wish to harm the child? Will they ever escape the shadows pursuing them?

Paperback ISBN 9781923097315   eISBN9781923097322

Coming 2026

Bound Down in Iron Chains

An Australian Historical Tale, set in the Boys' Orphanage in Sydney in 1818+

Smuggling, Rum and Ructions

Howard Marlow is a studious and honest London bookkeeper. When asked to help a friend's brother with his bookkeeping, he unknowingly helps a crime gang. He is arrested, convicted, and transported. On arrival, Howard is assigned to the boy's orphanage, where a possibly crooked soldier is in charge. He is asked to use his skills to decipher bookkeeping entries that make no sense. He discovers his love for the affection-starved boys at the orphanage.

Naomi Buckingham, a convict girl, is thrust into the harsh reality of the orphanage alongside Howard. She is assigned to the orphanage, but it is far from the refuge she had hoped for. The supervisor is a man who does not respect women. With no one to rely on but the new accountant, she grapples with the question of trust.

Naomi is the key to breaking the bookkeeping code and cracking the case wide open. Can Howard use his brains to save them both? How do they become involved with some of the worst criminals in the New South Wales penal colony?

Paperback ISBN 9781923097353 eISBN9781923097360

Coming 2026

Unlikely Convict Ladies Trilogy 1792-1840s

Dancing to Her Own Tune

Co-authored by Sheila Hunter and Sara Powter

Sydney 1790s to England 1830s

Annie White is released after serving seven years as a convict in Sydney. She has a visitor who helps her start a baking business. Annie is then asked to assist another ailing man, **Sam Corbett**. She nurses him back to health, and a relationship blossoms between them. They settle into a life together, barely making ends meet, when she realises she's expecting a child. Sam's past is laid bare, and he must come to terms with the revelations. They both must confront their accusers and discover that the answers to their questions are not what they anticipated. Their life experiences seem to cling to them, and unable to shake them off, they end up back in England. They must face their ghosts and recognise they are not who they think they are. How can they transform their anger and spite into love and forgiveness? The Dance of Life goes on.

ISBN 9780645110715 ISBN9780645110722

Long-listed for the Historical Fiction Company Competition 2022

Amelia's Tears

Parramatta 1828 – England 1840s

From Tears of Sadness to Tears of Joy.

Amelia Westaweller awaits her assignment in the Parramatta Female Prison. Forced to leave the relative safety of gaol, she is assigned and now faces her worst nightmare. A foul man claims her and makes her life a living hell. Then, her world goes black. A glimmer of hope arises when she hears from her brother, Jim, who has enlisted a friend to help her. She writes to Jim, pouring out her heart and telling him of the horrors of her new life. He encourages her to stay firm in her faith. All she can do is pray. When Major **Ned** Grace, her brother's friend, enters her life in Parramatta, he starts to ease her path. Things have changed, as now she has a child in tow. How can Amelia forge a new life for herself? What man could want her with her background and a child at her side? Who is the gentleman who turns her tears of sadness into tears of great joy?

ISBN: 9780645110739 eISBN: 9780645110746 Hard Cover ISBN 9798420617953

A Lady in Irons

England 1800s - Parramatta 1808+

Katy Harrington is mourning the death of her husband after he died in a shooting accident. Barely coping, she awaits the birth of their child. If it's a girl, she must hand the family home to her husband's brother. The day after giving birth to a daughter, she and her daughter are left on the side of a road. She collapses and is found by someone she thought had died in a fire ten years before. **Perry White**, badly scarred himself, nurses her back to health. They marry and move in with her widowed friend, Mary.

After some years, she discovers her husband and friend in each other's arms. Now living in a love triangle, she flees. Grasping the only straw available, she intentionally gets arrested and is sent to a colony far away. By doing this, her marriage can be annulled.

What happens in the Colony is different from what she expects. Governor Macquarie comes to her rescue, but what of Perry and her children?

ISBN: 9780645110784 eISBN:9780645441505

NO MORE, MY *Love*
Hunter Valley, NSW, 1820s

Jess Elkin is distraught when tragedy ravages her family. Now widowed, she becomes the victim of a carriage accident and is nursed back to health by the driver.

Marcus Ryan, a hard-headed woollen mill owner, was not expecting to fall in love. Yet, when Jess's fortunes suddenly turn for the worse, Marcus must decide how far he will go to pursue her. Years after following her to Newcastle, Australia, Marcus vanishes. Jess is left wondering if he will keep his promise to return to her… Will she ever see him again?

ISBN: 9780645441536   eISBN 9780645441581

Long-listed in the Historical Fiction Company Competition 2023

The Vine Weaver
Hawkesbury River area 1820s+
New Beginnings and Old Threats

In the 1820s, **Joel and Hetty Walker** lived on a secluded farm on the Hawkesbury River, which became a haven for the protection of young convict women. A series of events brings **Fran Rea** to Hetty's attention, and she is taken to the farm. Fran and Hetty develop a cottage industry under the compassionate eye of farmhand **Hector Macdougal;** Hector's loving words change lives. It is to him that Fran turns when threatened.

The vines now must draw them close to survive the future revelations, and of those, there are many.

ISBN: 9780645441512   eISBN: 9780645441529

Long-listed in the Historical Fiction Company Competition 2023

https://amazon.com/dp/0645441511   https://amazon.com/dp/B0C6Z552Y2

The story continues in "Scotch at The Rocks"…

Scotch at The Rocks
Glasgow, Scotland, early 1800s to The Rocks, Sydney 1830s

Orphaned children Brodie Stewart and Heather Anderson live on Glasgow's streets. Although hungry, they somehow manage to survive and stay out of trouble. Heather finds a job and looks to be settled; things go pear-shaped for them both. Eventually, they marry by declaration, but even that gets complicated, and they are both arrested soon after exchanging their vows. In 1838, they were transported to Sydney as convicts. Heather arrives within weeks of Brodie, and they are assigned close to each other. They are now living in the docklands of Sydney, known as The Rocks. They now have to forge a new life halfway across the world from their homeland.

Adventures abound, and Brodie gets press-ganged. While he's away, Heather's life changes and soon, she's officially selling Scotch Whisky at a shop in The Rocks.

You can take a Scot out of Scotland, but where did the Scotch come from?

ISBN 9780645441550 ebook 9781923097001 Large Print 9781923097254

https://mybook.to/ScotchatTheRocks

Waiting at the Sliprails
The Bathurst Road 1830s
A Convict's Tale

Bea Dawes's term of conviction nears an end, and she has few options other than marriage to a stranger or going on the street.

Jack Barnes, the hired drover, wants a wife. Bea accepts his offer; then, she discovers that he could be gone for months, leaving her alone with **Billy and Netty**, part of the tribe of an Aboriginal tribe who live on his secluded farm. Bea learns to love her husband and also this wonderful Aboriginal couple. Drought ravages the farm, and Jack must hit the long paddock with the flock. In his absence, a visitor arrives, threatening to destroy everything she has worked so hard for. Can Bea touch her heart? Can she cope? Will the drought ever end? And when will Jack return?

ISBN: 9780645441543   eISBN: 9781923097032

https://mybook.to/WaitingattheSliprails
August 2023

PenCraft Award Winner for Literary Excellence
Christian Historical Fiction 2024

Convict Shadows of the Past
Two Jennifers, two hundred years apart

When she discovers her convict family history, eight-year-old Jenny Kellow learns that she was named after a convict from nearly two hundred years ago. Inspired by her grandfather's stories, she delves into her ancestors' convict past. From him, she hears tales of bushrangers, convicts, and life in the early colony of Parramatta. She embarks on a journey to retrace the footsteps of her convict great-great-great-grandmother to honour her. Jenny's quest begins with microfiche in the 1960s, where she discovers a small tin mining town in Cornwall and the production of a cheese that set London alight. She uncovers that her ancestor, **Jennifer Kellow,** brought her cheese-making skills to Parramatta, where she taught others the craft. Echoes of the past can still be heard if you know where to listen. Who was the first Jennifer, and what does she have to do with cheese? Why is she so elusive? Did Jenny's ancestor, Jennifer, ever see those two small crosses carved into the bricks of the Female Factory? Would Jenny ever uncover her ancestor's story?

ISBN: 9780645783315   ISBN ebook 9780645783322
A NaNoWriMo 2022 book winner

In Defence of Her Honour
London 1800s to Parramatta 1819
Will the real man of quality please stand up?

Bill Miller was raised and educated with the sons of the family. The youngest, Bert Edison-Browne, had been his best friend. However, jealousy intervenes when Bill's excellent schoolwork begins to curtail their friendship. He wins a scholarship and enters Oxford University. When Bill's father dies unexpectedly, Bert insists that Bill take over as butler, but it's more to oppress him. Bert's jealousy grows and festers. He is now looking for a way to rid themselves of their new butler. A ruckus ensues, and Bill is arrested for assaulting Bert.

Molly Ross, the housekeeper's daughter, will vouch for him. It's too late; Bill has been arrested and is soon to be sentenced and transported. With Bill gone, Molly now fights to defend herself from Bert. After hitting him with a pan, she, too, is arrested and sent to Sydney. Bill and Molly arrive with letters of introduction and compensation from Bert's father. Soon, they will be running the best inn in Parramatta with an endorsement from the governor.

ISBN 9780645441567   ISBN ebook 9781923097049
Long-listed in the Historical Fiction Company Competition 2024

J Can't Stop Tomorrow
Irish Famine 1840s to Avoca Beach, Australia

Escaping bigotry and prejudice in Ireland, the O'Shane family lives on a secluded farm on the west coast of Ireland. The potato blight soon decimated their farm. It's always darkest before dawn, and the two remaining girls cling to the hope of a new life. With the kindness of strangers, the eldest girls, **Clare** and **Kerry O'Shane**, head to their cousin, Sal Lockley, in Parramatta, Australia. A new, wonderful life awaits them both. **Shéamus Connor** is the annoying teenage boy who reluctantly draws Clare's affection. However, living in a convict town means ruffians abound.

John Moore is a bad-tempered and troubled Irishman who is content to live alone on another secluded farm until he discovers Clare and two other lads need rescuing.

Can John protect her from the pain inflicted by an evil world?

Can Shéamus find his lost love, who has fled?

ISBN: 9780645441598   ISBN ebook 9781923097056

Madeline's Boy
England 1830s to New South Wales 1840
The race to protect an Orphaned Boy
All is not straightforward when money and titles are involved.

Orphaned, afraid and on the run, Chip must flee.

Madeline was his mother's best friend. Maddie now needs to keep her charge safe and alive. She must give up her life to protect the boy she has loved since birth.

Months after Chip's parents' demise, Maddie sets out to deliver Chip to his Uncle Humphrey, who lives in Sydney. Through him, she meets Chip's uncle's friend, Tim, who falls for Maddie —but will they find happiness?

The menacing presence soon finds Chip, and Maddie needs to hide him again. They are relocated from hidden farms to secret valleys, ultimately ending up in an Aboriginal encampment.

Can Tim find a way to be with Maddie? And if so… Will Chip ever be safe?

ISBN: 9780645783308   ISBN ebook 9781923097094
Long-listed in the Historical Fiction Company Competition 2024

Jam or Marmalade for Tea
England 1820s to New South Wales 1825 (Governor Brisbane Era)

Martha Hamilton is the eldest of four orphans struggling to survive on their own. She is caught stealing, tried, convicted, and transported to New South Wales. With her family gone, she becomes despondent. Life holds no meaning for her, and the ocean waves look inviting.
Captain Guy Manning is a frustrated and injured redcoat soldier returning to Sydney for a new assignment. He notices Martha trying to jump overboard and rescues her. How do two cats bring them together?
A convict ship is no place for romance, and she's far too young anyway, isn't she?
Can Guy save her and forge a life together for them? What connections does he have to try to save her siblings? Why is marmalade important for their future?
Paperback ISBN 9781923097933   eISBN9781923097285
A NaNoWriMo 2023 book winner
https://mybook.to/JamorMarmaladeforTea

A prequel to 'The Lockleys Parramatta' series
(Free novella with newsletter signup)

Unshackled Lives
Set in England & Australia in the 1800s
Australian historical fiction of early colonial days

Ned Lockley is the second of four sons of the Duke and Duchess of Gracemere. As his mother's favourite, his childhood years were blissful, but he needed to grow up, and quickly.
A whirlwind romance is followed by a loved one's betrayal. The following emotional turmoil is particularly challenging for Ned to cope with, especially amid a collapsing and immoral society.
Ned can't stay as his family is falling apart. His mother's words to remain true to himself and his faith make him leave everything he knows. How did Ned end up in New South Wales in charge of placing female convicts? Will he ever find happiness or discover who Charles is?
ISBN 9781923097377   eISBN 9781923097384   LP ISBN: 9781923097391

A 100-year, six-part Australian Colonial series
The Lockleys of Parramatta 1800-1900

Hands upon the Anvil
A blacksmith's life and love are more than work
Parramatta 1830s

Eddie Lockley's parents were transported for their crimes. Can a steadfast lad rise above his origins and guide others to succeed in a land of opportunity?
Ten-year-old Eddie longs to help his mum and dad. Living in a convict town with his family, the keen youngster has been working with the local blacksmith since his sixth birthday. But when a lieutenant doesn't stop abusing his older brother, the young boy yearns for the day when he can stand up and end the torment. Though he's thrilled when his mentor offers to send him off to learn his letters, Eddie fears he won't be around to watch his siblings' backs. But as he takes on the biggest adventure of his life, the brave believer soon discovers that God is looking out for everyone he loves. Does this young man in the making have what it takes to change everything for the better?
ISBN 9780994578235   Ebook ISBN 978-0-9945782-5-9   Hardcover 9798496177368
https://mybook.to/HandsUponTheAnvil

Out Where The Brolgas Dance
Gold is found, and so is love
Parramatta 1840s
How can a question change so many people?

It's the 1840s, and discoveries across the Blue Mountains continue. Major Mitchell's new road is complete, and towns are planned and being built. Abundant land is available for those who want it. Eighteen-year-old **William "Wills" Lockley** has laid a solid foundation for a respectable career as a blacksmith, but the Lockley lust for adventure flows deeply within his veins. He dreads the monotony of work at the blacksmith's forge and yearns for adventure in a new frontier. Wills meets six Englishmen *(Coping with what is now known as PTSD)* who have the means to make his dreams come true. What they discover changes the Colony and their lives forever. Gold fever ensues. While in the West, Wills must deal with an uncertain romance. Does Cathy even want him?
ISBN 9780994578242 Ebook ISBN 978-0-9945782-6-6 Hardcover ISBN 9798755445504
LP ISBN 9781923097155

Diamonds in the Dirt

Diamonds, love and money… but there is much more to life.

Parramatta 1850s

The youngest Lockley son, **Luke Lockley**, has completed his university education, and his life lacks direction. No job, no money, and no love. Desperately alone, he prays for guidance. How can Luke trust that God has a plan for him if he can't even find a job? He does the only thing he can … he prays. Within a week, life has changed … oh, how it has changed as his brother Wills turns up with a suggestion. Would Luke be interested in joining the expedition with John Evans? **Reverend William Clarke** needs assistance with a government mineral survey. The challenges, adventures and finds are life-changing for many. However, it gives Luke meaning, purpose and direction. The condition of his heart problems also takes a turn. Can he walk away? Will she wait for him?

ISBN: 9780994578273 Ebook ISBN: 978-0-9945782-8-0

Hard cover ISBN 979-8788011141

https://mybook.to/DiamondsintheDirt

The Earl's Shadow

Who or what is the 'shadow'? How does it affect so many?

Parramatta 1860s

Charles Lockley is the Earl of Coxheath. He spent his youth as a convict in Parramatta and had no idea he was an Earl. He had minimal education and few social skills; his eldest son, **Charlie**, is no different.

Now faced with mortality, Charles has to work out how to live the remainder of his life after a near-death experience. He is called to step way out of his comfort zone in London. His action will change the world for many. The echoes from the past still haunt Charlie. London is calling the family, and they can't postpone the trip. How does the Cobb and Co. coach driver **Jim Leslie** fit in? And precisely what is *'The Earl's Shadow'* that he speaks about? What happens if the 'Shadow' is gone?

ISBN: 9780645110708 Ebook ISBN 978-0-9945782-9-7

Released June 2022

https://mybook.to/TheEarlsShadow

Once a Jolly Swagman

An old black Billy Can contains the secrets of an incredible life

An Australian Historical Novel Inspired by the songs of The Seekers

Set in 1870s Parramatta and Kent, UK

Rick Lockley, struggling to escape his family's expectations, runs away to find himself. **Jack**, a jolly swagman, takes him under his care. Even after years together, Rick knows little about the old man.

On his death, Jack leaves Rick his precious billy can; the contents reveal Jack's identity. Stunned, Rick must travel to England to finalise Jack's wishes. There, he uncovers Jack's life of love, betrayal and a link to his own family. Rick also discovers there is much more to learn about this enigmatic man.

ISBN 9780645110753   Ebook ISBN 978-0-6451107-6-0

Released Sept 2022

https://mybook.to/OnceaJollySwagman

Jonty's Journey

Gems, Love, Artists and a Golden Lion

Australia and South Africa 1880-1902

Sydney Jeweller Jonty Evans's passion for gems takes him to Africa at a volatile time. There, he finds the diamonds he wants and is given a lion cub. However, Jonty is all but kidnapped. His experiences in the Transvaal plunge him into questioning everything he knows about life. Soon, nightmares haunt him. (This is now known as PTSD.)

Upon returning home, he nearly ruins his chance with **Lottie** before it even begins, and he finds adjusting hard. Lottie's father, **Luke** Lockley from Parramatta, takes him under his wing and directs him to someone who can assist.

Jonty is then called back to Africa as a liaison and reunites with his lion, Chimbu, after saving the life of his security detail. His life journey introduces him to remarkable artists, politicians, poets, rebels, and the scapegoat soldier Harry Breaker Morant. Can Jonty lay the past to rest and find his lost peace?

ISBN 9780645110777   HC ISBN 9781923097124   Ebook ISBN: 978-0-6451107-9-1

Released Feb 2023

https://mybook.to/JontysJourney

Sheila Hunter's Australian Colonial Trilogy 1840s

Co-Winner of 1999 NSW Senior Citizen of the Year, In the Year of the Senior Citizen

Mattie

The Story of an Australian Convict Child
An Australian Historical Story inspired by real Life.

An orphaned child, Mattie, is convicted of petty theft, sentenced to seven years, and sent to Australia. She meets another convict woman who, at her death, gives Mattie a chance for a new life. She makes the most of everything that comes her way, earning her freedom, falling in love, marrying, and becoming a mother. But life is not kind to her.

She meets bushrangers, moves to the gold fields in Bathurst, and starts a store. Yet, she is the kind of woman who made Australia what it is today. Can she survive alone in a man's world? She is a remarkable woman who breaks down all her barriers.

(Mattie's story continues in The Lockleys of Parramatta - bk 4 & 6)
ISBN 9781503252370 & ebook AISN BOOTTEDBTO
(The story continues in The Earl's Shadow & Once a Jolly Swagman)
Released 2015
https://mybook.to/Mattie_sh

Ricky

A boy in Colonial Australia

Ricky English and his mother immigrated from England to join his father in the new Colony of Sydney. Upon arrival, there was no sign of his father. Ricky's mum uses the tiny amount of money they brought to get lodgings in a run-down building. Things go from bad to worse when his mother dies; he is thrown out of the hired rooms, and the caretakers confiscate all their possessions.

Ricky lives on the streets of Sydney Town as a street waif. Ricky finds safe places to sleep and befriends freed convicts who can help him survive. One day, he encounters a lost child and helps reunite her with her family. These people try to help him, but he insists on doing things his way because of his stubbornness. However, he has found a mentor and confidante. The story follows him through his life. He survives and turns his life around, helping others along the way. *(Will's story continues in Jonty's Journey)*

Paperback ISBN 9780994578211   Kindle ASIN: B00MLYN6IG
Released 2014
https://mybook.to/Ricky_sh

The Heather to The Hawkesbury

Four Scottish families brave a new life in a strange land.

Mary Macdonald and husband **Murd** and family; her brother **Fergus** MacKenzie; sister-in-law **Caro** MacLeod; cousin **Alex** Fraser and all their families who have had to emigrate from the Isle of Skye during the "Clearances."

The story follows the four families from Scotland as they sail to the NSW colony in the 1850s. Mary does not cope with the changes and losses that occur in the first months in the colony. The other women in the family rely on her, and she nearly crumbles. The families struggle together through accidents, losses, trials, floods, and hard work, forging a strong bond with their new country. Trials, tribulations and triumphs see the four families make a firm mark in their new homeland. The immigrants from Scotland helped make Australia what it is today.

ISBN 978994578228   ebook AISN B01A21JYWQ   Large Print ISBN1533473641
Available on Amazon/Kindle & Large Print
Released 2016
https://mybook.to/TheHeathertTHawkesbury

Sara's Author Bio

Sara Powter

PACIFIC WANDERLAND PUBLICATIONS

Sheila Hunter and Sara Powter were a passionate mother-and-daughter team of amateur genealogists. While working together on their family tree, they made many captivating discoveries. Our most significant discovery was finding four convicts who held very different perspectives on life in the colony from the military. These four felons were transported to Australia between 1792 and 1814, during the height of convict transportation. Before her passing in 2002, Sheila adapted some of these histories into enchanting stories, known as her Australian Colonial Trilogy. Sara later had these published. Sheila left a fourth unfinished story, inspiring Sara to complete it. However, before she did, **The Lockleys of Parramatta** were created to see if she could do justice to her mother's work. The first two in the series were completed before attempting to finish **Dancing to Her Own Tune** for her mother. (*Sheila wrote the first 30k words*)

Vividly living through the Colonial Era, these books delve further into the theme of overcoming adversity in Colonial Australia, and how it developed, the demise of the Convict system and the discovery of mineral wealth.

Sara skilfully intertwines precise archival data with a captivating narrative to craft a collection of stories about faith, love, loss, and redemption.

Two hundred years after her family arrived in Australia, Sara continues the Australian Colonial stories that start with **Gentle Annie Soames**, a saga about the First Fleet. Her **First Fleet Trilogy** is now complete. Following this chronologically are **The Hunter to Macquarie Collection,** the **Unlikely Convict Ladies Trilogy**, and The **Lockleys of Parramatta**. **The Convict Birthstain Collection**, set in the mid-1800s, follows. All the stories are stand-alone novels. There is a chronological list of her books on her web page.

See Sara's web page to keep up to date with more stories.
An online store is available for a signed copy of Sara's books.
https://www.sarapowter.com.au/ *(Australian Postage only)*
Feel free to email her at
saragpowter@gmail.com

Amazon Aus QR

BOOK BUB
https://partners.bookbub.com/authors/6273615/edit

FACEBOOK https://www.facebook.com/profile.php?id=100063887262514

Do you want the book *"Unshackled Lives" for free?*
Download from Book Funnel after you sign up.

FREE Newsletter signup
From my web page.

www.ingramcontent.com/pod-product-compliance
Lightning Source LLC
Chambersburg PA
CBHW050909250626
47155CB00001B/164